Dedicated to

Neil and Margaret Waterman
You got us into this whole mess! What with your bedtime reading, your love, and your ability to question everything. The sense of gratitude cannot be properly conveyed….

Books are nothing without readers. Special thanks to the following for their invaluable assistance:

Rob Condon
Marie Isenberg
Dan Schmidt
and, of course, Ellen.

Ends of the World

ISBN 978-0-9967962-0-0

Cover design by Matthew Waterman.
Inset cover and image courtesy of Dan Schmidt

EOTW Publishing

www.MatthewWaterman.com

by
Matthew
Waterman

MATT

The next day Matt went back to work. Because, really, what else was there to do? It's not every day one nearly kills a little boy. He'd returned to his apartment the previous night and been confronted by the abject normalcy of it—dirty dishes from that morning's breakfast still sat in the sink and his unmade bed was just as he'd left it. Though the encounter had been gut-wrenching, life would go on. He'd been aware he could stay awake all night, re-playing the events over and over in his mind—what he could have done differently, what he should have done differently—but that would accomplish nothing. The world hadn't come to an end and he'd still be expected back in the office.

The subway that morning—roaring along in its jarring, yet vaguely rhythmic clatter—was lined with the usual cast of characters. Leaning against the closed door was the unshaven man on his way home from an overnight construction job—the ashen dots on his boots suggested he was a welder, in fact. More obvious to Matt was the fact that his mother constantly harassed him about the college degree he'd never pursued and that was the main reason he resented visiting her. Nearby, a 20-something man in a shirt and tie checked his phone far too ostentatiously in a crass attempt to illustrate his importance. Matt could see that the young man had struck out at the bar again and that, over time, the kid was beginning to resent his friend who accumulated more women's phone numbers than he. Meanwhile, a few feet away from him, a middle-aged, dark-skinned woman clung to the pole with her whole body pressed against it. She peered out at the world with an angry, stern expression and the simplest conclusion was that she was selfishly hoarding the area around the pole. Matt recognized there was more to it than that, though. The woman, a mother of four who doted on them—and everyone else on her block—was actually petrified, scared that she might be accosted at any moment in a city far from her birth. And despite her kind, generous nature, her reflexive defense mechanism was a demeanor of hostility. Matt saw many of these characters on a semi-regular basis—The Angry Consumer, The Big Bag Carrier, the Stoic Man, the Foot Tapper, The Messenger—enough personalities to populate a Grecian epic. He knew their stories, their histories and desires, and on every trip a new tale revealed itself to him.

Matt arrived at his stop and climbed the stairs out of the subway station into the grey of the morning. The Fall air was sharp, the sidewalk hard. Normally the concrete of the city held on to the summer's heat well into September and, sometimes, October. But a mild summer meant that battle had already been lost; winter was on its way.

Matt's march to his office often entailed at least one close encounter with a cab and this morning was no different. Just as he stepped off the curb in front of the throng of people assembled at the corner, a cab driver gunned his car to make it through the yellow light. Matt heard the engine revving, hesitated, and the car flashed in front of him close enough to nick the edge of his bag and rip it off his shoulder. He struggled to gather it off the pavement even as the mass churned past him, automatons oblivious to his plight. Welcome to another Tuesday morning.

"The numbers aren't tying out." Those were the first words spoken to Matt that day. Not, "Hello," or, "Good morning." Instead they were: "The numbers aren't tying out," in Abby's deliberate, overly enunciated cadence. Matt's high-strung co-worker was prone to fits of anxiety-driven overstatement but the news nonetheless caused a drop in his already dour mood. The report had been submitted; it was too late to correct data discrepancies.

"Damn," Matt grunted. "What happened?"

"The numbers from the Datachariot feed were Bid Price, but the ones we used last quarter were Ask Price."

"Wait. What?" said Matt, confused. "We didn't need use Datachariot for Friday's report."

"No, no, no. I'm talking about the reconciliation review for next week."

"Ugh," he grunted, dropping his bag on his desk and finally taking the time to remove his coat. Based on Abby's urgency, Matt had jumped to the conclusion that she was referring to a major quarterly project they'd just completed, not an internal review that wasn't due for a week. "Give me a second and I'll look at it."

Working in the back office of an investment firm was not the way Matt had envisioned spending his life. Crafting fiction was his true passion, his true focus. But he needed to pay the bills. His work at the firm was a stark contrast to the nights spent writing and, he reasoned, it was a good division of labor: His workday role involved hard numbers and the mitigation of red tape so, away from the office, his creative process should've been able to operate unfettered. The fact that he was often too exhausted to conjure any worthwhile prose after a stressful day was the logistical serpent he often battled.

Matt managed to solve Abby's dilemma quite easily once he got settled. Her nervous energy could be irksome, particularly when all he really wanted to do was get some coffee. As transfer request specialists, it was their job to be a bulwark when machines failed. Most transactions occurred via simple computer-driven programs but, on occasion, quirks would occur outside the normal processes. Transfers might go to the wrong account; reallocations might not process before the close of business; that sort of thing. Matt's group was charged with navigating a labyrinth of accounting standards, technology interfaces, and rules enforced by the Securities and Exchange Commission to ensure the dollars and cents of all transactions were fully reconciled. The investment gods located upstairs in the higher floors of Fitzgerald Tower might be paid the big bucks to enact their investment schemes but somebody had to ensure the client's money actually moved to the requested funds at the end of the day.

Everyone on the floor worked in a cubicle, creating what amounted to an angular, cell block-style atmosphere—there were days when Matt might speak to no one except when he arrived and left. On the one hand, it was nice to have a discrete area that he could call his own because intrusions and distraction could be kept to a minimum. Yet, on the other hand, the division only served to partition his life further, a literal structure within his own metaphorical division of labor. Factoring in his desire to vanquish any thoughts of his encounter with the little boy, the work-life demarcation that morning took on new levels of meaning.

In fact, so structured was his daily routine that it was only when he turned to retrieve a protein bar from his bag—two hours into his day—that he realized it was open. Crap. He must've forgotten to zipper it closed when he left his apartment. He pawed through it, found the bar, and nearly swiveled back around before he stopped. Something was wrong. More carefully, he checked the contents of his bag again and concern began to grow within him. The tickets to Wagner's opera, *Götterdämmerung*, had been delivered to him at the office yesterday. Where were they? He was positive he'd put them in his bag immediately upon receipt but, after last night's events, he was also positive he hadn't taken them out when he arrived home. Frantically now, he took item after item out of the bag one by one, inspecting each before setting them aside. An old report he'd been meaning to review on the subway; printouts from a conference held three weeks ago; the paperback he was reading at the moment. Each of these were extracted and examined until the only thing left in his bag was an old ATM receipt and a handful of spare change.

The tickets weren't there! What the hell? Matt looked up from the bag to the cubicle wall but his thoughts were a million miles away. They could've fallen out at any point last night, he supposed, if the bag had been open the whole time. He certainly hadn't been in the right state of mind. Then he remembered the cab that morning, that goddamn cab—he'd lost the bag when the cab grazed it. Among the throng of people and the rush of the busy street corner, it would've been entirely possible to miss the envelope if it'd fallen out.

Matt slammed the palm of his hand on the desk. "Dammit," he blurted. Each ticket cost $600! More importantly, Wagner was his girlfriend's favorite composer and the Metropolitan Opera was concluding a special, commemorative showcase of, *Der Ring des Nibelungen*—it was essentially a once-in-a-decade event and *Götterdämmerung* was the climax of the four operas. Meda had been looking forward to it since it was announced. How could he have lost them?

Once again, he struck his desk in frustration, saying nothing this time.

"Is everything okay over there?" came Abby's voice over the cubicle wall.

"Yeah. I'm fine," Matt growled. For a long period he stared at the empty bag in mute disbelief, angry at that stupid cab and berating himself for gathering the bag so hastily. How stupid! He should've taken an extra second to be sure nothing was missing, should've taken better care of such precious items.

The loss hung over the rest of his day like a toxic cloud. To his additional frustration, urgent requests rolled in non-stop and it was impossible for him to make any plan to rectify the situation. Meda was going to be livid. She'd paid for the tickets and entrusted him to take care of them. In fact, it was only due to the unreliable mail system in their neighborhood that they'd decided to have them sent to his office. Now, having lost them for such a stupid reason, he knew Meda wouldn't be satisfied without her pound of flesh.

When 6:00 finally rolled around it felt more like a death row march than an eagerly anticipated end to the work day. With the forlorn unease of one looking under the hood of a smoking car, Matt turned and stared inside the bag again. Nothing had changed. Its former contents were still strewn beside it and the emptiness within was like that of a blank sheet of paper, daunting in its vacancy. He had to do something about the lost tickets. But what? They'd sold out almost instantaneously–it was only through a clever gambit by Meda that they'd managed to acquire them in the first place. Normally he could escape the office at 6:00, head home, and start writing. Now, instead, he swiveled back to his computer to begin the dispiriting task of locating new tickets. He started searching the typical online ticket agencies, preparing himself for the anticipated sticker-shock, when:

KRACKOOM!!!

Matt ducked on sheer instinct. Abby yelped. In the cubicle opposite him, a co-worker cursed. Then, in the immediate aftermath, he took stock: It sounded like a bomb had exploded. Yet there was no devastation, no smoke or fire. The floor had shaken but no one cried as if injured. He stood up and found others popping their heads out of their cubicles in similar fashion, each wearing expressions of concern and confusion.

"Is everyone okay?" asked Abby to no one in particular.

A gradual murmur began to grow and, out of the buzz, Matt heard someone describe a bright flash. That's when he realized what it was: Lightning.

"I think it was lightning," said Matt.

Wait a minute, that doesn't make sense. He began to doubt himself. He'd experienced countless thunderstorms in his office building yet he'd never heard such a loud thunderclap. Normally the sound of thunder rolled down the Avenues, slow-moving and growling. It was never so acute. Also, skyscrapers were designed with lightning rods on top for safety, weren't they?

"You think so?" asked Abby, appearing outside his cube.

"I'm—I'm not sure," he said vacantly.

"It was a heck of a flash," said Conrad, approaching from the cubicle across the hall.

"You saw a flash?" asked Matt.

"Yeah. Definitely. I can still see the image when I close my eyes. It hit right outside the window there."

At that the trio turned their gazes to the location of the purported lightning strike. The floor-to-ceiling windows of the office reflected the artificial light inside, making it hard to see the world beyond initially. After staring for a moment, though, the three discerned the sheets of rain slapping the side of the tower. Like the starting gun of a race, the bolt had signaled a torrential downpour. At the same time, the commotion on the floor was only increasing. Matt glanced around, saw that certain co-workers were donning their fire warden vests, and he put two and two together—someone had made the decision to evacuate the floor.

"I thought towers were built with rods on top to absorb lightning strikes," said Matt, amid the growing commotion. It didn't make sense to him that lightning should strike the side of the building and his mind was unwilling to dismiss such an odd occurrence out of hand.

"I don't know, man. I saw it," said Conrad.

Just then, Bill Nevers, the officious twit in charge of omnibus transfers, appeared. "We have reason to believe the tower was struck by lightning. Security has asked everyone to move to the ground floor for their own safety," he declared robotically before moving on.

Matt rolled his eyes. Five minutes earlier and he would've been on his way to the subway! Now, with the elevators taken out of service, the entire floor would be forced to descend the stairs. Making matters worse, many were gathering their coats and bags to leave for the night, further delaying the evacuation process. Contrary to expectations, corralling thousands of people in twenty-nine floors of offices down to the ground level could actually be done in an orderly manner—it just took forever. With decorum at a maximum in such a situation, no one panicked or descended the stairs recklessly. Instead, it was often a tiresome procession that moved one halting step at a time. Matt surveyed those around him and shook his head grimly as he envisioned the evacuation taking well over an hour to complete.

By the time he reached the ground floor he wanted to scream. Already dispirited by the lost tickets and the obliterated writing time, he saw that he still had to trudge through the downpour. Once outside, he stomped down the sidewalk, his umbrella crashing into those carried by others, and by the time he reached the subway entrance he was half-drenched anyway.

Rush hour had eased and, when a train finally arrived, it was nearly empty. Nonetheless, Matt glanced up and down the car as was his normal habit. He slumped into his seat and it took him a moment to register what he'd seen. That was The Stoic Man. At the far end of the car. The same guy he often saw on his morning commute—including that very morning! Matt marveled at the coincidence: What were the chances he'd ride with the same person on his way to work and on the way home? Considering how many cars are available in every train, with new trains arriving constantly, the odds were astronomically low. Sure, Matt recognized certain familiar faces from time to time, but never on both ends of the commute on the same day.

For a long time he sat with the crashing, hypnotic roar of the subway filling the air. Then, given how exhausted he was, he began to doubt whether that truly was The Stoic Man at the end of the car. He'd only noticed the man while in the process of sitting down—it was entirely possible he'd misjudged and jumped to the wrong conclusion. So with nothing else to occupy his thoughts, he decided to take another peek just to be sure. As nonchalant as possible, he began to bend forward to get a better view of the car. But there was no need. The Stoic Man was standing directly beside him.

"What do you think you're doing?" the Stoic Man asked.

MATT

"That's the problem with art these days: It's all about money!"

Matt smiled. He disagreed with his friend but was willing to humor him for the moment.

"No really," insisted Magee, sensing Matt's lack of concurrence. "The art collectors rule everything. It's all just...*investment* to them."

"But that doesn't—or at least it shouldn't—impact the creation of the art itself," countered Matt.

"It shouldn't. But it does! I don't want to pour my heart and soul into a painting only to have it bought and shoved into a warehouse where no one will see it...just because some art collector thinks it might be valuable after I die," said Magee, concluding with a joyless swig of beer.

The bar was quiet—perhaps six other people, total, scattered about the establishment—and two of them shared Magee's scraggy-beard and thrift-store appearance. Happy hour at Matt and Magee's favorite pub was a place for 30-somethings who had no interest in a club atmosphere—a premium was placed on the ability to actually hear each other speak and, when one's sole encountered a sticky patch on the floor, it was just part of the charm. They'd agreed to meet to discuss replacement tickets to the opera but, two hours after arrival, the topic had yet to be addressed.

"Why can't you just create the art you want and forget the critics? No one forces you to sell the stuff," pushed Matt.

"Matt, Matt, Matt," moaned Magee. "It's not that simple. You know that."

Matt smirked but said nothing. This wasn't the first time they'd engaged in such conversational sparring and it certainly wouldn't be the last. A pattern had emerged over their years of friendship wherein Magee railed against the state of affairs in the world of art, Matt attempted to provide some perspective, and Magee replied with some version of, "It's not that simple." Depending how many beers they'd consumed the argument might continue longer—often with numerous convoluted, downright painful digressions—but it always seemed to conclude with the notion that Matt was too naïve and that art wasn't revered in society anymore.

Magee didn't comment on Matt's smirk. Instead, he took another sip of beer, glanced out the window, and asked, "So...anyway. How's the apocalypse coming? Last time we talked it seemed like you were making some headway."

"You mean, '*Ends of the World*'?" asked Matt. Magee was referring to a collection of short stories Matt was writing. The tales were to take place in the days leading up to Armageddon, with the fates of each protagonist somehow linked together. "It's going well so far. I've got a lot of ideas; still rounding out the characters. The theme common to each story is some level of disillusionment, either through promises broken, false expectation, or some other recalibration of goals. I feel like so many people—be it college students up to their ears in debt or older people who'd hoped to retire prior to the market crash—are dealing with unexpected disappointment. Like they'd been sold a dream that didn't come true."

"So...light hearted romps all?"

Matt smiled. "Some are! I think many of the characters will experience some kind of redemption. Not necessarily the one they want or expect. But: S*omething*. If every story is a depressing ode to unfulfilled dreams I'm not sure readers are going to react too well."

"There you go again," said Magee, rolling his eyes. "Why do you always have to dilute your work with concerns like that? If you want to create gloomy, depressing snapshots of real life then do it! Don't flinch."

"I haven't told you the best part yet," said Matt with a mischievous smile.

"What?"

"Product delivery."

"Did you just refer to your writing as 'product'? Seriously, Matt. You know how I hate that term."

"Product delivery. I plan to price each fifteen page story at seventy-five cents. People will be able to knock out a story when they're in line at the DMV if they want. Ideally, once they start reading, they'll get addicted and need to keep reading in order to fill in the blanks of the other stories. Before they know it—if all goes according to plan—they will have read a novel's worth of material, all eighteen stories in the collection, and paid $13.50—the price of a full, regular novel."

Magee stared at Matt for a long time, stone-faced. "That's a terrible idea."

Matt laughed once more, Magee not sharing his mirth. "What? What's the problem?"

"Good lord, where do I start?" moaned Magee, his palm going to his forehead. "The fact that you're trying to trick people into reading your material? The fact that you're creating this artificial fifteen page limitation which is bound to impact the work? The fact that you're even considering this crap at all, when you should be focused solely on the writing? The list goes on!"

"Everything's changing, man," said Matt with a shrug. "You have to change with the times. It's all about instant delivery now; people can download music or books with a click of a button. The printing press allowed for the creation of the novel and that was great—it changed human history. Now technology is allowing for the creation of something else."

Magee, ignoring Matt's comment, pointed an accusatory finger and said, "Weren't you the one that *just* said the market shouldn't impact the creative process?"

"That's different."

"How?" snorted Magee. "Because it involves me?"

"No, no," said Matt defensively. "It's different. You were saying you don't want to paint anymore because it's just going to disappear into some vault somewhere."

"Right."

"I'm *still writing*. I am just reacting to a market that is changing. If I expect people to read my stuff I have to at least acknowledge the change."

"So why don't you write children's books? Or romance novels?"

Matt leaned forward, the joviality in the conversation decreasing. "I see where you're going with that. You're implying that I'm selling out."

"Yep," agreed Magee.

"Just because I'm changing the method of the delivery of my writing, does *not* mean I've compromised the work."

This time Magee didn't reply, instead merely raising an eyebrow.

"Oh, get off it," said Matt, falling back into his chair again. "Not everything's black and white, dude. It's always easier to sit back and critique than it is to go out and actually do something."

"Buddy, do you know how much stuff I'm doing now?" asked Magee, his tone rising. "I'm juggling five different projects. Including juggling!"

"You're learning to juggle?" asked Matt, incredulous.

"Yep."

"Why?"

"Why not?"

Matt shook his head. "Must be nice to live without a day job."

"Except for the untidy fact that I *have* a job that keeps me up until 4:00 AM."

Matt shifted in his seat. He wanted to take the comment back. Magee worked nights as a bartender and, while the job might only result in thirty hours a week, they were grueling hours nonetheless. Each took another sip of beer and, eventually, Matt said, "Anyway, I wanted to ask you about those opera tickets."

"Oh right," said Magee.

"It's a special show. Sold out immediately. I looked online and the prices of the few available were astronomical. So I figured I'd check with you to see if any of your connections could help."

"Wagner, right?"

"Yeah, *Götterdämmerung*. Saturday, in two and a half weeks. The tickets Meda bought were first tier but at this point I think I'd take anything."

"Okay. I'll check," said Magee, jotting down the information on a piece of paper. "I can't think of anyone off the top of my head...these aren't exactly Springsteen tickets...they're not the kind of tickets that come up in conversation often, y'know?"

"Yeah, I figured."

"Meda doesn't know?"

"No, I haven't told her. I wanted to get my ducks in a row."

"You're that scared of her?"

Matt cocked his head to the side. "I'm not scared of her, you ass. It's a big deal to her. She's really looking forward to it. Once I tell her I lost the tickets, she's bound to fly off the handle. So I want to have potential new tickets lined up before I even broach the subject."

Magee laughed. "It was an honest mistake. You lost the tickets. Big deal. You think she's going to take your head off?"

Matt looked away, embarrassed but unsure why. "Probably not. But I'm not about to risk it."

At that, Magee's phone began ringing. He pulled it out, looked at it, and said, "Let me take this. This guy might be able to help us out."

Magee answered the call, grew serious, and then took the conversation outside. Matt continued to sip his beer, peering up at the television while his mind wandered. When Magee returned, though, his mood was nearly giddy: He'd received exciting news about a short film he was hired to shoot. After weeks of negotiations, the producer had received permission to use an abandoned warehouse and he wanted to tell Magee himself. The news altered the trajectory of Matt and Magee's conversation and, in a celebratory mood, the pair ended up staying at the bar for another two hours. And though Matt had multiple chances to do so, he never brought up the strange events that had occurred in his life in the preceding days.

MATT

So anyway, that little boy Matt may have killed? Matt had barely slept a wink since the encounter. Haunted by guilt-ridden reflections and hazy memories, he couldn't achieve closure until he was positive the boy was alive and well.

The night had begun straightforward enough: After getting home from the office he drove to a small library to work on his novel. He intended to focus on character sketches and overall plotting, and knew the isolation of the tiny branch would be ideal—once there, there was nothing else *to* do but write. And, as expected, he found a secluded spot behind the reference encyclopedias without a soul in sight.

Crafting eighteen stories, each intended to be intertwined with the others, required a decent amount of planning. Writing the stories was the exciting part but Matt recognized he had to wrap his head around a number of the storylines before starting. Therefore, he created a calendar-like table with the names of the characters across both axes to project how they might interact with each other in their respective tales. It didn't need to be exhaustive—every single character didn't have to interact with every other one—and, actually, it would be a mistake to try to plot out all the stories so far in advance. But some type of over-arching vision was required. As opposed to the creation of a classic, linear narrative, plotting so many interactions required his thoughts to be more scatter-shot, more flowing, and the solitude of the library was the perfect place to enter such a meditative state.

Matt spread out his materials on the table before him and began to scribble short notes into the various boxes. One character might run into another on the street and then, soon afterward, have a conversation with a third. The goal was to show how the protagonist in one story might be viewed by the protagonist in another, and vice-versa, creating a mesh of viewpoints that didn't always jibe with the characters' own self-perceptions. Each character would be telling their particular story but it would be up to the reader to figure out where the truth lied among the respective narratives.

Matt got lost in his thoughts and, gradually, his movements grew more frenetic. He scribbled short, one-sentence notes in his character matrix then jumped to his notebook to write more involved details about the interaction. A blurb about two character's interaction on the matrix might lead to an entire sheet of details in the notebook. He flipped through the pages manically, adding a sentence to one character's description here, a key detail to the overview of a second character there. At one point, it occurred to Matt—as if viewing himself from outside his own body—that he probably looked like a mad scientist, feverish in his focus. Time passed, of course. But it didn't feel like it to Matt. Something had happened to him and it was only when he saw a member of the staff turning off the lights that he checked the time. It was 12:21. The library had been closed for almost two hours.

"Holy," Matt muttered, startling the older woman.

"What do you think you're doing?" she demanded.

"I'm sorry. I didn't—"

"You have to leave, sir. I don't know what you were planning but you have to leave. *Now.*"

"What? Heh. Okay, I'm sorry," said Matt, grinning in embarrassment. Clearly the woman thought he had some nefarious scheme planned, as if he intended to spend the night in the library. "Really, this is an honest mistake. I didn't realize."

"Gary! Gary, we're going to need the keys for the front door," the woman hollered down the hall.

Matt grew flustered and began shoving everything into his bag. He didn't take the time to fold up his matrix properly and it was a minor miracle he remembered to grab his coat off the back of his chair.

Given the opportunity to make another comment, the woman added, "I could have you arrested, you know."

The threat brought a new level of reality to the situation and Matt stammered, "I'm really sorry. Shoot, I didn't," before trailing off.

"If I see you in here again I will be calling the police. If this were any other place of business you would probably be explaining yourself to them already," she continued.

"I know, I'm sorry," said Matt, before blurting, "I won't be back. Don't worry."

He hurried away with his materials pressed against his chest and his tail between his legs. At the door he was met by a disappointed-looking young man, his key already in the air as if he was ready to insert it into some invisible lock. "I'm really sorry," Matt said again.

"It's okay. Happens to the best of us," he said. As much as the man's words glossed over the incident, there was no mistaking his annoyance, however. Once on the other side of the glass, Matt gave another, final nod but the man had already turned away.

Matt ambled to his car, more shaken than he would've expected. It was as if he'd been sleeping and awoken to find himself in the library. So lost was he in his thoughts that he was having trouble coming back to the real world—despite the frigid air, he was within five steps of his car before realizing he hadn't put on his coat.

Slumping into the driver's seat, he replayed the night's events in his mind as if watching a movie. He'd told the woman he wouldn't come back to the library. Why did he say that? Yes, he was embarrassed and caught flat-footed. Yes, she was threatening him with police action. But that was clearly an overreaction on her part, right? It was silly to think he was attempting anything devious. Now he'd volunteered not to come back—even though it was possibly the best place to plot out his novel. He cursed himself for losing track of time so terribly and the woman for such unneeded hostility. But with nothing else to do, he slipped the car into gear pulled away.

The most straightforward route from the library to his apartment wasn't long in terms of distance but it could take an inordinate amount of time due to the stop-and-go traffic. So, instead, Matt preferred to take a path that wasn't nearly as travelled, a unique one that entailed passing through a district composed mainly of warehouses. The route ran on a service road beside one of the borough's main arteries and was far more likely to be travelled by delivery trucks than soccer-mom minivans. As opposed to traditional city blocks, the route had few stoplights or stop signs and Matt could sail along with comparative ease. The downside, however, was that the area was downright desolate at night—so bereft of people that, when it snowed, the sidewalk might be free of footprints for hours. If anything were to go wrong on that stretch it would be a very lonely place to find oneself.

The journey had possessed an ethereal feel that night, though, a sensation that only grew as Matt drove. Part of the reason was his speed—when did he ever cruise at such a clip down city blocks? Another aspect that added to Matt's sense of dislocation was the geographic unfamiliarity—he'd travelled the route on a number of occasions but he would never be at ease with the complete and utter dearth of people. Put side-by-side with Matt's mental state after the incident at the library, it made him feel like a traveler in his own body, no longer in control of his direction or goals. He was aware, on a logical level, that his corporal body had been at the library and that he was now barreling down a city street. Yet, at the same time, he didn't feel like the movements were his own, like he was the one actually *doing* any of it. He glanced up at his rearview mirror, first seeing himself in it and then the road travelled. It offered him a sense of where he'd been, as if to give validation to his literal existence.

Then: His ears heard it first, a dull -*thud*- like the sound of a potato thrown at the wall. Next his eyes took it in, even before his mind fully processed it: A flash of movement directly in front of the car, the headlights reflecting off something far too close. And he felt the slightest of shocks through the car.

Then his body took over. It slammed on the brakes. It swung the wheel away from the point of contact. It issued a strained, pathetic curse word. And then its arms created a vice grip on the wheel until the car came to a screeching halt.

Only then did his conscious thoughts catch up. He'd hit something. It *had* happened. This was reality. Somewhere inside, he wanted it to be a misperception, yearned for it all to go away somehow, some way. But his mind asserted that it wasn't and it wouldn't.

"Oh my God," Matt said in a state of terrible awe. All of it had occurred in the space of a few scant seconds. But once the car's motion ceased he was in action, ripping off his seatbelt, and leaping out. His car had come to a stop directly under the harsh incandescent light of a streetlight, however—this allowed him to scan the immediate area inside the light instantaneously yet it made it practically impossible to discern anything beyond. He peered about manically, his feet shifting as he searched the area. There was a warehouse building close beside him to his right. A fence with barbed wire atop was on the other side of the street. Beyond those basic features, though, he could see only darkness. In his mania it took him a moment to recognize the light's influence but then, once identified, he sprinted outside the cone. "Hello?" he cried, over and over.

As he ran, it became apparent that his night vision was lacking—he could make out dark graffiti on the wall and could discern the steel garage door but he couldn't see anything in great detail. "Hello? Is anybody here?" he screamed even more urgently—if someone was hurt, he didn't have the luxury of waiting for his vision to adjust.

He continued to dart further into the darkness and then, barely, he heard a light, metallic *-ting-* at his feet. He glanced down and saw a knife lying on the asphalt. Then, immediately, he saw a second nearby. They were long, unorthodox, and appeared to be composed entirely of silver. At a complete loss, he bent to get a better look, to ensure he was actually seeing what he was seeing. And, upon closer inspection, he confirmed that they were knives—and they had blood on their blades.

"What the—?" cried Matt, reeling in horror, his eyes still locked on the blades. Could that be? What was happening?

His mind was no longer functioning properly—thoughts were shooting like fireworks in myriad directions, one having nothing to do with the next. He'd hit someone with his car? Why knives? Should he have locked the car door? What if the person was dead? Was he in danger? Blood?

"Hello?" he cried desperately, as if he, himself, was the one that needed to be saved.

Then he heard it, the slightest whimper originating from his right. His gaze snapped to the source, first seeing the doorway and then peering into the dark with piercing concentration. All was still for a moment and the only sound to be heard was Matt's ragged breaths. And then he was off, tearing towards the spot with deranged intensity.

It was a little boy. Huddled at the base of a doorway atop the second of two concrete steps, the boy was nearly invisible in the black of the shadows.

"Oh no," Matt muttered to no one. As he sprinted the roughly twenty steps to the boy, time seemed to lengthen. Each step brought him closer yet took longer and longer to pass. His mind raced with unarticulated fears yet the closing of the distance didn't aid his vision like he'd expected. In fact, even as he arrived at the boy's side, Matt could only barely make out the boy's baggy coat and boots.

"Are you okay? Hey, are you okay?" Matt had fully intended to seize the boy, to look him up and down to confirm he was conscious and uninjured. When he arrived, though, he stopped short of doing so. It may've been the knives. It may've been the boy's appearance. It may've been vague rationalizations regarding the dangers of moving a person who'd suffered an injury. But Matt didn't touch the boy. Instead, he let his hand hover just over the boy's shoulder as if to wake him from slumber. Matt's mind conjured images of the boy going feral, biting his outstretched hand, and he tried his best to dispel such fears. Yet, as he bent closer, he remained on the balls of feet, ready to retreat.

"Can you hear me? Are you okay? Please tell me you're alive," Matt rambled, practically begging. The boy's head remained cocked to the side, his face in the corner of the entrance offering only a partial view.

But then, from the darkness, came a feeble, "I'm not dead."

Matt's body relaxed by a degree. He appraised the boy again, unsure what to do next. "Did I hit you? With my car?"

"No," said the boy, his voice surprisingly lower than Matt would've expected. It wasn't like that of a man, or even a pubescent teen, but was, instead, serious in nature—not at all like that of a child.

"You—you sure?" said Matt. His mental cacophony had calmed only slightly. Echoing from a distant chamber, his conscience acknowledged that he might be *too* ready to take the boy at his word, that he should be asking different questions.

"Yes. You didn't hit me with your car," the boy said, sounding to Matt's ears as if he was growing impatient.

It dawned on Matt that the boy might be homeless or an illegal immigrant, that he might be so withdrawn because he didn't want help. Matt hesitated, saying nothing for the moment. Whether the boy was homeless or in the country illegally didn't impact his responsibility in the situation. Yet the voice in the back of his mind had gained purchase—"If he doesn't want my help, what can I do?"

"I need. I need to know that you're okay," Matt fumbled, instantly embarrassed by his words. "Please. I'm sorry."

"You have to be more careful," said the boy, his words blunt and definite.

Matt took a small, single step back, wholly unaware he'd done so. Though he didn't recognize it at the time, the boy's admonishment was, paradoxically, very liberating. Two entities had been battling within him: One that was responsible and aware he had to make things right; the other that was childish and fearful, hoping to just run away. By telling him he should be more careful, the boy suddenly appeared much less a victim. Who was he to tell Matt what to do, right? Matt knew he'd messed up—he didn't need this kid to rub it in. Matt re-appraised the boy, even though he could barely see him. He didn't spot any blood or obvious injuries—"What about the knives?" a distant voice in the back of his mind asked—and he seemed lucid enough, plainly conscious. What more was there to do?

"Okay," said Matt, as much to himself as to the boy. "I'm going now."

The boy didn't respond.

At first, Matt didn't move. He remained paralyzed on the empty sidewalk in a sort of purgatorial state. Inertia-less, he said once more to no one in particular, "Okay."

Then, finally, Matt turned to go. His movements were tentative, a reflection of the turmoil inside him. The first step was the spiritual equivalent of a sigh of relief, yet every step thereafter was fearful, as if he was being pulled back to his car rather than walking towards it. The path to it was diagonal across the street yet his gaze remained cocked, staring back at the boy with an expression that teetered on both concern and panic. When he arrived at the car he opened the door, glanced back in the direction of the boy for a final moment, and, eventually, fell behind the wheel. And after a silent, torturous pause, he drove off into the cold night.

MEDA

So cute. The boy and his puppy, playing on the sidewalk on the opposite side of the street. Meda's sweaty yoga pants still lay in a heap on the floor and her phone had at least five unread texts, but she couldn't take her eyes off of the duo. Which one was cuter? She couldn't say. She knew she had things to do (for starters, putting on some actual clothes rather than Matt's ratty old T-shirt). But, for now, she was smiling.

It was almost 8:00 and Matt would be arriving soon. The couple tried to save Thursday as, "date night," to ensure they spent time together mid-week. Between her job, Matt's writing, and myriad social obligations, it was all too easy to lose track of time. Some of her friends thought such structure in a relationship was weird but the arrangement was actually her idea. Too many times she'd realized too late that weeks had passed and they'd seen each other exclusively on weekends. By circling Thursday night on the calendar, she forced herself to get out of the office. That such pressure also created time for yoga class was an ancillary bonus.

"Carlos! Ven acá!" came a voice from inside the apartment complex across the street and the boy snapped to attention. He gathered up the puppy and scampered inside, breaking Meda out of her hypnotic spell. With the smile still on her face, she rifled through the clutter on the table beside the window and found the pack of White Buffalo cigarettes with the familiar Native American iconography on the cover. The Biendava account needed its focus group report finalized in two days, she needed to get a present for Janet's baby shower, and the drip in the shower wasn't going to fix itself. But all that could wait. Smoking after class wasn't ideal (enough people had offered that helpful tip already) but she didn't care. A single clove cigarette was not the end of the world.

She had spent her twenties working. When she recalled that period in her life, her memories were, essentially, limited to two categories: The hours she'd put in at her public relations firm and the nights she'd spent at the bars with those co-workers. It had been grueling and she'd sacrificed a love affair with singing in the process. But she'd operated under the notion that it was an investment in her future, that if she put in the long hours in her youth she'd be set up for greater things in life later. Then the bubble popped. The majority of her firm's clients were companies that sold operating materials to financial services companies; everything from small, boutique furniture stores to established stationary suppliers. When the money dried up for everything except the head honchos' bonuses, her company stagnated. Rather than becoming a Director at the age of thirty-two, she was still a Senior Associate for the sixth year in a row. She recognized she had a decent job and she was in a better position than many people. But, if asked at the age of twenty-two if this was where she expected to be a decade later, she would have no option but to reply in the negative.

The buzzer for the door downstairs came to life just as she was stubbing out the cigarette. (Perfect timing!) She buzzed, opened her apartment door, and, when Matt arrived, he gave her a surprised smile.

"Wow, hon," he said, taking stock of her half-naked state.

"Oh, get over it," she said, as they exchanged a quick kiss. "I'm not dressed like this to titillate you. I just got back from the gym and haven't taken a shower yet. I don't think you *want* to get too close just yet."

"Not true. I love when you titillate," said Matt, placing a bag of groceries and a bottle of wine on the small kitchen table.

"God, why did I use that word?" moaned Meda in faux-lamentation.

"What? 'Titilate'?"

"Stop."

"Tit. Il. Ate," said Matt, over-enunciating every syllable.

"I swear, I think the little boy across the street is more mature than you," said Meda, waving towards the window.

Matt's eyes widened briefly, an expression that suggested he'd forgotten his keys or failed to turn off the stove. Then, craning his neck to see out the window across the room, he asked, "What little boy?"

"Oh, he went inside. Forget it," said Meda, unwilling to prolong the conversation. "How've you been, baby? I missed you."

"I missed you, too."

"What'd you get us?" she asked, tugging at the side of the bag to sneak a peek inside.

"I was going to throw together a chicken and rice dish. Simple, one skillet."

Meda smiled. It was perfect. "Thank you. You're the best," she said, adding, "Are you getting excited for our night at the opera?"

Matt's complexion changed in a heartbeat. It was as if a cloud had blotted out the sun and, suddenly, the walls of the room felt a foot closer on every side.

"I—we have to talk about that," he said, eye contact lost.

"What? What happened?" asked Meda.

Matt's gaze shot up, angry now. "See? I *knew* you were going to react that way."

It was then that Meda became aware of how haggard Matt appeared, his frown producing previously unseen stress in his complexion. "What do you mean? What way?" said Meda.

"I lost the tickets, okay? I'm sorry," said Matt, throwing his palms out in a Jesus Christ pose.

"Oh no," moaned Meda, deflated.

"See?" repeated Matt. "I knew you were going to be like that. I just knew it."

"Be like what? Calm down, babe," said Meda, feeling disorientated by the abrupt change in the tone of the conversation. "How did you lose them?"

"I don't know *how* I lost them. Otherwise I wouldn't have lost them!"

Meda shifted her weight to one foot. "You don't have to be mean."

"I think they fell out of my bag," said Matt, essentially ignoring her comment. "It got knocked off my shoulder by a cab and it was during the morning rush. I think they fell out and I didn't notice."

"Oh that's awful," said Meda.

"See? I knew that was going to be your reaction," snapped Matt again.

"My reaction? You mean: Disappointment? Well, yes. Of course I'm disappointed."

"No, you know what I mean. You blame me. You think it's all my fault."

"What?" said Meda, her patience dwindling. "What's going on with you, Matt?"

Matt's expression glazed as if he was having trouble finding the right words. "I said I was sorry," he said finally, throwing himself on the mercy of the court. "I don't know what else to say. I knew you were going to blame me and I'm ready to take my medicine."

"Take your medicine? Who do you think I am?"

"I was afraid you'd be a bitch about it. I held out hope you wouldn't but—"

"Bitch?"

"Held out hope you wouldn't but here you are, putting it all on me—"

"Did you just call me a bitch?"

"An honest mistake that I'm so, so sorry for and you can't just—"

"Did you just call me *a bitch*?" she demanded, more loudly.

"You can't just accept that I made an honest mistake. You have to twist that knife—"

"I think you'd better go, Matt."

That stopped him dead. He paused and, after avoiding eye contact the entire time, peered up at her with an expression of genuine surprise.

"I don't know what's going on with you," Meda continued. "You look terrible. You're putting words in my mouth. And, and, I just don't think it's a good idea for us to be together tonight."

Matt's expression turned to one of hurt, anguish. Then, just as abruptly, his brow dropped. "So that's it, huh? I lose the tickets and now you can't stand the sight of me?"

"You. Are acting. Nuts," said Meda slowly, palms up and towards him as if to tell him to stop.

"Well, I'll have you know that I've got Magee working on new tickets as we speak. We should still be able to go once—"

"It's not about the tickets!" Meda blurted, nearly stomping on the floor. "I don't care about the tickets! I care about this Jekyll and Hyde routine when I asked a basic question!"

"You don't care about the tickets?" asked Matt, appearing hurt and confused once again. Meda wished he could see himself in the mirror, how drastic (and scary) the changes appeared.

"You know what I mean," she said, at her wits end. "Of course I want to go. I'm just saying: This. You." She trailed off, waving her hand at him as if the difference was plain to see.

"I think you're right," said Matt, angry again. "I think I should go."

"Fine," said Meda, exhausted.

"Fine," repeated Matt and he turned to leave.

At the doorway he paused, as if she might have something further to add but, when she didn't utter a word, he closed the door and stomped down the stairs. Meda, still reeling, watched him leave from the window. It was all so sudden, so severe. It was the exact opposite of how she'd anticipated spending the night and her expectations were still catching up to the reality. She took a shower, she made dinner, and, resisting the urge to call him, she went to sleep alone.

MATT

Matt stalked away from Meda's apartment, peering about the street as he went. There was an old man putting his garbage out, a miscreant in his day, no doubt. Sure, he'd settled down into the life of a law-abiding citizen, after he'd aged and didn't have use for violence anymore. But ask the man whose jaw he'd broken or the couple whose business he'd robbed, and they'd tell you what they thought about such a sweet old man.

In the previous four days Matt had slept a combined ten hours—and the majority of those had come only as the result of the drinks he'd shared with Magee. His conscience was suffering from an infestation—every time he thought he achieved a modicum of peace a new reminder appeared out of the corner of his eye. He tried to push worries about the little boy out his thoughts. Yet, when he actually succeeded, he replayed the ethereal scene from the library instead. And if he managed to stop ruminating over that, he obsessed about the strange encounter with the Stoic Man on the subway. During the day the banality of his work served as a distraction but, at night, there was no respite from these demons.

A pattern had emerged every time he attempted to sleep—he would lie down in bed and, despite his best efforts otherwise, he'd begin thinking about the boy and the accident. He'd relive the impact on the car and he'd rue all the actions he hadn't taken. Eventually he'd move to the computer to begin searching the internet, to divine a new way to ascertain the boy's status. Yet he'd find nothing. It was New York City—hit and run stories went unreported all the time, particularly with regard to the homeless. Making matters worse was the fact that, on the night of the accident, Matt was so out of his mind that he couldn't remember the location where it occurred. He could only approximate vague coordinates based on how far he'd driven. And that didn't even address the fact that the boy could've wandered for blocks before seeking help. There were so many possibilities, so many uncertainties—yet his mind could not stop ruminating.

Matt continued on his way from Meda's apartment, her reaction a devastating exclamation mark on his already raging sense of estrangement, and he arrived at an intersection with a four-way stop sign. Matt checked for oncoming cars and then stood a moment longer at the crossroads. In one direction was his apartment. In the other, his car. Matt wasn't looking forward to going home—another torturous, sleepless night was unavoidable. What if he took a drive instead? If he could discern the location of his encounter, at least, he could achieve some modicum of progress. He peered up the avenue towards his apartment, pondered, and instead headed towards his car.

Normally jumping into the driver's seat was an automatic affair, something done with barely any thought. This time was different, though; everything seemed familiar yet foreign. He realized that the last time he'd been behind the wheel was that fateful night and, with a flush of memories, his perceptions changed. Technically nothing was different—three discarded coffee cups lay upside down on the passenger seat floor, just as they had that night, and old reports from work were still scattered on the back seat. Yet Matt felt as if he was a completely different person. It occurred to him that his sense of dislocation was permeating things as commonplace as his car and, in an odd sense of accomplishment, he felt as if he'd done the right thing by deciding against going home.

He began to drive and quickly realized that traffic at 8:30 was far different than what it was at midnight. Rush hour was not yet over. In particular, many were still getting out of work in the warehouse district through which he drove. Matt had anticipated driving slowly, cautiously, with the opportunity to eye up the streets he passed to check for familiarity. Yet it took mere moments for a line of cars to stack up behind him and the honking to begin. He couldn't see down the streets adequately without creeping but he risked another accident if he continued to take his eyes off the road in such traffic.

Matt pulled over a few times to let the cars pass but, each time, another line built up as soon he began to drive. He repeated the process several times and then, frustrated, stopped at the curb and threw the car into park. He was too frazzled, too sleep-deprived and he knew he was bound to create an accident if he continued. Several cars zoomed past in harsh, strobe-like waves of light and Matt slammed the palm of his hand into the wheel. All he wanted was to find out what happened to that little boy! But, despite his best intentions, he couldn't even divine where they'd met.

"Damn!" he hollered to no one in particular, looking about the area feebly, as if the asphalt and concrete might have anything to offer.

He shifted his car back into gear and was about to pull a U-turn—hoping against hope that he might actually get some sleep when he got home—when his headlights landed on some graffiti on the wall under the overpass. It wasn't a word or even traditional English-language letters. Instead, it looked like a combination of letters smashed together, one atop the other. Though created with crude spray paint, it was nonetheless perfectly circular and certain portions were so precise that a stencil would've been required to produce it. "Holy," muttered Matt, before parking the car and, then, jumping out to investigate.

"Dirty Lord," he whispered in awe, approaching the wall with an air of spiritual reverence. He raised his hand to it without thought, as if to verify that it was real, and touched his fingertips to it.

A decade earlier, Matt and Magee had arrived at the exact spot after evacuating a particularly lame house party. After suffering through a few penniless years in New York City after college, things were finally starting to look up for the pair—Matt had landed a decent job and Magee's art had begun appearing in shows. They'd decided to leave the party, though it was still relatively early, and begun to wander with paper-bagged bottles in hand. And, for whatever reason, their odyssey had taken them to the graffiti at this location.

"What d'ya think that's supposed to say?" Magee had asked as the pair approached.

"I think that's an 'R'," said Matt, after appraising the symbol for a moment, tracing with his finger where he saw the letter.

"And an 'I'," said Magee, doing likewise.

"And two 'D's. See them? On either side."

"Oh yeaaaahhh," said Magee.

Each became more focused, taking time to appraise it as one might do a painting at a gallery. "And a 'W', I think," added Matt.

"No, a 'Y'," corrected Magee. Matt nodded, re-evaluating his initial thought, and, Magee continued, "Dir...D-I-R..."

"Dirty!"

"Dirty Lord!" cried both simultaneously, each coming to the same synchronic conclusion though such a result was preposterous. They looked at each other in awe for the briefest moment then burst out in guttural laughter, falling into the other's shoulder in the process.

"Dirty Lord: Master of those who dwell under the bridge," Matt announced in a deep, falsely earnest tone. "Patron saint of the misbegotten wretches who live their lives out of their minds."

"Caretaker of nonsense," added Magee. "Instigator of insanity."

The two continued to giggle, constructing first the Dirty Lord philosophy and then his origins. They decided that he had elves that worked for him, ones who made people lie about their age and create fake IDs; that he could come out of the graffiti whenever he wanted but could only be forced out by yelling gibberish to an unsuspecting person in a loud room; that he was older than all the other world's gods and goddesses, but he had never gotten off his ass to establish any rules.

From there, Dirty Lord fused into the pair's lexicon and their friend's as well. Then the expression morphed, changing from the name of the entity to a verb whose meaning was never established. "Dirty Lording," became a pseudonym for getting drunk, or for doing something undesirable while in an inebriated state. Eventually, they used the phrase too much. It became trite and, with time, they stopped using it altogether.

These memories came back to Matt in a rush as he stood in front of the improbably located graffiti. The sight of it brought back a flood of reminiscence, recollections of people and things he hadn't contemplated in years. Those times seemed so simple, so naïve. It had been an article of faith that Magee was going to be a world-famous painter and that Matt was going to be a best-selling author. Their friend Cynthia was going to be one of the best chefs in the country and Ben's films were going to win awards. It was all so straightforward and there was never any entertainment of other possibilities. "What happened?" Matt nearly asked. But he didn't. He didn't want to.

Instead he sighed. He wasn't overtly sad, nor was he happy. Instead, the two emotions merged, causing him to feel a strange version of wistful. The frustration he'd felt earlier metastasized with his meditation on times past to produce a sensation of rueful acceptance. With a nod, he turned to leave, unsure where he was headed.

He took a few contemplative steps back towards his car and, absentmindedly, looked up. The area was dimly lit, even as car headlights flashed past on the six-lane expressway beside. But across the highway was a storefront that caught Matt's attention. It had the appearance of any other corner bodega, garish and bright but otherwise nondescript. Yet something caught Matt's eye. He continued to stare at it, the bright yellow awning announcing, "Two Rods Deli," to the darkness while the lottery sign tantalized people with the amount of the latest jackpot. It was anachronistic, offering an odds-defying chance in spite of the harsh backdrop of asphalt and concrete.

Then it hit Matt. All at once, the idea came, the light in the dark. It shot like a jet in his mind with promises of hope. That was what Carol needed. Carol, the character in one of the stories for his novel. All along, he knew she needed something else, some *reason* in spite of it all. And there it was. The lottery numbers. Staring him right in the face.

Matt's hand moved to cover his mouth. He began to bounce on his heels, more rapidly with each passing moment. Then, in the alembic illumination of the bodega sign, he jumped behind the wheel of his car and sped off.

CAROL

It was only a single word, one tantalizingly distant word that prevented Carol from finishing the crossword puzzle she had been laboring to complete for almost four days. Normally crosswords were a breeze for her. Often she could complete them without even slowing down from word to word. And it wasn't as if she needed some fancy college degree, either; forty six years in the school of hard knocks was all the experience she needed. But, for this particular collection of puzzles, a friend had challenged her, stating that the book would be impossible to complete. So, naturally, Carol was bound and determined to finish it in its entirety. And now this single word—eleven letters, with 'E' as the second letter, 'I' as the fourth, 'E' again as the sixth, and 'TU' as the ninth and tenth—stood in her way.

It was 7:50 AM and she'd stayed awake too late the previous night working on that darn puzzle. Her shift at Walmart started at 8:30 and, though it was only a twenty minute drive to the store, she knew she had to get moving. Dropping the contemptible book onto the table, Carol shot up from her chair and got her sweater out of the closet. She wasn't about to let that book get the best of her but, for now, it would have to wait. Money didn't grow on trees and her mortgage wasn't about to pay for itself.

The air that morning had a bite to it and Carol was reminded that she'd have to wrap up the rose bush before the first frost. That had always been Steve's job. But as she got into the car seat, re-checking the mirrors to make sure they hadn't changed, she reminded herself once again that everything was her job now. There was only one person in this world that she could count on now and that person was Carol Beckworth.

As usual, she was the third person to arrive. Renita would be in the accounting room, getting the cash ready for the day, while Nick, that jerk of a manager, would be unlocking the door for employees. Garrett, the long-haired dolt in the garden shop was supposed to be there already, getting pallets of merchandise out to the sidewalk in front but, of course, he was nowhere to be seen. Carol got out of her car and cast an eagle eye up and down the parking lot to see if he was en route but, with no sign of the simpleton, she huffed in displeasure. If Nick expected her to drag fully loaded pallets around he had another thing coming.

"Hi Carol," sighed Nick, his keys jangling as he opened the door.

"Hello Nick," said Carol through a taut, grimacing smile.

Carol strode to the back of the store, exchanged pleasantries with Renita while picking up the drawer for her register, and proceeded to her spot in the clothing and apparel department. Not a day went by that she wasn't shocked at what the girls were wearing. Just when she thought she'd seen it all, an even skimpier piece hit the market. Carol didn't blame the young girls; she believed in the right of free expression, of course. But she also recognized that, untethered, children would not always do what was best for themselves. Instead, she blamed the parents. What might seem cool to the children now was merely a gateway to laziness and welfare later. She'd seen the process with her own eyes and, when the day came that a parent asked her what she thought, she had her response ready.

It didn't take Carol long to realize that Shanice had left the department in shambles yet again. Carol had to clean up after those kids on the night shift every single day; it was as if they didn't do any facing of the merchandise at all. Complaints to Nick disappeared into the ether and any snide comments made to Shanice seemed to escape the fool's comprehension. So, with a sigh, she set about organizing and re-hanging the merchandise. The first customers of the day began to appear and, gradually, Carol almost forgot about the crossword puzzle.

⋈ ⋈ ⋈

Steve had left seven years earlier. For nineteen years she'd kept a good home and performed all her wifely duties. Then one Saturday morning she found out it had all been for nothing. She'd put her education aside in the beginning of their marriage, frittered away her most fertile years while he hemmed and hawed over having children, and endured his mid-life crisis which had occurred ten years ahead of schedule. And in the end she had nothing to show for it. He'd tried to appear gallant, leaving her with the house and virtually all their possessions but that only served to infuriate Carol further. She saw his conciliatory actions for what they truly were: A way to clear his own conscience. As if he could make everything right by leaving her with simple material goods. Part of her wanted to forsake all of it, to prevent him from achieving any type of societal exoneration or victory. But, upon overwhelming pressure from her friends, she'd relented and kept the empty, ridiculously outsized house.

Her last communication with him had occurred four years ago, a mundane matter involving old tax issues. Yet she still thought about him every day. All those years squandered and now he was off with that hussy! Every backache she suffered from shoveling the driveway, every new wrinkle she found when looking in the mirror, every time someone called her, "ma'am," she was reminded of Steve. The best years of her life were gone, down the drain. All because of him.

At the end of her shift that day, Carol passed the customer service center at the front of the store and spied a man who'd just received an application from Sheila. He was a husky young man with a shaved head, a tattoo running up his neck, and jeans that looked like they'd been through a war. She'd seen his type before: Men in their mid-20s with the maturity of children, the type that appeared on the courtroom television shows and were last seen in the paper after being busted for drugs. Her pace slowed as she continued to dissect the man with her eyes, watching him leave and then strut out to the parking lot. Despite her reservations about Sheila, she had to find out what was going on.

"Please don't tell me we're planning on hiring that convict," said Carol.

Sheila sighed. "He just wanted an application."

"Well, yes, I can see that. But we're not going to actually hire him are we?"

"I don't know. He asked for an application so I gave it to him. Just that simple. Anyway, we're already down two people in shipping since Bill and Juan left."

"But that doesn't mean we take in any ruffian off the street to handle the merchandise."

"Carol, it's not my decision to make anyway," said Sheila, growing frustrated as she attempted to close out her register for the day. "He hasn't even filled out the application yet, much less had an interview."

"Well, I was just pointing out that we should be careful," said Carol. If Sheila didn't care who they hired then Carol wasn't about to concern herself either: Let the place go to hell if that's how everyone wanted to act. She pivoted, waited a beat for Sheila to say goodbye and, when it appeared no declaration was forthcoming, she continued on her way.

On the way home she pulled into the familiar gas station where she bought her nightly lottery ticket. She'd been playing those numbers for nearly a decade: A combination of her birthday, her mother's birthday, and the anniversary she'd formerly shared with Steve. After dutifully buying them day after day, year after year, she was loath to change them, should they actually come in the day she switched. Yet the dissonance involved in rehashing her former anniversary was a picked-at scab whose irony wasn't entirely lost on Carol.

"Hello, I'd like to buy a ticket," said Carol, mustering a congenial smile.

The scruffy young man behind the counter appeared dazed when she spoke and an awkward pause occurred before he seemed to wake up. "Oh, I'm sorry, the machine's broke, ma'am."

Carol eyed it up. The LED lights across the front continued to flash the night's drawing and everything appeared to be in order. "What's wrong with it?" she asked.

"I'm...I'm not sure," said the boy, shifting his stance. "It's just broke. I'm sorry."

Carol peered at the machine again and then looked back to the boy. Despite stopping at the gas station every day for years she didn't recognize him.

"We have another store down on Delaware Ave. I'm pretty sure that one's working," he added. The words sounded too practiced, however, as if he'd already spoken them thirty times that day. Put side-by-side with his shifty body language, Carol saw that it was an obvious attempt to shoo her out the door.

"Are you new here?" asked Carol.

The boy smiled for no discernible reason and proudly proclaimed, "Yep. Just started yesterday."

"So," said Carol, picking her words carefully, "are you sure the machine is broken? Or is it simply a matter of not knowing how to work it?"

"Oh no, I'm pretty sure I know how to work it," said the boy with false bravado. "Linda, the manager, showed me how." Then, when the silence hung a beat too long, the boy plugged once again, "I'm pretty sure the one at the store on Delaware Ave. is working, though."

Carol frowned. She'd watched innumerable employees enter the numbers through the years; it wasn't rocket science. They had idiot-proofed the machine enough that she was certain, once she took stock of the keyboard, she'd be able to do the transaction herself. In her most appeasing, schoolteacher-esque tone, she said, "How's this: Can I come back there and take a look at the machine with you? We can enter the numbers together just to be positive it's not broken? Then, if it works, you'll know how to do it yourself."

"No, it's broke, ma'am," the boy said flatly.

His statement surprised her with its obtuse, blunt defiance. Whereas previously the boy had seemed like a guileless simpleton, he now transformed into a stubborn, arms-crossed troll. Carol had tried her best to be polite but now he was testing her patience.

"Young man," said Carol, mustering a plaintive smile, "I've been buying my tickets at this location for years. While I'm not superstitious I'm sure you can understand the importance of tradition with something like this. I truly do not want to go to another location if at all possible, especially when this machine is clearly operational. If you could just humor me: Let me come back there and show you how it works. Then we'd both be better off."

"No, I'm sorry but we can't let people back here. Against the rules. It's definitely broke, ma'am. I'm pretty sure the location at Delaware Ave. has one that—"

"Yes, I heard you the first time you said that! And the second time," interrupted Carol. "I do not want to drive to the Delaware Avenue branch when there is a perfectly fine machine right here. All I need is thirty seconds behind the counter to show you how it's done. I can assure you I am not going to rob you."

The boy chuckled at the suggestion, oblivious to the fact that he should've been embarrassed by his own ineptitude. "Oh, I know. I didn't think you'd rob me. It's just...y'know...the rules."

"The rules," Carol repeated. She wanted to ask if any of these rules stipulated that he actually know how to do his job. The know-nothing boy only shrugged in return, however, an obstinate nonchalance that shot Carol's ire to new heights. She recognized the reality of the situation, though: If she went behind the counter and forcefully created the ticket herself there was the strong chance that it would be disallowed if, in fact, she won. It shouldn't come to that, obviously. This simpleton shouldn't have the power to stand between her and something so dear. Yet that was the reality she had to accept.

"I pray for this generation," Carol said as she yanked her purse off the counter. The boy seemed more relieved than angry, however, adding an exclamation point to Carol's already blazing frustration.

It was a minor miracle that Carol got home without a car accident. She raced to lights that were still red and blew through at least a couple stop signs on the way. She should've simply marched in back of that counter and threatened to create the ticket herself; that would've spurred that halfwit into action. She should've called the manager or the store's headquarters; another plan of action that might've gotten the punk's attention. Heck, she should've started embarrassing him in front of other customers; anything to make that lazy slug get his butt in gear. Yet, even as she continued to obsess over the things she could have or should have done, she took pains to exonerate herself. The problem was his, and his alone. She had no reason to blame herself. Who knows, he might've saved her some money. Think of all the money she'd thrown away on that foolish game through the years. Maybe, actually, it was time to give up on it. Maybe that fool had done her a favor. But if those numbers came in and she didn't have the ticket?

Carol's ire remained undiminished even as she stomped into her otherwise tranquil home. She threw her purse on the table in mute rebellion and didn't bother to hang her sweater in the hall closet. Then, for a long moment she stood, peering about the room with her hands on her hips and a scowl slashed across her face. She considered going right back out, buying a ticket from a different store, establishing a different pattern, and never giving that terrible gas station another red cent. But then she considered how foolish she'd feel if the numbers weren't winners. To think what a sucker she'd be, after a long day of work, to go out again for something she knew damn well was going to result in nothing.

"Huagh!" she grunted, seizing the top of one of the kitchen chairs, lifting it, and slamming it down again. It was immature and petulant. But she didn't care. Or, at least, she didn't care until the vibration caused a book on the table to shift and slide towards her. It was the crossword puzzle she had yet to complete, the page still pulled open with the cover tucked underneath. There in all its glory was the unfinished puzzle, six empty squares bereft of letters staring up at Carol.

She twirled on her heel stiffly, her nostrils flaring as she strode to the living room. Her movements were tight; her arms pencil straight at her sides and her head cocked at an odd angle. So robotic were her steps that it almost appeared as if something else was controlling her movements. She had no goal in mind; she just felt compelled to leave the kitchen. It was only when she spied her answering machine that her rigid stature lost a slight bit of its edge.

Its light was flashing, indicating that a single message had been left. She hadn't seen that in quite some time. When Dottie called she almost always called in batches, often remembering one more important thing she forgot to add. Yet it was too soon for her job to be calling; she'd only just left. So, with a mix of annoyance and curiosity, she punched the button on the machine.

"Hi Carol, this is Michelle. Long time, no talk, sis! I'm sorry I didn't get back to you sooner: You positively need to start texting. It makes everything so much easier."

Carol showed the briefest flash of a grin. Michelle was six years younger and hopelessly irresponsible. But it was nice to hear her voice.

"Anyway, I wanted to tell you: Y'know how I used to go to school with Steve's younger sister, Lorraine? Back in college? Well I ran into her the other day. I know: You and Steve didn't exactly break up on the best of terms so I thought you might get a kick out of this. Apparently, Steve passed away! He was out scuba diving and something happened. He came up too quick or something. Lorraine said this happened like almost two years ago. Crazy, right? I mean: Steve out scuba diving? No wonder it all went wrong, right? Anyway, I just wanted to share that tidbit. I'll see you soon, dear. Bye!"

If, previously, Carol was a barely restrained coil of bound tension, she was now made of stone. There was no hint of agitation, no expectation of sudden, violent movement. Instead, there was merely silence. It was immutable, an absence of anything whatsoever.

She should've been jumping for joy. She recognized that. She should've been kicking up her heels and pouring champagne to celebrate the lout's demise. But that wasn't how she felt. And that sensation was as stark and barren as the news itself.

Instead she felt stiff, frozen in place. Cold. A vague corner of her mind tried to reassure her that these sorts of moments never played out the way one imaged. But that voice was small and unsure of itself. Carol didn't trust it.

It was bad enough that Steve had wasted nineteen years of her life in that sham of a marriage. Worse yet was the fact that he'd remained in her thoughts since its dissolution, day-in, day-out. But to find out that he hadn't even been on the planet for two of those seven years? It made Carol feel foolish, deceived. Why hadn't she been told until now? All that time spent wondering about him; all that mental energy spent being angry at him; it was all a complete waste. He hadn't even been alive! In a way, it felt as if he'd won somehow from beyond the grave. But in another, more horrible way, Carol suspected there had never been a contest in the first place.

The revelation represented an end. An end to what, she couldn't say. But with nothing left to do, she began to make her way up the stairs, as if in a trance. She didn't bother turning off the lights, she left her sweater on the sofa, and she clutched the banister tight. Then she cried for hours before finally, mercifully drifting off to sleep.

⋈ ⋈ ⋈

The following morning she put on her tattered robe and retrieved the newspaper from her porch, as was tradition. She still felt numb. She still had an empty chasm in her thought process, a gnawing, undefined absence. But in the act of retrieving the paper she had a purpose, at least, however transitory.

Immediately she flipped to the section that listed the previous night's winning lottery numbers. Her traditional combination, the one incorporating her and Steve's anniversary, had not come in. It wasn't even close. She knew she should feel relieved; the devastation she would've felt if her numbers were the winners was unthinkable.

Yet it was a pyrrhic victory nonetheless, one that only reinforced the sense of helplessness within her. She realized she could probably forget to buy the tickets again and there'd be no terrible consequence. There was no need to be so diligent, so formal in their purchase. In fact, part of her thought that she could likely stop buying them altogether. Because it just didn't matter.

She got ready for work the same as she did every other day. Thoughts of Steve came into her mind and she was almost successful shooing them away. And, on her way out the door, she snuck a passing glance at the book of crossword puzzles. She hesitated, pursed her lips as she stared it down, and then turned to go.

At least a different person was behind the counter at the convenience store the next morning. Gone was the simple-minded dolt and, in his place, was a young lady who appeared much more clean-cut. "Hi, I was hoping to get a ticket," said Carol, motioning to the controversial lottery machine.

"Sure thing," said the girl, jumping to help.

Carol eyed her up, saw that she had much more going on behind the eyes than that previous fellow, and decided to pose a question. "Out of curiosity: Has that machine been giving you any trouble?"

"What? No, it's been fine," said the girl.

"It wasn't broken? Hasn't been repaired recently?"

"No, not that I know of. In fact, if it was, I think I'd have to call a technician from the state lottery commission. It's under their authority."

"I see," said Carol, nodding smugly, satisfied that she'd been vindicated.

"Okay, what numbers would you like?" asked the girl after queuing up the machine.

Carol began rattling off the numbers and, while doing so, spied an open book behind the counter. While the young girl entered the numbers and printed up the ticket, Carol grew curious. She asked, "What are you reading?"

The girl glanced over at the book and, with a wave, said, "Oh, it's for school. We have a quiz in a week and when it's slow here I try to get some reading done."

Carol didn't necessarily approve of such dereliction while on the job, but she was impressed nonetheless. "Oh, well that's quite industrious. What subject?"

"English 212: Desideratum of Voice in Modern Literature. It was supposed to be an easy class but the professor is much more...."

The young girl's words trailed off in the background; Carol was no longer listening. Instead, her eyes glazed over as if doing complex math equations in her mind as she focused on the word the girl had just spoken: Desideratum. It was eleven letters long. The second letter was an, "E." The fourth was an, "I." Another, "E," was the sixth. That was it! That was the last remaining word for the crossword puzzle!

After a few seconds, the girl realized that Carol was in her own world and, with awkward awareness, she stopped talking and moved to the cash register. "That'll be one dollar," said the girl.

It was enough to snap Carol out of her enthrallment. "Oh!" she said, louder than she would have liked, and she was sent digging into her purse. "Thank you," she added, abstractly, as she did so.

"No problem," shrugged the girl.

"No, I mean it. You've been a great help," insisted Carol before seizing the ticket and rushing out.

She had the word! The puzzle would finally be complete! All that toil, all that mental energy spent on that dastardly crossword and, finally, she'd be able to put it to rest. She leapt into her car, fully intending to drive home and fill in those magical letters with delight.

But then she realized what time it was. She was due at her job in fifteen minutes. There was no way she could get home, complete the puzzle, and get back to work in time. As instantaneous as her enthusiasm had risen upon finding that long sought-after word, it now plummeted just as precipitously. She hadn't expected such a revelation on the drive to work.

The knowledge of the word should've been enough, she recognized. She told herself that it shouldn't matter when she literally filled the letters into the boxes. Yet, all the same, she yearned to complete that darn puzzle. The craving made her feel foolish, childish. She shouldn't care so much about a stupid crossword in a silly old book. And she especially shouldn't consider risking her livelihood for such a petty desire. Yet the urge to drive back to her home was practically overwhelming

For a long time she sat stock-still in her car, torn between rushing back home or going to her job. Her brow was fixed in an ant-like frown and her hands gripped the steering wheel with white-knuckled intensity. Resentment roiled within her as she told herself that it was just a crossword puzzle, that she could fill the word in later. Then, shaking her head side-to-side with grim fatalism, she decided that she had to get to work.

She shifted the car into gear and it was a minor miracle that she didn't run over the man who'd materialized in front of her car. The car had only rolled a few feet yet, when she was forced to slam on the breaks, an emotional thunderclap cracked inside her. She had made her decision to go, as loathe as she was to do so, and she didn't want to give herself any chance to reconsider. She was doing the right thing! She was going to her job, stifling every instinct for fulfillment! Yet here was this grotesque mockery of a human, a man who'd probably never denied himself anything, wandering about in a stupor in front of her car.

"You're a druggie!" she cried, yet the man didn't move. Instead, he remained fixed in place, a slack-jawed road block that prevented her from moving.

Carol's hands trembled. She inhaled two quick breaths, nearly hyperventilating. Then desperately, plaintively, as if appealing to higher power, she cried, "Well? Move!"

Then finally, mercifully, the monster began to amble on and Carol jammed her foot on the gas pedal. She had cried into the pillow the previous night and she had no intention of doing so again, especially on the way to work. Yet, despite herself, her emotions boiled over at the first stop light and she was forced to yank a tissue out of her purse. Damn that man! Damn Steve and his floozy wife! Damn the lottery and her rundown house and all those wasted years! Damn them all!

She managed to compose herself in the parking lot, wasting precious minutes in the process. Her stride to the employee's lounge was tight and quick and, apart from curt pleasantries, she didn't say a word to her co-workers as she passed. She managed to clock in only two minutes late and, still silent, she started her day as the first customers arrived. And later, when a handful of people at the front of the store witnessed a growing orb of energy that illuminated the store with a harsh, piercing light, Carol's thoughts were still occupied by the unfinished crossword puzzle.

MATT

Matt called in sick to work that Friday. The epiphany he'd experienced at the sight of the Dirty Lord graffiti and the bodega sign across the highway had provided the perfect means to humanize his character, Carol. With that final piece of the puzzle in hand, he'd spent the night writing and any sense of time or place vanished—the only break in his frenzy came when he took five minutes to leave a voicemail for his boss and feign sickness.

"*Ends of the World*," was Matt's novel. While the title referenced exactly what happened in the stories—the apocalyptic end of the planet—it also served as a double entendre regarding the personal revelations of the characters. At its heart, each story had to be about the individual, the end of *their* world, their expectations and hopes. The financial collapse had crushed people's dreams, college students were graduating to a hostile work environment, and technological progress was changing human interactions at an ever-accelerating rate. It was as if many had been told a big giant lie, that they'd built their expectations based on a world that no longer existed. Yet, despite such changes in trajectory, people found something important to keep them going. Whether characters achieved their goals, had them dashed, or arrived at some other conclusion, the overarching thrust of each story involved the motivation that kept humans going, the secret desires that made them get out of bed in the morning.

Just as critical was each character's awareness of their motivations. Everyone has a vision of what goals are most important in life; many of these dreams revolve around common themes like family, friends, religion, or career. Yet, in many cases, those weren't the desires that literally drove people to action. Often, peoples' actual identities were formed by far less tangible forces, motivations that they, themselves, might not even recognize. A career woman, successful in every regard, may still be fighting ghosts from high school; a priest may have serious doubts about religious leaders yet pursue his vocation due to his love for mankind. The tides beneath the surface could be more important than the easily visible waves atop.

In terms of the apocalypse—the actual end of the world—Matt had a plan. He didn't want to get too hung up on the details, inadvertently turning his work into a hard-core science fiction piece in the process, but he recognized he had to have some explanation for such a cataclysmic event. There were many ways that life on earth could be extinguished but so many required expositions that'd been trodden over already. If he had to spend a page or two of every story explaining an asteroid collision, for example, he would've already lost sight of the respective character's path to self-discovery. In the end, he'd settled on a possibility which was unlikely but probably no more unlikely than many of the other common scenarios: A global apocalypse resulting from experiments run in a particle accelerator. According to one theory, the act of smashing subatomic particles together in a collider might create a new, previously unobserved particle that would then fuse with matter surrounding it, converting more and more matter into this new material. In such a situation, a chain reaction would result as the converted matter—strangelets—grew exponentially larger. In a matter of moments it would engulf the earth and turn it into one gigantic blob of strangelets. While such a cataclysmic outcome was quite remote, it seemed suitably enigmatical for a work that explored people's inscrutable motivations.

With that in mind, one story in the collection had to be about the person conducting the experiment at the particle collider. There could be no overarching narrative without an actual explanation of how the end of the world came about. Beyond that, Matt knew he had to craft at least one story about parenting, and the bittersweet realities of such dreams achieved. While a newborn baby might represent untold amounts of hope and joy, some parents are surprised by their feelings of frustration and resentment when dealing with a screeching hellion at 3:00 AM. Similarly, when dating or getting married, some people experience complicated emotional reactions when they find the person of their dreams. One man may realize, too late, that his wife isn't exactly what he expected and blame her for his disappointment; another might decide that his own expectations were unfair and live happily ever after.

Not every story had to involve changes that were quite so momentous, though. The shifts in the trajectory of one's life weren't always as right-angle obvious as a newborn or a wedding. Sometimes, the decision to go to a particular store could send one down an entirely unexpected path, the importance of that decision only appreciated in hindsight. Taking a picture of a thunderstorm could lead to a lifelong photography obsession; running into an old co-worker could prompt an entire re-evaluation of one's career. There had to be a place for those stories when exploring the end of a person's worldview, as well.

Carol's story was an example of this. The happenstance re-discovery of the Dirty Lord graffiti had led to Matt's view of the lottery sign across the street and, through that, he'd found the key ingredient to propel the tale. Previously, he'd feared Carol might come across as an unsympathetic character to some readers and he knew that her persona might require nuance. So he thought he could add some depth to her motivations through the use of lottery tickets and a crossword puzzle, things that might be so inconsequential to readers yet represent so much to Carol.

The result was that, with his creative impasse bulldozed, Matt had no choice but to avoid the office—he collapsed into bed at eleven o'clock the following morning and was unconscious for almost twenty-four hours. His sleep patterns had been non-existent since Monday and, in practical terms, that was the biggest reason he crashed so hard. But, beyond literal exhaustion, his shamanistic fervor while writing was the volcanic release atop such fatigue. It was only fifteen pages—a few hours of work for some writers. For Matt, though, such impassioned writing sessions led to a peculiar rearrangement of his sense of self. After conjuring such material, he often required time to disconnect and actively remind himself of his real, corporeal existence.

Sunday he awoke, ate breakfast, and gradually accepted the fact that he had to patch things up with Meda. He was the one who'd lost the tickets so it didn't matter if he thought her reaction had been over the top or not—he was the one who had made the mistake. Their argument had been essentially forgotten during his writing binge but, as he came back to reality, he recognized how terribly he'd acted.

On the way to her apartment he picked up a bouquet of flowers. It was lame and he knew it, yet he wanted to offer some acknowledgement that he was wrong. Then, immediately upon arrival, he explained how he hadn't been sleeping and that he had no right to take out his frustration on her. "I know I should've contacted you earlier," he said. "It's not a proper excuse, but I was on a tear writing and I didn't want to stop when the juices were flowing. I knew you were mad and I shouldn't have left you hanging since Thursday."

"I wasn't mad at you, you idiot. I was worried about you," said Meda, frowning but not angry.

"Worried? About what?" asked Matt.

"You weren't yourself the other day, babe. It was weird."

"Well, yeah. I was still angry at myself for losing those tickets and I felt like I needed to explain."

"Forget about the stupid tickets," said Meda. "You lost them. It was an honest mistake. Big deal."

"I guess I figured you'd be angrier."

"I'm disappointed, yes. But it's not the end of the world," said Meda, laying a hand on Matt's arm. "Besides, that day was turning out to be very hectic anyway: It looks like Janet's baby shower will be that afternoon."

The mention of the baby shower triggered a response of horror in Matt's mind. The day spent writing had allowed him to keep thoughts of the little boy he'd struck at bay but, upon such a cue, the guilt and frustration came roaring back. The whole point of his drive Thursday night was to reconstruct what'd happened. Yet, upon viewing the sibylline Dirty Lord graffiti, everything had taken a ninety-degree turn.

The rumination froze Matt, his face blank for a protracted moment. He didn't reply to Meda and, with the awkward silence only lengthening, she asked, "Everything okay?"

"What? Yeah. Yeah—sorry. Everything's fine," said Matt, broken out of his stupor and returning to reality.

"You look like you just saw a ghost."

"I'm fine," Matt said with a sheepish smile. "I just remembered something. I'm sorry."

"Okay," said Meda slowly, a new edge in her voice. She looked Matt up and down and, without realizing she was doing so, took a step away from him.

Matt didn't want to tell Meda about the boy. Not yet. Just as he hadn't brought it up to Magee several nights earlier, he had no desire to confront the topic when he didn't have all of the facts. He told himself that he needed to gather more information, that he didn't want to worry loved ones unnecessarily. But there was also another, more pragmatic reason he was avoiding the issue: If anything terrible *had* happened to the child, any discussion held might make them accessories to the crime. Better to just keep the topic under wraps, he reasoned.

"I had just forgotten about the shower, that's all," said Matt, moving closer to her.

"Yes, I'm sure that's it," said Meda, her words frigid.

"I'm sorry. I just zoned out," Matt said, recognizing the sudden change in her demeanor. He moved to hug her but she only barely reciprocated.

"Okay," she said simply, after disengaging from him. Then, after a moment she added, "Let's just forget it."

The pair spent the rest of the day together: Matt managed to keep thoughts of the child at bay much of the time and Meda temporarily dismissed Matt's odd reaction to the baby shower. They enjoyed themselves and put their respective concerns on the back burner. Yet something remained lodged between them, an ill-defined presence, like that of a neighbor peering in through the window.

MATT

Matt awoke the next morning possessed by a new fervor: He had to find out what happened to that little boy—if not for the boy's sake then, at the very least, for himself. While his time spent at Meda's had been loving and relaxing, he now recognized the wedge that'd been dropped between them. He couldn't continue to hide the events from her while, at the same time, pretending that everything was fine.

To spur himself to action, Matt downed a cup of coffee on the way to his car, adding a fourth empty cup to his growing collection of detritus in the process. He reasoned that the best place to begin his search was the resumption of the drive he'd taken a few nights previous. If he could just find some evidence that the boy was okay he could put the whole matter behind him—he wouldn't have to tell Meda, or Magee, or anyone about the incident.

Driving down the service road ramp on a Sunday morning in daylight was much easier than Matt's previous foray. This buoyed his spirits and he glided past the Dirty Lord graffiti with a grin. He shifted forward in his seat as he drove, leaning into the wheel to get a better view of each street he passed. Stop signs were sporadic in the area, appearing at irregular intervals, which meant he had little time to view certain streets he passed. Diminished traffic notwithstanding, it was nonetheless an effort to peer down each street and assess it instantly while still keeping an eye on the road.

He passed one street, peered up it, and saw a gas station at the end. It couldn't be the one he was seeking because he had no memory such a station. He passed the next—no fence present, just buildings. Couldn't be the right one either. Passed the next; a red building. Matt didn't remember a red building. Passed the next; a weird sign. Passed the next; just didn't seem right. Passed the next; the Stoic Man was walking down it. Passed the next; Matt didn't look down it.

Matt slammed on his brakes and a car, its horn blaring, whipped past. He checked the rearview mirror, confirmed it was safe to turn up the next street, and managed to pull over to the curb. What was that guy doing there? It was him, right? It had to be him. His mien was so distinctive—the embodiment of an 11th grade chemistry teacher. The man's eyes were glassy yet observant; his features hard yet unremarkable. He blended into the background of the subway and, miraculously, never blocked anyone's path. Yet, once Matt had taken notice of him, he was impossible to miss. That was how Matt was so certain it was him. On that random street. While Matt was investigating.

Matt's memories flashed to the subway ride that Tuesday night, when his mind was already reeling from the lightning strike at his office. The Stoic Man had materialized beside him, like a chameleon emerging from camouflage. Matt had been readying to glance down the car when, out of the blue, the man appeared and asked, "What do you think you're doing?"

"Ah. Excuse me?" Matt asked, caught utterly unprepared.

"I asked: What do you think you're doing?" the man repeated, automaton-like.

"I'm taking the subway home?"

"No. With your life. What do you think you're doing with your life?"

Matt's condition went from surprise to outright befuddlement in a fraction of a second. Questions abounded: Why was the man there, at that exact moment? What did he want? How had he snuck up on him so effortlessly? Before Matt could say anything, however, the Stoic Man added, "Because I might have the answer for you: The Tarot."

Then the man reached behind him and produced a deck of Tarot cards, still sealed in plastic as it might appear on the shelf of a big-box retail store. Suddenly, Matt's mood took another turn, this time moving to one which was both relieved and disappointed. It was only a sales pitch! The man was trying to sell him something.

The man held the deck in front of Matt for a long moment. Matt had assumed he would launch into a monologue regarding the potency of the cards and their ability to bring fulfillment to one's life. But no. He just held them there. He didn't smile, he didn't waver—he didn't do anything. And with the awkwardness hitting a bizarre crescendo, Matt said, "No thanks. I think I'm all set."

"I'm sorry to hear that," said the Stoic Man, withdrawing the deck without another word. If that was his normal pitch, Matt mused, it would be a miracle if he ever made a single sale. Then, after another awkward pause, the man added, "Let me offer you this: The Moon. The artwork on this card is exquisite and I'm sure it will pique your curiosity."

The man produced a single card out of his front pocket and offered it to Matt. Matt was ready to resist, to say he wasn't interested—what was he supposed to do with a single Tarot card anyway?—but then decided to accept it if only to make the man go away. Matt gave it a cursory glance: The card showed a rugged, moonlit landscape with two wolves beside a body of water, howling skyward. He would admit the image was striking but, hoping to put an end to the encounter, he shoved the card in his bag and said, "Thank you. Now please. I had a rough day." For another long moment the pair remained as statues, Matt's eyebrows raised. Then the Stoic Man nodded and, without a word, walked back towards the opposite end of the train.

Unto itself, seeing the man on both subway rides that day was a large coincidence. Then, having such a weird exchange with him that night was unsettling. But to see the man again, walking down the street Matt was investigating in search of clues about the boy? Matt was positive something else was at work, something outside the boundaries of random chance. He reappraised the situation: His goal was to find the area where he'd hit the boy and take his cue from what he found. In a perfect scenario he might find the boy on a street corner nearby. He recognized the chances of that were low, however, but thought he could scour local basketball courts or other places kids congregated. And, on the likely chance those plans didn't produce results, Matt hoped to at least ascertain the location of the encounter.

Now the Stoic Man had appeared again, though, triggering an ominous thought: If Matt was unwilling to believe his appearance was just a coincidence, was there anything he should be afraid of? He knew it was common for criminals to return to the scene of a crime and that police patrolled such areas frequently for that exact reason. Could the Stoic Man actually be associated with the authorities, staking out the area to see who might show up?

Matt weighed his options. Giving up on the search because of the Stoic Man's appearance seemed like a lazy, unethical rationalization. Yet the consequences of pushing forward without a plan could do more harm than good. Dammit! He wished he hadn't seen the man, that he'd been able to explore the area in peace. Now that sight might haunt his thoughts the entire time—could he survey the area appropriately or would he jump to a hasty conclusion out of fear? The situation elicited an eerie sense of déjà vu as he found himself, once again, alone on a deserted street and facing a crisis of conscience in which his own mind might be his worst enemy.

He decided to go home. Matt rationalized that he could always come back another day, when he'd feel more secure and when there'd be less danger. Better to return and investigate properly than do it half-ass, right? And just because he wasn't exploring the exact area didn't mean he was out of options. He'd tried using a computer to determine the boy's status a number of times already on those nights when sleep eluded him. But what if he tried again now that he was no longer sleep-deprived?

Once home he plopped down behind his computer, determined to try everything he could to locate the boy. The world was so interconnected; there *had* to be a way to find out the boy's identity. He attempted to drill down from every pseudo-lead he could find, refining his searches and exploring every potential dead end as if it were a real possibility. He pounded away for almost two hours and, devoid of possibilities, he took a moment to gather his thoughts. Mindlessly, he peered out the window beside his desk, as if to receive some kind of inspiration. It had begun to drizzle and he could hear the bells of the nearby Church. The kind old ladies were probably trudging through the miserable weather at that moment, on their way to attend mass even though they might catch a cold in the process. His mind wandered and he mused how frustrating it might be for hospital personnel to see former patients putting their health in danger for such an intangible reason. Then Matt frowned and, almost imperceptibly, his posture improved. The reverie gave him an idea: Rather than searching for news about a child who'd been struck by a car—a veritable needle in a haystack and rife with false-positives—what if he checked the hospitals in the area? While they didn't publish a list of every patient admitted, he thought he might find a lead if the incident was noteworthy.

Matt attacked the keyboard once again. His initial results regarding hospital admissions largely focused on professional athletes, celebrities, and politicians. Not surprised, he continued to work. He tried to conduct his search in an orderly fashion, refining by date and exhausting all available options regarding one hospital before moving to the next. He located many mundane articles, ones that required tedious investigation, but he knew he had to be thorough. Then, scrolling through a seemingly inconsequential result, he saw the words, "...boy found on sidewalk in front of hospital..." and, with dreadful temerity, he clicked on the article. Immediately, the blood dropped from his face and his mouth went dry. He read the write-up posted by the New York Hospital in Flushing four times, hoping against hope that he was mistaken. But he was not. The final lines read, "The unnamed boy passed away at 12:21 that night. Anyone with information should contact (718) 666-2124."

MEDA

Sunday nights were the worst. Meda put such hope, such expectation into every weekend and, inevitably, Sunday night showed up on her doorstep with menacing Sweeney Todd-eque flair and a clock in hand. Another work-week was imminent; another week in which she'd be forced to admit she had no clue what she was doing with her life.

She and Matt had reconciled after their weird blowup Thursday, so she was happy for that. Yet, while the Matt she knew had returned, he was still just that: The Matt she knew. She saw his expression when she mentioned Janet's baby shower. She understood what it meant. It wasn't like she was one of those girlfriends who constantly nagged about marriage, or used threats or machinations to force a proposal. (In all actuality, if she was so certain she wanted to marry him, she felt no compunction against proposing to Matt herself.) But his sheer avoidance of practicality gave Meda pause at times. She was thirty-two years old yet Matt shoved his head in the sand whenever the conversation turned to parenthood. Meda didn't want to be a mother tomorrow (she wasn't even positive she wanted to be a mother ever!) but the topic had to be addressed. If Matt checked out at the mere mention of a baby shower, she wondered if they'd ever have a mature conversation on the matter.

Janet wasn't the only one expecting. Another friend, Mackie, was also in her fifth month and Carrie had already moved upstate with her growing brood. Meda was happy for them, of course. But they were also living reminders that time moved on. Seemingly overnight, the topics of conversation amongst her group of friends had shifted from pop culture and life goals to strollers and baby vomit. And social events (whose frequency was already dropping precipitously) had become segregated affairs in which the new moms inevitably paired off with the other moms while Meda joined the remaining single ladies. She didn't resent being lumped in with them (though the reasons she remained un-married were in no way similar to Karyn's inability to date less than three men at once). She was merely frustrated that such a schism seemed so unavoidable in the first place.

There was a knock at her door, which was unexpected since she hadn't buzzed anyone in downstairs. Meda glanced in the mirror on the way to the door to be sure she didn't appear too horrid and then squinted through the peephole. It was Mrs. Javier from two doors down (a sweet, kind lady who, nonetheless, possessed the supernatural ability to be in search of conversation at the worst possible times). Less than five feet tall and with a nervous, fragile demeanor that made her appear even smaller, she possessed the eyes of a baby: Wide and unblinking as if every word in a given conversation held gravitas beyond measure.

"Hey there," said Meda, as she undid the chain.

"Hello dear. I'm so sorry to disturb you. But I wanted to ask: Have you seen Mr. Goldt around? That carbon monoxide scare happened the other day and I wanted to make sure everything was okay."

"No, I haven't seen him. I didn't even know there was a carbon monoxide issue," said Meda, catching up on the topic quickly (and resisting the urge to add that, if she *had* seen Mr. Goldt she would've been sure to remind him about her leaky faucet as well).

"Oh yes, it was a real ruckus Friday afternoon. I suppose you were probably at work. The fire trucks came and everything."

"Oh, I had no idea."

"It was in Mr. Webber's apartment downstairs. They said the batteries were running out in his fire alarm. But, oh you know, I just want to be sure," said Mrs. Javier. "That boiler is very old."

"Well," said Meda with a grin, "at least we're on the second floor. If anything goes wrong the first floor will get it before us."

Mrs. Javier flashed an expression of horror and it was clear that Meda's sarcasm had gone over like a fart in church. "Yes. Well. I just wanted to find out if you'd seen him. (He never tells us anything.)"

"I'm sure everything's fine," said Meda, trying to reassure the old woman in the wake of her ham-fisted attempt at humor. "The fire department wouldn't have left if they thought anything was wrong. It's been two days."

"Yes, I suppose you're right," said Mrs. Javier, as if engaging in some sort of internal monologue before, apparently, deciding she was satisfied. The women smiled then, breaking her countenance of utmost concern and added, "I must say the truth, though: You young girls. Nothing scares you."

Meda laughed. It was an odd yet earnest compliment. "I suppose I just know when to pick my battles," she shrugged.

"When were you born?" asked Mrs. Javier, staring upward with inquisitive power.

"What?"

"When were you born, dear? I bet you're a Leo. So confident, so strong," said Mrs. Javier, referencing astrological signs like others might talk about the weather or their commute.

"Oh," said Meda. "No, it's Gemini. My birthday is June 2nd."

"Ohhhh," said Mrs. Javier, her eyes growing impossibly wider and appearing to take a step backward. "Gemini. The twins. So you have the dual nature."

"I guess," Meda shrugged, hoping to conclude the conversation without any offense to the old woman's beliefs.

"It means, for all your confidence, dear, that there is also the opposite feeling within you. Some level of fear, some insecurity. You don't pursue what you want and it pains at you."

"I'm okay," said Meda, suddenly feeling defensive.

"Don't let insecurity rule your life. Confidence is good. But false confidence can be deadly."

"Um," muttered Meda with a frown, feeling awkward (agitated, actually).

"Fear is a terrible thing, dear," continued Mrs. Javier, unbowed. "You are so confident on the exterior; don't let your inner, opposing voice gain too much power. You need balance. You can't allow either to get too powerful or it will tear you in half."

"Thank you, Mrs. Javier. Thank you for your concern," said Meda, effectively speaking over Mrs. Javier. She loved the sweet old woman and often humored her when her stories rambled on. But she didn't have the patience for such silliness, especially when the woman was nearly insulting her.

"Be careful, dear. Be careful," said Mrs. Javier, glancing at Meda's hand on the door and intuiting that the conversation was at an end.

"I will," said Meda.

Mrs. Javier paused for a moment, ponderously, and then added, "And I'll let you know if I hear anything from Mr. Goldt."

It broke the tension and Meda smiled, saying, "Thank you, Mrs. Javier. I'll do likewise."

Meda closed the door, feeling guilty at her impatience with the old woman. It was frustrating for her on a couple levels because that would've been the perfect chance to have a pleasant conversation with the woman. Mrs. Javier was sweeter than sugar yet, invariably, she always appeared after Meda's worst day at work. Meda tried to be cordial but, more often than not, she just wanted to get home and relax. Now, with the time and opportunity to talk, she'd practically slammed the door in her face.

Meda didn't want to dwell on it. Just as she didn't want to dwell on Matt's odd reaction to her mention of the baby shower. Overall, she had enjoyed a relaxing weekend so she didn't want to focus on any negativity. She told herself that a two minute conversation with an old woman about astrology shouldn't cast a pall over the entire weekend. Yet the sensation lingered. Maybe it was the fact that Monday was around the corner or maybe it was something else looming she couldn't quite articulate. For whatever the reason, though, as much as she tried to forget the woman's words, she couldn't quite suppress the surprising amount of animosity she felt towards them.

MAGEE

Paint cost too much. And even if he could afford it, trekking to the store promised to be a nightmare. The piece would've been perfect...but it just wasn't going to come together.

Magee surveyed his current work, unsatisfied with the way the strands of paint had set on the doorway sized mirror. The problem was minor...the edges of the lines were flatter than he'd anticipated. He'd envisioned a rounder, thicker feel to the paint but couldn't make it achieve such height with the brand he'd chosen. Normally, this wouldn't have been an issue...Magee knew not to paint on an existing mirror...better to paint on simple glass and get it silvered later. But he'd found this ancient pane in a trash bin outside an old building and it was just too perfect *not* to use. The thing had to be 100 years old. In discrete places the silver backing was either scratched away or aged off, creating a negative-space effect that could never be replicated in a studio. Miraculously, he'd even gotten it home without cracking it. Now he was attempting to conjure up the vision he'd imagined on such unorthodox material...an act which was becoming no easy feat.

The phone rang. Good. A needed respite. Magee answered it, expecting it to be a return call about the tickets he was tracking down for Matt.

Instead: "Magee," said his mother, extending the enunciation in a dramatic, world-weary manner.

"Hi Mama," said Magee, not dismayed but not overjoyed.

"I haven't heard from you in the longest time, dear." Her Greek accent was thick, despite living in the states for almost forty of her sixty-six years, and every word carried an extra ounce of flourish.

"I called Thursday," said Magee, deadpan.

"You should call more often," she said, allowing a long pause before continuing. "Anyway, I just wonder if you could join me at liturgy this weekend. Rosarie's daughter is coming and—"

"Mama."

"I just thought it could be so nice—"

"Mama."

"if you met her. She's—"

"Mama, please. Seriously," said Magee. It was a dance they'd repeated often, never with a different result. Despite living three hours away, Magee's mother would plead for him to go to liturgy with her in a transparent attempt to hitch him up with a woman of her choosing...as if he needed his mama's help finding a girlfriend. The most frustrating part of these entreaties was how they ignored all those made previously...as if she was going out on a limb, pleading for him to join her *just this once*. "You know how I feel about organized religion...please respect my views."

"You didn't let me finish. This girl, she is young and cute and she has a steady income at a museum."

"What museum?"

"It was...what was it? Oh! I know! The Rhode Island School of Design."

"Oh come on, Mama," said Magee.

"No, listen. It's good. You can move back here. She has a steady job. While you're getting settled—"

Magee, chuckling, interrupted her again, saying, "Mama, I've got a life here. It's just...no way."

At that, there was a knock at Magee's studio door. He barely registered it, in fact, because it was so rare to get visitors. But, when he glanced out the window and saw the brief flash of a shirt sleeve, he confirmed someone was there.

"You haven't even—"

"Mama, I'm sorry."

"—given her a chance."

"Mama. Mama, I'm sorry, there's someone at the door. I have to go."

"Oh Magee," said his mother, her words dripping with sadness.

"I love you. I'll call you tonight."

Magee darted across the room to the door, opened it, and before him stood a little man. Squat like a toad, with cheeks and eyes to match, the man couldn't have been much more than five feet tall. He wore stained, olive-colored coveralls and Magee could practically see his odor.

"Hello?" said Magee.

"Hi," said the man, shifting his stance. "Taylor contacted me. Said you were looking for tickets."

"Ah, yes. Yes, that's right" said Magee. He'd spoken to Taylor about the opera tickets yet he couldn't believe *this* was the man who was going to broker the deal.

"You buying?"

"Yes, I'm buying," said Magee, before adding, "Well, for a friend."

At that, the man's left eyebrow shot up. "A...friend?"

"I'm buying them but for a friend of mine. How much are they again?"

"Whoa, whoa, whoa," said the man, his palms up. "Slow down."

"What? What's the matter?" asked Magee, digging in his back pocket for his wallet.

"What's the matter? I can't sell you the tickets if you're not the one going."

Magee frowned, pausing for a moment before asking, "Excuse me?"

"You heard me. I can't sell them to you if you're going to pass them to some other malakas. What if this friend shows up in a clown suit? I'm the one who loses my connection. Can't do it."

Magee attempted to wrap his mind around the situation...it was the opera, not a congressional hearing. "Okay," said Magee dismissively. "Forget that. I'm going. My girlfriend and I are going. Now how much are they?"

"Too late. You already told me they're for a friend of yours. I can't risk it."

Magee stopped, shook his head. "Okay...this is crazy. My friend isn't going to show up in a clown suit...he's not going to do anything embarrassing. How is this even an issue? No one will know they were your tickets. You mean to tell me that you only have access to two seats, event-after-event, at the Met?"

"Nah, I have a bunch."

"Then...." Magee stopped himself from saying something that might make the situation worse. Five minutes earlier his artistic creation was his only concern. Then, suddenly, he went from deflecting his mother's passive-aggressive entreaties to navigating a business transaction that was hard to take seriously...yet, for Matt's sake, he couldn't mess it up. "Is this a bargaining tactic?" he asked, taking a different tack. "Is this a way to drive up the price of the tickets? Because I'm not sure where you're going with this...."

"It is not," said the man. "I'd love to sell them to you...but I can't."

"So what then?" said Magee, frustrated. "You just lose the business because you don't want to trust me?"

"I'd have to meet this friend of yours," said the man, with a disinterested shrug.

"But...." began Magee, ready to point out the insanity of such a request. He wanted to the tell the man that such a vetting process was useless, that he could bring the head of the local PTA and there'd be no way for him to verify if that same person went to the performance. Instead, he stopped himself once more. No need to make the ridiculous situation worse. "Okay. Okay!"

"Good," said the man, smiling for the first time, though it appeared more similar to a grimace. "What do you propose doing, then?"

"I'll get in touch with him, find out a time to meet. It shouldn't take long, right? There won't be any forms to fill out?" asked Magee with acidic sarcasm.

"No, there will not," said the man, still leering. "It shouldn't take long."

Magee took down the man's phone number, the stilted awkwardness between them unrelenting. It all seemed so preposterous...such a waste of time. But what could he do?

Magee closed the door behind the man, broken out of his creative mindset, and for a long time he peered about his studio. He wanted to keep working. Knew he should. But now he didn't feel like it. He was still exhausted from bartending over the weekend, he presumed he'd have more time tomorrow to focus, and he was sure he could come up with other excuses to call it a day if he required. He thought of other things he could be doing: Re-canvassing another piece...practicing his juggling...figuring out how he was going to pay rent while also buying more supplies. But the concomitant pressure of the obligations only served to discourage him further. It was too much static. Finally, grimacing, he lit up a joint and promised himself he'd get back to his art later.

MATT

After that, Matt was haunted. The confirmation of the boy's death was tangible now, irrefutable. He was dead and Matt was responsible. The sleepless nights wracked by doubt were a torment night after night, yet he'd suffer those again gladly in place of the dread certainty that now afflicted him.

He recognized the need to go to the police. Now that he was certain of the boy's fate there was no choice but to be accountable for his actions. Yet the lack of detail bedeviled him. What was he supposed to say? Was he to go to the cops and announce that, a week ago, he'd hit a little kid with his car and fled the scene? And that he couldn't remember what the boy looked like despite having a full conversation with him? They'd nail him to the wall with such vagaries in his story, possibly implicating him in other crimes he never committed. He needed to be precise and pick his words carefully, all the while aware that his story would be put through the ringer.

Predictably, the subway ride to the precinct was hell. The characters around him were no longer benign entities waiting for their story to be told. Instead, they'd become more sinister, more insidious. Matt was reminded of folklore monsters in countries around the world, often products of the treacherous world outside those societies. Before modern times, the forest and the night were far more dangerous places and, long before automobiles and GPS, the prospect of getting lost meant the very real possibility of being taken down by a wild animal. As a result, legends of vampires, werewolves, and witches manifested. But what types of comparable creatures might be found in the congested, modern world where the fear of the wild had been replaced by the neurotic fear of *too many* people instead? Wolves were no longer the problem—the single psychopath on a crowded subway platform was.

He imagined a creature below the subway car, flat like a stingray and clinging to the underside of the carriage with hawk-like talons. Its moist, leathery skin would remain unseen from the platform even as it snatched up vermin from the tracks below. And when the ground became too dry, when there weren't enough rats to satiate its hunger, it might reach up to the platform in search of other prey. Matt's gaze shot to the bottom of the subway doors, searching for evidence of the creature's talons. It all seemed so real, so possible.

Then he thought of the disease in the air around him, the inevitable result of so many people packed so claustrophobically into such an unsanitary space. Virtually everyone was holding on to one of the metal poles or handlebars. He scanned a number of the riders' hands, spotting the filthy fingernails of one and the cracked, desiccated skin of another. Those metal poles always displayed an odd sheen, an indescribable wetness that resulted from the touch of so many strangers' hands. What if the sheen was alive? What if it moved up and down the entire car like blood through a person's veins? It could pass under someone's hand, infect the person, and grow more virulent by exposing itself to a constant parade of antibodies. By the time victims began to show symptoms, it would be too late—the pustules on their hands would've already leaked more of the invisible sheen before it slid away, like mercury, down bathroom drains and into the water supply of the city.

Thankfully, the train was approaching his stop. Flights of fancy such as these, a normal activity under other circumstances, were gaining far too much traction in his mind's set of possibilities. His confidence in the tale he intended to tell the authorities was precarious enough without seriously entertaining notions of unseen subterranean creatures.

"Excuse me," he said, as the subway doors opened. He was buried deep in the subway car and it was always a hassle to extricate oneself in such a crowd. No one moved, however, at Matt's proclamation. The mass of people simply stood in place, zombie-like, and Matt realized he'd have to get more aggressive. "Excuse me!" he announced forcefully.

Still locked in place, Matt saw the languid, waiting mass on the platform begin to enter the car and his unease grew in earnest. He placed his hand on the back of the person in front of him and issued increasing pressure until the man got the message and took a small step forward. No words were exchanged—it was as if the person was asleep—and the crowd entering the car was now fully blocking the entrance. They began to push against the bodies in Matt's path, even as he attempted to usher the same people aside. Then, with dread, he realized the majority of those on the platform were now inside—the doors would seal shut momentarily and the train would churn forward with Matt trapped in the middle of the somnambulant throng.

"Excuse me!" he shouted to the dumbfounded stares of those around him. Their faces were dead—their only desire was to be left alone irrespective of anything happening around them.

His sense of decorum exhausted, Matt shoved two people aside and heard the familiar chime of the subway door's impending close. "I have to get off!" he cried, to no discernible response. The doors began to move and panic welled up within him. Matt used both hands to push one stone-faced man out of the way and he arrived at the last person, ready to barrel through the zombie. She was elderly, however, staring up at Matt with eyes that seemed as large as her entire face. It made Matt pause—he couldn't shove an old woman out of the way. The doors were nearly closed and, instinctively, Matt's hands shot up over the diminutive woman to hold them open. The doors halted at the pressure of his grip. He was now locked in place, however, unable to trample over the woman, yet holding the doors open as if stuck between two pillars. The moment lasted interminably long. Around him, the grey commuters finally began to awaken and issued hostile stares at the intrusion on their commute. Finally, the woman took the slightest step to the side, allowing Matt to slither past. "Scorpio," she hissed.

Matt nearly fell onto the platform, bursting forth from the car and losing his balance in the process. Then, when he glanced back at the car, he found that every person inside was staring at him from behind the glass. He glared back, angry and resentful. The subway pulled away yet the grim eyes of the passengers never left him.

It took Matt a long moment to compose himself. What the hell had just happened? He was relieved to have escaped the car in time yet disgusted by the other passenger's utter lack of awareness. Their sallow, lifeless expressions frightened him in a way he couldn't articulate and, with armpits now drenched in sweat, he cursed the surreal ordeal. Why did that have to happen on the way to the police precinct?

Matt exited the subway station and started to make his way to the police precinct. He was still bedeviled by the experience on the train, however. It made him doubt himself, made him wonder if he was overacting to what was an otherwise normal experience on the subway. Was it his fault for not approaching the door earlier? Did he look like some maniac–shouting and shoving people aside–and was that why he drew so many stares? Or was the incident truly unique, possibly related to his ongoing series of bizarre events? His confidence wavered and doubt began to creep in.

He was so distracted that he nearly didn't look up as he approached the precinct, nearly didn't see the man standing at its steps. The Stoic Man. In a police uniform. Matt glanced up once, then down, then his gaze shot up again—the clothing was different, but it was him. It was definitely him. Matt's pace slowed and his jaw dropped. He was mere steps away from the man—too late to turn around. And then, in that split-second, his movement caught the man's attention. It was too late.

They made eye contact and the moment seemed to lock itself in time, Matt saying nothing yet dimly aware that his expression was anything but natural. Bodily, he froze, while an explosion of questions and frayed logic detonated in his mind. And the man's countenance morphed as well, from one of boredom to one of concern.

"Can I help you?" asked the man. His chest puffed up as he spoke and it was clear his police instincts were kicking in.

"I'm, wow. I'm sorry," blurted Matt, adding a nervous giggle that did nothing to ease the awkwardness. "It's just, I thought—this is going to sound crazy—I just thought."

The man continued to stare at him, squinting in the morning sun as Matt bumbled. His shadow seemed to stretch across the concrete to infinity, impossibly long and lanky. Seconds slipped by and the myriad questions in Matt's mind ricocheted chaotically like materials at a junkyard hit by a tornado. He knew he needed to come up with something to say, to offer some reason why he recognized the man. Yet the words at his disposal were a collection of wriggling salamanders, unable to clutch.

"I remember you. From the subway," said Matt, finally, with an exaggerated smile that suggested they were mutually guilty of some sort of etiquette breach. The Stoic Man did not reciprocate his levity.

"The subway?"

"Yes. You were selling tarot cards."

At that the man's air changed again, still cautious yet with the hint of a smirk at the edges of his lips. "Selling tarot cards?"

"Yeah, I know it was you. As crazy as it sounds."

The Stoic Man eyed Matt up and down, flashing his gaze from Matt's pockets to his bag and back to his face. "I," said the man, pausing for effect, "believe you are mistaken."

Matt burst out laughing and immediately regretted it. Clearly, the Stoic Man was not about to admit it. Then, taking a breath, Matt also realized he'd get nowhere by arguing with a policeman. "No, no," said Matt, holding up his palm apologetically, "it's cool. I mean—we all have to make a living, right? I'm not judging you or anything. I just know it was you, man."

The Stoic Man glanced over his shoulder, back at the precinct. His sense of concern had evaporated, replaced by one of mild irritability. "I suggest you move along, sir."

Matt's mouth opened but he said nothing. He knew he had no business haranguing the man but he felt insulted nonetheless. How could the man just stand there and deny it? And worse yet, treat him as if he was some kind of nuisance?

The cop looked back at Matt with an expression that asked, "Are you still here?" when another officer emerged through the station's doors. "Sorry, sorry, sorry," said the pudgy, beleaguered officer. "Stella ran into me. Wouldn't shut up."

The Stoic Man offered the second officer an irritated glance and, in turn, that officer eyed Matt up and down. "What's going on?" he asked.

"Nothing. Forget it," said the Stoic Man, turning from Matt and walking away. The second officer did another passing review of Matt and then turned in tandem with the Stoic Man.

Matt was left standing on the concrete sidewalk in front of the police station, dumbstruck. Before approaching, he thought nothing would've dissuaded him from taking responsibility for the child. Now, however, he wasn't even confident in his own sanity.

He stood in front of the building for many moments, stock still yet frenzied in thought. Then, practically on auto-pilot, Matt took out his phone and dialed Magee.

"Hello?"

"It's Matt. I think I'm losing my mind."

There was a pause, then a chuckle. "Aren't we all? I'm glad you called, though. I spoke to this guy...."

"No, no. I'm serious. It's such a long story. It's too much to get into over the phone. Can you meet for a beer? I feel like I'm going crazy and I'm afraid I'm going to do something stupid."

"Wow, holy crap, buddy. You sound shaken up," said Magee, now more serious.

"I am. I think I might have hit a little boy with my car last Monday."

There was another pause from Magee's end, before he guffawed, "You didn't run over anybody with your car! You would've told me when we got together!"

"That's just it," said Matt forcefully, "I was too scared. I didn't want anybody to know, to be potential accomplices, so I didn't mention anything. Now I'm not sure if I'm losing my mind because of it. It's all—there're too many strange things going on."

"Matt," said Magee, sounding like a 911 operator, "there is no way you did that. I would've noticed the difference in you. We've known each other forever. I would know if you were hiding something that important."

Matt readied his rebuttal but Magee continued, "It's the creativity. It gets too powerful sometimes...you lose track of reality. It's happened to me a million times when painting. It's part of the process. So, before doing anything else, you should get back to it while those juices are flowing."

Even as Matt wanted to argue the point, there was a small amount of wisdom behind what Magee was suggesting. Matt had never experienced full scale hallucinations when writing, much less ones that continued for a week. Yet it was common for him to lose all track of time and get so lost in his world that he was forced to spend time disengaging afterward.

"This is a good thing, man. Don't be frightened...you should use this. You should get writing and ride the snake. Who knows what you'll come up with."

At that, Matt began to nod, despite himself. While it might not have been Magee's intention, a rearrangement of the senses could be the best medicine to help him return to a proper state of mind. He'd done so in the past—perhaps he could do so again.

With Matt still silent, Magee added, "And besides, even if you *did* hit someone, a week has already passed, buddy. Time is no longer of the essence. You need to get your head straight first."

Matt searched for a reason to shoot down the idea but Magee was making too much sense. He recognized he couldn't go into the police station so distrustful of his own memories. That would be a recipe for disaster. Instead, if he could just get the voices in his head to quiet themselves, he might be able to think clearly. "So, if I decide to spend time writing, does that constitute a total admission of craziness? Because," said Matt, "if I thought that I was crazy, well, I guess I'd have more fun."

"It doesn't matter, buddy," said Magee with a jovial air. "As long as you get yourself together."

"Okay," said Matt finally, decisively, before turning to march back to the train station.

DORIAN

The worst part was the way she walked, Dorian decided. It wasn't the nasally whine issued forth when she was forced to make room on the couch. It wasn't the ill-fitting T-shirts which inevitably drew taught and revealed flashes of her pale, bulbous stomach at the worst possible times. It was the labored drag of her feet that'd annihilated any remainder of his libido.

Dorian knew Brynn would never be one of those bouncing, vivacious women he saw in the beer commercials. But, he figured, she could at least give a little effort. To watch her shuffle across his basement apartment, each step appearing more strenuous than the last, one would think she actually had a job or had accomplished something in her life. And ultimately, after blurting out his feelings about her locomotive failings, she'd left for good, a turn of events that Dorian hadn't expected.

In the past, their shouting matches had occurred with enough regularity that Dorian had learned to plan for them and, at times, instigate them. Without fail, Brynn would depart in a huff, leaving her recently purchased meth behind for Dorian to smoke at his leisure. Then, by the time she was ready to come back, she'd conveniently bring a new score for both of them to enjoy.

This time his familiar gambit had backfired, however. It was only now apparent that she wasn't coming back again, a fact Dorian grasped only after devouring the stash she'd left behind. This left him with an odd conundrum: He would have to find his own fix.

Already the first tingles of restlessness were setting in and his fiendish insecurity was growing. Brynn had been coming over to his place for almost two years and, in that time, he'd never had to buy his own drugs once. While he was confident one of his old sources would be holding, it was unfamiliar territory nonetheless.

Dorian peered at his phone, vaguely aware that he hadn't used it for anything other than texting in months. Using a phone to actually speak with someone seemed weird, retro actually, like he was reaching out of his cocoon back into the real world. He punched in the digits with child-like caution and, after six rings, the call was answered. "Hey! Roderick! It's Dorian!"

"Who's this?" asked the voice at the other end before Dorian had finished speaking.

"It's Dorian. I haven't—"

"Who?"

"Dorian. I was Brett's friend. I used to see you all the time at the—"

"I don't know no Dorian."

"Sure you do. Remember, I always wore the hat with—"

"I don't know. No Dorian."

Dorian sighed. "Listen, man: I really need your help. I'm all outta ice. Trust me, we used to meet up. You, me, and Brett. We—"

And the phone clicked, conversation over. For a long moment Dorian stared at the device in disbelief. What an asshole! If he'd only let him explain he was sure Roderick would've recognized him. Seconds passed and eventually his eyes flicked back to life.

The dealers he knew were accustomed to seeing him in person, Dorian decided, with unsteady confidence. Their phones were probably bugged; they couldn't talk business over them. He nodded knowingly, almost proudly, at his deductive ability. While preferable to have someone deliver the stuff to his doorstep, Dorian greeted the problem as a challenge, an adventure almost. Possessed by a nervous, jittery energy, he began darting about his apartment before, eventually, locating his coat on the chair in front of him.

As it turned out, he didn't need it at all: It was a radiant autumn day with nary a cloud in the sky. Dorian had not been outside in the middle of the day in months, however, and the sunlight nearly knocked him over when he emerged. Instinctively, he shot his forearm up to cover his eyes, groaning as he did so, and once up the stairs he leaned against the building for a long period.

It was an inauspicious start to his adventure and Dorian mentally lashed out at Brynn for forcing him into such dire circumstance. A vein of anger pounded a path across his forehead, no doubt agitated by such ferocious sunlight. When he finally gathered himself enough to shuffle down the sidewalk, his gaze shot to and fro and a mother pulled her son closer to her side as they passed

The convenience store where Bill worked was only three blocks away and, gradually, Dorian began to acclimate in his own unique way. He felt light-headed, something akin to the high long-distance runners experience after pushing their bodies to the extreme. The pounding in his skull continued unabated yet, at the same time, it was as if he was merely a traveler in his body. He felt as if he could stop and examine the intricacies of a tree or a garbage can for hours if he allowed himself. Each new concrete slab of the sidewalk became a new rectangle of opportunity and he grew hypnotized as he passed over one, then another, then another. On one level, he was aware they were no different than the last time he'd walked them. Yet they seemed new this time, magical almost.

Before he even realized how close he was, Dorian arrived at the convenience store. In fact, the only thing that broke him out of his stupor was the end of sidewalk as it gave way to the small asphalt parking lot. He came to a halt, grinning as he reappraised his journey. How far he'd come!

His confidence grew and Dorian strode up the blacktop towards the store. Then, nearly halfway there, an explosion of sound assaulted him. His body jumped, nerve endings jolted alive like yanked strings of a marionette. It took him a full two seconds to realize that it was a car horn, that a car had come within two feet of hitting him. Dorian was levels beyond surprised and he could only stare in awe with his world so savagely rearranged. He had been on the sidewalk. Then he was going to be in the convenience store. Yet somehow, someway, in between both of those states, he'd almost been run over.

"You're a druggie!" shouted the librarian from behind the wheel.

The accusation broke Dorian out of his stupor and he began to giggle. He knew he should've been angry, violent even, with this wench that'd almost hit him. But her allegation was just too silly. "You're a druggie." Who says that?

"Well? Move!" she hollered, laying on the horn as she did so. Dorian might've stood there giggling for another ten minutes but the car horn was too jarring. His palm shot to his temple and, weakly, he stepped away. He felt defeated in some vague way yet he couldn't stop giggling. "You're a druggie," she'd said. Holy friggin' shit.

The car tore away and Dorian tried his best to salvage his dignity by shouting, "You. Shouldn't drive so fast. At a gas station."

But the car had already zoomed into traffic, hurtling towards a red light by the time he'd completed speaking. He was left alone, his heart still racing in the wake of the encounter, and only then did he become aware of the handful of gawkers who'd witnessed the exchange. He remained fixed for a time, slack-jawed. Then he resolved to get his drugs and get the hell out of there.

Dorian entered the convenience store and went straight to the cashier. Black disappointment washed over him, however, when a frail girl with bad skin emerged from behind the comparatively mountainous cash register. She wasn't Bill. She wasn't close to being Bill. And Bill was the contact Dorian needed.

"Where's Bill?" asked Dorian.

"What?" said the girl, her face blank.

"Where's Bill?" Dorian asked a second time in abject bewilderment. Who was this girl? And why wasn't Bill there? Nothing was going as planned.

"I don't know who you're talking about," sneered the girl, shifting her weight and raising an eyebrow.

"Bill!" Dorian demanded. "I'm trying to find Bill. He works here. I need to talk to him!"

"There is no Bill here."

Dorian dragged his fingers through his greasy hair, making it even wilder in the process. Seething with belligerence, he said, "Okay. I get it. Bill isn't here now. I get that. But do you know when he is going to get here?"

The girl, moving her hands to her hip, only repeated, "There is no Bill here."

Dorian glared at her, his fists balling in rage, though he said nothing. Then, the girl evidently registering the barely-contained tension in his body, explained, "I'm serious, okay? There is no employee here named Bill. There are two people named Mike, a Lisa, and a Jorge. And me. But there's nobody by the name of Bill. So I don't know what to tell you."

For a long, interminable moment Dorian simply stared at the girl. Her logic was immutable. Yet it represented such utter desolation to his worldview. He'd come all this way...almost gotten run over in the process...and there was no Bill. He worked out the notion in his mind further and realized that he hadn't scored from Bill in years, actually. He probably didn't work at the store any more. The girl was telling the truth.

Dorian raged, slapping his hands down on the counter and emitting a guttural, "Uaagh!" Then he whirled around and crashed through the door to the open air outside. Just as when he'd emerged from his apartment, the sunlight blasted him again and he shot up his hand up to cover his eyes. He stumbled, caught himself on the wall, and momentarily considered going back inside. For the first time he appreciated how stifling the air had become. It wasn't merely heat; it was the vast openness of it all. There was nowhere to get away from the sun's rays, no place to hide. It made the walls of the store appear waxy, as if they'd been coated in a thick, synthetic sheen.

Dorian tried to formulate a new plan amidst his turmoil, stumbling to the corner of the building to regroup. He considered finding Bill, going to his home, but remembered that he'd never met him there. He grew nostalgic, wistful, remembering how natural it had been to stop by the store, pick up some ice, and go to the club. A bead of sweat trickled into his eye, though, and after cursing at the salty sting his reminiscence turned sour. When did doing drugs become so hard? When did they require so much work? Years ago, or actually a decade ago, when he first started smoking up with Chester, it was all so fun and new. When did it become about...going out in the daylight, fighting off librarians and prissy little girls behind the counter of a convenience store?

Then Dorian began to doubt himself. He felt like he couldn't trust those memories now, that, just like the wall behind him, they were fake and covered in wax. He began to wonder if Bill was even real? Had he actually existed? And, taking that even further, had Dorian, himself, existed? Or were those fake memories, too? Implanted ones? Memories made in a computer or by aliens? His thoughts were zig-zagging now, random shots of unfocused inquiry. It was terrible.

Dorian shook his head, as if to clear out cobwebs. He re-focused his eyes on the ground in front of him, the blur coming into focus. Yes, Bill was real, he told himself. But he was not at the store. And there was no way to locate him. So if he intended to score any meth he'd better accept that and figure out another plan. With a loud huff Dorian pushed himself off the wall and began walking. He didn't know where he was going. He just knew that he had to do something.

This time the sidewalk lacked any sort of wonder. Dorian stomped his way down the concrete slabs and began to examine the world around him with a singular focus: Procurement. Would there be any dealers at the auto mechanic? Probably not. At the fast food place? Maybe, but he couldn't just walk in and announce his desire. What about those kids with the skateboards over near the railing? Dorian stutter-stepped briefly but figured while, sure, they probably had some weed, they probably wouldn't have any ice. So what was the point?

He continued down the street, his hands buried deep in his coat pockets even as sweat continued to broaden the wet circle around his neck. He flashed his gaze about with manic precision, peering into every nook and cranny for the possibility of someone who might be holding. He was leaning forward in his charge and was so focused on divining a supplier that he nearly careened headlong into a woman passing in the opposite direction.

According to Dorian's perceptions, everything about the encounter was recorded a split-second late. He had been walking alone, no one else around. Then suddenly this woman was inches away from him. In that moment, he peered at her face, her cheeks, her lips, as if pulling out of a camera's fisheye lens. He recorded the woman's beauty, how luxuriously her hair flowed out behind her like an exploding star. The surprised expression on her face made her appear vulnerable, tender, and he only barely kept himself from caressing it in an attempt to ease her pain.

"Agh!" cried the woman, leaping backwards a moment before the collision.

Dorian halted and said, "You're the woman." Then he realized he couldn't remember the rest of the words he intended to speak. She began walking again, deftly sidestepping him, and in a turnstile-like motion he twirled with her. She passed and, in the process, he was certain he saw her flash him a smile.

He wanted to hit on her, attack her with his best pick-up line. But he lost the moment as he stood pondering. Another second passed and the woman was well on her way. Dorian shrugged, deciding not to give chase since a woman like that wouldn't be carrying anyway. Still, though: She was hot! And he'd managed to get a smile out of her! Dorian still had it! He would've taken more time to bask in the glory but the itchy sensation settling in across his abdomen reminded him that he'd better keep moving.

He continued to shuffle along on the barren sidewalk for a very long hike, the realization dawning that his need for ice was even more acute than he'd first imagined. Trickles of sweat had formed a marsh across his skin and, in a vague way, as if it was happening to another person, he acknowledged that his strained mouth-breathing was only making him sound more hoarse. He couldn't go on like this.

Then, as if presenting itself like an oasis in the middle of the desert, a building appeared before him. Dorian had no reason to think anyone would be selling drugs at it. In fact, from the back, he couldn't discern its function at all. The important point was that it was a structure, something to provide shade and get him off the terrible sidewalk for a moment. In all reality, Dorian knew he would've spotted the beautiful location earlier if he'd only looked up. But that was all in the past. No use crying over spilled milk.

He staggered up and around it to get a better view and he realized the place was actually a casual dining establishment. In the front was an area for outdoor seating containing generic, white tables and chairs spread across the pavement. Encircling the area was an aluminum barricade and Dorian yanked it aside before collapsing into a chair in the corner. Only a handful of the tables were in use and those patrons were all alone, sipping their morning coffees or checking their phones. He enjoyed an excellent view of the landscape and, immediately, he noticed the woman in her mid-thirties in a pantsuit a few tables away. She definitely didn't have any drugs on her but she succeeded in catching his eye nonetheless: For an older lady she was pretty hot! Her hair was cut too short and she probably would've looked better with more make-up. But still. After a few seconds she glanced up at him, frowned as if remembering something, and then went back to her phone.

Dorian smiled. Granted, getting an old lady's attention was like shooting fish in a barrel. Who would've thought he'd get a look from a lady like that so early in the morning, though? He hadn't even showered. Then he reminded himself not to get distracted; he still hadn't come close to locating any ice. He was about to move his attention to the other patrons of the restaurant when, seemingly out of the blue, a young woman appeared in front of him.

"Hello," she said, "how are you this morning?"

Dorian's gaze flitted from side to side. He was completely befuddled. What did this girl want? Why was she asking him how he was doing? Did she have any ice? Feebly, he examined the girl up and down: She wore a button-down shirt but still looked okay and a weird apron was tied around her waist.

The far-too-perky girl tried again. "Can I start you with a cup of coffee?"

A light bulb virtually appeared over Dorian's head when, viewing the pad and pencil in her hands, he realized she was a waitress. His wide-eyed expression collapsed. He didn't want to order any food! What kind of crap was this?

"I'm fine," said Dorian, all but waving her away.

"Oh, okay then. Do you know what you'd like to order already or do you need a moment?"

"No. No," said Dorian, shaking his head irritably as he resumed his scan of the establishment.

"No, you don't know what you want?" asked the waitress slowly, her spry demeanor turning less chipper. "Or no, you don't need a moment?"

"I just want to sit here," snarled Dorian through gritted teeth.

The waitress paused and, with a sneer, said, "I'll give you a moment to figure out what you'd like."

"Yeah," muttered Dorian, relieved the girl finally left him alone. With that distraction out of the way he began to investigate yet again. The older business woman sitting nearby, while good looking in her own way, was a lost cause.

Beyond her, he noticed a much younger girl sitting alone as well. She was a typical, non-threatening suburbanite, probably enrolled in college somewhere, though Dorian wouldn't hold that against her. In fact, as cookie-cutter boring as she was, he couldn't help but notice she was okay looking, too. And at a table beyond her, he spied yet another woman, this one clad in spandex and sneakers who was also appealing but just a little too skinny. And, sitting at a table even further away, was a weirdly attractive woman in a green evening dress and sporting a bouffant hairdo like she'd come from the 1950s.

Then, in a creeping realization that drew all remaining moisture from Dorian's mouth, he realized that every person at this oasis was a woman. And not just that: Every interaction he'd had all morning was with a woman. Conspiracy theories lit up his mind like erratic strobe lights, each thought only barely related to the next and all possessing fatal flaws in their logic. Were the women out to get him? What had they done with the men? Was he the last man on earth? He shot accusatory glares at the various women. Then he peered inside the establishment to see the waitress talking conspiratorially with a woman who appeared to be the manager. He grew even more agitated and craned his neck to look up and down the boulevard. An older woman was in her car, idling at the stoplight. Another woman could be seen pushing a grocery cart in the parking lot across the street. Another woman was walking up to the café itself, apparently ready to take a seat.

What was going on? Dorian's mind was manic now, screeching loud and red without any notion of what the danger actually was. Abruptly he stood up, his chair falling back and sounding a plastic –boing– on the pavement below. The professional woman nearby eyed him up again and he squinted at her with suspicion as he attempted to ascertain her inscrutable intentions. Then, with his vantage point altered, Dorian re-appraised the newly arriving woman: The way she walked was unmistakable. He scolded himself for not recognizing her immediately. And a conspiratorial connecting-of-the-dots took place in his thoughts. It was Brynn. She was behind it all.

She took her seat nonchalantly, as if she didn't know what was going on, and Dorian recounted the events that'd brought him to this point: It was all her fault he'd run out of drugs. She was the reason he'd been forced to venture out at such an hour. Now, somehow, someway, she'd made sure there were no men around. Why would she do that? He didn't know. But he was positive she was behind it!

Dorian wiped his forehead and returned with a palm as drenched with sweat as if he'd dunked it in a toilet. He needed to score some drugs and he needed them now. He needed... He needed.... Wait! He realized: Brynn was here! He'd become so focused on the bevy of women that he'd wholly forgotten the most important thing! Whatever nefarious purpose Brynn had in mind didn't matter: She was right there, in the flesh, and she was bound to be carrying.

The impulse to charge rose within him, an almost carnal desire to just run and grab the item of his affection. He tried to calm down but it was getting harder and harder for him to control his taught, flexing muscles.

Then Brynn stood up. Dorian's attention snapped, analyzing every movement. It was simply too perfect. He steadied himself, waiting to see what would happen next. Then, with the sound of an angel's chorus accompanying the movement, she made her way indoors into the restaurant with that horrible, bedraggled, unsightly walk of hers. And, glory be: She left her purse on the table!

Dorian licked his lips. His heart was pounding and his nerves were aflutter. He knew it would only be a moment longer and she'd be inside, out of sight and he'd have his chance. His body was bouncing with nervous energy and, at the edge of his vision, he noticed the businesswoman outright staring at him now.

Then a thought occurred to him, like a screeching bat shooting in from the fringes of his consciousness: What if someone else was sizing up the purse at the same time? It lit fear into his soul as he imagined the purse disappearing before his very eyes and the terror unleashed his body, sending him into a desperate sprint.

It was a minor miracle he didn't break his neck. He misjudged the very first chair he encountered, slapping it away yet still tripping over its leg. He spun, crashed into another, and then a third, and barely avoided falling down altogether. After regaining a small portion of his balance, he attempted to fit between two more and got caught on both simultaneously. His eyes remained focused on the purse as he bumbled, however, and he somehow moved within a few feet of it. At that point he gave up any attempt at subtlety and dove onto the table like a football player would a fumbled ball. It collapsed and he slammed to the ground awkwardly, clutching the purse to his chest rather than using his arms to break his fall.

Elation hit: He had it! He had the purse! Then he remembered he must keep moving. He got to his feet gracelessly and took a quick scan of the establishment: Everyone was staring at him with expressions of shock. Haha! he thought. I've beaten you at your own game. They never expected that! "You have to wake up pretty early!" Dorian bellowed before darting off.

No one gave chase and, after sprinting about six blocks between houses and across burned out lots, he slowed to a walk. Only barely did he keep himself from stopping and smoking too early. When he somehow managed to locate the perfect alleyway, he was proud that he'd waited, though. It was dark and secluded with very little foot traffic on the sidewalk beyond. And the club next door wouldn't open for hours.

He staggered to the back of it, gasping for air, and crashed into one of the trash bins. Immediately, he began rifling through Brynn's purse. He was well aware of the concealed slot where she hid her stash and tossed her wallet and mascara to the side in his quest to reach it. With orgasmic joy he first felt the wad inside the pocket then pulled the tinfoil out. There it was. The moment had finally arrived!

With jittery, trembling hands he crammed the wad into her pipe and put the lighter's flame to it. He was nearly hyperventilating from his sprint, his body in utter revolt, yet somehow, he found a way to take a deep, long pull. It didn't taste normal and volcanic heat seared his lungs. But he didn't care. Pleasure and pain churned together in his mind and in his lungs, and a wild spate of coughing burst forth from within him.

Holy crap that stuff was harsh! Why hadn't she brought anything like that around when they were together? With no hesitation, Dorian immediately went for another pull, lighting it again just in case. It felt like a thousand tiny daggers were plunging into his lungs, miniscule cuts that stabbed his air sacks and injected their power.

Coughing yet again, even more brutally, he went back for yet another pull, trying his best to keep it contained in his lungs. He failed, but he knew he was on his way. His eyes watered and his mouth dropped open, gasping for air, even as his brain flashed with endorphins. The torture in his lungs was matched only by the ecstasy in his mind and, without conscious thought, he looked skyward in euphoria. At the very edges of his vision, a bright light began to appear, growing in strength and power. It was like nothing he'd ever seen before and he forced himself to continue staring even as his lungs went molten. Then Dorian felt his body shudder and, majestically, he was consumed by the light.

MATT

"You seem a lot better, buddy," said Magee, sizing up Matt. "On the phone earlier...you didn't sound normal."

Matt smiled sheepishly. He'd spent the night in a feverish bout of writing and had grown perhaps too comfortable in Dorian's skin. It'd been frighteningly easy to lose himself in the mind of a meth addict and, when he'd called his boss to tell her tales of an afternoon spent at the doctor's office, he became acutely aware how far away from reality he'd travelled. "Well, I'm not sure I'm back to normal," replied Matt, keeping any mention of Dorian to himself. "But at least I've made some progress."

Matt and Magee had decided to meet for drinks that night and, judging by Magee's apprehension, he must've been worried. "So what's up, buddy? What's going on with you?"

Matt peered from side to side at the other bar patrons and then, leaning in conspiratorially, said, "I told you: I hit a boy with my car last Monday night. And ever since then my life has been a total mess."

"Okay, let me just get a couple things straight," said Magee, clearly suspicious. "You say you hit a kid. How do you know? Are you sure you didn't hit, say, a dog or something?"

"No, I'm positive," said Matt. "I got out of the car and checked. He claimed to be fine."

At that Magee grew more serious. "You actually pulled over and talked to him?"

"Yes."

"Did he...seem okay?" Magee asked. "I mean, was he walking? How hard did you hit him?"

"He wasn't walking. He was on the ground, hunched in a doorway. I think I only nicked him with my car but I'm not sure of anything."

As Matt spoke, Magee's body language continued to change, his expression becoming more concerned. Then, blinking, he asked, "Wait. You're not sure of *anything*?"

Matt rubbed his forehead, appearing both embarrassed and frustrated. "It was late. It was dark. And—this is going to sound crazy—but it all happened so fast. I wasn't really there."

"What do you mean you weren't 'really there'?"

"I mean—I was at the library, writing and organizing the novel. And—again, it's hard to describe—but I completely lost track of time. Just, poof, hours disappeared. I actually got kicked out by the librarian. Nearly arrested. And, even driving home, I still didn't feel right. I felt like I was a passenger in my own body just along for the ride. And then, all of a sudden, there was this rush of movement and I realized I hit something. So I got out of the car and I found this figure huddled in a doorway. It was the boy. We spoke and he said he was going to be okay. But still, to this day, it feels like everything that happened that night happened to someone else. I have the memories—as vague as they are—of being there but I don't feel like it was *me* there."

Magee listened intently. Then, when Matt was done, he said simply, "It sounds like you were drugged."

"That's what it felt like."

"No, I'm serious. I think you were actually drugged."

The notion brought Matt to a standstill after he'd agreed so cavalierly. He began to say something, stopped, then frowned. "I don't think I was drugged. I mean, you'd think I would've known."

"What you just described to me sounds exactly like someone under some sort of outside influence. A drug is the most logical choice. Or possibly a panic attack...something like that."

"No, I wasn't panicked. If anything, I was the opposite: Too focused, too spellbound. While, yeah, I was terrified after I hit the boy, I didn't feel like my heart was fluttering out of control. Instead, it was a sense of dis-reality—as if I couldn't believe it had actually happened."

"Yep, that sounds like something chemically-induced, buddy," said Magee gravely, taking a sip of beer. "It doesn't mean you're going crazy. But it doesn't mean the accident didn't happen either."

Matt frowned again, slowly shaking his head from side to side. "I haven't even told you all of it, though. After that, after I decided the boy was okay, I went home and tried to carry on with life as if nothing happened. I couldn't sleep, though—that night or the rest of the week. I couldn't stop thinking about him. In the meantime, these weird events started happening. Like, for example, I lost the tickets to the opera. Then my office got struck by lightning. And I keep seeing this man—he keeps appearing everywhere I go. It's all so strange to say aloud, without context. It's as if I can't trust what I'm seeing anymore. Even if I was drugged that night it wouldn't explain everything afterward."

"Everything you just described could be related, though," said Magee. "The cause doesn't have to be an illicit drug. It could've been a reaction to a combination of drugs."

"Who'd want to drug me anyway?"

"Look, I'm not saying some CIA agent dropped LSD in your coffee for the hell of it. I'm just pointing out that each of those experiences you mentioned involve sensory experience and, therefore, relate back to chemicals in your brain."

Matt peered at Magee, taking a swig of beer as he did so. If he accepted Magee's suggestion that a chemical imbalance in his brain was the cause, that would explain the rash of strange events and he could seek out some sort of treatment to keep hold of his sanity. But it didn't let him off the hook with regard to his responsibility for the boy. If he rejected his friend's assessment, however, his sanity remained in question but his conscience retained a vague plausible-deniability regarding the boy.

"What do you think I should I do?" asked Matt, finally.

"Wow. I think you have to go to the police," said Magee with uneasy gravitas. "If you don't, this is going to hang over you for the rest of your life. You checked with the kid and he seemed okay...at least you did the right thing. I don't think that'd be considered a classic hit and run."

Matt nodded impatiently. "Magee, I already told you—that's where I was this afternoon when I called you."

"I know but...at the time, I didn't know it was this serious. What happened? What made you call me?"

"When I went there," Matt paused and glanced down at the table before continuing, "I saw this guy. He's this man, very stoic, who I've been seeing everywhere: On the subway, on the street, everywhere. Well, *he* was the cop. He was the police officer I encountered at the station. I have no explanation for it. And he refused to admit that he was the same man I'd seen previously. I called because I didn't know what else to do—I felt like I couldn't trust my own mind, like I wasn't sure what was real anymore."

"Well, again, it goes back to the possibility of those drugs."

Matt continued, undaunted. "From what I understand, it's often hard for a crazy person to recognize the true nature of their insanity. On some level they might know that they're not normal but, on another, they might not see how far their perceptions deviate from reality. I recognized that something was wrong. I knew that I shouldn't make any statements to the police, offer them anything incriminating, when I couldn't even be sure who I was anymore."

Matt stared at Magee intently, preventing any interruption. "I am well aware that I have to go to the police. But do you see my dilemma? Do you see why I'm so frustrated? I have to admit my guilt or I'll be haunted by this forever yet I can't go to the authorities until I'm positive I'm in the proper state of mind."

Magee began to nod, gaining new appreciation for the Catch-22 nature of his friend's quandary. But just then his phone went off, lighting and vibrating on the table in front of them. "Oh come on," muttered Magee.

Matt's balloon deflated instantly at the intrusion and, at first, Magee reacted similarly until he glanced at the message. "Hey...I know this is terrible timing," said Magee, "but it's the guy with the tickets. I didn't get a chance to tell you: I found somebody who's willing to sell tickets to that opera. Long story but, for some reason, he wanted to meet you in person before selling them."

"What? Really?" asked Matt. The lost tickets had gone from a calamity to a nearly forgotten annoyance but it was good news nonetheless.

"It's crazy. He showed up at my studio earlier today and was ready to sell them. When I mentioned that they were for a friend, though, he started acting weird and refused to let me buy them. He said he'd have to meet you to make sure you wouldn't embarrass him. I texted him that we were going to be here but I didn't expect him so soon. Apparently, he's here but doesn't see us. I have to find him."

"Oh, okay. Do it. Go ahead," said Matt.

The bar had grown crowded as the night progressed and Magee slipped away to cut a path through the congestion. He'd been gone less than a minute, however, when Matt felt the presence of someone on the other side of the table. Matt expected it to be Magee but, when he looked up, he found himself eye-to-eye with a short, dumpy man in drab coveralls. Though the bar was hardly a fashion expo, the man still appeared out of place and his large, out-sized eyes stared at Matt with a mix of recognition and suspicion.

"You," the man said.

"Me?" said Matt with a nervous laugh.

"Are you Magee's friend?" asked the man.

"Oh! Yes, I am," said Matt more attentively, sitting up in his chair and offering his hand to shake. "I'm Matt. Are you the guy with the tickets?"

The man looked at Matt's hand like it was a dead rat and took a step backwards. For a long, awkward beat he simply stared at Matt and, eventually, Matt dropped his hand when it was clear it would not be shook. Then the man's apprehension gave way to outright anger, a deep scowl forming on his anuran forehead before he erupted, "You gotta be kidding me. Did they send you straight from the Azeri embassy or what? You guys think I'm that stupid?"

"What?" said Matt, perplexed.

"Y'see," said the man, to no one in particular, "*this* is why I check this stuff out. I tell ya...."

"I think there's been a mistake," said Matt, trying to smooth over the situation without even knowing what he was smoothing over.

"Yeah, there's been a mistake all right," growled the man. "You think I'm stupid? You think I'm gonna get involved in *that* crap?"

"No. Wait. Calm down," said Matt. "We were just trying to get some tickets to the opera. I don't know what—"

"Well, not from me, you're not," said the man, whirling to go. "I shoulda known. 'A friend'. Ha! Tell Magee he's seen the last of me. He's got a lotta nerve!"

"Wait," cried Matt as he jumped off his stool. But the man had already barreled his way through the crowd with a gruff, "Scuse me!"

The scene had created a handful of onlookers. And as Matt peered about, suddenly aware of the eyes upon him, Magee appeared at the opposite edge of the crowd. He'd missed the exchange but, based on his expression, he could sense that something very strange had occurred. Yet all Matt could do was hold his palms up, unsure what'd just happened.

MEDA

I hate them. I hate them. I hate them. It was a mantra for Meda, cantillated over and over in her mind, as she trudged home from work. The downpour began at 9:40, precisely the moment she'd left the office, and it had followed her to the subway station in Manhattan. Then, as if the timing wasn't bad enough, it started to freeze when she reached her neighborhood, making the journey that much more perilous. Working late was nothing new (the term "late" had become a relative statement to her long ago). But, having grown older, her patience tired exponentially quicker for such hours when the reasons behind them were incompetence or ego-driven self-aggrandizement. At 3:00, the project had been complete and ready to send, with the head of the firm's blessing. Delivery had been held up, however, by a cadre of 'strivers', five weak, insecure men who required validation and felt the need to conduct a final review, despite the fact that they couldn't make any edits after the CEO's sign-off. If Meda had left an hour (hell, ten minutes) earlier she would've avoided the frigid rain and sleet. Instead, she struggled to carry her laptop (which seemed to grow a pound heavier with every block walked), her purse, and her umbrella while chanting her bitter refrain. This, most assuredly, was not what she'd signed on for when she'd picked her career.

"What do you think you're doing?" came the voice, eliciting a momentary cringe from Meda. It was Mrs. Javier. Meda was steps away from her apartment, yearning to get inside, rip off her soggy clothes, and make the day go away. Instead, initially blocked from view by Meda's umbrella, Mrs. Javier was there to greet her on the porch stoop. (Why was she sitting outside in the freezing rain?)

"Hi, Mrs. Javier," said Meda, looking up.

Mrs. Javier was in a chair under the awning, safe from the rain but lodged perfectly in front of the door. Until she moved, there was no way for Meda to get under cover or into the building. "A lady in your condition, carrying all that heavy stuff," said Mrs. Javier, ignoring Meda's greeting and, instead, continuing her admonishment.

"What?" said Meda, blinking.

"An expectant mother, in weather like this," said Mrs. Javier.

"Oh. Oh! No, I'm not pregnant, Mrs. Javier," said Meda. She was trying to be patient with the old woman, aware that she meant well and that the exchange should only take a few moments. Despite her mild amusement (and irritation), she was still standing out in the cold rain, still getting wetter despite her best efforts with the umbrella.

"You're not?" said the woman, incredulous. "But you've had that glow. I know that glow when I see it."

"I'm not. Trust me on this one."

"Are you sure?"

"Yes, I'm sure, Mrs. Javier," said Meda, forcing a grin. (Come *on*, lady!)

"Oh, well, I suppose you would know."

Mrs. Javier trailed off and Meda took the opportunity to take the first step up the stairs. Apparently, the woman had no inclination to move so Meda decided it was time to give her a not-so-subtle hint that she was in the way.

"Have you gone to the doctor?" asked Mrs. Javier.

"No. No, I haven't. Because I haven't felt the need to do so." (Gritted teeth.)

"Well, let me tell you: I know a doctor over on 34th. A lovely man. He's very nice and—"

"Mrs. Javier. I'm sorry, but I need to get inside. I'm sopping wet. And you're blocking the way."

"Oh!" said the woman, glancing from side to side. "No me digas! I'm so sorry, dear. Here I am, jabbering away, and you just want to get in out of the cold."

The woman jumped to her feet to move the chair, in the process stepping out into the rain herself.

"I'm sorry," said Meda, suddenly uncomfortable. She hadn't intended to be brusque; she just wanted to get indoors. Now she felt like she'd forced the old woman out into the freezing rain. Self-consciously, she repeated, "I'm sorry, Mrs. Javier. We'll talk again soon."

"Yes, dear. Of course," said Mrs. Javier as each rotated around the other clumsily in the cramped space of the stoop. The strap of Meda's laptop bag caught on the chair, yanking the bag off her shoulder and further adding to her vexation.

"Oh shit," Meda blurted, instantly embarrassed.

"It's okay, dear. I'll get it," said Mrs. Javier, freeing the bag while getting poked in the forehead by Meda's umbrella.

"I'm sorry. Thank you. I'm sorry," stammered Meda, struggling to get inside the building and extricate herself from the situation. She felt like a toad for being so rude. Yet she also felt vague resentment at being forced into such a predicament in the first place. Her face was burning hot, despite the frigidity in the air, and the dampness in her underarms was revolting. Once in her apartment (after fumbling with her keys for about three hours), she dropped everything and exhaled. Initially, she merely stood in place.

Then she caught sight of herself in the mirror at the end of the hallway. She looked wretched. Rather than peeling off her coat, as she'd intended, she began to move towards the mirror with cautious, furtive steps. So entranced, so horrified was she by what she saw, that she didn't care about the soggy footprints left in her wake—she had to get a better look at herself, at this terrible woman she saw in her apartment. (That couldn't possibly be her, right?) Her eyeliner had run down her cheeks, sodden strands of hair were plastered to her forehead in stringy clumps, and there wasn't the slightest trace of confidence in her stance. The veneer was gone, a notion that struck her both literally and figuratively like a sudden nausea. This was who she was now. She was no longer the carefree twenty-something that wanted to conquer the world. And it didn't matter whether poor decisions, lack of ability, or bad luck had led to that moment. This was *who she was*.

She sobbed. The concomitant emotional drain of the workday; of the terrible trek home; of the gnawing doubt about her life's goals; of her relationship with Matt; of the guilt at how she'd treated Mrs. Javier; of the sight of herself stripped of all illusions: They all hit Meda at once. She felt like a wimp for crying and her embarrassment fused with her frustration to produce even more tears. Her palm went to her face, covering it, and she stood for a long time heaving in silence.

The only thing that brought her back to life was the ringing of her phone. It was muffled, originating from the inside her bag, which remained in a heap at the front door. She didn't want to answer it, fearing the call involved some last minute dilemma at her workplace. In fact, she didn't even move until the second ring. Then, finally, with lead-laden footfalls, she trudged toward it. As far as she was concerned, the call could go to voicemail. The phone was still ringing when she picked it up, though, and, seeing that it was Matt, she hurried to answer it.

"Hello?"

"Hey hon, it's me. Can I come over?"

MEDA

Meda didn't need a savior riding in on a white horse. She wasn't a damsel in distress. But two hours after that embarrassing display at the door, she would agree that Matt's appearance had utterly transformed the atrocious trajectory of her day. Her encounters with him had been unusual lately so, at first, she was apprehensive when he asked to come over (seriously didn't need another argument on top of everything else). Instead, Matt had surprised her by picking up groceries again and, as they worked to create dinner together, her post-work meltdown was almost forgotten.

"So why *is* she getting married?" asked Matt as he leaned across her to reach the salt.

"That's just it: I don't think she knows. It seems like she's doing it only *because of* the expectation that she's supposed to do it," replied Meda.

"I mean, if Donald was pressuring her, that'd be one thing," added Matt. "It doesn't sound like he's chomping at the bit to get hitched, either. I don't understand where the pressure is coming from."

"Exactly. Even back in our first year of college, Brenda was always the diligent, responsible one. She made me seem like a wild child. I never would've expected her to rush something so important."

"Excuse me, hon," said Matt, "I just need to reach the sink."

"Oh, of course," said Meda, sliding out of the way. "So it appears we have to start looking for a place to stay next month. She didn't even block hotel rooms for guests."

"Yeah," said Matt with a chuckle. "Definitely unlike like Brenda."

The banter was light, easy, exactly what Meda needed. Without conscious effort, Matt had provided a means for her to forget the day and move to a better headspace. So when his expression grew more serious at the break in the conversation, she tightened, mentally and physically.

"I have something to tell you," he said. "I'm not even sure where to start."

Meda said nothing. She wanted to tell him that he didn't have to start, that there was no need to alter the path of the night they'd been enjoying. Everything was fine.

"I guess," continued Matt, whether Meda wanted him to or not, "it all began last Monday—God, it seems so much longer ago than that. I was at the library working on the novel. And I got so wrapped up in it that I lost all sense of time. It's hard to describe. The librarian kicked me out."

"Okay," said Meda, elongating the word, unsure where Matt was going with this.

"So I left, still feeling a little messed up in the head and."

"And what?"

"I think I hit a little boy with my car."

"What?" Meda shot to attention.

"In fact, I know I did."

"You *what*?"

"I stopped and talked to him."

"Why didn't you tell me? No wonder you were acting so strange last week. I knew something was up. Why didn't you just tell me? You could be arrested!"

"I know! And that's not all of it," said Matt slowly, his tone sheepish.

"What? What else is there?" She snapped harsher than she'd intended. With the air taken out of the room and her momentarily bliss eradicated, she wasn't sure she wanted to hear any more.

"Ever since then, I've been experiencing all these strange events. Weird, crazy encounters. It's hard to describe. I feel like I'm going crazy."

"What's going on, babe?" asked Meda, growing concerned.

"I keep seeing this same guy everywhere: On the subway; walking down the street; in a cop uniform. The same guy all the time. But he claims he doesn't remember me. He—"

"Wait," interrupted Meda, "a cop uniform? Did you go to the police?"

"Yes. I mean, yes, I intended to go. I went to the station. Once I got there, this man was outside, though. So I left."

"Matt!"

"I know! It sounds so insane when I describe it this way. I just felt like I couldn't trust my senses anymore. I didn't know what was real and what wasn't. I didn't want to say anything incriminating. So I left before entering the precinct."

Meda reeled. From the time she'd left work to the conclusion of Matt's confession, her emotional state had whipsawed. In a bout of practicality she darted to the stove to turn off the burners. Concern for Matt collided with anger at him for withholding the information so long. Betrayal was too strong of a word yet the edges of it were within sight.

"I don't know what to say," she admitted, wide-eyed. "Why didn't you tell me sooner? At the very least, why didn't you tell me before you went to the police? This involves both of our lives. What happens to you impacts me. I know you probably thought you were doing the right thing. I just wish you would've mentioned it to me."

"The boy is dead, Meda!"

"What?"

"I looked it up. On the internet. The thing is, I pulled over and spoke to him after I hit him. He insisted—*he insisted*—he was okay."

"Oh my God."

Suddenly her emotional state didn't matter. Her job didn't matter, encounters with Mrs. Javier didn't matter. When Matt began it was obvious he had something serious to tell her. But she never expected *this*.

"I thought he was, maybe, homeless or an illegal immigrant. And that was why he didn't want my help. I think he even said I didn't hit him. It's so hard to remember."

"Well, are *you* positive you hit him?" asked Meda, her tone a mix of hope and cross-examination.

"Yes. I heard the thump on the bumper. I think I only grazed him. But yes, I'm virtually positive I hit him."

"Did he appear delirious? Was he speaking coherently?"

"He seemed fine. He sounded like he didn't want to be bothered. He was huddled in the corner of a doorway. It was dark. It happened in that industrial section over near the service road next to the expressway. East Elmhurst, I think. There was no one else around."

Meda was at a loss for words. She blinked and, multiple times, her lips moved as if she was about to begin a sentence. No words came out, though.

Matt added, "Sunday night I searched online for news about hospital admissions. A boy was dropped off on the sidewalk in front of the New York Hospital in Flushing. He died that night."

"So what are you going to do?" asked Meda slowly.

"I have to go to the police."

"But it's been so long now," said Meda. The disappointment in her voice echoed the weariness of a beleaguered mother whose infant had thrown dinner on the floor. "Why did you wait so long, Matt?"

"I know. I'm sorry," he said, addressing her chagrin. "I didn't know what to do. I feel terrible. I can't put it into words how bad I feel inside. Who knows, maybe that's *why* everything has been so insane lately. I just don't know. That's the scariest part."

"Oh babe," said Meda, growing more sympathetic. She didn't mean to hurt him or add to his guilt; it was obvious he was distraught. Though aware she had every right to be angry, furious even, twisting the knife was not her intention. Most importantly Matt needed guidance and, placing her hands on his shoulders, she said, "Let's think. You said you pulled over and checked on him. What happened, exactly, when you hit him?"

"Oh boy. Like I said I was a little out of it. And it happened so fast," said Matt gloomily. Meda didn't interject, however, forcing him to continue, "He must've darted out in front of me. It was dark and I think one of the street lights was out."

"Okay, good," said Meda, nodding. "All of that works in your favor. Are you positive there were no witnesses? No other cars around?"

"Nope. Nobody."

"Okay."

"So, if you were in court, you could state affirmatively that the boy jumped in front of your car and that you checked on him to be sure he wasn't hurt?" Meda was asking the question as much as she was rehashing the narrative to herself. "I guess that's a positive, at least."

"You think I might not be in trouble?"

"I have no idea," said Meda quickly. "From the sounds of it, you did the right thing. And legally, you have something resembling a defense. Apart from forcibly bringing an unwilling child to the hospital, I don't know what else you could've done."

"Yeah," agreed Matt.

"That doesn't change the fact that you have to tell the police, though."

"I'll go to the precinct tomorrow," said Matt, earnest and contrite. Then he added, "tomorrow after work. I haven't been in to the office since last Thursday."

"Jeez, Matt. You idiot."

"I told you: It's been a weird time for me. I've been trying to get my head together. At this point I don't think it'll matter whether I go to the cops in the morning or after work anyway. If I don't get my butt into the office, though, I might be giving them reason to fire me."

Meda didn't like the delay; her sour expression required no words to convey that. But she also recognized his need for continued employment. Finally, in a hushed tone, she gave permission to his plan with a simple, "Okay."

MATT

Matt fidgeted. Then scolded himself for doing so. Throughout his commute that morning he'd been preparing his story—he'd missed a total of three days of work and needed some sort of an explanation. He recognized that his tale had to be believable and that he had to have the details tight in case his boss asked any unexpected questions. Yet, he needed to tell his yarn in a manner that was believable and didn't sound overly rehearsed. Silly fidgeting, left unchecked, might take an otherwise believable story and make it look like a excuse concocted by a little boy.

"Hey Louise," he said, entering his boss's office.

"Why hello, Matthew. How are you feeling?"

"Better. Not a hundred percent. But definitely better than I was."

"That's good to hear. What happened?" she asked, barely looking away from her monitor.

"It was mess," said Matt, with a practiced laugh. "They thought I had West Nile Virus at first."

"Oh my."

"Yeah, it was a scare. Apparently the symptoms are very similar to that of a regular flu and I had been bitten by a mosquito recently."

"Then tests ensued, I presume."

"You guessed it. Apparently, they have to track the number of cases. It turned out that I only had a simple flu virus. It was still an ordeal."

"Of course," said Louise, now wholly distracted as she began to type something. "I'm glad you're feeling better."

"Me too," said Matt, nodding, then leaving.

See? No big deal. Matt smirked at his needless worry. He should've known no one would care, that there'd be no Gestapo-style interrogation waiting to trip him up.

Then: "Matt!"

The screech came from the neighboring cubicle the moment he dropped his bag.

"Hi Abby."

"Are you okay? You were out three days," she said, materializing at the entrance to his cubicle.

"Yeah, I'm feeling much better," he said, barely avoiding a roll of his eyes. He had expected to explain himself to his boss but had overlooked his excitable co-worker.

"What did the doctor say? I heard you were having tests done."

Matt wanted to ask how she'd heard about any tests he'd taken so quickly but didn't want to prolong the conversation any longer than necessary. "Yeah, at first they were concerned it was West Nile Virus. Fortunately it wasn't. Just the flu. A real pain in the butt, though."

"Oh, absolutely. My friend's mother needed an MRI for that. That's serious business."

An MRI? That didn't sound right. West Nile Virus doesn't warrant an MRI, does it?

"Did you have to have one?" Abby persisted.

Matt hesitated. "Ah, no. No, actually. They just, um, took my blood. No MRI."

"Oh. How long did it take to get the results?"

"Not long," said Matt, trying to hide his gritted teeth. "But, um, you know these hospitals—speed is a relative thing at them sometimes, right?"

"Absolutely," said Abby, blinking. "I wonder: Maybe my friend's mother had the MRI because she was older. Maybe that's why she required it and you didn't."

"Yeah," said Matt, far too enthusiastically. "That's probably the reason. I didn't hear any mention of an MRI so it must be something they do as a precaution for older people. Or something."

"Yes," said Abby again, nodding and then smiling. "Well anyway: I'm glad you're back."

"I am, too."

By midday, Matt was sick of telling his tale. The conversation with Abby had unnerved him and he'd lost confidence in his ability to manufacture a storyline on the fly. Suddenly he needed to be careful with the details lest he contradict himself inadvertently. Some co-workers were concerned for his welfare while others saw it as a simple way to start a conversation, but in every conversation the exchange was no longer natural or spontaneous. Normally he went to lunch around 2:00 PM but, by noon, he could take no more and headed outside.

Once downstairs, Matt was reminded why he waited so long to go to lunch most days—the sidewalk was packed. At noon, a virtual flood of hungry office workers hit the concrete, creating chaotic sidewalk congestion and lines at the delis that extended out the doors. Matt surveyed the sidewalk and sighed—couldn't anything just be normal anymore?

He decided to dive down a small side street that was partially hidden from view. It would be hard to describe any street in midtown as a secret but the cobblestoned enclave was the closest approximation to it. The boutique eatery at the rear was too expensive and the portion sizes were laughable but at least Matt could escape the bevy of people.

Then, from Matt's left, someone said, "Hey!"

Initially, he didn't even look up. With so many people having so many different conversations, exclamations like that were merely part of the auditory background. So, casually peering upward to find its source, he didn't truly expect that it had been directed at him. Then he saw the now familiar face of The Stoic Man. And he nearly rolled his ankle coming to a halt.

"I was hoping you'd arrive," said the man. He was far more casual than Matt had ever seen him. Rather than a formal shirt and tie or a police uniform, the man was now sporting chinos and a polo shirt. He even sported sunglasses dangling from the shirt pocket. Yet, without a doubt, it was the Stoic Man.

"What—? How—?" Matt stammered, too many questions popping up too quickly.

"I couldn't speak candidly when you came to the precinct the other day. I knew my partner was coming."

"What?" Matt repeated, completely befuddled.

"I know you wanted to make your confession. But I couldn't let you do that."

"How—How did you know I was going to be here? Be here right now?"

The man shook his head to dismiss the question. Instead he continued, the urgency in his tone only increasing. "You're going to have to forget about that boy. He was lost anyway, doomed. In fact, he's better off dead."

"What?" cried Matt, louder than he intended. He scanned the immediate area but no one batted an eyelash.

"Don't worry about him, Matt," the Stoic Man persisted. "You need to focus on yourself now. Yourself and Meda."

"Wait. How did you know her name?" said Matt in an attempt to slow the conversation. The encounter had occurred so suddenly, so utterly out of the blue, yet there were still so many basic questions left unanswered. The fact that the man knew Meda's name—when Matt was positive he'd never mentioned it to him—set off new alarm bells in what was already an abrupt mental fire drill.

"You're going to have to watch her. I'm not positive if she is *in on it* or not."

"In on what?"

"Those tickets to *Götterdämmerung*—she picked them out, right?"

"What? How the hell did you know about that? What's going on?"

"The tickets. Did. She. Pick. Them?"

"We both did. We had them sent to my office. I don't understand."

"No. She picked out the seats, the exact location of them, correct?"

Matt searched his memory. He felt like he'd been ambushed and that made him wary. Yet he was forced to admit: The man was right. Meda *had* chosen the seats.

Though Matt said nothing, his expression evidently betrayed him because the man nodded, "I was afraid of that. It might just be dumb luck—but I doubt it. Of all the available seats in the opera she picked those exact ones."

"Why? What's so special about them? I'm so confused."

"Listen," said the man intently before scanning the immediate area as if someone might be listening. "This is bigger than both of us. I can't stay here much longer on the chance someone's been tailing you. The Armenians? Their beef with the Azeri goes back centuries. You shouldn't get involved in any of that."

"What? This is crazy," cried Matt, now hopelessly lost.

"There's going to be an assassination attempt. In those exact seats. I saw the intelligence on it. And here's the thing: The authorities are going to let it happen. I'm not even sure why. Azerbaijan is the gateway to western Asia, though. So I have to think someone in a high place is involved."

"This is—" said Matt before being interrupted.

"Let me finish. I'm running out of time. You have to be careful around Meda. Do not go to the police with any information about the boy. He's important—critically important. But in the grand scheme of things you have to watch out for yourself now. You have to keep yourself alive, first and foremost. Do you understand?"

"No, I don't," said Matt, practically laughing at the absurdity of it all.

"You have to be serious, Matt! Do you understand?"

"Yes! Fine! I understand!"

"Okay. Good," said the man, gathering himself and peering about the area again. "I have to go—I'll be in touch. Don't go to the precinct. Be careful around Meda. Stay safe."

"Wait, I have so many questions," said Matt. Before he even finished the sentence, however, the Stoic Man patted him on the arm and darted away. Matt took a step to follow, hesitated, and then watched as he disappeared into the crowd on the sidewalk.

For a long period Matt stood, staring down the path, his mouth agape. Once again, he felt as if he was a passenger in his own body—physically, he was cognizant he was there, that he existed at that present moment. Yet the previous two minutes seemed as if they'd occurred somewhere far away and involved a different form of his self.

Matt tried to focus on the facts: The Stoic Man knew his name and Meda's , he knew she'd been the one to pick out the tickets, and, somehow, he knew that Matt was going to wander down that side street at that exact moment. It was all so serendipitous that it lent an enigmatic authority to the man's bizarre claims about Armenia. In fact, hadn't Magee's ticket seller mentioned something about an embassy the other night? Matt still had no idea what any of it *meant*, however. How could that young child have anything to do with a country on the opposite side of the globe? How could Meda be involved in an assassination attempt? The problem wasn't simply that Matt had too many questions; it was that he didn't even know which were the most important.

He felt the urge to shake his head, as if he was a cartoon, in an attempt to bring himself back to reality. His mind was spinning and he couldn't get a handle on what to actually *do* next. How could be go back to work after that? How could the tedium of account transfers compare to everything he just heard? Yet what else could he do at that very moment?

In a stupor, he wandered into the eatery, ordered the first sandwich on the board he saw, and took it back to his desk. Then he immediately began researching Azerbaijan's relationship with Armenia. Apparently the Stoic Man was right: The two countries had been at odds for ages, with violent, gruesome conflicts occurring at multiple times in the previous century. Further, like many other countries in the region, the area had been contested by rival powers over the centuries, creating a history of violence and genocide. Matt had known almost nothing about the countries but, very quickly, he became fascinated. Transfer reconciliations piled up yet his curiosity couldn't be denied—everything the Stoic Man had referenced appeared to be true. Matt didn't want to believe, couldn't believe, that Meda was involved in an assassination plot. Yet the stakes were so high—literally life and death—that he didn't want to summarily dismiss the man's warning. He needed more time to think. That was paramount. And by the time he left work, Matt decided his most immediate goal was to create a believable story to tell Meda why he hadn't gone to the precinct as he'd promised.

MEDA

The project was out the door. That was all that mattered to Meda. After the late firedrill yesterday, she'd spent most of the day following up on loose ends. It required various degrees of lies and apologies to people she'd been avoiding but, finally, she was caught up on her work. The project could officially be declared complete and, after all the aggravation, she sauntered out of the office at five o'clock on the dot.

When she emerged from the subway in her neighborhood it felt like something was wrong. She stepped to the side to take stock and, gradually, her grin blossomed. Meda hadn't arrived home while the sun was still shining in weeks. It was a suspiciously odd (good) feeling, as if summer was in bloom all over again, and it caught her off guard. The joys of leaving work on time!

Meda approached her apartment building, already making plans for this cornucopia of newfound time. Yoga class was always an option; the leak in her apartment still needed to be fixed; and then there was that book languishing on her nightstand she'd been intending to read. The possibilities for her night were endless.

Once inside and up the first set of stairs, however, she stopped dead in her tracks. Her apartment door was open. It was only ajar the slightest crack but that didn't make it any less worrisome. Had someone broken in? And if so, were they still there? Or had she simply failed to close it fully when she left that morning? She took one hesitant step down the landing towards it, unsure what to do next. Startling a would-be thief might make the person more dangerous. Yet if she ran away to call the police, the person might have the chance to finish the job and get away.

She took another furtive step closer, listening intently for any movement beyond the door. She was still at least ten feet away and could flee, if necessary. Instead, without taking her eyes off the door, she took her keys from her pocket and balled them into her fist.

Another step and Meda was nearly ready to make her presence known. She recognized that, if an intruder was still inside, the worst thing to do would be to enter the apartment; better to stay in the hallway with a reasonable chance of escape. Announcing herself was also a risk, ruining the element of surprise, but survival was most paramount (better to lose a few possessions than get locked inside with a psychopath).

Then, just as she was about to holler, the door swung open. Meda tensed, ready to fight or to make a mad dash down the stairs. A person came into view. It was Mrs. Javier.

Meda's shoulders dropped and she issued a breath that seemed to deflate her entire body. Yet, for her part, Mrs. Javier still hadn't realized Meda was standing there. The old woman was fully focused on something she was carrying, a small item wrapped in cloth.

"Mrs. Javier?" asked Meda incredulously.

"Oh!" cried the old woman, practically leaping out of her skin. "You scared me."

"And *you* scared *me*," said Meda, affronted. "What were you doing in my apartment?"

"Oh, I'm sorry, dear. I thought you'd be at work. You're home early," said the old woman, clearly shaken.

"I am. But why were you in my apartment?" In the immediate sense, Meda was relieved that a six foot guy in a ski mask hadn't emerged. Following that initial relief, though, she wanted answers.

"Oh dear," said Mrs. Javier again. (Just answer my question, enough with the 'dear'.) "This must look so strange."

"Yes, it does," said Meda, growing angrier by the moment.

"I just wanted to give you a gift."

"A gift?"

"Yes. Well," said Mrs. Javier, pausing sheepishly, "I was afraid you wouldn't accept it."

"What? Why?"

"Because it's a fertility idol," she said, producing a small statue from the cloth in her hand. The idol appeared to be ancient, depicting a woman with what looked like thick wings and two lions held at her side on either hip. "I realized some ash from the incense was on it and I was about to clean it up."

"What?" said Meda, squinting, nearly volcanic at the audacity.

"I wanted to put it in your apartment. To help."

Meda shook her head from side to side. She didn't know where to begin. "Y'know what, Mrs. Javier?" she began, taking a gulp of air and ready to unleash a torrent. (Scared half to death, all because this woman felt it her right to stick her nose in and)

"Yes, dear?"

The words halted Meda. (The woman's wide eyes, her earnest expression.) There were a million questions Meda wanted to accost her with, a million different repudiations regarding her need for the woman's help. She wanted to scream at her, curse her out for daring to assume she required assistance getting pregnant and for breaking into her apartment with some creepy idol. But to what end? Meda could verbally tear the old woman asunder, reduce her to tears. But what would be achieved?

Meda took another breath and stared at the ceiling for a long moment in an attempt to compose herself. "Mrs. Javier," she said, fully enunciating each and every syllable. "I *appreciate* your concern. But please, *please,* do *not* go into my apartment ever again. Please do not offer me any advice regarding child rearing. Please do not leave anything in my apartment without telling me. If I have any reason to think you were in there again, I will call the cops."

Meda felt terrible as she spit out the last sentence, but she wanted to let the woman know that she meant business and that there'd be real-world consequences.

"Yes, dear. I'm sorry," said Mrs. Javier, before adding, "I was only trying to help."

It nearly set Meda off. A muscle in her back twitched involuntarily and, for the third time, she took a deep, nostril flaring breath. She wanted to scream that it wasn't her job to help, to berate the woman for making her feel guilty when she was the one that'd been wronged. Instead, she swallowed. "Okay," she said. Then Meda strode past Mrs. Javier into her apartment.

"Have a good day, dear," said Mrs. Javier finally, turning to go.

"You too," said Meda. And she closed the door.

Once inside, she dropped her bag. The impact of the encounter cast a grey shadow (she'd been in such a good mood, too!) and she glanced around her apartment, taking stock. While nothing seemed out of place, an air of "foreignness" lingered. The knowledge of a stranger's presence infected her surroundings and she viewed everything with a vague amount of skepticism: Was there anything missing from her bowl of change? Had she really left that cabinet door open in the morning? Was there a tiny statue lurking inside the bedside drawer? Meda saw the idol in the old woman's hands, so, clearly, it hadn't been left in the apartment. Yet just the thought of something like that lurking mere feet from where she slept made her shudder.

In the end, she couldn't identify anything that was missing. She did find another rag, though, one similar to the cloth Mrs. Javier was carrying. With renewed disgust, Meda tossed it on the shelf in the bathroom and proceeded to change out of her clothes.

She'd been so busy at work that she never had a chance to think about Matt's meeting with the police. Once she relaxed and settled in, however, the seriousness of Matt's predicament returned to her anew. The newfound time on her hands was a fantastic luxury but it also offered more opportunity to worry, so she decided to call him to get an update. He didn't answer, as she might've predicted, and she left him a voicemail.

Four hours later, he still hadn't returned the call. "Matt, let me know when you get this," she said in a new voicemail. "I'm getting worried, baby. I'm guessing you're still at the precinct. Thought you'd be home by now. I hope everything is okay and you're not.... Anyway. Call me, okay? I love you."

Then, when he still hadn't called by midnight, she left yet another, more urgent message. And, eventually, she resigned herself to sleep, still fretting about her thoughtless, immature boyfriend.

MAGEE

There were too many distractions in life. That was what Magee concluded. How could one be expected to make a fearless leap into the creative maelstrom while worrying about the laundry or errands or social media? In the previous three days, what should've amounted to roughly twenty hours of studio time had been summarily gobbled up by dreary life mundanities like a carcass besieged by piranha. He was relieved to have finally found a birthday present for his aunt and, unless he planned to wear those jeans a fourth time, a trip to the laundromat had been an absolute necessity. The fact that he'd only spent a total of three hours in the studio, however, was an utter disgrace.

The other, less obvious drawback to so much lost time? Art was no longer actively on his mind. So when he forced himself to go down to the studio that Wednesday afternoon, he had no firm creative vision...no real idea of what he expected to produce. It was hardly the best way to work and, in similar circumstances, he'd produced as many bad pieces as he had good ones. Still...he had to at least try. He glanced at the piece he'd been working on previously, his image in the mirror reflecting back at him, and a sensation of resentment arose within him. He began to rationalize that he'd be better off doing nothing than ruining a piece with such potential. Then the phone rang.

"What now?" shouted Magee, as if he was already elbow-deep in paint. He shot a glare at it...why had he even brought it with him? He had no intention of answering it. Yet, in a fit of curiosity, he gave it a quick glance. A 917 area code...it was local. The person's name wasn't programmed into his phone, however. Who could it be? It rang two more times, Magee content to ignore it, when he realized: It was the man with the tickets to the opera.

“Hey,” came the gruff voice as soon as Magee answered, dispensing all formalities. “What’s up with your friend?”

“What?” said Magee.

“Your friend. The one that wanted the tickets.”

“Matt?” said Magee, taken aback. Matt had asserted that the guy wanted nothing to do with him ever again. So not only was the immediate inquisition jarring but the call itself was wholly unexpected.

“He freaked out on me. Wasn’t talking sense.”

“He...? Really?” stammered Magee. “What did he say?”

“I don’t know. Buncha crap. Something about Armenia.”

“Armenia?”

“Yep. He was all riled up. Total freakout territory.”

“That...doesn’t sound right,” said Magee.

“Well, it’s what happened,” said the man, matter-of-factly. “Between you and me, it scared the crap out of me. I heard rumors that something involving the Armenians was going down at that opera. Hadn’t thought much of it at first. Figured it was a simple drug deal or something. Then, just that afternoon I heard it’s something bigger, though. Assassination, possibly.”

“What? Assassination?” said Magee.

“Something like that. Something shady. Oh! I almost forgot: Your buddy? He turns around and asks who sent me. Like I was out to get him or something. Crazy talk.”

At that, Magee hit a mental pause button. He and Matt had only recently been talking about Matt’s anxiety in the wake of his accident. The word ‘crazy’ was getting a lot of use suddenly.

“Anyway,” continued the man, emitting a sour wheeze, “does he want the tickets, or not?”

"You still want to sell them to him?" asked Magee, now free-falling in the conversation.

"Sure. Why not?" said the man. "I don't care what he does once he's there. As long as I don't have to deal with him anymore. I could give a damn who gets assassinated."

"But...I thought...you needed to meet the buyer to...."

"Look: I needed to make sure he wasn't a cop. He ain't. So does he want the tickets or not?"

Magee paused, then blurted, "I'm...I'm sorry, this is all very weird. I don't know if he still wants them. Let me check with him. Is that okay? I'll check with him and give you a call back?"

"That's fine," said the guy before hanging up, just like that.

For a moment Magee stared at his phone, thoughts of his artwork forgotten. Clearly, he trusted Matt more than this shady toad man. Yet something wasn't adding up. Magee had been skeptical that night at the bar...Matt's story hadn't made any sense. From what Matt described, it must've happened in an incredibly short period of time: How had Magee not run into the man? Why hadn't Matt calmed the guy down? Why hadn't he chased after him? There were too many questions left unanswered, details that didn't seem quite right.

He decided to call Matt. Practically speaking, he had to find out if Matt wanted the tickets. On another level, though, Magee needed to satiate his own curiosity. The two versions of the events were so far apart, so irreconcilable...where was the truth in the story?

It rang four times before Matt answered. "Magee?"

"Hey, I have some good news: Those tickets to the opera...for you and Meda? It turns out the guy still has them and wants to sell them."

"What?"

Secretly, Magee had hoped Matt would volunteer some nugget of information at the mention of the ticket broker. Instead, he sounded like he'd just woken up. "I just got off the phone with him. All I have to do is call him back and the tickets are yours."

"Really?" said Matt, as if he was doing anything but comprehending the conversation at hand. "That's crazy."

It was hardly the reaction Magee expected. "The guy...he and I actually spoke for a bit." Magee paused, offering Matt an opportunity to interject. When he didn't take it, however, Magee continued, "He had an *interesting* take on the conversation you guys had that night."

"He did?" said Matt, suddenly perked up.

"Yep. He said *you* were the one that actually...lost your cool."

"What?"

"He said you freaked out on him. Said you had asked him who sent him."

"What?" said Matt, growing more forceful. "No. That's not right. It was the exact opposite. That was what he asked me!"

For an awkward moment there was silence. Magee didn't want to dispute Matt's claim yet he didn't know where to take the conversation. "Weird, right?" he said finally, trying his best to commiserate with his friend despite the stilted exchange.

"You've got that right," said Matt, affronted and borderline shouting. "I can't believe that! I mean—come on!"

The juxtaposition was too intense. Matt had veered from distracted malaise to anger in a heartbeat and, put side-by-side with the contradictory accounts of the incident, Magee was more baffled than ever. "So anyway," he said, hoping to at least get an answer out of Matt, "you still want the tickets, right?"

"Oh," said Matt flatly, "those."

After another beat: "Aren't you interested?"

This time there was an even longer pause, the lengthiest in the conversation, and Magee very nearly began speaking out of sheer social pressure.

"Let me think about it," said Matt, swaying back to inattention again. "I don't know right now."

"Okay. Whatever you say."

"I—" began Matt, halting. "It's hard to explain. I'm not sure we want them anymore."

Whatever enlightenment Magee had hoped to glean from the call hadn't come. In fact, the situation had only become more obfuscated. He didn't want to be rude to his friend but he was frustrated nonetheless. He concluded, saying, "Okay. Just...let me know, okay?"

"I will. I will."

RYAN

"I mean, it's not as if I expected a hero's welcome. I know what those old timers went through back when they came home from Vietnam," said Ryan, swishing the remaining dregs of beer in his mug in a slow circle. "But I guess I still expected something, y'know?"

Across the table, Mark shifted uneasily. This was their first time hanging out together, even though Ryan had been home for almost five weeks. Mark appeared as if he wanted to say something but was too embarrassed by the words.

"I don't mean to complain," said Ryan, appearing self-conscious suddenly and leaning back in his chair. "How about you? How have you been?"

"I'm good. I'm good," said Mark. "Just very busy at work. It never ends."

For a moment silence hung in the air, one which would've never shown its face back in their high school days. Ryan took the opportunity to survey the bar, saying, "Man, I can't believe we're back here again. Some things never change, right, bro?"

"You're right," said Mark through a forced smile. He was dressed in a shirt and tie, and appeared tired after a day at work. The bar, Mulligan's, which normally catered to underage kids when it wasn't in trouble with the law, wasn't a trendy happy hour spot and Mark was the only one not wearing a T-shirt.

"Do you see that guy Macino in here still? I remember: Every time we were here, every single time, he was camped out at that corner of the bar."

"No. I, uh, haven't seen him," admitted Mark.

Ryan paused. "Wow, that's surprising. Did he stop coming? Or...wait. When was the last time you were here?"

Mark's eyes shot down to his half-finished beer and, with a guilty smile, he admitted, "I think I was here a few months ago."

"Oh, I see now," crowed Ryan with a gale of laughter. "You! You were the one that stopped coming!"

"Well, y'know," smiled Mark, trailing off as Ryan's laughter did the same.

"It's okay. I'm just kidding. You've been busy and all."

"Yes. Exactly," said Mark, and each proceeded to take a sip of beer.

The conversation continued for the next few hours, Ryan throwing back two beers for every one of Mark's. Though their exchanges had become more infrequent as time went on, the pair had kept in contact throughout his enlistment. Yet they'd only hung out in person two or three times over the period: Ryan was rarely eligible for leave and, even when he was, Mark was often away at college. That'd been the case with most of Ryan's friends, in fact.

If there was one difference that irritated Ryan in the weeks since his return, one change in virtually everyone, it was in the way they listened to him. Everybody seemed to wear this overly earnest expression, as if they were having a conversation with a child or an elderly person. He recognized that most people meant well; they were just trying to empathize with him. But Afghanistan wasn't something a civilian could understand. The fact that he'd survived didn't mean he was, alternately, a god or a mental patient. He was still just regular Ryan Newsome.

After passing out that night at his parent's house, Ryan awoke the next afternoon and decided to visit Mr. Parchett, his old high school teacher. Apparently, he'd opened up a hardware store and, according to Mark, the store also carried technical devices for computers and mobile devices.

Ryan knew he'd have to find a job one of these days and he figured the skills he'd learned in the service would translate well to a position at such a place.

"Mr. Parchett!" Ryan bellowed upon entering the store. It was dimly lit and the merchandise seemed a little dusty. The moment he spied his former teacher, however, those details were instantly forgotten. The man was half-hidden behind his newspaper and his formerly salt-and-pepper hair had turned entirely white, but, with no one else in the store, it was easy to conclude it was him.

For his part, Parchett seemed startled at first, his body tensing at the disruption. Then, realizing that he wasn't in any danger, he began sizing up Ryan as if he was a raccoon who'd wandered in from the dumpster. It was far from the reunion Ryan had anticipated.

"Ryan? Ryan Newsome?" The old man spoke slowly, gradually gaining confidence as he decided he was correct.

"Yes! It's me. Ryan!"

Ryan strode to the counter and threw his meaty hand out to shake, Parchett's smile now beaming.

"Oh my! How have you been, son?"

"I'm great," said Ryan, nearly shouting in excitement. "It's great to be back for good. Just getting into the thick of it."

"'Back'?" repeated Parchett.

"I did three tours in Afghanistan," said Ryan, an odd embarrassment in his tone. "Great to be done."

"Oh my," said Parchett, his smile shifting to that expression of awe that Ryan was quickly starting to loath. "Good for you, son. Good for you."

"Well...thank you. It's all a little weird being back."

"I'm sure it is," said Parchett, nodding his head for a long moment before shifting gears. "So what can I do for you

today? Are you starting a big project or just odds and ends around the house?"

"Oh, no. None of that. I'm actually here to see if you're hiring," said Ryan with a broad smile.

Parchett's disappointment was obvious. "Oh. Oh my," he said, scratching the top of his head. He peered back behind the counter, as if he'd forgotten something, unwilling to make eye contact any longer.

Ryan, inwardly deflated, had nonetheless prepared himself for such an eventuality. "Not hiring, huh? Wrong time of the year?"

At that, a new expression appeared on the old man's face, as if someone had dropped a spoonful of salt in his coffee. "What is the right time of year nowadays?"

Ryan stuttered, then chuckled nervously, unsure how to respond. "It's...um. It's pretty rough these days."

Parchett peered up at him, as if he wanted to say something but was holding back. Finally, he said, "Well, it could always be worse, I guess. Right?"

"That's the right attitude, Mr. Parchett. That's why I always loved you, man."

"Yes. Yes," said the old man, taking a seat on his bench again and eyeing up the newspaper he'd dropped on the counter. The conclusiveness of his words left a gap in the conversation and, unsure what to say next, Ryan gazed about the store with feigned interest. The tapping of Ryan's foot was the only thing to break the silence and, eventually, Mr. Parchett succumbed and picked up the paper.

Ultimately, since Mr. Parchett seemed disinclined to exchange goodbyes, Ryan left the store without a word and the jingling of the chime on the door was the only sound to mark his exit. He walked to his car, the lone one in the lot, and found himself sad in a new, unexpected way. It wasn't as if Ryan had assumed he could walk in and get a job just by asking for it. Whether he wanted to admit it or not, though, he had put some hope in that exact possibility. Instead, the joyous reunion he'd anticipated had gone nothing like he'd imagined.

Feeling more rudderless than ever, Ryan simply drove. He didn't have a destination at first; he just wanted to leave the parking lot. His mission that morning had been to get a job at Mr. Parchett's store so, recalibrating his expectations, Ryan began to formulate an alternate plan. Before leaving for boot camp he'd worked at the local Walmart for almost two years. Perhaps, he reasoned, he should check that place out?

There was no sense of homecoming when he arrived there either. In fact, he didn't recognize a single soul. On the drive to the store he'd fancifully wondered if Jill might still be at the service counter or if Gloria, the girl virtually every guy in the place had a crush on, might still be working the registers. Instead: nothing.

"Hi, I'm Ryan Newsome. I used to work here," he announced to the woman at the service center.

"Okay," she responded, blank-faced.

"I..." began Ryan, before halting. "Well, I was thinking of coming back to work here again."

"You're going to have to fill out an application," said the woman, any hint of a smile still conspicuously absent.

"Um, okay," said Ryan with a nod. Then, in one continuous movement, the woman turned to open a drawer, pulled a sheet off the top of a large stack, and handed it to him.

"There you go," she said, already moving her attention to the next person in line.

"Thanks," he muttered, half-stepping and half-pushed to the side by the customer in back of him. The formality and the speed of the exchange left him feeling like something had been overlooked. For a moment he stood, staring at the application without even knowing what he was looking for, before, eventually, he turned to go. And that was that, he thought.

Ryan walked back to the car and began to pull out of the parking lot, mulling his encounters that morning. He was lost in thought, wondering how everything could've changed so much, so quickly. Then the cardboard-puncturing pop and sudden jolt to his car knocked him out of his distraction. Instincts learned in Afghanistan nearly made him dive onto the passenger seat and it took him three full seconds to realize he'd been in a car accident. Embarrassed by his near-dive for cover, he looked up to see the blue Honda's front end butted up against the front left side of his car. The other driver, a man in his early 40s, was already stepping out of his car wearing a disappointed expression.

Ryan also got out while the man surveyed the front of his car. At first, neither said anything. Once he realized the accident was his fault, though, Ryan blurted, "Geez, I'm sorry. I didn't see you coming."

"Doesn't seem too bad," quipped the man, half-distracted as he investigated.

Following suit, Ryan began to check as well. The front driver's side quarter panel would have to be replaced but it didn't appear as if the damage was too extensive. "Oh man," he muttered. "My mom is going to kill me."

The man nearly smirked, appearing as if he wanted to say something but was holding back. Sensing the man was ready to laugh at him, Ryan added, "I just got home from

Afghanistan. I haven't had a chance to get a job or anything yet."

At that, the man's expression did an about-face: His demeanor became downright apologetic and, bowing ever so slightly, he said quickly, "Oh, I'm sorry, son. I didn't know. We are all really proud of your service over there. I didn't mean to.... We're all just really proud of what you guys are doing."

"Thanks. Thank you, sir," said Ryan, nodding.

"Actually," said the man, his head swiveling in an odd, amiable way, "the damage isn't that bad. I think my car'll be fine. If you, y'know...if you don't want to report this to insurance that's fine by me. Those rates are killer after an accident and I'd hate to...y'know. After you just got back and all."

Ryan peered at the man, dumbstruck. He moved his gaze to the car and then back to the man again. The fellow seemed like he was offering to do Ryan a favor yet he couldn't help but wonder if it actually was a favor. Wasn't this the exact purpose of insurance? Then again, though, he wasn't even positive his parents had put him on their policy. If they hadn't, what kind of trouble could they get in? He felt like an alien navigating such an odd, counterintuitive scenario.

"Thank you. Thank you, sir," said Ryan finally, shooting out his hand to shake. Fundamentally, he didn't want his parents to get in trouble and that trumped any financial concerns. This man seemed like he was offering to help and he didn't want to look a gift horse in the mouth.

"It's no problem, son. Seriously, it's the least I could do," the man said, still shaking Ryan's hand vigorously. He was smiling now, chummily so, as if celebrating some secret mission, and it was starting to grate on Ryan.

Eventually Ryan pulled his hand from the stranger and the man stepped back to his car. "Just take it one step at a time, son," he said, waving as he got into his vehicle. "Drive slow. You'll get the hang of it again."

Ryan said nothing but only nodded, a slightly perplexed expression showing. He surveyed the damage to the car one final time and, with nothing more to say or do, he hopped inside. He didn't go home, though. After the encounter with Mr. Parchett, his experience at Walmart, and the car accident, he needed a drink. It may've only been two in the afternoon but he couldn't listen to his mother complain about the car all afternoon. So, instead, he decided to stop by Mulligan's yet again.

"Ryan!" came the holler as soon as he stepped through the door. "I thought that was you coming!"

The man was already off his bar stool and closing in on Ryan quickly. Lost in his thoughts, Ryan felt an immediate fight-or-flight surge and momentarily stood locked in place. If he had a sidearm he might've drawn it. Then, with vague embarrassment, he recoiled, as if he'd been reminded of someone's birthday a week after it passed. Though the man had lost most of his hair and gained probably forty pounds, Ryan was ashamed at his failure to recognize one of his best friends, Mikey Petronella.

"Mikey!" hollered Ryan in return as the men's bodies slammed together in the middle of the otherwise vacant bar.

Their friendship was odd, something akin to perpetual long-lost friends. The pair had been best friends throughout grade school but had drifted when each went to a different high school. Mikey had fallen in with a bad crowd and gone down a worse path than Ryan. On the odd occasions they ran into each other there was always a vague reunion vibe present, complicated by an unarticulated awkwardness at the turns each of their lives had taken.

"Holy crap, how have you been, man? I haven't seen you in ages!" shouted Ryan.

Mikey, still grinning, dropped his gaze for a moment and said, "Well, y'know. I was with this woman. We were living out in Eldon Falls. It was all messed up."

"No! Not you," laughed Ryan. "I was the one who was away! I just got back from Afghanistan!"

Mikey's cherubic yet simultaneously weathered face lit up. "Well hell, why are you giving me crap, man? You're the one who left."

They grabbed a pair of stools at the bar, Ryan still chuckling. It was the most natural, most relaxed he felt in days. Catching up with his other friends had become increasingly dispiriting, a parade of interactions that only highlighted the glaring differences in their lives. Yet here was Mikey, in his leather jacket and jeans, the same as he'd always been. Their first four beers went down like water and, for the first time, Ryan didn't feel like an alien walking around in the skin of Ryan Newsome.

"See, here's the thing," said Ryan, feeling lubricated and talkative. "Everything was great when I first got home. I mean, shoot, that was all I was looking forward to the whole time I was over there. At first it was like being on permanent leave. Every day was a party. Now, though...now it's like: 'What am I doing?' It's weird."

Mikey nodded in agreement with a respectful frown.

"I feel like: Why am I doing 'this' when everyone else is doing 'that'?" continued Ryan, using his hands to suggest a physical item to either side of him. "Does that make sense? I feel like I should be having a good time but everyone is just

constantly bringing me down. Like I disappointed them or something. I figured I was doing a good thing."

"Dude, dude," said Mikey, one hand in the air. "You didn't disappoint nobody. You're a freaking hero, man. What's with this talk?"

Ryan grimaced. He didn't want to be a hero anymore. He just wanted to be himself. "I just," Ryan began, before starting again. "I just want to live my life. I didn't die in Afghanistan. But...I don't feel like I have a life here anymore either."

Mikey rolled his eyes. "What do you mean you don't have a life? You survived Afghanistan, man! If you can survive there you can definitely survive here. You just need to find a starting point."

"What?" said Ryan. He could see Mikey was trying to help; he just didn't think it would work.

"Over there, you came up with a plan and you did it. Right? Enemies all around. What do you do? Well, do the same here. Figure out a starting point."

"Well," said Ryan, hesitating. "Today I applied at Walmart."

Mikey nearly spit out his beer. "No, no, no, dude. Don't put me on! I mean something real. Something important to you."

Ryan thought back: What was important to him when he first left for boot camp? It wasn't an easy question. After the life and death struggle he'd witnessed everything else seemed so trivial, so insignificant. How could something like football or a car compare in importance?

"Go back to when you enlisted," continued Mikey. "What was your thought process? You had to have a reason for joining back then."

Ryan grinned, replying half-sarcastically, "I liked firing guns."

Mikey cocked his head to the side as Ryan laughed, but he wasn't about to let Ryan off the hook that easy. "Okay," he said. "Guns. Got it. Seriously, though: There must've been something else there. The guns were a perk but they weren't, like, the real reason you went over to fight in a foreign country."

"Yeah," Ryan conceded.

"So what was it then, man?"

Ryan pondered for a long moment, peering up to the ceiling and then down into his mug as if he might find an answer there. Then, like a grade school student finally admitting his guilt to the principal, he said, "I don't know. I guess I just wanted to help people."

"Bingo!" said Mikey, jabbing his finger at Ryan, practically celebrating. "There you go!"

"What? What do you mean?"

"I mean," said Mikey, taking a long gulp of beer, "that's where you should start now."

"What, like go volunteer? I gotta pay the bills, man. I can't live with my parents forever."

"No, no, no. Don't be dumb."

"Well what?" said Ryan, growing agitated. "You're saying I should be a cop or something?"

"Hey," said Mikey, raising his eyebrows suggestively. For a long moment he said nothing else, letting the thought sink in, and then added, "You still get a gun."

"A cop?" Ryan cried. "We hated cops!"

"Yeah," said Mikey. "But that was back when we were kids. We're not kids anymore, man."

That stopped Ryan. In fact, for a long moment, he wore the expression of someone who'd found a fly in the bottom of the glass. He stared forward at nothing, his lip curled. A cop? How could he ever become one of those pricks? It seemed like only yesterday he and Mikey were getting nailed for penny-ante traffic violations because those pigs needed to meet their quotas. He couldn't believe Mikey would even suggest it. How could he ever trust a cop, much less consider joining their ranks?

In the space of Ryan's silence, however, Mikey's attention span hit the wall. Oblivious to the seriousness of the conversation a moment earlier, he mused, "Hey remember that time the cop busted us with the beer? We totally knew he was going to go drink it himself. You asked if he wanted the ice, too!" Mikey burst out with a guttural laugh. "You had brass ones, man. I'll tell you."

After a beat, Ryan joined in the laughter as well. Yet, amidst many beers consumed throughout the rest of the afternoon and night, the notion of becoming a police officer gained strength in his thoughts. Despite his initial, knee-jerk repulsion, he accepted that there was a certain amount of logic to the suggestion. First and foremost, it would be a way to pay the bills. With no other opportunities in sight, it was a job at least. He recognized that his heart wasn't in it and, for a job like that, he probably should be more enthused. But he'd spent enough time trying to do the right thing; for now he just wanted to move out of his parent's house. And the next morning, rather than waking up and wondering what to do with the day, he finally had a goal.

Ryan wasn't so naïve to think that, as a former GI, he could just go down to the local precinct and immediately enter the force. But he knew there were programs for returning soldiers to help them get on their feet. In the past he'd been skeptical of them after some of the stories he'd heard but, in this case, he thought some information might be helpful. So he planned to go to the library first, do some research, and then head to the local VA.

His mother was surprised to see him awake so early, and in a weird way, it made him happy. His head hurt a bit from the previous day's activities but it was nice to be out doing something before noon for once. He was still on Cornet Street, only halfway to the library, when he saw that traffic had backed up. There was no traffic light at the intersection ahead and Ryan groaned at the hold-up. This trip was not starting out well.

He rolled to a stop and saw that some people were actually getting out of their cars. It became evident that simple traffic congestion wasn't the cause and Ryan's disappointment turned to concern. He shifted the car out of gear and then, his curiosity too great, he turned the car off altogether and stepped out.

Once outside with a better view, he immediately spotted the source of the commotion: A house was on fire. It was about ten car lengths ahead of him, almost at the end of Cornet, and a small crowd of people had gathered in front. At first walking to the spot, Ryan spotted a woman in hysterics and he picked up the pace, nearly sprinting by the time he arrived.

It was an odd time of day—after rush hour but before lunch—and everyone in the crowd apart from the woman was a senior citizen. One man was trying to keep the woman from going back inside and, as Ryan got closer, he heard her crying, "But my baby's inside!" Ryan circled the crowd, proceeding directly to the woman, and confirmed, "There's a baby inside?" She'd barely nodded when Ryan followed up with, "Where?"

"The top floor. Right there!" she said, pointing. There were no firefighters on the scene and flames were pouring

out of both sides of the bottom floor. There was no way she or anyone else present could get up there. So without a second thought Ryan darted up the stairs on the porch, climbed up the first floor banister, and, with a leap, grabbed hold of the railing on the second floor. Behind him, someone offered a weak, "No. You shouldn't." But Ryan paid no heed.

On the second floor porch, Ryan saw that the main door was open with a screen door in place. He didn't have much time. While the ventilation meant the heat and toxic fumes hadn't been fully trapped inside, it also meant the flames would engulf the floor quickly. The air at the top of the rooms would still be toxic and smoldering but at least he could gain entry if he stayed low. He took his shirt and pulled it over his mouth and nose, just as he'd done in Afghanistan when an RPG had ignited their barracks. Then he charged in. Immediately to his left was a room and, in it, he saw adult furnishings. Farther down the hall, at the stairs, he could see the haunting image of flame where it shouldn't be. He advanced towards it and threw open a door on his right. Inside, he saw pink carpeting and balloons on the wallpaper.

Bending at the waist, Ryan leapt to the side of the crib. If he'd experienced relief at the sight of the pink carpet he practically gushed at the sight of the baby. Being careful to stay as squat as possible, he picked the baby out of the crib and held her low. Then he raced to the air outside, purposefully avoiding any glances over his shoulder to see how close the flames had crept.

Gasps emanated from the crowd when he emerged and, already coughing, he tried to identify the mother again. She broke away from the man, shouting, "My baby! My baby!" and motioned for Ryan to drop the baby to her. Ryan couldn't scale down the banister with her in tow so, with bated breath, he leaned over the railing as far as he could and let go of the baby. The mother caught her. Cheers broke out and, now allowing himself to peer back, Ryan turned to see the flames already reaching the trim atop the length of the hallway. He climbed down and was greeting by a celebration and pats on the back. It was exhilarating, he would admit.

Someone in the crowd said, "Wow, you're a hero, son!" Ryan's grin was modest, without teeth, and it practically spoke the words, "Aw, shucks." He nearly corrected the person. Instead, he demurred, his silence serving as a humble acceptance to the claim. And when the flames began to spill out of the porch above, the crowd of people was so enthralled that they didn't see the growing orb of light on the horizon behind them.

MAGEE

Magee entered Meda's apartment with a grin. During their history as young twenty-somethings, the pair hadn't always seen eye-to-eye. Whereas Magee often wanted to do another shot at the bar, Meda usually knew when to call it a night. Though Magee might encourage Matt to quit his job after a particularly onerous day, Meda would tell him to stop and think things through. The dynamic was never outright acrimonious but it was a clash that'd occurred with remarkable predictability. And though the tension had receded as the three had grown older, the history remained.

"Hey, thanks for taking a second to talk," said Magee. Despite the fact that they'd spent countless hours together through the years it still felt awkward to stop by Meda's apartment without Matt present or aware of the visit.

"No problem at all," said Meda with a wave. "I could use some company after the day I had."

"At least tomorrow is Friday."

Meda nodded at the pleasantry and said, "You sounded so serious when you called."

Magee pursed his lips. "I know. Sorry. I didn't mean to scare you."

"Oh, not at all," said Meda, each taking a seat on the couch. "I only meant that it was unlike you. Actually, it made me curious."

"I'm worried about Matt," he said flatly. He allowed that to sink in, Meda saying nothing, and then continued. "Normally, if he's acting strange I know why. Work problems...stress about the novel...predictable stuff. This time, though...it seems a little different."

"I know," said Meda.

"You do?"

"I've noticed it, too. Did he," asked Meda cautiously, "mention anything about a little boy?"

Magee peered at her with serious eyes despite his best efforts at a poker face. He hadn't known, in advance, if Matt had told her about the boy so his relief was palpable. "Yes," he said, hesitating. "And...the car?"

Meda nodded, similarly comforted by the knowledge that she wasn't breaking Matt's trust. "He said he ran over a child somewhere out in Queens."

"Ever since then...." Magee shook his head as he spoke, letting his words trail.

"Ever since then he's been *different*."

"Yep. He told me, in his exact words, he thought he was going crazy."

"He said something similar to me," said Meda, leaning towards Magee ever so slightly. Both relaxed, allayed by the knowledge that the other had noticed the difference in Matt. The commonality seemed to create a bridge and, after the pause, Meda rose and moved to the kitchen. "I'm sure the guilt is getting to him. I hope his confession to the police will alleviate some of those feelings."

"Wait," said Magee, his concern evident. "He's going to turn himself in?"

"He promised me he would. We didn't see any other choice," said Meda. Then, pulling two bottles of beer out of the refrigerator, she added, "You want one?"

"Um, yeah. Sure," said Magee, sounding distracted. "Okay. I...I wasn't aware he decided to do that."

"We talked about it Tuesday. I never heard from him yesterday or today, though. I called him three times. No reply. It's like he just decided to disappear. That's why, frankly, I was glad you called."

Meda rejoined Magee on the couch and handed him the beer. He had an odd air about him, as if he wanted to say something but was reluctant. Magee mulled his words while, in the background, a television personality breathlessly reported about someone who'd been pushed in front of an oncoming subway train. "I spoke to him last night and...I don't think he went to the cops."

"I knew it," said Meda, far less angrily than Magee expected. Actually, she sounded disappointed.

"Also, our conversation last night...it was weird," continued Magee.

"Why? What did he say?"

"It's..." began Magee, his gaze shooting skyward momentarily. "It's not a matter of what he said, per se. It's not that simple. What worried me was how *out of it* he sounded. The other night we were at a bar, right? I'd arranged for him to meet one of my contacts about those tickets."

"Oh, the opera tickets? Yes. Thank you for your help with those," said Meda.

"No problem," said Magee with a wave of the hand. "Anyway, somehow Matt ran into the guy after I'd stepped away and, in the interim, the whole introduction went to hell. I have no idea what happened. Here's the important part: This guy called me back later and his version of the events were the exact opposite of what Matt described. It was insane. I mean, of course, I presumed Matt was telling the truth. Later though...when he and I spoke, Matt's reactions were so strange, so inappropriate. I couldn't help but wonder if the ticket broker's story was the correct one. The more I thought about it, the more I started thinking about...y'know, Matt's sanity. We all say we're going crazy sometimes as a figure of speech, but I'm starting to wonder if Matt truly meant what he said."

Meda took the story in, her concern growing as Magee spoke. Matt and Magee had found themselves in many tough spots through the years yet Magee's blind Pollyannaism had rarely flagged. Even when a potential DWI charge threatened to ruin Matt's career, Magee had kept perspective and, with the help of a well-placed associate, he'd gotten Matt off with a comparative slap on the wrist. Something had to be seriously wrong for Magee to be worried.

"What do you think we should do?" asked Meda.

"I don't know. That's why I thought we should discuss it."

Again the pair paused. Their initial relief abated as each, independently, recognized the need for an actual plan of action. Adding to the tension, the television grew unexpectedly silent and the only sound to be heard was Mrs. Javier shuffling in the hallway outside Meda's apartment.

"I don't think we should turn him in," said Meda, as if establishing a starting point.

"No. No, definitely not. If he goes to the police it has to be of his own accord."

"Agreed," said Meda, to the tangible relief of each.

"In fact, I don't think we need to involve anyone besides us two. At least not at first."

Meda drew back ever so slightly. "Yes. At first."

"So what do you think we should do? Should we sit him down and ask him what's going on?"

"That sounds like a good start," said Meda, still pondering. "With both of us present in-person he'd see we mean business. I think–"

Meda was cut short by the harsh vibrating sounds of her phone on the glass coffee table. Her mood soured as she reached to pick up the device, saying, "Oh. Oh crap. I'm sorry. There's this thing at work."

She trailed off, reading the message while Magee waited. He tapped his finger and the newscaster droned on about a comet and the discovery of a binary star system far away.

"Magee, I'm really, really sorry. I have to reply to this now, from my laptop. It'll only take a second." She glanced around the room, still holding the phone aloft as if it was a holy relic. "Here. Here's the remote control. I'll only be a second. Just make yourself at home."

"It's fine," said Magee, half-sincerely, but he wasn't sure she even heard. He scowled at the remote control, dropped it on the couch, and headed to the bathroom. He wasn't mad at Meda in the classic sense. But it did serve as a reminder of their imperfect history together. This was Matt's welfare they were talking about...clearly more important than a bunch of numbers in a spreadsheet. Work could wait another fifteen minutes.

Once in the bathroom he splashed water on his face. It was Thursday night and another long weekend tending bar loomed. While the tips generated paid for his existence, the three nights were the busiest, most aggravating portions of his week.

He took stock of himself in the mirror and then noticed something odd behind him. In an otherwise spotless bathroom was a cloth thrown haphazardly on the shelf next to the shower. Everything else in the room possessed an impeccable sense of arrangement: From the tissue box to the bottles of moisturizer, virtually everything was aligned perfectly and shared an overriding sense of order in their placement. Everything...except that cloth. Without even knowing why, and without consciously intending to snoop, he turned and leaned towards it to get a better look. His curiosity only growing, he took a small step closer.

Then he saw the label on it. He read the words, processed them, and then picked up the cloth to make sure he wasn't mistaken. They read, "PRODUCT OF ARMENIA". His mind reeled, echoing the ticket broker's words about Matt's ravings and tales of assassination plots. Magee's gaze went up the mirror, his jaw dropped as he locked eyes with himself. He didn't want to believe it...almost couldn't believe it. But he knew what he had to do.

MATT

That Friday, Matt went to the police station. Completing the story about Ryan had been cathartic and had helped him exorcise much of the uncertainty in his mind. In the process he'd all but blown off Magee's phone call and he'd called in sick to work yet again, his second occurrence in four days. But Magee was right—writing the stories about Dorian and Ryan had reduced his mental clatter.

On Wednesday the Stoic Man had warned him about Meda and, owing to the man's inexplicable knowledge and timing, he'd avoided contacting her. Yet, once he'd finished Ryan's tale, Matt couldn't follow the other portion of his advice. In the midst of Ryan's story, he and Mikey had entertained the notion of Ryan becoming a cop—that was something Matt hadn't planned prior to the point. While it seemed to help the story, Matt recognized that thoughts of the police were now creeping into his writing, consciously or unconsciously. And, if he accepted the fact that he'd have to confess at some point, better to do it in his current state than to allow such fear to infect more of his work.

He arrived at the police station and stood in the same exact spot he had at the beginning of the week. This time the Stoic Man was nowhere to be seen. Matt had considered calling a lawyer to get a professional opinion but quickly ruled that out. As foolhardy as it may be, he felt like he had to take advantage of his current state of mind and do this alone. He began to ascend the marble steps and the stone beneath him was solid and unflinching. Rather than any feelings of fear or trepidation, he instead experienced a sense of fortitude—now that he'd taken these literal and metaphorical steps, he was positive he was on the right path.

Then he opened the door to the station. Inside, it was bedlam. The lobby was full of bodies—some in a lethargic stupor, others chasing children across the floor, and still others appearing to be on the verge of violent explosion. Garbage was strewn beneath unsteady tables and it appeared as if a pipe along the wall was leaking unabated, a brown, fetid pool of liquid in front of it. Making matters worse, the room's lighting was haphazard and sinister—some of the overhead lights were non-functional while others were on the fritz, casting strange shadows in sporadic strobe-like bursts. Matt felt like he'd stepped into a nightmarish asylum from the 1800s that had incorporated the languor of bureaucratic neglect.

He told himself to remain calm even as menacing glares shot up at him. He identified a front desk, spotted the beleaguered police officer behind it, and, on shaking knees, proceeded towards it. The desk was built high, so that the officer might peer down upon those who approached, and as Matt got closer—each step requiring exponentially more courage—he took stock of five empty coffee cups strewn across it. The officer was busy writing in a large ledger and appeared wholly unconcerned by the clutter, however. As if the oppressive atmosphere of the lobby wasn't intimidating enough, a new sense of trepidation arose within Matt—he was about to come clean about a potential murder to people who couldn't be bothered to clean up their own garbage?

Matt arrived at the desk and rested his hand on it. The officer had yet to acknowledge his existence and Matt reminded himself that it wasn't too late, that he still had the opportunity to turn around and walk away. Instead, Matt cleared his throat.

"Hello?" he said, nearly stuttering.

The officer kept working, saying nothing.

Matt's brow furrowed, then he repeated more loudly, "Hello?"

"Domestic dispute or dispute with a neighbor?" said the officer, still scribbling on the paperwork.

"What?"

"What are you here for?" said the weary officer, cocking his head to one side after finally looking Matt in the eyes. "Domestic dispute or dispute with a neighbor?"

"Ah. Neither," said Matt, taken aback, barely resisting the urge to just run away. "I'm here to turn myself in."

The officer sighed loudly and put his pen down with a hard snap. "Turn yourself in for what?"

"I think I might have killed someone. A child," said Matt, preparing for apocalyptic judgment to rain down upon him.

The officer said nothing, however; a virtual statue.

Unnerved by such blasé enmity, Matt began to blather. "I—I think I ran him over. With my car. This was two weeks ago. Almost two weeks ago. I read in the paper that he died at the hospital. I *did* stop, though. I got out of the car and talked to him. He said he was fine. He insisted that I go, actually. I want to be clear on that. I definitely checked on him."

"Killed a child, huh?" the officer mused. "That's a new one. Okay, come with me." The officer stood, using his arms to push himself up and he walked slowly—maddeningly slowly—to the side of reception desk.

Matt gulped and shifted his feet a number of times. This was it, he told himself. Despite his best efforts to stifle his babble, he added, "I pulled over and checked on him. I want to be clear about that."

"That's fine," grunted the officer. "Come with me."

The officer began to amble down the hallway beyond the door without so much as glancing at Matt. Matt followed, of course. What else was there to do? It was now too late to turn around yet his sense of regret had grown to epic proportions.

The back of the precinct was in better shape than the lobby but it was still far from perfect. The ceilings were lower and the incandescent lights harsher, only serving to highlight the general grunginess of the place. Matt followed the officer and they passed offices, each possessing angry men who peered up at Matt as they passed. Somewhere, beyond the wall, Matt heard what sounded like two or three officers using loud voices but he couldn't ascertain if they were arguing or celebrating.

The officer took a left turn and then a quick right one down another hall. Matt nearly lost the officer and, after a brief second of confusion, caught a glimpse of him and hurried to catch up again. By then the officer was turning left down yet another hall and, his disorientation bordering on child-like fear, Matt scampered to close the gap.

"Do—do you get these kinds of cases often?" asked Matt, trying to establish some sort of rapport with the officer.

"No," said the man.

The officer made yet another turn and, with Matt close behind, they arrived at a seating area composed of three folding chairs inside an otherwise barren cubicle.

"Here," said the officer, with a lethargic wave towards the chairs. "Wait here and someone will be with you."

At that the officer began to walk away, leaving Matt in the middle of the office with no knowledge of how he got there or how to get out. "Wait," said Matt, unsure what he intended to ask. "What's—I mean—who's going to meet me? What's going on?"

"An officer will take your statement soon," said the officer. "Just wait there."

Then he left. Matt wanted to stop him, ask how long it might take or what to expect. But it was too late. Even if he could hold the officer's attention for more than a few seconds it was clear he wasn't going to volunteer any more information than absolutely necessary.

So Matt sat. And he waited. At first he stiffened whenever he heard footsteps, ready to make his confession to the approaching officer. Each person passed without so much as a glance, however, time after time. If he had been in the front waiting area—as gruesome as it was—he would've stood up and asked for an update. Left as he was in a veritable catacomb of the office, however, he had no recourse but to wait for someone to arrive. It was infuriating.

Time continued to march, plodding and elephantine, and with no real reason to do so Matt pulled out his phone. He considered calling his office, if only to make his alleged medical relapse sound more realistic. Louise had been very forgiving the last time he missed a number of days—he recognized he might not be so lucky a second time around. Pursing his lips in dissatisfaction, he took a quick peek outside the cubicle door. It didn't look like anyone was coming so he sat down again and prepared to dial her number.

Then: "Hey, sorry that took so long. Happens around here sometimes. Believe me, I don't like waiting either."

The detective had blown through the entryway of the cubicle, clipboard in hand, with no pleasantries attempted. His shirt sleeves were rolled up, he wore a perpetual grimace, and, as he whirled a chair around to sit, his words strung together in one unbroken sentence.

"I hear you wanted to turn yourself in? Something about killing a kid? What's your name?"

"Um, yeah," said Matt, gulping. "My name is Matt and on the night of October 3rd I ran over a young boy near Astoria Boulevard. I got out to check on him and—"

"Wait, you hit him with your car?"

"Yes. I said that to the officer in front. I pulled over to make—"

"Okay," announced the officer, appearing annoyed. He began rearranging the papers on his clipboard and, for the first time since he'd appeared, there was a brief moment of silence. "Now that we've got that cleared up. You ran over a kid, hit and run. You said near Astoria Boulevard. Do you have an exact address?"

"Well, wait," said Matt, distressed. "It wasn't actually a hit and run. I—"

"Did you call the police?"

"No, but—"

"Well, there you have it," said the detective, making a mark on the paper.

"Wait, just—slow down, okay?" said Matt, leaning forward. It was immediately apparent that the detective didn't approve of his assertion. "I just want to explain. I did hit him with my car but I also pulled over to check on him. I talked to him and he was conscious, aware of everything I was saying. He told me he was fine."

"Okay," said the detective, annoyed yet again. "So what you're telling me is: Not only did you *not* kill a kid outright but you have no reason to think he was even hurt?"

"No, no. I do have a reason," said Matt, dropping his gaze. "I did some research. There was a young boy that was dropped off at the New York Hospital in Flushing the night of the accident. He died."

The detective leaned back in his chair, cocking his head at an angle and peering at Matt from beneath his furrowed brow.

Nothing about the confession was going the way Matt had expected—from the madhouse in the front of the station to the manner in which the detective had begun the interview. He'd barely asked his name! Matt had imagined making a more plaintive case, walking an officer through the exact sequence of events in order to tell his story correctly. He'd never intended to just blurt out key details! And it was clear that the detective, formerly in such a hurry, was now seeing Matt in a different light.

"Sir," said the detective, his voice low and impassive, "the boy that died that night was nine years old. He was murdered."

Matt's heart sunk.

"He was strangled to death."

Wait. What?

"We have the suspect in custody now. It's his uncle."

Matt looked up at the detective, incredulous. The detective wasn't smiling but he appeared as close as he might come to doing so.

"You mean—?" said Matt.

"I mean: You had nothing to do with that boy at the hospital. We have no reports of any kids being hit by a car that night. You didn't kill anybody."

MEDA

Meda spotted Matt striding closer and intercepted him in front of her apartment. The work week was (thankfully) over and he'd sent her a text suggesting he had some important news. "Hey there," he said, giving her a quick peck on the cheek.

"Hi baby," said Meda, immediately recognizing that Matt appeared more chipper than normal (he almost looked stoned, actually). They made their way up to her apartment and, before they even took their coats off, Meda continued, "Okay, so help me out here. I'm dying for the big news. What's up?"

Matt smiled. It wasn't broad or joyful but, rather, was one of relief. He moved to hug her and said, "I went to the police station this morning."

"You did?" She hugged him in return but then, absent-mindedly, wondered why he hadn't called her sooner.

"I wanted to tell you in person," he said, as if to address her mental quandary. "It's complicated, honey. Here's the important part: The kid that died? The one I read about that showed up on the steps of the hospital?"

"Yes?"

"He wasn't hit by a car. It wasn't me."

"Right! I knew it!" she exclaimed, practically leaping in the air. "I knew you were jumping to conclusions!"

"I know, I know," admitted Matt before she planted a big, long kiss on him. Matt wasn't going to jail!

"I'm so happy, baby," said Meda.

"Yeah, me too," said Matt, his gaze dropping to the floor.

Meda noticed his hesitation and peered at him quizzically. "So tell me more! How did it go? What did the police say?"

At that Matt left Meda's embrace and shifted to gaze at her more directly. "It was *weird*. It wasn't at all like I expected."

Meda didn't lose her smile but she grew cautious nonetheless. "What do you mean?" (More to the point: Why does everything have to be so complicated with you, Matt?)

"The whole place—I'd never been inside that police precinct before. I don't know what I expected but it definitely wasn't *that*." Meda raised an eyebrow but said nothing, and Matt continued. "The place was a mess. There was no sense of order, no one seemed to care about anything, and the back of it was like a maze. Worse than any office building I'd ever been in. It was just this bureaucratic nightmare."

"Well, if it was such a mess, how do you know—"

She stopped herself mid-sentence and Matt eyed her up. "How do I know what?"

"How do you know everything's okay?"

"That's why I wanted to discuss this in person, hon. I couldn't explain it in a text."

Meda frowned, wary of what might come next.

"I'm positive I didn't kill the boy that arrived at the hospital," said Matt. "The detective I spoke to—as crazed as everything else was at the station—this detective seemed to know what he was talking about. He gave me details about the boy that died, specific details about how he was choked to death and how they had the suspect in custody. That is definitely not the boy I hit."

As Matt spoke, Meda grew more and more conflicted. She was relieved to hear Matt was cleared yet that initial moment of unadulterated jubilation was gone. It was as if Matt had unduly prepared her for something that wasn't especially terrible. She listened, weighed the implications of his words, and, despite her best efforts to avoid interrupting him, muttered, "So what's the problem?"

"Here's the thing," Matt continued, as if anticipating her misapprehension, "he didn't have any information about any children being struck by a car that night."

Meda frowned again. The fact remained: Matt hadn't killed the boy. After waiting a beat, she said simply, "So?"

"So: I'm certain I hit a little boy that night. I'm certain *something* happened to him. Legally, I might be fine. But I still don't know if that boy is alive or dead."

Meda wanted to sympathize, to confirm that his concern was morally justified, but a part of her felt cheated. They'd just experienced a moment of perfect, life-altering relief at the news that Matt wasn't about to be charged with murder. Couldn't they have a moment to be happy? They had their lives back!

"Come on, Meda," said Matt, seeing her reaction.

"Okay, I get it. Legally you're fine. But you're still worried about the child."

"Yeah."

"Well then what's next, exactly? You seem unwilling to let it go. Do you have any plan in mind?" She waited a beat, offering Matt a chance to chime in, before adding, "Because I can't think of anything."

Matt stared at her for a moment, his lips pursed. He appeared stumped yet resistant to admitting such. "Well, I can't just forget about him."

"I'm not suggesting you should," said Meda. "At the same time, you shouldn't torture yourself needlessly. You, *we*, received some great news today! You're safe. Let that sink in. Embrace it. Then, tomorrow, if you still don't feel right, you can figure out what to do. I see that you're holding back and that you're not allowing yourself to move on, baby. It's sad. And it's unnecessary."

She touched his arm and Matt moved closer to her, hugging once again. He wanted to resist such temptation; he didn't want to give up on the boy so easily. Yet he had to admit she was right—he *was* safe and that was a monumental reprieve. And, unless he could think of a way to locate the boy, he had to let go of him.

MAGEE

His name was Sergei Dimitrioff. Locating the ticket broker's name and address had required some creative detective work and a couple leaps of faith but Magee was confident he'd isolated the correct person. Certain commonalities had emerged in his conversations with others who'd worked with him and, Magee had determined, the only other men with a similar name and comparative details were either miles away or hopelessly older than the man he encountered. If this guy in Brighton Beach wasn't the man he was searching for Magee might as well give up the quest.

It wasn't a wise decision to hunt down the man at home, though. Magee recognized that. Sergei clearly valued his privacy and, the deeper Magee dug, the more he'd learned of the man's nefarious connections. So as an alternative Magee had divined a bar he was known to frequent and hoped to intercept him there. Surprising him there was also a risk, but Magee knew he might have to take a chance if he expected to get to the heart of the matter.

By all accounts Matt was acting erratically, if not losing his mind outright...Magee wanted to give his friend the benefit of the doubt but it was clear he was no longer himself. Meanwhile, Magee had found an Armenian-made towel in Meda's bathroom. Unto itself, he would've thought nothing of it. However, the country had been mentioned twice in recent conversations, each instance incorporating whispers about some sort of assassination plot. Magee didn't want to believe Meda could be involved in anything like that...at least, not of her own volition...but the timing of the discovery was very troubling.

Any attempt to put the pieces of the puzzle together necessitated a trip to the southern part of Brooklyn and, unfortunately, train service on a Saturday night could be excruciatingly tortoise-like. To occupy himself, Magee began to plan what he intended to say to Dimitrioff. He knew he'd have to allude to Meda's potential connection to the assassination plot without providing any reason to implicate her. He didn't think the guy would have any direct antagonism towards her...Sergei clearly wanted to stay clean of the whole affair. However, he also recognized that such information would be valuable to certain people and had to assume the guy might capitalize on it. So before he started dropping Meda's name, he'd better be damn sure she was involved.

Magee arrived and took stock on the street corner. For decades Brighton Beach was a destination for Russian immigrants and, while the exact concentration may have waned in recent times, the influence was still readily apparent. He smelled the stuffed cabbage from the food cart nearby and heard the obnoxious, disco-esque music blaring from a nearby club. Opposite the club was a large billboard featuring twin girls, each reaching towards the other through either side of mirror and creating an optical illusion in the process. Magee scoffed...he'd created a similar image in art school more than a decade earlier and couldn't help but wonder how much the creator had been paid for such tripe.

Magee had mapped out where Masis was located and knew it was in a far different part of the neighborhood. As opposed to the club generating such maddening noise, Masis was not a destination for the young, hip crowd. At best it appeared to be a hole-in-the-wall bar...at worst, a bar that was a front for other, illegal activities.

By the time Magee approached it, he had travelled through a number of successive mini-neighborhoods. The area known as Brighton Beach was not huge but it possessed many of the same features as other nearby neighborhoods: A collection of trendy bars and restaurants near the subway station...a series of smaller eateries and grocery stores as one moved on...and row houses and apartment buildings after that. Magee had passed through those to the sketchier area beyond, to a less desirable area located beside the intersection of a number of busy highways and side streets. During the day the auto-body shops would host some activity and the main traffic arteries would be congested. At night, however, apart from the few lonely cars speeding down the empty highway, the area was virtually deserted.

Above the bar hung a plywood sign with peeling paint and, inside, the bar was so dimly lit that it was impossible to be certain it was open. Beside it stood a dubious looking auto-design shop and, after a tight alleyway on the opposite side, there was a check cashing building. Both were closed.

Magee gulped and, upon opening the door to it, time seemed to freeze. It was as if every patron had looked up at him in the same choreographed movement and then remained locked in place. Even the bartender, a weathered, thick-boned woman, took notice, first peering at Magee with an expression of surprise and then with one of disappointment.

Magee, with the weight of the stares upon him, drifted to the bar and sat down on one of the many available stools. Eastern European music blared in the background, overly joyful and incongruous against such a morose backdrop, and the bartender reluctantly meandered over.

"What do you have on draft?" asked Magee.

"Bud and Bud Light," she replied, as if disputing a false accusation.

Magee could see that there were other beers on tap, ones with names he didn't recognize. But he decided bad service was better than no service. "I'll have a Bud."

The place was small and it wasn't crowded but Magee was nonetheless surprised by the amount of people. Virtually everyone was male. Some were old and some were young but all were the type that conveyed anger even when they smiled. Based on Magee's cursory view, there was a paradoxical air of community about the place...as if everyone was acquainted but didn't automatically get along.

Opposite the bar was a skeevy set of couches in the front corner, framed by wood paneling that had probably been installed when Carter was in office. Four of the youngest people in the bar were gathered there, stolidly smoking their cigarettes despite a decade-old ban on doing so indoors. Further down the bar was the entrance to a side room but Magee could discern nothing inside. And in the back of the bar was a room with a pool table, a light dangling above that created a milky glow on the cloud of smoke within. If Dimitrioff was in the bar he had to be in the side room or hidden from view in the pool room in back.

Magee sat, sipping his beer and casting quick, furtive glances about the bar. Most of the glares that initially fell on him had moved, though some returned from time to time. So he didn't want to create additional suspicion by ham-fistedly investigating the rooms in search of Dimitrioff. Better to bide his time, settle in, and appear like a harmless, lost tourist.

After awhile, the bartender approached Magee again and, since he'd finished his beer, he readied to order another. Instead, before he had a chance to speak, she asked, "What do you think you are doing?"

It caught Magee by surprise. "What?"

"What are you doing here?" she asked, her accent now more pronounced. "You would have to be a fool to not see that you do not belong here...but you do not have the eyes of a fool. I will you a new beer but first I ask: What are you doing here?"

Initially, Magee felt cornered, as if he had been busted in some way and felt a flash of antagonism. Then he realized that the question was an opportunity, a chance to make his desire known without prolonging the visit. "Oh...I'm, ah, looking for someone, actually," he said.

"Who?"

"His name is Sergei Dimitrioff. I'm pretty sure—"

"I know Sergei. How do you know Sergei?"

"He...ah, helped me out once. And he sorta gave me a warning. So I have a few questions for him. I—"

"He warned you about what?"

"He told me...told me something that makes me think my friend might be in danger." The bartender's interruptions had made the conversation combative and halting so, in an attempt to avoid interruption and defuse the tension, he began to ramble. "Look: I didn't come to create trouble. Sincerely. Sergei helped me out with some opera tickets. That's all. If I was cop with any intention of busting him I wouldn't have come in and had a beer. I would've just busted him on the spot. I don't want to know anything about his other activities. As far as I'm concerned he's a plumber that had an extra ticket. It's just, during the transaction, he gave me a warning. So now I think my friend might be in trouble...I think he might get killed."

Throughout Magee's explanation the bartender's hand had remained on her hip. At the same time, a bearded man at the opposite end of the bar had perked up. It was impossible for Magee not to notice he was listening. Magee resisted the urge to speak to him directly and kept his focus on the bartender but it was obvious the man's attention was rapt.

Magee finished and, for a long beat, her expression remained unchanged. Then, without a word, she turned and nodded to the bearded man. In return, he ducked into a doorway beside and, though Magee couldn't see him, he could hear his footsteps ascend a staircase behind the bar.

"Thank you," said Magee to the bartender, relaxing back on his stool.

She nodded ever so slightly and said, "We shall see."

Her response was odd and Magee felt as if a shadow had passed over the already-darkened bar. He didn't want to leave when he was so close to speaking with Sergei, though. A nervous minute passed and then Magee heard footsteps emanating from behind the bar. It sounded like a group of people this time and Magee got off his stool, ready to greet Sergei.

Sergei did not appear, however. Instead, three men...three very large men...emerged, tailed by the bearded man formerly at the bar. One of the three was bald with a deep scar across the ridge of his skull, each wore a leather jacket, and all possessed deep ridges in their brows indicative of perpetual scowls. Their eyes did not leave Magee as they made their way around the bar.

Magee, warning bells roaring within him, was about to say something. But before he got a chance the bearded man, from behind the three, pointed an accusatory finger and said, "That's him. That's the guy who killed Boris."

MEDA

Meda was awake and roaming her apartment. She wasn't sure why. It was a Saturday night, Matt was in her room sleeping like an exhausted eight year old, and she should've been doing the same. Down the hall, Mrs. Javier could be heard shuffling about her apartment (Did that woman ever sleep?) but such faint rustling had never kept her awake in the past. And though the moon was beaming, bright enough to illuminate her apartment without the need for any additional light, the glow alone shouldn't have interrupted her slumber either. It was something else, something at the edge of her thoughts that fed her restlessness.

Meda stared out her kitchen window as she sipped some tea. A friend had sworn that a particular variety helped her sleep and, for extra emphasis, had stressed that, "it *really* worked." After nearly forgetting about it, Meda sensed an opportunity to finally put it to use and had dug it out of her pantry. So far? The somniferous qualities of the tea seemed to have been grossly exaggerated.

As if in a dream, she floated from the kitchen to the couch. She felt no need to turn on the television or pick up the latest edition of Harper's or The New Yorker; such distractions would only prevent her from getting to the root of her dilemma. Her vexation lay in the fact that, if she were to be perfectly honest, there were parts of Matt's story that didn't add up. She didn't want to cast aspersions on such a welcome revelation yet there she was, wide awake and reviewing the tale over and over again.

They'd spent the night together and she'd continued asking him questions about the experience, eager to get more details regarding how he'd received such great news. But with each new detail he provided, Meda grew less and less comfortable. Matt said he'd gone to the police station and the lobby was utter bedlam. Meda could believe that, perhaps. While a bit surprising, she could conceive of an over-worked, under-staffed police force that didn't have the ability to keep the waiting area in tip-top shape. Matt also described his journey through the bowels of the station as if he'd marched miles of hallways and corridors. That seemed less plausible. Could such an ill-kept precinct be so massive? And Matt said he'd been left alone in the cubicle for an hour. That seemed downright impossible. A man makes a murder confession and the officer at the reception desk can barely be bothered to find a place for him? Meda was aware that people sometimes confessed to crimes they hadn't committed. But the police couldn't possibly be so cavalier with every professed killer who walked in the door, could they?

It was so frustrating. His story was full of details that, if they weren't outright falsehoods, nonetheless lacked veracity. Yet what alternative did she have but to believe him? If she concluded his tale didn't ring true, she had two choices, each presenting a unique dilemma. On the one hand, she could write off Matt's description as unintentional fabrication or exaggeration. Yet a story like that wasn't just the product of an overactive imagination—it was the hallucinations of someone who was mentally unstable. On the other hand, if she decided that wasn't the case, it meant that Matt had concocted the whole account and never gone to the police in the first place. While more rational, that choice implied conscious deceit on Matt's part rather than mental illness. In the end, neither option gave Meda the peace of mind she craved.

Confounding matters further was the fact that Meda was well aware she had every incentive to believe Matt's story. She yearned for Matt to be free and clear so they could move on with their lives together. Further, she knew the human mind could convince itself of almost anything if it wanted to believe the information strongly enough. (Just ask William Miller's followers!) She recognized it would be hard, if not impossible, to be truly objective about Matt's story without her unconscious mind engaging in some level of wishful thinking.

She knew that choosing to accept Matt's story at face value was the best available option. She told herself to stop trying to find problems, to put her mind at ease. Yet it wouldn't stay at ease. And that was the source of her greatest consternation: Every time she felt as if she'd made peace with her conscience, her mind began to rehash the same details all over again. Wearily, she peered out the living room window at the moon once more.

Then, ever so distantly, she heard something. It emerged from the background, as if it was present all along only she hadn't noticed it. Though she'd been sitting in the moonlight in what she'd presumed to be utter silence, a sense of wonder came over her at the recognition of the music. She focused on the rhythm more attentively and realized it was coming from inside the apartment building. And at the same moment it occurred to her that she hadn't heard Mrs. Javier's movements recently.

Meda stood up and began to move closer to her front door. She progressed gingerly as if she was approaching an injured animal. In the blue moonlight of her apartment, she didn't stop to wonder why she was approaching so carefully; it just seemed appropriate relative to the distant harmony. She deposited her empty tea mug on the kitchen counter as she passed, careful to avoid any noise. And as she moved, the song became clearer and clearer. It was glorious.

Meda didn't recognize the language. That did nothing to diminish its power, though. She'd grown up listening to Verdi while other children were watching cartoons; she'd revered the Three Tenors while her friends were listening to Nine Inch Nails. Yet this was unlike anything she'd ever heard. Then, as if she couldn't be any more astonished, the source of the song dawned on her: It was Mrs. Javier. Just as the sound had seemed to be omnipresent prior to Meda's recognition, so too came the now-obvious realization that she was the person singing it. Of course it was her; who else could it be?

For a long time she stood stock still at her door, listening. Some time passed and she became aware she couldn't stand there forever. She didn't want to miss anything, though, and she backed away from the door just as daintily as she'd approached it. She stared skyward as she moved, her mouth agape as she strained to hear. Then she slid the armchair from the living room to the door. She settled in, mesmerized, and continued to listen to her remarkable, improbably talented neighbor as she belted out the mysterious arrangement. And as the minutes stretched into hours, she fell asleep against the door, balanced on the chair with her arms wrapped around her legs as if floating in a protective cocoon.

MAGEE

Magee took two lunging steps to the door. That was as far as he got. Then he felt a jolt and glimpsed a moment of blackness. Another jolt, and then the ground was rushing towards him. Instinctively, his arms went to cover his head, barely in time to cover a kick which would've connected with his skull. In the abstract, he knew he was being attacked. But his mind was still processing that fact. It'd happened so quickly. There was no time to act. Only react.

It was all boots, connecting with his ribs and bashing the back of his palms. He couldn't concentrate, couldn't formulate a plan. He knew he had to get out of the bar but one of the men was positioned in front of the door. What now? What now? The unmistakable taste of blood in his mouth; some indecipherable shouting Magee could barely register. And the boots kept coming down.

Then: "Wait. Hold on."

Another half-hearted kick to his ribs.

"Hold on! Hold on!" more emphatically. A pause. "I do not think it is him."

The accent was heavy, vaguely Eastern European. Magee wanted to get a peek at voice's owner but couldn't risk exposing his face.

"What do you mean it's not him?" A second voice, the accent not as thick.

"I mean: It does not seem right."

"Seem right? How could he have known?"

"This man.... He could not have killed Boris. Look at him."

"What do you mean? He probably surprised him," said the second voice, growing desperate.

"Look at his hand. No wedding ring."

"So? What does that mean?"

"It means he does not have a wife, simpleton. So he probably does not have a child."

"What? Are you kidding me?"

"No," from the accented voice, defiant. "I do not think it is the right man."

Magee heard a groan of frustration and there was a moment of tense silence. He considered bolting for the door while he had the chance. But he knew it would be a virtual admission of guilt to...whatever crime they thought he'd committed.

"Hey." It was a new voice, yet still accented like the first, and Magee felt the tapping of a boot in his side. "What are doing here? Why did you come here?"

A second ticked by, then another, and Magee felt the pressure on him to respond. Without fully uncovering his head, he pivoted slightly and said, "I came here to get information for a friend. That's it. I swear on the holy bible. I have *no* knowledge of anybody who was killed. Whatever happened to your friend, it was *not* me that did it."

"You said something about a friend that might get killed." For the first time Magee saw the face of the man who'd spoken first, the owner of the heavily accented voice. He was the one with the scar, the largest of the three, and his words were rigid, authoritative.

"I did," said Magee quickly, in an attempt to sound honest. He was about to blurt out something about the opera, decided against it, and began to babble. "He just wanted to get these tickets for his wife. It was her birthday. He lost them and felt terrible. Sergei was helping to locate new ones. In the process, he tried to warn me about some sort of danger."

"Okay."

"I just didn't want anything to go wrong. I didn't want my friend—"

"Okay."

"—to get in any trouble."

"Okay! I understand. Now get out." The men continued to scowl at Magee and it was clear no apologies would be forthcoming. A second ticked by, Magee didn't move. Then: "Go!"

Magee used the bottom of the stool beside him for a boost and shocks of pain shot through his ribs and hands. Despite the various injuries that announced themselves as he moved, though, he knew he didn't have time to dawdle. On unsteady legs he rose. Then he burst through the door into the cold night, the air hitting his face like North Atlantic seawater. He was sweaty, his skin was flushed and throbbing, and the frigid wake-up was a welcome relief. He stumbled five steps and stopped to take stock of his surroundings. Then, telling himself that he should just get out of there as quickly as possible, he picked a direction at random and went. And, further up the street, he broke into a full-on sprint.

By the time he slowed down he was hyperventilating. The frigid air had reduced his lung capacity but at least he was away from that bar. His mind was still processing what'd happened...coming to terms with the fact that he very well could've died back there. He felt thankful to be alive but, at the same time, incensed that he should feel that way in the first place. He wanted to take revenge, to go to the cops and get those thugs arrested. But then he felt like a coward when his common sense told him otherwise. It was safe to conclude those guys had connections, dangerous ones, and that pursuing vengeance or legal action would only make the situation worse. And that sense of helplessness fed back into Magee's sense of outrage.

The only silver lining to be found was that he was now certain Meda wasn't involved in any plot or scheme. There was no way she'd associate with that crowd. Though that concern had been the driving force behind Magee's visit, he'd stumbled on a much larger hornet's nest instead. Clearly, there was more going on than any of them knew.

Magee continued to walk for a long time. He was aware he should probably go the hospital to confirm he didn't have a concussion and, with every step he took, he could feel myriad bruises and wounds filling with blood. But an emergency room visit might involve police activity, insurance hassles, or other unintended consequences. Before doing anything he wanted to think everything through...both in the short term and the long term.

Then his phone rang. Begrudgingly, he took it out and glared at it. Hardly in the mood for chit-chat, he grunted, "Hello?"

"What do you think you're doing?"

Magee paused, taken aback. "Excuse me?"

"You went to the bar tonight, right? Masis?"

"Who is this?"

"It's Sergei, you jerk." Magee recognized the voice once he identified himself. "Why the hell'd you go and do something like that?"

Indignation surged in Magee. Not only had he been beaten to a pulp but now this lowlife was suggesting it was his own fault? "Hey listen, *pal,*" he shouted, "your buddies nearly killed me!"

"You shouldn't have gone there," said Sergei, far too dismissively for Magee's taste.

"Oh? Oh, that's it? I shouldn't have gone there? That's all you have to say?"

"What d'ya expect me to say?"

"I don't know, maybe, 'I'm sorry.' Or, 'Wow, I can't believe that happened.' I mean...what kinda crap is that? You're saying I deserve to get killed for going to the wrong bar?"

"Look, it was a stupid thing t'do. I don't know what you was hoping to accomplish but now...now, it's too late."

"Huh? What do you mean it's too late? Too late for what?" Magee remained angry, yet the inflection in Sergei's voice gave him pause.

"I didn't know at the time. About the Armenians. About what happened to Boris."

"What? What didn't you know?"

"That friend of yours...the one who wanted to get the opera tickets?"

"Matt? What about him?"

"*He* is the one those guys at the bar are looking for! *He* is the one that killed their friend!"

"What? No. No way! That's impossible."

"Oh yes he did. And they have the videotape to prove it."

BENEDICT

Benedict went to a psychic once, many years ago. He'd gone on a lark, never expecting to take anything she said seriously. Early in his reading, however, she told him he was, "a man in hell." He had, of course, called her a vile name and stormed out without giving her any compensation. Yet not a day passed since that he didn't ruminate upon the encounter.

Now he lived in Switzerland, having emigrated from America years earlier. It was perfection. There were none of the tedious familiarities of his hometown, none of the distractions that undermined his efforts. No, in Switzerland he felt pristine, undiminished. He could continue his work at the particle collider at CERN and, at the end of the day, proceed home without fear of running into an old acquaintance or nosy neighbor. At CERN, his life had a singular goal and that was exactly the way he wanted it.

His father had been an award-winning architect. Benedict was sure he disappointed the man. Not only had he not followed in his footsteps, as seemingly everyone anticipated, he hadn't even attempted to claim a seat at the company his father founded. The fact that he'd become a particle physicist at the preeminent organization for scientific research mattered little. Instead, the common refrain was the notion of lost opportunity, that he'd missed the chance to take over an established architectural firm when it was right there for the taking.

For as long as he could remember he'd been fascinated by the arrangement and symmetry in the world of science. An indelible mark had been left at an early age when he'd learned that most complex atoms—the foundation of every plant, every animal, every building, everything in existence—were created in exploding stars eons ago. The notion had offered him structure: The world around him wasn't a hostile, unknowable jumble of parts beyond his mental capabilities. It was the opposite. Atoms were the fundamental building block of everything, like the brick and mortar of one of his father's buildings. If every human was composed of this matter, then eventually all of the desires, all of the longings of humans could also be understood. Benedict had no interest in creating tiresome office buildings for people. He wanted to show people what they were.

"Terrible weather we've been having, eh?" said Talbot. Talbot was a rotund, dullard of a man. He had a mind capable of solving the most complicated, byzantine math equation in moments while also possessing an encyclopedic knowledge of pop culture minutiae. Yet he'd never once ironed his pants correctly. In Benedict's opinion, Talbot could've actually done something with his stockpile of facts—write a book, create a database, something—but, instead, he seemed content to win an argument here and there with random strangers on the internet.

Benedict and Talbot were co-workers and, most days, the pair went to lunch together. Oftentimes it was a regretful tradition that bordered on obligation for Benedict, but he nonetheless felt like he should have some level of human interaction in the course of the day.

"I find weather to be predictive," said Benedict. "When it is dreary, our co-workers tend to be more focused on their work. Some would say this is counterintuitive since popular opinion suggests they'd be tired or morose. On the contrary, I believe pleasant weather causes distraction. They begin to think about life outside of work rather than focusing on their jobs. Have you noticed such a trend?"

"I think..." said Talbot, "that people like good weather. And they don't like bad weather."

"Mm. Yes," said Benedict.

Benedict glanced around the cafeteria. As an American, he was in the minority. While most of the time this wasn't a problem, there were instances when his co-workers made assumptions about him. Benedict despised that. Usually it was subtle, not intentionally malicious at all. These were scientists, after all, educated individuals who were accustomed to working with people from all walks of life. Yet, on the odd instances he'd been told to slow down, or when he'd been asked to withhold judgment until all the facts were disclosed, he felt the implied accusation: You are an insincere Yankee without decorum. It made Benedict want scream that he was not defined by his birthplace, that they had no right to judge him without truly knowing him.

Benedict spotted Katerina at a table nearby. She often worked in a lab nearby and she possessed one of the most symmetrical faces Benedict had ever seen. She sat alone, reading and lost in her novel despite the activity in the crowded cafeteria.

"She's pretty, yes?" said Talbot.

"Excuse me?"

"That lady. Katerina. I saw you looking at her."

Benedict frowned. "I wasn't looking at her. I was noticing how crowded it is in here today."

"You were doing that. And then you stopped looking when you laid your eyes on her," said Talbot with a satisfied grin.

Benedict paused, still frowning. Then, dismissively, said, "Don't be foolish."

Talbot took a bite of his sandwich and, for a moment, the only sounds to be heard was the background buzz of the cafeteria. Then, after chewing for a long while, Talbot added, "She probably wouldn't be interested in me anyway."

⋈ ⋈ ⋈

Of course Benedict understood perfectly well what Talbot had been inferring. But the simple truth was Talbot was dead wrong. Benedict had no interest in Katerina. None at all. Even if Benedict hadn't planned to end the world the following day, there was a practical reason he had no interest in Katerina: She reminded him of another woman, one he'd known a lifetime ago. If Benedict saw that woman by the side of the road, dying of thirst, he wouldn't so much as touch the car's brakes.

The woman in question's name was Gloria. She'd introduced herself after inadvertently locking her keys in her car and, at the time, Benedict couldn't believe his luck: A beautiful, intelligent woman offering to give him her phone number! He'd driven her home just as particles of sleet had begun to fall and then driven her back to the parking lot once she picked up her spare set of keys. Yet he'd purposefully avoided entertaining any notions that it would lead anywhere. Why set himself up for disappointment? But she had given him her number all the same.

He called the very next day, of course. Then they met again for coffee two days later. The truth was he didn't drink coffee but it had seemed like the thing to do. He proceeded to spill some on his shirt with the very first sip, however, and he very nearly streaked out of the shop in shame. Yet, at the end of the night, despite the accident and his abject loss of any semblance of confidence, she'd still asked when they could get together again. It was unreal.

Soon, she began to introduce Benedict to her friends. How foolish and naïve he had been! Gloria began by inviting them to join the pair at social settings such as concerts or the park—never bars, however. Benedict was so happy to be with Gloria that he took it as a compliment, proof he was an important part of her life. So enamored was he that he never noticed the gradual shift in the location of their outings. Over time they met less in public and, instead, began to gravitate to one specific friend's place instead. These gatherings were much more serious.

The location was Jack's apartment and, for a reason he couldn't pinpoint, Benedict always felt mildly out of place there. It was as if Gloria's friends were too comfortable: They knew where everything was stored and could help themselves to whatever they wanted, yet Benedict didn't have the same camaraderie. He hadn't worried about it, exactly. He'd merely assumed that the group had known each other a long time and that he wasn't privy to the in-jokes and togetherness.

They also began to discuss religion more often. Rather than talking about everyday trivialities, the group began examining the purpose of one's life, quoting scripture from the Old Testament, and producing ragged, well-worn copies of the Bible from their back pockets. Often, they'd cross reference other material, esoteric sources ranging from Freud to Aleister Crowley to forgotten prophets from the Middle Ages, and produce fantastical elucidations. Sometimes, the conversations grew heated with members offering differing interpretations up to Jack as if he was the ultimate arbiter. Once in awhile the gatherings would veer off topic and Benedict might finally have something to add. Yet, inevitably, the conversation always came back to similar spiritual and philosophical discussions.

This went on for several months and Benedict spent time exclusively with Gloria less and less. Rather, every time they met it was amidst the larger group of friends at Jack's place.

Benedict was still so charmed by Gloria and the notion of dating a woman like Gloria that he didn't mind, exactly. In fact, even if he had minded, he wouldn't have known how to indicate his displeasure anyway. Yet, on another level, that inaction continued to humiliate Benedict to the present day.

The catalyst to change was simple, a single word that'd been utilized accidently. Benedict had picked up Gloria at her apartment and they were on their way to Jack's apartment, as had been their custom. He was relating a story about something that'd happened at work, something inconsequential, and he'd referred to Gloria as, "girlfriend." It wasn't a purposeful mistake, not a sneaky way for Benedict to confirm their status together. It was simply how he thought of her.

She had grown silent, however, the smile plummeting from her face. Benedict was driving and couldn't engage her fully, but he recognized the tangible shift in her demeanor. She hadn't moved yet it felt as if she'd curled up against the passenger side door. He'd made a joke, something to cut the tension. It hadn't been successful. Then they'd parked and entered Jack's apartment as if nothing had happened.

The normal pleasantries were exchanged and for an extended period Gloria seemed to hover at the periphery of the group. Then, after everyone had settled in, she made an announcement. "Everyone? Everyone, I think it's been awhile. Too long. I think it's long past time we re-affirm our love for Jack. He is our leader and provider and I don't ever want to take him for granted. I love you, Jack."

To Benedict's horror, others immediately joined in, no questions asked.

"I love you, Jack."

"I'll always love you, man."

"I love you so much, Jack."

And then he saw Gloria's stare fixed upon on him, anticipatory and accusing. He would always remember the heat in his face at that moment: It was as if boiling water had frothed up beneath his skin, red and molten, and brimmed under his cheeks and forehead. His sense of betrayal and humiliation was exquisite, only surpassed by his outright confusion. Yet, within him, social pressure fused with those emotions to form a tempest of insecurity. All eyes were upon him. He wanted to rage, to bludgeon his way out of the place, to run away like a child who'd wet his pants. But they were his friends. He didn't want to embarrass himself in front of them. In front of Gloria. With each passing second the gravity increased, the situation growing more and more unbearable.

"I...I love you, Jack" he had muttered.

A sense of relief had passed over the group and Gloria's smile beamed as she touched Benedict's arm reassuringly. He'd even stayed through the night and brought her home. But he never spoke to her, or them, again. The phone rang without answer for weeks and he didn't own an answering machine. He endured his days with stoic resolve and spoke to no one after his shift was over. He ate. He slept. He went back to work the next day. He did that for years.

The Large Hadron Collider was the prime mover that broke Benedict out of his stasis. Professionally, he'd excelled in the intervening years. Personally, he'd remained all but inert. When, first, the Barrel Toroid was switched on and, at roughly the same time, rumors of the Collider began to heat up, Benedict found himself consumed by the possibilities.

Everything else in life was secondary to him, a farce. The arts? There was no true creation of anything; all matter was already pre-existing. All humans were doing—all they'd ever done—was take already-available matter and rearrange it in a different pattern. That's it. Painting...literature...even childbirth: Humans insisted on labeling these activities as acts of creation. Yet Benedict knew it was all a lie. The semantics were quite straightforward. No human had ever literally made something from nothing.

The Large Hadron Collider was unique, however. It allowed humans to break down matter to its fundamental components, to what it was at the very beginnings of the universe. For the first time in human history people weren't simply dredging up some dye from the earth and splattering it on a cave wall. No, the Large Hadron Collider, by smashing atoms together at tremendous speeds, allowed humans to create matter that was literally new.

The following day, Talbot was nowhere to be found at lunchtime and, instead, appeared in the doorway of Benedict's office at the end of the workday. Talbot's work demanded he be in a different area after lunch so his appearance, particularly when many were leaving for the night, caught Benedict by surprise. Unprepared for the late interruption, Benedict reminded himself what day it was and that he needn't get cross, even when Talbot came plodding in without any offer to do so.

"To what do I owe this pleasure?" said Benedict, standing, his hands on his hips.

"I was just thinking of something last night. And, well, I couldn't stop thinking about it," said Talbot. He was never a man who displayed superior confidence of movement but he now appeared particularly nervous. He shifted to and fro listlessly and covered and uncovered his hands a number of times, all within the brief moment of his appearance.

"Okay," said Benedict, simply.

"Yesterday, when we were in the cafeteria?" Talbot paused, waiting for affirmation that Benedict did, indeed,

recognize the occasion to which he was referring. "Okay. Well, I maybe gave you a hard time about that woman, Katerina. And I just wanted to say I'm sorry."

Benedict laughed, both surprised and relieved, at the fact that the announcement was so trivial. "You came over here just for that?"

"Well, yes. I thought...we are both grown men. We don't need to fight over a woman."

"We don't indeed," said Benedict, chortling even more. "I can assure you, though: I do not fancy Katerina in any way. If you're seeking my permission to pursue her, you most assuredly have it."

Benedict lost Talbot's attention by the end of his statement, however. It was an abrupt change considering how concerned Talbot had been a moment earlier. Instead, he'd become distracted by materials on Benedict's desk, the paperwork he'd been admiring when Talbot arrived. "What's this then?" he said, pointing to the papers.

Benedict chided himself for his carelessness. This was the exact reason he hated visitors. Especially those who showed up unannounced. To most co-workers, the paperwork would've seemed like a jumble of hieroglyphs, numbers, and letters combined in altogether inscrutable equations. Given Talbot's experience, however, Benedict saw that he recognized some of the immediate implications.

"Oh, it's just something I'm working on," said Benedict dismissively. He could've swept up the papers, hidden them from view, and Talbot probably wouldn't have challenged him. But he knew it was all too late anyway. Instead, with the slightest amount of pride evident, he stood by while Talbot read.

"What is it?" asked Talbot, even as it was clear he had an inkling what was literally represented.

"What do you think it is?"

"It seems like," began Talbot, pausing in a mix of trepidation and skepticism, "like a stable, negatively charged particle with three quarks: The up quark, the down quark, and...the strange quark."

"That's right," said Benedict, now smiling.

"A strangelet. Why? It's been proven these can't exist in nature. They decay too quickly."

"Look again."

Talbot shuffled through the papers, concentrating more intensely. "You're suggesting it's stable to two seconds? Or more? Do you know what this means?"

"Yes," said Benedict, his smile beaming.

"If enough of those are made...for that long of a period," said Talbot slowly, carefully, while Benedict nodded in agreement. "Those strangelets will convert the matter around it into strangelets. And so on and so on. It won't stop."

"Of course."

"But...how? Why?"

"Gaze at the heavens, my friend," said Benedict. "What is the most cherished particle on this planet? Formed strictly in the hearts of stars light years away before landing on the planet? Gold."

Talbot was still locked in concentration but a brief sense of recognition seemed to pass over him.

"Mankind has been pursuing gold since it was first discovered in caves," continued Benedict. "Most often it was for the wrong reason: Base avarice. That was cowardly, bestial. I believe there is a higher purpose. Something one might consider almost...holy."

"What?"

"Alchemists throughout the ages have tried to convert lead into gold," continued Benedict, virtually ignoring

Talbot's question. "We already have the ability to do so through nucleosynthesis here at the collider. To alchemists of old that, alone, would have been tantamount to seeing the face of God. But for us to be truly heavenly, we have to go one step further. We have to take that gold, that energy, and create new matter."

"Strangelets?"

"That's right. Only gold has the exact mass necessary to create the energy required. Think of the Golden Ratio, witnessed in everything from the arch of a seashell to the Egyptian pyramids—the naming convention was transcendently appropriate. The muon begins the process and, following the bounce, the transmutation occurs exponentially thereafter. Gold!"

As Benedict spoke, Talbot's expression changed. Previously he'd appeared curious and befuddled but, as he listened, his concern grew. "Wait, are you pursuing this? Are you actually going to try to create these here?"

"Yes. Today, in fact."

Talbot's eyes went wide. "Today?"

"Yes. It's been years in the making. I had to live a monastic life to save up the necessary bribery funds, garner favor with sundry technicians, understand every security protocol, maintain the patience to wait for the perfect time. It was not easy, I will admit. Particularly difficult was the fact that I couldn't allow one group to know what another was doing."

"But," began Talbot, nearly at a loss for words, "if this works. And it's stable. That group of strangelets will convert the earth into one giant mass of strangelets. It will be the end of the world."

"Precisely."

Talbot shook his head. "Why would you? What do you think you're doing?"

Though Benedict had been grinning the entire time, he now smiled more broadly than ever. "I will make the earth pure."

"Pure? What? Everyone will be dead!"

"Humans have had it all wrong," said Benedict calmly, as if speaking to a child. "The answer has been in front of us all along. It's right there in the numbers. Allow me to explain. One, the number one, is a singular point, correct? It is the number that denotes a singularity, like the universe just prior to the big bang. The number two is two points. Two dimensions. In other words, when connected, they form a line: Something that divides and creates duality."

Benedict began to use his hands for illustration purposes during his sermon while Talbot listened intently. "The number three is three points, the triangle. It's one of the most powerful numbers due to its ability to encase. We see in three dimensions. Our whole worldview originates in that number. It's no wonder that, in many of the world's religions, the godhead takes the form of a trinity. The number four represents the first solid object of the world. Four points, when put together, create a tetrahedron, the pyramid. The Egyptians knew this. So long ago, they appreciated the importance of that number."

"Five," said Benedict, his words dripping with disgust, "is the number associated with man. It is practically evil insofar as it forms nothing new. At best it creates a pentagram, a reversion from the solidity of the pyramid back to two dimensions. Five is a terrible, barbarous number."

"Six, however," said Benedict, nodding and smiling once again. "Humans were wrong about the number six. Throughout the ages it's been associated with satan, the

devil. Humans thought God was represented in the number seven so, with childish simplicity, they concluded that six was less and, therefore, associated with the devil. I know better. Six points allows two attached planes to form side by side. Think of the corner of two walls: Two independent bodies nonetheless joined together. Just as string theory predicts! And here is the important part: Six is also represented in the number of quarks found in a strangelet. People called the Higgs Boson the God Particle? They had no clue what they were talking about. The strangelet is the literal God particle."

Talbot listened in awe. His expression was frozen in a state of dumbfounded fear, utterly motionless, as if in a photograph. Finally, he said, "I can't let you do this."

Benedict smirked. "Let me? How do you propose to stop me? You know the procedures. It's too late."

"N-no," stuttered Talbot. "I'll pull the fire alarm."

At that, Benedict faltered. Pulling the alarm wouldn't halt the process automatically, but it might delay it. It might force protocols to be re-checked, meaning that at least one of his carefully orchestrated pawns might grow spineless and abort their required task. He had to think quickly.

"Talbot," began Benedict, with a beatific smile, "can't you see we're on the verge of something important here?"

"We?" said Talbot incredulously.

"Yes. 'We.' We are the only people in the entire world who know what is about to happen. Isn't that awe-inspiring? In Buddhism they have a name for it: Bodhisattva. He who brings enlightenment."

Talbot was grimacing, skeptical, and not saying a word.

"All your life has led to this moment, Talbot. This will be the literal apex of humanity."

"But," said Talbot, "I will die, too."

"Correct! As will I!" proclaimed Benedict. "We will be the final dying gods of the world!"

"That's silly," said Talbot and nothing more.

Benedict nearly lost his temper with his childlike colleague. After so much work he couldn't allow this imbecile to ruin everything. Instead, he calmed himself and tried a different tack. "Let me ask you: What do you hope to do with your life?"

"What? What do you mean?" The question aroused insecurity in the man and his body language changed.

"I mean," said Benedict, pausing, the smile returning. "You love your science fiction shows. You love your action thrillers. But wouldn't you like to be a part of one of them? So often, they promulgate some semblance of higher purpose, some reason for being. Do you want your life to be the consumption of potato chips and passive television observance? Or do you want something more?"

Talbot was about to respond, to protest in some way, even as the dissonance in him raged. He didn't have the ability to refute Benedict's accusation directly but he knew he could drag the conversation out, as he was so adept at doing online. Then Katerina walked by. She was on the phone as she passed and, quite clearly, both Talbot and Benedict heard her say, "I love you, Greg."

For a long time there was only silence. Benedict eyed up Talbot in the aftermath of the revelation as one might a suicidal person, careful not to upset the man. By gradual degrees Talbot's shoulders drooped and his mannerisms became more languid, more lethargic. Benedict, if pressed, would admit that he never expected the man to take Katerina's words so ruinously. He was not about to look a gift horse in the mouth, though, and, in response, Benedict grew more sure, more confident. Talbot gave another glance at the paperwork, one that was rueful and mourning, but he didn't speak a word.

Seconds ticked by. Then minutes. Eventually, with no further threat from Talbot, Benedict motioned first to the clock on the wall and then to the window of his office. He moved to the window and, after hesitating one final time, Talbot shuffled over to join him. And in the vacant, isolated silence of the office, Talbot and Benedict waited and watched the end of the world.

MATT

The sun was shining, the subway was running on schedule, and even the yapping Chihuahua next door—often the bane of Matt's morning—greeted him with tail-wagging excitement. For the first time in almost two weeks Matt didn't feel as if the Sword of Damocles was hanging over his head. He'd ripped out a complete new story on Sunday—one of the most crucial, in fact, since the tale detailed the literal end of the world—and, even more importantly, he'd been cleared of any wrongdoing in the death of the little boy. Though still concerned about what happened him, Matt knew that if he wanted to keep the widening gyre of his life from spinning wholly out of control, he had to return to his writing. Ironically enough, crafting the story about the world's end had provided a new beginning and, with a new day dawned, everything seemed golden and radiant.

So relaxed was he that he almost overlooked a strange set of paperwork on his desk at the office. Then, investigating more closely, he saw the name, Abaddon Gupta, atop. Clearly, his twitchy co-worker Abby had been in his cubicle and left it behind by mistake. Under normal circumstances, he would've been angry at such a breach of privacy and concerned about potential snooping. Instead, smirking, he said, "Hey Abby?"

"Yes?" she said, appearing at his cubicle door almost supernaturally fast.

"Did you leave something here?"

Matt held up the papers and her expression shot from embarrassment—as if she'd been caught red-handed—to a sense of relief.

"Oh my God!" she shrieked, seizing the papers from him with both hands. "I've been looking *all over* for those!"

"Yeah, they were just sitting there," said Matt, still smirking.

"These are my health insurance elections. I was absolutely terrified I'd have to request them again. The deadline is in three weeks. Oh my God, thank you," babbled Abby, rattling off each sentence as if she'd called in an emergency to 911.

"Hey, no problem," said Matt calmly. Then, after a moment, he added, "Just one thing."

"Yes?"

"Why were they in my cubicle?"

Abby flashed an ingratiating smile and bobbed her head to the side before she began speaking. "I—I just don't know. I was in here over the weekend. Y'know, the reconciliation of the retail Class B account is such a pain. I hoped to get a jump on it. It's so hard to do during the week with all the interruptions here, y'know? And—I don't know—I was just absolutely tired. This job is so draining, y'know?"

Matt nodded along, fully aware that she had in no way explained her intrusion into his cubicle. But if he heard her say, "y'know," one more time he feared his brain would explode. So, to make her go away, he said, "It's fine. Don't worry about it. I'm glad you got them back."

"Thank you *so much*, Matt," Abby effused, before disappearing back to her cubicle.

It was a hiccup in Matt's otherwise zephryean morning and he was determined not to give it undo significance. Instead, he moved on and, by noon, he'd accomplished more than he might in an entire day. It was a good feeling after seeing the stack of work which had built up in his absence. Apart from his brief conversation with Abby, he didn't say a word to anyone and, when a call came in from Magee, it seemed like a nice break after such a productive morning.

"Hey, are you in a safe place?" asked Magee conspiratorially as soon as Matt answered.

"Well, if you consider my office to be safe," replied Matt.

"I'm serious," said Magee, the urgency in his voice undiminished. "I think you're in danger."

"What?"

"Those Armenian guys? They think you killed one of their friends. And, apparently, they have you on video tape."

"What?" repeated Matt, even more skeptically.

"I haven't seen the tape. But Sergei, the guy who was selling the tickets to the opera? He gave me a call...probably put his own ass on the line in the process. He warned me that these guys were looking for you."

Matt leaned back in his chair, his brow furrowed. He'd been through the ringer lately, his life turned upside down ever since he hit that boy. He wasn't ready to give up the peace he'd finally achieved without a fight.

"These guys are dangerous, man," continued Magee gravely, reacting to Matt's silence.

"So wait," began Matt, "you're telling me this guy—this ticket scalper who has already proven himself to be a little unhinged—warned you that some Armenians are out to get me? And, despite the fact that I only met the guy once, very briefly, and despite the fact that I most assuredly haven't *killed* anybody...you choose to believe him?"

"Buddy, it doesn't matter whether you actually killed anybody! They *think* you did. They're really bad guys, members of the Armenian mafia. And they're coming for you."

Matted rolled his eyes. "So anyway, I've been meaning to tell you," he said, blatantly changing the topic of conversation. "I was driving recently and I saw that graffiti we found years ago under the bridge. It started the whole Dirty Lord expression. Remember? I couldn't believe it."

"Matt, are you paying attention?" asked Magee, disgusted. "I'm trying to tell you your life is in danger and you're talking about that? Come on. Get serious."

"Okay, okay," said Matt, trying to at least humor his friend. "So hypothetically...even *if* the ticket broker is telling the truth and *if* some guys in the Armenian mafia are out to get me: Why should I care? There's no way they will find me."

"You're not listening! These guys are dangerous! I've got two fractured ribs and a possible broken finger to prove it. Not to mention the fact that my cheek is swollen to the size of an apple."

"What?" asked Matt, more concerned.

"That's right. These guys, they jumped me in a bar because they thought I killed their friend. And that was only because I asked a question! Sergei called me after that. One of the guys at the bar must've told him I was looking for him and he put two and two together. Turns out, he recognized you from the videotape they have. That was why he freaked out on you at the bar. He thought he was being set up."

Matt listened. His joviality was gone but his skepticism remained. "Have you seen the videotape? Do you know what he's talking about?"

"No, I haven't seen it," admitted Magee. "But that doesn't matter. Whether you killed their friend or not is irrelevant. They think you did. And they're out for blood."

"So what should I do?" asked Matt, as if they were discussing a parking ticket.

"I'm just trying to warn you, man!" said Magee, exasperated at Matt's cavalier reaction. The last time they spoke Matt was half-wracked with anxiety, worried he was going crazy. Now Magee was describing an actual, legitimate threat and Matt couldn't muster enough concern to stay on topic for more than five seconds.

"Okay, okay. Thank you for the warning. I do appreciate it," said Matt congenially, his tone suggesting he was more concerned about hurting Magee's feelings than any danger. He recalled the Stoic Man's warning about Meda and, after avoiding her for almost two days, how unfounded that concern turned out to be. He was sick of these secret dangers lurking around every corner—he was safe and all was well.

Magee recognized Matt's ham-fisted attempt at reconciliation, however, and it only served to frustrate him further. "Look," said Magee, "I'm trying to tell you your life is in danger. It's up to you to take this seriously."

"I am! I am!"

"You're going to have to be more careful," continued Magee, disbelieving Matt's insistence. "You're going to need to keep an eye out...be aware of anyone following you...that sort of thing."

"Okay. Fine. Sounds like a plan," said Matt, already checking his latest emails.

MEDA

Another day at work, another trip home from work. It seemed as if Meda's entire life was spent merely moving between her office and her apartment, never deviating from the assigned path. Sure, she and Matt had gone on vacation for a week the previous summer (Seriously, though: Was she supposed to spend the entire year looking forward to a single week off?) And at odd times in the past she and Matt had mused about getting in a car and just driving without a map or a destination. Yet there was always a reason they couldn't do it, some deadline or obligation that had to be met before any such journey took place. It was good to be done with her work day, if only to put Monday behind her, but it nonetheless felt a little empty, a little structured to be walking back to the familiar walls of her apartment yet again.

On the sidewalk before her the last remaining bands of the day's sunlight sent splashes of color on the concrete and, up ahead, she saw Mrs. Javier sitting in her familiar spot.

"Hello," said Meda warmly. "Beautiful day."

"Well hello yourself, young lady," smiled Mrs. Javier. "And yes, glorious isn't it?"

"The days are getting shorter. We should enjoy these sunsets while they last," said Meda. As atrocious as the old woman's timing could be and as creepy as she'd been of late (no one should have to deal with hidden fertility idols after a long day at work), Meda actually welcomed the banter. She needed something to break her out of her malaise and if it was one thing Mrs. Javier had in spades, it was positivity.

"You're right, you're right. Winter will be here soon enough." Mrs. Javier paused, then continued, "I've been meaning to ask you."

"Yes?"

"I was at mass yesterday and it occurred to me: Have you noticed any water pooling around your sink? I've—"

"Wait, wait, wait," interjected Meda, her hand in the air and chuckling lightly. "Mass? You go to Catholic mass? Just last week you were carrying around a fertility idol. And, before that, you seemed pretty intense about your astrological beliefs. What gives?"

Meda's words had been jovial and light-hearted but, for a brief moment, she worried she might've offended the woman. Mrs. Javier's smile allayed that concern. With perfect serenity she said, "No one says you can't believe it all."

Meda laughed in earnest then and blurted, "The church itself says you can't!"

"No," corrected Mrs. Javier. "They say you're not supposed to. I can believe whatever I want. I just might have to pay for it later."

"But," began Meda before stopping. She was at a loss for words (more appropriately: A loss for how to express her surprise at such tortured logic without dismantling an old woman's spiritual belief system). "But you still go to mass knowing you're not supposed to worship false idols."

"Well, we're all sinners, dear."

"That's different!"

"How?"

Mrs. Javier had uttered the word with a wry smile and Meda was flummoxed even further. She'd always intuitively suspected the old woman had a spiritual side. Yet she was having a hard time articulating a description for such a contradictory belief system. It was like voting for all of the political candidates or betting in favor of both sports teams. Some things just don't work that way!

Before she could say anything, however, Mrs. Javier added, "I just like to play it safe."

(And there you have it.) Meda nodded, still unsure if it was appropriate to laugh. "Well. Okay then. Whatever works for you, Mrs. Javier."

"Indeed," said the old woman.

Meda smiled. Her previous lassitude had been vanquished, replaced by an appreciation for this old woman who had seemed merely superstitious and nothing more. Her easy spiritualism was a breath of fresh air and, as Meda peered up at Mrs. Javier, the sun broke from behind a cloud and dropped a luminous beam directly on her.

"I heard you singing the other night," said Meda.

At that Mrs. Javier appeared wary, startled almost. "You what?"

"Saturday night. I couldn't sleep. I was awake and I heard you singing." Then Meda added, "It was beautiful."

Mrs. Javier's eyelids fluttered in a mix of embarrassment and gratitude. "Oh. No one was supposed to hear that."

"Well, I did," said Meda, "and I thought you were excellent. I actually nodded off to sleep while listening. What song was it?"

"The song? Oh, it was one I used to sing a lifetime ago: 'The Youth and the Streamlet,' by Sayat Nova. I am afraid to say, I was much better back in those days. What you heard the other night?" And Mrs. Javier concluded with a dismissive wave, as if she was ashamed.

Meda shook her head from side to side in awe. "If that was you on a bad night, I can't imagine what pipes you had in your youth."

"Pipes?"

"Your vocal chords," said Meda, her grin transforming into a light chuckle. "You must've really been something special. From the sounds of it you had all the potential in the world. What happened?"

Mrs. Javier grew more serious, raising her eyebrows and lamenting, "What happened? Life happened. My family moved here, to America, when I was young. Soon after that I met Manuel. But he, he was from a different neighborhood. My parents? They didn't approve. So: We were on our own."

Mrs. Javier halted for a moment, cocking her head to the side ever so slightly and raising her palms in an expression of helplessness. Then she continued, "Little Manny was born. Then Perry. And then Alan. Suddenly, there were three babies to take care of. I still sang my songs. Mostly when Manuel and the kids were not home. But: It was different."

She finished and, for a long moment, Meda stood speechless. She wanted to console the woman but didn't know how to do so without casting aspersions on her decisions or her family.

"I don't have any regrets," added Mrs. Javier, as if sensing Meda's inner dilemma. "I loved Manuel with all my heart. And my boys, they are still my pride and joy. They will always be my little babies. I wouldn't do a thing different. But sometimes I do wonder. I know I would've never put food on the table with my voice. My songs, (America was listening to beach music, the Beatles) no one would care for old folk songs from a foreign country. Sometimes, though: Sometimes I just wish there could have been another way."

Meda offered a smile through pursed lips and placed her hand on the woman's arm. "It sounds like you had a very fulfilling life, Mrs. Javier. I don't think I would've changed a thing either."

Mrs. Javier sent a smile up to Meda, one which was beaming and appreciative. "You're such a good girl. So nice."

Meda chuckled, despite the serious tone. "Thank you, Mrs. Javier."

MAGEE

Magee knew it was a terrible idea...even worse than his original plan to track down Sergei at the bar. Yet he also recognized that he wasn't going to get through to Matt. Jesus, himself, could come down from the mountain to warn Matt about the danger and he still wouldn't listen. Magee knew Matt wouldn't take the threat seriously unless he was presented with absolute proof...and that involved tracking down Sergei yet again.

Going back to the bar was suicide...out of the question. Therefore, Magee had only one other option: Go directly to Sergei's apartment. Magee had found it via his previous sleuthing but, prior to the assault at the bar, he'd thought surprising the man at home might not be the best choice. Everything was different now, though.

For a time, Magee loitered outside the apartment building assessing the entrance. He'd decided to make the journey early Tuesday morning rather than Monday night. Fundamentally, the extra foot traffic at rush hour made it much easier for him to sneak into the apartment building unnoticed. Perhaps even more importantly, it offered the chance for more witnesses if something went wrong. Satisfied that the doorman on duty wasn't on full alert, he took the opportunity to duck in the open door just as someone was leaving. With downcast eyes he made his way to the elevator and quickly punched the button for the sixth floor. He arrived and emerged, trying to look inconspicuous while appraising the hallway. Sergei's apartment was the ninth on the floor and, thankfully, nothing seemed amiss, no extra surveillance or obstacle to confront. He approached and knocked on the door with three quick raps of his knuckles. For a tense moment there was only silence. Then he heard a grunt followed by, "Coming."

The door opened. Magee grinned, saying nothing, and Sergei's manner drooped. "You," he said.

"Yep. Me," said Magee, nodding obsequiously. "I...was wondering if you had a moment."

"What?" said Sergei, disgusted. His hair was a mess, his eyes were hateful squints, and he wore a ratty, stained robe.

"Look, I'm sorry to surprise you like this," said Magee, raising his palms in hopes of allaying the man's ire. "I just had to get in touch with you. Not by phone. In person."

Sergei hadn't stopped scowling since answering the door and Magee's words only seemed to drive the ridges in his forehead deeper. "How the hell did you find me?"

Magee chuckled, still trying to disarm the man. "The internet is a hell of a thing. With enough digging...."

Magee trailed off, hoping Sergei would come around if he made a joke. Instead, Sergei shot his head out through his doorframe, glaring down the hallway in each direction before yanking Magee inside. "Goddamn it. Get in here."

Momentarily relieved to at least gain entry, Magee then surveyed the place. It was an absolute pigsty. Food delivery containers were piled three-, four-deep beside the couch, the crack in the coffee table was only partially hidden by the papers strewn atop it, and the rug was a relic from the 1970s. It was so bad that it caught Magee off guard and he muttered a low, "wow," without even intending to do so.

"What?" said Sergei, still angry.

"Nothing," said Magee, before repeating, "Nothing."

Sergei nodded slightly and his glare fell on Magee like an interrogation light. It was obvious he'd registered Magee's judgment and, in the silence, Magee squirmed self-consciously. Yet, rather than challenging him, Sergei instead muttered, "So. Why're you here?"

Magee composed himself and began, "The other day on the phone...you told me my friend was in danger...that those guys at the bar think Matt killed their friend."

"Yeah."

"And you mentioned some video they had. Something that proved Matt had done it."

"Yeah. I've got it in my phone."

"You do? Excellent!" said Magee, displaying obvious relief despite his attempt to appear impassive. An actual recording of the event was precisely what Magee had hoped to see.

"Hold on," grunted Sergei, gradually accepting Magee's interloping presence in his sanctuary. He began rifling through a heap of receipts and odd materials, adding, "You know these guys...they're not people you want to mess with."

"Oh, I know," assured Magee, the pain in his ribs an every-present reminder.

"No, I ain't kidding. I do some things with them now and then. I've seen their work. It ain't pretty. I don't think your friend knows what he's gotten himself into." At that, Sergei peered up at Magee, meeting him eye-to-eye. He was no longer scowling and, to Magee, this solemn visage appeared even more disquieting in its own right.

"Okay," said Magee, less flippantly. "I appreciate the warning."

"Don't worry about it," muttered Sergei before producing his phone.

"Do you mind if I record it with my phone?" asked Magee.

Sergei stopped, peered at Magee's phone suspiciously, and then looked back at his own. "Sure," he said, with a shrug. "It'll probably come out like crap anyway."

"I know. But it's better than nothing," said Magee.

Sergei started the video and Magee couldn't see anything...the blackness on the screen was so absolute that it was a veritable mirror. He could hear movement, like that of someone walking, and he detected the rustling of fabric. In fact, initially, it sounded as if it'd been a mistake, an accidental call from someone's pocket. But gradually Magee connected the dots based on the incidental noise, the heavy breathing, and plodding footfalls: It was a recording created by someone who'd been running for a long period and was dead exhausted.

The audio, lacking visual presentation, went on for a long time and eventually Magee looked up to Sergei with an inquisitive glance. In return Sergei held a single finger aloft to indicate patience and, after an anticipatory moment, he pointed it back towards the phone.

There was a harsh, sudden grunt. Then another. They weren't angry, though; they sounded like they were born from terror or agony. Then a quick smattering of shuffling footsteps and uncoordinated scrapings on blacktop could be heard, along with an extended wheeze. And then, after a brief moment of abject silence, there was a hard, dull thud. It was brutal in its immediacy and for the first time the video offered something visual, a momentarily light which flashed across the screen. After that, another thud could be heard, this one more wet. It was again followed by silence and the visual display turned black. Gradually, however, Magee realized the darkness wasn't absolute...it appeared different but he couldn't identify how, exactly. Then he noticed three or four of the vaguest pinpricks of light scattered across the screen, unmoving, and he realized they were stars in the night sky.

Now all was silent...no rustling of clothes or ragged breaths...and Magee briefly wondered if the video had ended. Sergei anticipated his confusion, gave a knowing nod, and Magee peered back at the screen attentively. He heard another quick series of footsteps. Then there was a flash across the screen, practically imperceptible.

"Did you see it?" asked Sergei gravely.

"No. No, I didn't," admitted Magee. "It happened too fast."

"Hold on," said Sergei, drawing the device closer and pressing a few buttons.

Magee waited in silence, on pins and needles. The dry pit that'd formed in his stomach gave physical sensation to his sense of foreboding.

Then, holding out the device once again, Sergei said, "Here." On the screen, paused in mid-frame, was a moment halted in time. And there was no doubting the fact that it was Matt.

MEDA

It occurred to Meda that she had never called Magee after their meeting the previous Thursday. The weekend had come and gone and after spending time with Matt she realized she should've at least given Magee a ring to let him know Matt was doing better. She took a final swig of coffee, her second of the morning, and vowed to call him as soon as she arrived at the office.

When she opened the front door of her apartment building, however, she was surprised to find Mrs. Javier on the front stoop. (It was as if she never left!)

"Mrs. Javier. Hey," said Meda, caught off guard but happy to see her nonetheless.

"Oh, hello dear," said Mrs. Javier, craning to peer up at Meda with those child-like eyes. Meda worked her way around the chair and then Mrs. Javier, smiling slyly, added. "It's back."

"What? What's back?"

"The glow, dear," effused Mrs. Javier. "You can't fool me. I see it again. Are you sure you're not pregnant."

Meda laughed. She recalled her aggravation the last time Mrs. Javier insisted she was with child and, slightly embarrassed at the memory, Meda replied, "I am *positive* I am not pregnant, Mrs. Javier. Thank you for the compliment, though."

Mrs. Javier pursed her lips, as if she still didn't believe her.

Meda expected Mrs. Javier to add something but, when it was clear she would not, Meda moved the conversation along a different path. "What a beautiful day, huh?"

Mrs. Javier nodded. "Indeed. Not a cloud in the sky. The people on the television are saying we might be able to see that comet tonight. Even with the glow of the city and all."

"Oh, I hadn't heard," said Meda. "I didn't turn on the news this morning. I was thinking of stopping at the new Farmer's Market on the way to work and didn't want to get distracted."

"Oh yes," said Mrs. Javier impassively.

"Have you been there?"

"Yes. It's nice," she said, unenthused. Then she added, "I must say the truth, though: It's a little crowded inside. The aisles: Too tight."

Meda smiled at the old woman's cursory summation. She was cute without even trying to be. "So why are you up so early? I never see you in the morning."

"Oh, I'm always awake, dear. I may not be out here but I'm awake," said Mrs. Javier with a finger in the air, setting the record straight. She peered about and, returning to Meda's question, she said, "Mr. Goldt is supposed to come by today. I want to be sure to catch him on his way in."

"Why? Still worried about the carbon monoxide scare?"

"Well, yes. I want to find out about that. I also think I've got a leak. And you know how he is: He comes in, does a quick fix, and scampers away. Then we never see him again until the end of the month."

Before Meda could concur, a loud crack split the air above the pair. Each glanced up to glimpse the falling tree branch a split-second before it crashed to the street in front of them.

"Oh my!" said Mrs. Javier, startled.

Meda jumped to hover over Mrs. Javier protectively then scanned the tree above to ensure no other branches were coming. A second passed and, satisfied that they were safe, she added, "Wow."

After the immediate surprise, each took stock of the branch lying on the asphalt. It was rotted, rife with lichens. Meda wondered why it would fall now, of all times (why not during the last rain storm?) but decided that didn't matter.

"Well that's one way to start your morning," said Mrs. Javier with a laugh, breaking the tension.

"Indeed," added Meda.

Then Mrs. Javier pushed herself up from her chair and began to descend the stairs. "Well, only one thing to do."

Meda, a second late, realized Mrs. Javier was planning to move the branch out of the road and followed after her. "What? No, wait, Mrs. Javier. I can do that."

Mrs. Javier was already in front of Meda on the stairs, though, and Meda wasn't about to barrel over her to get in front. Then, once they hit the sidewalk, they encountered two cars parked very close together, offering only a narrow path to the street. Meda was chuckling and frustrated at the same time, unable to outflank the old woman.

"Mrs. Javier, come on," pleaded Meda after failing to jockey for space.

"Nonsense," said Mrs. Javier, waving a dismissive hand. "You wanted to go to the market. And you have to get to work. I've got all day."

"Mrs. Javier," groaned Meda. She knew she could move the branch with about a tenth of the effort as Mrs. Javier; it was silly for the old woman to struggle with it when she could handle it so easily. As stubborn as she was acting, though, Meda couldn't exactly push the woman aside. Instead, she remained at the sidewalk, sulking and with her arms crossed.

Mrs. Javier picked up the branch and began to drag it across the asphalt, an air of determination about her which Meda was loath to squash. "Mrs. Javier. I'm serious," said Meda, "let me help." But now there was no way she could reach the branch without impeding Mrs. Javier's progress. The woman had managed to drag it between the two cars and, with the pathway blocked, it became a one-person job out of necessity.

The seconds continued to tick by, Mrs. Javier grunting and yanking on the branch, while Meda felt more and more awkward with each passing moment. She prayed none of their neighbors could see the scene unfold: Meda standing by idly while the old woman did all the work.

Finally, Mrs. Javier managed to maneuver the tree limb through the gap between the cars and, with a final heave, hurled it on the sidewalk. “There,” she said breathlessly, flashing a proud smile.

Meda smiled back. The whole exercise remained totally unnecessary in her mind. Yet, while she regretted not making a more decisive move for the branch, she could appreciate how symbolically important it was for Mrs. Javier.

After taking a moment to recuperate, however, Mrs. Javier’s eyes wandered back to the street behind her. There were at least seven or eight smaller twigs remaining. They weren’t big enough to affect traffic or do damage but, clearly, Mrs. Javier’s interest was piqued. Her prideful smile still present, she turned and began to amble back into the street.

Again, it took Meda a moment to realize what Mrs. Javier intended to do (it wasn’t enough that the old woman took it upon herself to act as the Parks Department for the block, she also had to be sure the street was returned to its previous, pristine condition). When she did, however, she cocked her head sideways and said, “Mrs. Javier, you’ve got to be kidding me.”

The woman persisted, however, bending painstakingly to pick up each individual twig. If left alone, they probably would’ve blown away anyway. There was no need for Mrs. Javier to trouble herself. But she was undaunted.

“Mrs. Javier,” muttered Meda, taking a few quick steps between the cars toward the road. “At least let me help.”

At that, Mrs. Javier looked up to Meda, her eyes wide and cherubic, her smile gratified. She parted her lips to say something.

Then everything happened too fast. In a blink, Mrs. Javier was gone. There was a deep, dull thud and a rush of movement, a flash of black. And in the time it took Meda to hear and register the rev of the car's engine, Mrs. Javier vanished. Meda shuddered. In shock, frozen. Then she heard a second, lesser thud. And as the car sped away Meda sprinted into the road, screaming for help.

BRYNN

Sometimes the days blended together. Was it Tuesday? Was it Thursday? Did it matter? When Brynn actually had a job it was often as a bartender, so the end of the week for most people signaled the beginning of the week for her. Those positions rarely lasted long, however. Most bar owners were scumbags and, if they weren't, the customers were. In fact, she often spoke with a note of pride about how many bars she'd been fired from. The reality was she'd never really wanted those jobs; they were actually just lame attempts to convince her father she was "doing something with her life." So, as the result of such instability, she eventually stopped worrying about what day it was altogether. Why bother establishing a schedule when it was all going to get demolished soon enough anyway?

"You're so zen," said Devon, her skinny best friend with hair that was too red.

"Actually, I don't believe in religion," said Brynn. "It's always trying to tell people what do."

Devon laughed. "No, zen isn't a religion, silly. It's a state of mind. Like being one with the world and stuff."

"Oh!" said Brynn. "That's okay then."

It was two o'clock in the afternoon and they were on their way to get something to eat. They'd only recently awoken after another amazing night—if asked, they would say it was, "literally amazing." And now they were famished. They didn't know which fast food place they intended to hit but the usual suspects were located within a three block radius. So, for now, they simply headed in that general direction as Brynn waxed intellectual about her reasons for leaving Dorian.

"Anyway, it's like: I'm not actually trying to be zen or to have this, like, big plan or anything," continued Brynn. "I just felt like...we'd been seeing each other on and off for awhile now, right? And we were always doing the same stuff. And actually that's fun and cool, right? But I just didn't have a reason to go back this time. And when I didn't it was like, 'oh, okay' and suddenly everything was different, y'know?"

Devon nodded knowingly.

"So, like...I just haven't been back. That's all. It's funny actually: I feel like there should've been this big momentous thing, right? I mean...we were always fighting, of course. I don't mean, like, just a regular fight, y'know? I mean something bigger, like something crazy going down. But there never was. Instead it was just like, a whimper, not some big explosive thing. Know what I mean?"

"Oh, totally. It's like society expects a couple to have some terrible, dramatic ending: Somebody caught cheating with a best friend, or going to jail, or something. But it doesn't always work out that way."

"Right! You get it."

The autumn afternoon was unusually warm and the desiccated concrete sidewalk mirrored the cotton-mouth each was suffering. On one side of the pair was a two-lane highway with cars speeding past and, on the other, was the concrete wall of a large industrial building. For most it would've felt confining and claustrophobic; though there was a sidewalk present, few pedestrians actually used it. Yet the pair ambled along, oblivious to their precarious position.

They approached an intersection where another two-lane highway crossed and, at the light, a car came to a halt a few feet in front of them. Neither had been paying attention to the cars zooming past so, at first, neither took particular notice of the car or its driver. Then, with it idling in their path as they began to cross, Devon squeaked a tentative, "Randy?"

Brynn thought she'd misheard Devon and was a second late realizing it was, in fact, Randy behind the wheel. For his part, he appeared as if he hadn't noticed the girls either and, upon hearing Devon say his name, he mumbled, "Huh. Oh…hey."

"Heyyyyy!" cooed Devon. She wobbled to the car, came to a stop, and then stood beside it awkwardly. It was clear she wanted to reach through the open window and hug him but he hadn't reciprocated the invitation.

Brynn, initially surprised, crossed her arms and cocked her head to the side.

"How are you, baby?" gushed Devon, still marveling at the serendipity.

"I'm great. Damn. Good to see you, sweetie," he said, clearly caught flat-footed by the encounter. He glanced at the red light overhead and added, "We gonna see each other tonight?"

"Totally!" said Devon, nodding and smiling.

"Okay. Cool. I, uh…think I gotta go soon," said Randy, pointing to the light.

"Sure. Sure, okay," said Devon.

The light turned green and, after a clumsy nod, Randy drove away. Devon took a couple steps backward to get out of the street and for a long time neither spoke.

Then: "You're seeing him again?" It was not so much of a question from Brynn as it was an accusation.

"What?" said Devon, avoiding eye contact.

Brynn frowned. She was disappointed to learn her friend was back with that bastard but she was even more bummed that Devon had hidden it from her. "How has he been?" she asked stone-faced.

"He's been great!" said Devon, over-enthusiastically. "He really has changed. For real."

Brynn stared at her. Devon met her eyes, looked away, then peered up at the traffic light. It turned red again, signaling they could cross, and Devon glanced back at Brynn as if to suggest they should proceed. Brynn hesitated, a step behind Devon, and then began to trudge forward. She wanted to talk some sense into Devon, to stop her before something awful happened. But what could she do?

The pair eventually got something to eat, did some meth at a friend's apartment and, when Devon left to be with Randy, Brynn stayed behind to smoke even more.

⋈ ⋈ ⋈

Brynn wasn't sure what made her happy. Sure, a good meth buzz was a priority and she loved to hang out with her friends. Late night fast food was another item high on that list. But on a deeper, more fundamental level, as much as she might enjoy transitory contentment, she feared she had no idea what true satisfaction entailed.

On TV it seemed like everyone had some dream they were trying to attain or some overarching goal in their life. Brynn didn't know anyone like that, though. Sure, Walter claimed to be a writer, even though she'd never read a single page of his work, and, okay, Kevin used to have his eyes set on the NFL before flunking out of college. Hell, when she was younger, even Brynn had, alternately, wanted to be an actress or play music in a band. But those ideas seemed so distant now, so juvenile. She didn't need fake, media-created notions of happiness to be satisfied. And upon consulting the internet, Brynn found that Devon was correct when she'd told her she was zen—she pretty much did just flow from moment to moment. Why buy into all those silly dreams they tell kids they can reach? Better to have no expectations and, therefore, have no disappointment. If that was zen, Brynn was glad to be it.

While not exactly a goal she was working to achieve, she knew she needed to leave her godforsaken town, though. It totally sucked. If she could get to a bigger city like Scranton or New York City she'd at least have a chance to do something. Her father lived in Connecticut and was never coming back. The money he sent was more important than his presence anyway. The only other person she knew who'd left—without eventually returning—was her scientist uncle who'd moved to Switzerland. But he was a total weirdo. She didn't view his escape the same way she viewed her father's.

A number of days had passed since she'd last seen Dorian. The pair had been on-and-off practically from the start, it seemed, yet inevitably she always found herself stumbling back to him. He was a drama queen and he thought way too much of himself but at least there was safety with him. He never got violent with her or became one of those guys that slept around with other girls. It just wasn't in his genes. She'd always come to the conclusion—after every mean comment, after every stupid dispute about money—that it was better to get high on the sofa with Dorian than to get smacked around by some guy with six-packs abs and designer clothes.

So she wasn't sure why she hadn't gone back to him this time. Yeah, he'd hurt her feelings. Yeah, she was more-than-tired of supporting his lazy ass. And yeah, it'd all stopped being fun a long time ago. But it wasn't as if he'd crossed some line or done something unforgivable. As she'd explained to Devon, she just didn't feel like going back to him. Why seek him out for another round of reconciliation when it was just easier not to?

It was midday and it looked like another terrible bright and sunny one outside. She was so sick of this heat! It was the Fall! Go away, summer! The cardboard duct-taped in front of the windows blocked most of the light yet, on days like this, the few rays that managed to break through appeared all the more searing. She was wearing only her sweatpants and bra when there came a tapping at her door. What now? No one came to her apartment at such an hour. "One second," she moaned, shuffling back to her room to find a shirt.

She was still in the process of pulling down her shirt when, upon cracking open the door, Devon collapsed into her. Reflexively, Brynn hugged her, holding her aloft, and that was the only thing that kept her from falling to the hard tiles of the basement floor. "Oh my God, I'm so glad you're home, Brynn!" gushed Devon.

"Whoa, whoa, whoa!" said Brynn, startled by the entrance. "I got you."

"I didn't know where else to go," continued Devon, still in Brynn's arms.

Brynn hadn't gotten a good look at her when she'd crashed in but, with a moment to process the streaks of makeup, she realized Devon had been crying. And she was craning her neck at an odd angle, hiding her face.

"Holy crap. Are you okay?" asked Brynn, using her finger to guide Devon's chin to get a better view of her face. The damage was apparent instantly. One side of her face was swollen like a prizefighter's, her eye nearly shut. The makeup made the effect worse: While half of her face was clean, the bruised, swollen side still had black rivulets streaming around the outside of her cheek, as if Devon was afraid to touch it. Brynn was all but speechless, saying simply, "Devon?"

Devon only nodded, still weeping. Her lips pursed as if she was about to say something but no words came forth.

Then Brynn noticed the marks on her neck. Four small scratches, aligning perfectly with the fingers of a person's hand, ran down the left side of Devon's throat. They didn't appear as horrific as Devon's cheek but the implication was, in its own way, worse.

"Oh my God! Devon!" she cried, pulling her friend close to her again. It was a maternal reflex as Brynn put it all together. Devon sobbed with renewed intensity and, after kicking shut the front door, Brynn guided her to the couch. "Come in, girl. Come in."

Brynn sat beside her on the couch, heartbroken and awash in anguish for her friend. But that sorrow was quickly turning to anger. And the anger was growing.

"It was Randy, wasn't it?"

Devon said nothing but nodded ever so slighted. She looked embarrassed. She looked terrified. Worst of all, she looked weak.

"That bastard," Brynn muttered through clenched teeth. Her hands balled into fists and her muscles tensed. She didn't know what to do with herself; she just wanted to rage, to destroy.

And then Devon whispered, "It'll be okay."

Brynn glared at her. "What?" she hollered in disbelief, Devon cringing at the intensity. Then, without forethought or an actual goal, Brynn leapt from the couch. And emitting a bestial growl, she punched the wall, her fist easily puncturing the drywall.

"Brynn!" shouted Devon in disbelief.

It didn't achieve catharsis, however. Instead, Brynn's rage only continued to multiply at the thought that Devon intended to go back to him. Here she was, with a bashed-in cheek and choke marks on her neck, and she'd already decided it was going to be okay?

"He. He did this?" said Brynn. It was only a half-question and she didn't wait for a confirmation. "Have you gone to the police? You have to press charges. Look what he did to you. He could've killed you. This is serious. Come on, Devon."

Throughout Devon was shaking her head from side to side, however. It began lightly at first but then grew more pronounced as Brynn continued. It transmuted Brynn's fervor, even as her words continued to shoot forth in rapid succession. Despite her initial fury, she could see what Devon's protests meant. Brynn's expressions became more pleading, more desperate and, when she was done, she slumped down next to Devon with wide, imploring eyes. The implication was clear: She couldn't force Devon to press charges against Randy. She couldn't make her leave him. Moments earlier she could barely contain her rage yet, now, she was overcome by a resigned sadness. Anger implied she could do something, that she could put such frustration to use somehow. Yet if Devon was unwilling to make a change, Brynn realized, she was going to lose her friend.

⋈ ⋈ ⋈

Randy had to die. It was the only logical conclusion. Devon had returned to him at least five times and each time the violence had escalated further. Brynn saw what Randy was about, saw he would never change, no matter what lies he told Devon. There was a cycle at work and she knew Devon would never break herself out of it unless something terrible happened. The police couldn't help: If she called them, not only would Devon refuse to help the investigation but Randy would blame Devon for getting him in trouble. No, this was something Brynn had to do on her own. If the situation had to end in tragedy, Brynn was going to make damn sure it happened to Randy and not her friend.

Brynn's main problem was that she didn't have a clue how to author such a plan, no idea where to even begin. She'd never fired a gun. Of course, any plan to use a gun presupposed she'd either have access to one or possessed the ability to obtain one. She didn't. Running him over with a car was an option but it involved too much risk: Brynn was terrified she would accidentally hit someone else in the process and, further, she didn't trust her ability to get away from the scene once she did the deed. Besides, those ideas were too silly; this was serious business.

Brynn spent the ensuing twenty hours obsessing about Devon's situation. In fact, after Devon left, she smoked up by herself and never left the apartment. Then, throughout the night, she scrawled figments of plans across a wild assortment of papers, mailings, and anything else nearby. Some included detailed minutia of certain aspects of a plan while others were more akin to wide-open philosophical questions. And, upon reviewing these notes the next morning, Brynn quickly realized virtually all were unfeasible or downright moronic. It wasn't like television: She couldn't just decide to do something in a rage and expect it to work out. This needed careful planning. And that was something she had never excelled at, exactly.

Discouraged, she found herself sitting on the floor in the kitchen with her back against the cabinet below the sink. Gradually, she began to see the idea, the whole notion of killing Randy as a microcosm of her life. There was silly little Brynn, with all these big plans and all this fire and drive to get something done...except she always got lost in dumb details and frivolous distraction. She imagined the other students from high school and former co-workers laughing at all the crazy notes she'd written, many completely illegible.

She was just brain storming! Come on! They weren't meant to be fully reasoned plans or anything. Yet this was always the way it seemed to go; Brynn couldn't deny the evidence right in front of her. There was always some big inspiration, some reason to get super excited, yet in the end it always amounted to crap. It made her want to vomit.

Unsure what to do next, she peered about her apartment. It struck her how, as her gaze passed from item to item, nothing was right. Everything she surveyed had some sort of asterisk attached to it: The table she'd found on the street with the wobbly leg, the ashtray Dorian had made for her that he'd proceeded to break, the gas stove that needed matches to light because the ignition was defective. She had totally reasonable explanations why the water leak inside the wall hadn't been fixed and why her dirty laundry was stacked in the kitchen corner, but none of those excuses seemed to help now.

It was the concomitant weight of those flawed items, each whispering, "failure," that overwhelmed Brynn. She felt ashamed, helpless. Tears welled up and her shoulder blades tightened. Why couldn't anything ever go right? This was her best friend! She didn't want Devon to be another broken ashtray, another broken appliance!

She punched the cabinet behind her. It was childish and awkward, the bottom of her fist connecting with the door to her back. But at least it was some sort of release. The movement caused her tears to break free and stream down her cheeks, and she quickly rubbed them away with the back of her hand. It was all too stupid, too dispiriting. Could she do anything right, ever?

With her forearm against her cheek she glanced down, sniffing hard. In the process she noticed that the cabinet door had been knocked open by her punch and, as the result, she spied something inside. For a long moment she peered at it, impassive. Her tears began to dry and the sorrow in her expression changed, morphing to a calculating stare.

The item which had elicited such a reaction was a canister of chemicals used to unclog blocked drains or pipes. Specifically: The crystalline form of them. Crystals that appeared very similar to certain types of meth. Brynn's mind began to formulate a vague notion of a plan and, reaching in to retrieve the container, she also spied a bottle of bleach in back of it. Even better!

She lurched away from the door and pulled out both items at once. She had forgotten she even had these! She unscrewed the top of the drain opener and peered in. The crystals were too large and had a different texture: Anyone who'd done meth more than a handful of times would see the difference immediately.

But. What if she poured just a little bit of the bleach over the crystals? Just enough to reduce their size a tiny, tiny bit and, maybe, make them seem a little more weathered, as if someone had been carrying them around in their pocket awhile? It was worth a shot, right?

Brynn stood up and plopped both items on the countertop. With jittery vigor—she had a plan!—she threw open the cupboard door above the sink and yanked out an old takeout container. She placed it on the countertop and poured in the crystals, her mouth forming a cute 'O' as she did so. Next, she opened the bleach and eyed it up excitedly, holding the bottle with both hands as an added precaution. She tilted it and let a few droplets fall over the crystals—carefully, carefully, she didn't want to make soup!

Immediately she smelled something acrid and foul, and smiled to herself. It was working!

Then her phone rang. She frowned, peering first at it and then at the crystals in front of her. Initially, the timing seemed awful and she didn't want to be bothered. After a moment's consideration, though, she realized she'd probably poured enough anyway. The crystals were different already and some were beginning to meld together. That was good: She could break them apart later and make them look even more like real meth.

Satisfied, she darted across the apartment to retrieve her phone, now on its third ring.

"Hey, it's me," said Devon, before continuing apprehensively. "I...I've got something I wanted to ask you. Do you think—Would you be able to come out and meet up with Randy and me? We've talked a lot. A lot. I know you don't like him. But I want you to see that he's changed. I want you to see the real him, y'know? Can you do this? For me?"

"Yes. Yes, I think I can," said Brynn with a sly, nefarious grin.

In fact, on the entire walk to the restaurant, the grin never left her face. She wasn't sure if the crystals would actually kill Randy. If she had more time, she might've done some research. But she knew, at the very least, smoking those chemicals would make him sick. That meant he'd have to go to the hospital and, when they asked him why he smoked the stuff, he'd have to admit he was a junkie. Then, once the cops arrested him, Devon would be safe with him behind bars. Brynn had it all figured out. She couldn't have been more proud.

For perhaps the first time in her life she arrived early for an event. She checked her phone and realized it was a full fifteen minutes before the time Devon suggested. That was okay, though. The restaurant had a nice outdoor seating area and, in the late morning, it wasn't crowded. It gave Brynn a chance to get settled before her friend and the asshole showed up.

The hardest part of the plan would be sneaking the chemicals into Randy's wallet. From previous experience, Brynn knew he kept his ice in a hidden flap inside his wallet. That meant that, while she had an obvious place to put it, she nonetheless had no idea how to separate him from the wallet. It was often in the back pocket of his jeans and Brynn couldn't exactly mug the guy to get it. She had a vague idea that she might be able to get to it if he paid the check. But it wasn't a fully realized plan.

She decided to go to the bathroom. The morning was unusually hot and, combined with her hike to the restaurant, she'd begun to sweat. If her goal was to play it cool, calm, and collected, a sweaty brow was the last thing she needed.

Once inside, her conspiratorial mindset went into high gear. There was no one else around and, unhurried, she took her time preparing. She was reminded of a scene in a movie in which a gun was taped to the back of the toilet; she imagined a crime boss counting on her to take out the rat. It gave her a sense of purpose, a feeling like she was on the verge of something important. In the mirror, she stared into her eyes with fierce intensity and began mouthing the lyrics to one of her favorite hardcore songs. This was actually going to happen. She was going to make it happen.

Marching from the bathroom through the restaurant, she held her head high and stared straight ahead. One of the waitresses eyed her up with an odd expression and Brynn merely nodded. She was going to save her friend, whether her friend wanted to be saved or not!

When she arrived at the outdoor seating area, however, she had trouble locating her table. She couldn't remember its precise location and, adding to her confusion, it appeared as if a couple of plastic chairs had been knocked over. Then, her gait slowing, she realized the vacant area between those chairs was where her table had been. And that it now lay smashed on the asphalt below.

"Ma'am," said someone, but Brynn only barely heard the voice. Instead, she became laser-focused, scanning the area surrounding the broken table but not locating her purse anywhere.

"No," she said, as she picked up speed again. And she rushed towards the remains of the table, all the while muttering, "No, no, no."

"I'm sorry," continued the voice behind her. "This man. I think he stole your purse."

"Noooooo," cried Brynn in a defeated howl. This couldn't be happening! Her eyes fixated on the asphalt. Even as she moved closer to the wreck, she felt like she was going nowhere and, without intending to do so, her stride reverted to a bedraggled shuffle.

"I'm sorry, ma'am," continued the annoying voice. "You might want to call your bank and credit cards. You can use our phone. No problem."

It was like a different language to Brynn's ears. Bank? Credit Cards? What was the woman even talking about? She wanted her chemical concoction! She wanted to kill Randy! She wanted to finally do something with her life!

"We got a description of the man. Ma'am?"

That stupid voice! Shut up! Shut up!

But then, as if to grant her wish, the voice actually stayed quiet for a moment. And when it came back again, it sounded completely different, as if in a state of awe. "...holy crap...."

Brynn didn't care though. The tone of the voice didn't matter. What it said didn't matter. Everything was ruined. And as she continued to stare at the dilapidated wreck of the cheap plastic table, her purse nowhere in sight, she never saw the radiant, voracious light devour the horizon.

MATT

Seven cups of coffee later, with the morning sun poking through the clouds, Matt completed his second story in a three-day span. He hadn't anticipated such output but he wasn't about to slow down work on Brynn's tale once it took off. So lost in his work, he'd called in sick to his office yet again, summarily dismissed calls and texts from loved ones, and barely eaten. He didn't need a mirror to know how atrocious he looked—apart from the lack of nutrition, he hadn't shaved in days and had only taken one quick shower. Making matters worse, his writing sometimes took on qualities normally associated with athletic training. He might find himself pacing about the room, possessed by a coiled, pent-up vigor, before leaping to the keyboard again with frenetic abandon. Copious amounts of caffeine only made the mania worse. It was exhilarating, of course, but it was also a little creepy.

Eventually, when satisfied his output was exhausted, Matt tore himself away from the keyboard and took a shower. It was already past eight o'clock so he was bound to be late for work anyway. And, when he hit the sidewalk, he strode down it swiftly, confidently. He passed a burlap bag slumped next to a garbage can and, naturally, presumed it to be full of human body parts. Or a lost million dollars. One or the other. A black car idled by the side of the road and Matt assumed a husband, eager to pick up flowers for his wife's birthday, had unintentionally left it running in his haste. With a knowing smile, he inwardly applauded the man's efforts.

Then, when he emerged from the subway into the concrete of Manhattan, he tried to recall where he'd left off on key projects at work. Very quickly, it became evident that he was in a completely different mental state than the last time he'd been in the office. He'd reached an almost dangerous level of bliss and, now reminded of pragmatic, hum-drum concerns at work, it was hard to take them seriously. He found himself walking amidst a small herd of people and—as if it was an ancient memory from years past—he remembered he had to send an email Donna about the faulty BDT file processing.

The moving cluster of people continued through another intersection, some people in the group passing Matt, and his thoughts turned to the dreaded Dispensation Evaluation Update Meeting. Ugh—an hour of his day gone before he even stepped through the door. Still advancing, the entire cluster was now in front of him as they approached yet another intersection. Matt reminded himself to stop by Derek's cubicle since that was the only way to get the guy's attention. Then Matt was shoved to the ground.

It was sudden. Too sudden for his mind to process. He'd been walking. He'd felt a pressure on his back. And suddenly the ground was hurtling up towards him. He'd only barely gotten a hand up in time to break his fall and, before he could take stock of what'd happened, a loud, black car flashed past less than a foot from his head.

"Shit!" Matt cried. He shot his gaze about: The pack of people was on the other side of the intersection, marching on obliviously. The black car was tearing down the street, nearly out of sight already. And then, when he peered upward, his stare stopped and stayed in place. It was The Stoic Man, peering down at him impassively.

"You?" said Matt. His initial, knee-jerk response was anger—someone had pushed him! He quickly realized, though, that the shove had probably saved his life and a sense of gratitude overrode his anger. Then, when he saw The Stoic Man once again, he didn't know how to feel or what to say.

Matt pushed himself up off the concrete, staring at the man the entire time as one might a wild animal. It was obvious he'd saved him from the speeding car—Matt would've walked directly into its path. But why was the man there at that precise moment? What did he want?

"Th-thank you," said Matt, finally.

The man didn't reply. Instead, he only continued to stare back, his face bereft of emotion. All background noise fell away and in that moment, on a busy Manhattan street corner, Matt felt as if only he and the man were present.

"I don't understand," Matt blurted plaintively. Countless questions burst forth in his mind—it was impossible to settle on the single most important one. He was grateful for the man's intervention but dumbstruck by the serendipity of yet another appearance. And making matters worse was his sense of disappointment: Matt had finally come to terms with the car accident and the little boy! The weirdness in his life should be over!

The moment stretched on and, almost imperceptibly, the man seemed to lean in towards Matt. His feet didn't move yet somehow it felt as if he was closer and the lack of emotion on his face made the pseudo-movement all the more menacing. In fact, Matt was about to take a cautious step backward when the man, in a droll voice, said, "If you want to save the boy, you have to save yourself first."

Matt was rendered speechless. Still eye-to-eye with the man, he started at least three sentences but finished none. He wanted to ask the man what he meant, why he saved him, why he was there in the first place. He needed someone to tell him what the hell was going on but the only sentence he could produce was, "What the hell?"

Then, his phone came to life, both vibrating and jangling from inside his coat pocket. Matt sneered downward at the distraction, at the vicious timing of it. The Stoic Man said nothing more, however, and the phone rang again. Matt continued to eye up his sphinxlike counterpart but he was losing the battle—he had to do something about the phone. It rang a third time and, his lips pursed, Matt shoved his hand into his pocket and yanked it out. It was Meda.

"Hello?"

"Matt?" said Meda, her voice rising in distress. "Mrs. Javier is dead. She got hit by a car. Right in front of me."

Matt's world swirled all over again. Immediately he recognized the anguish in Meda's voice—so much that it took the briefest moment to remember who Mrs. Javier was. The shift in his mental gears was dramatic as he swerved from confused agitation at the Stoic Man's appearance to empathetic concern for Meda. "Oh no," he muttered.

"We were outside. She was fine. Everything was fine. Then this car. It came out of nowhere," said Meda in a rapid release.

Fifteen seconds earlier Matt had nearly been run over. Now Meda was on the phone in obvious shock. Matt's mind was paralyzed by options, too many to count. He managed to ask, "Did you call the police? Are you okay?"

"Yes. Yes," Meda replied. "The police are on the way. I'm fine. Physically, I'm fine. But Mrs. Javier. She's dead, Matt. She's dead!"

Without thought, Matt replied, "Hang on, honey. I'll be right there." It was an emotional reply, a knee-jerk response in the face of too many variables. Then, when he hung up, he took a deep breath and asked: Where was I?

It all came crashing back. Empathy for Meda had momentarily overridden his previous mental state but then, with a jolt, that sense of abject stupefaction returned. Questions sprung forth with renewed force and he readied to pick up where he'd left off. But, when he turned to address the Stoic Man again, he was nowhere in sight.

MATT

Matt glared back at the subway entrance. He needed to get to Meda, work responsibilities and questions about the Stoic Man be damned. Before he took a step, however, his phone began to ring yet again. Presuming it to be Meda—perhaps with something important she'd forgotten to tell him—he pulled it out and answered.

"Matt. It's Magee. We have to talk."

Matt grimaced and began walking towards the subway. "Hey Magee. Listen, I've got an emergency. I can't talk now."

"No, it's important," Magee insisted.

"Magee, whatever it is, it can't be that important. Meda just saw her neighbor die. I'm on way to see her now."

"Matt. It involves the boy. And the Armenians."

Matt stopped walking.

"I got more information," Magee continued. "I didn't think you were taking my warning seriously so I went to see Sergei at his apartment."

"Go on," said Matt.

"Well, I saw the video."

Now Magee had Matt's full attention and, with pedestrians nearly careening into him, Matt stepped into a doorway to avoid the foot traffic. "What?"

"I saw it," Magee confirmed. "It's from the night you hit the kid. Matt, I have a question and I need you to answer me honestly."

"Okay," said Matt tentatively, the gravity in Magee's tone a red flag.

"Did you get out of the car that night?"

The question was more straightforward than he'd expected and, after considering it only briefly, Matt replied, "Yeah. I did. I needed to check on the boy. Why?"

"Damn," muttered Magee.

"Why?" Matt asked again, after Magee said nothing more. "Why is that important?"

"Matt, you're on the video taken by their friend. Sergei paused the recording. It's clearly you."

Matt's brow furrowed. He wasn't connecting the dots.

"And the guy," continued Magee, "the one who took the video...he was stabbed that night."

Magee's statement dropped like a pallet of bricks in the middle of Park Avenue. "Wait. Stabbed?" Matt didn't even remember the man, much less anyone getting stabbed. "What?"

"It's why they think you did it, buddy. It's why the Armenians are after you." Magee paused and, with renewed earnestness, asked, "Matt, what happened that night? Tell me what *really* happened."

Matt listened and a sense of defensiveness arose within him. It was becoming clear Magee still had reservations about his version of the events and, perhaps, was entertaining the thought that he'd stabbed a man. So, with mild indignation, Matt began, "Okay, for starters, I don't remember anybody else there beyond myself and the boy. I searched the area. I'm positive no one else was present. So I have no idea how this guy managed to record me. And with regard to stabbing him, that's not even an option. I mean—disregarding the fact that I didn't even see the guy—it's not like I carry a knife. I wouldn't have had anything to stab him *with*! None of this makes any sense. There has to be some other explanation."

Magee was silent throughout. And the lack of response only served to make Matt feel more insecure, to keep him talking to the point of nearly blathering. In the space of a minute he had nearly been run over, had been saved by the

Stoic Man, and had learned that Meda'd witnessed a woman die. This new revelation was too much to take.

"I don't know what to tell you, buddy," said Magee, finally. "I saw the tape. It was definitely you. So either the man was there and you didn't see him or you're misremembering something. You were probably pretty traumatized. Didn't you say you felt like you were drugged?"

It felt as if Magee was making excuses for him, ones that were wholly unnecessary, and Matt didn't appreciate it. "Wait," he said, more confrontationally, "are you actually suggesting I might've stabbed somebody?"

"No, no, no," said Magee quickly, before adding. "I just think...there may be something more to the story. Maybe you're forgetting something. I don't know."

Matt glared up and down the sidewalk, as if to find a place to direct his ire. He couldn't believe Magee might actually think he'd stabbed someone. And, in the back of his mind, he also recognized that he couldn't stand around debating such a preposterous claim while Meda waited. "I'm sorry," said Matt, "I have to get to Meda. We'll talk about this more. I just can't do it right now. Can I call you later?"

"Yeah. Sure. Of course, buddy," said Magee, recognizing Matt's irritation.

They hung up and Matt stalked off to the subway, his mind underwater. The jarring suddenness of the series of events—one on top of the other, without the ability to adequately process any of them—made him feel like he'd awoken from a dream, like he needed to ascertain what was real and what was imaginary.

Meda saw her elderly neighbor die—that definitely happened. It was why he was headed to see her. He was nearly run over—that also definitely happened. He saw the car roar past with his own eyes, felt the blast of hot exhaust on his face.

But with regard to the events on that fateful night, the haze remained.

Matt was positive the boy hadn't died—of that, he remained certain. But what about the man Magee mentioned? Matt was nearly positive no one else was present that night. As Magee had hinted, though, he hadn't been in a sound state of mind. It's possible he might not have seen the man while his eyes were still adjusting. But how did the man get stabbed? As Matt noted, he wouldn't have had anything to stab him with.

Except. The memory, that of the knives—two bloody knives—lying in the street. Amidst the clamor of the subway car, the image flashed in his mind's eye. He'd virtually forgotten the knives; they'd become a recollection tucked away behind the more important memories of the night. At the moment he saw them, he was still trying to locate the boy. They'd been a peculiar sight but, in terms of priorities, ascertaining the whereabouts of the boy had been at the forefront. A sense of dread swelled inside him and doubt about his story began to creep in. Why hadn't he taken the time to figure out why two bloody knives were lying in the street? How could he have overlooked such an important detail?

He reviewed the night's events for perhaps the thousandth time, his memories still as fuzzy as ever. There was the moment he struck the boy. Then the moment his car came to a screeching halt. He recalled jumping out of it and realizing he couldn't see the area well in the halo of the streetlight. He remembered running, zig-zagging like a crazy person, trying to get a better view of the street. And he remembered the sound of his ragged breath.

Wait. How *had* his breath become so ragged in the first place? He shouldn't have been winded so easily. Why was he so short of air after sprinting such a short distance? His thoughts churned. Something was wrong. It didn't add up.

He focused more fully on the gasps he'd heard. He was positive he remembered hearing the sound of heaving, exhausted breaths that night. But what if he wasn't the source of them? And, if he wasn't, from where else might they have originated? Try as he might to avoid accepting it, he recognized the immediate implication—if the hoarse gasps had indeed come from the other man, how had Matt been close enough to hear them so distinctly?

Matt's subway stop was coming up. Finally, he'd be able to reach Meda and comfort her. Yet, within Matt, everything had changed. He now saw himself as a completely different person. Rather than a loving boyfriend rushing to console his distraught love, he was, instead, the perpetrator of a vicious stabbing.

MEDA

Meda sat on the stoop of her building staring blank-faced at the sidewalk. It was the same point at which she'd run into Mrs. Javier so often and a dark sense of guilt hung over her when she remembered her annoyance at the old woman's presence. She'd never been exactly friends with the woman, yet she was still having trouble coming to terms with the fact that she'd never be there to greet her again. The absence was much greater than she ever would've expected.

The police had arrived on the scene after her frantic 911 call, quickly followed by an ambulance. The officers were perfectly professional and had taken her statement of the events. Of course there'd been a flurry of neighbors and gawkers appearing in droves (seriously, guy in the Jets hat: Get out of the way when the paramedics are trying to work). The exact moment Mrs. Javier was struck had been so unreal but, after that, everything had shot into a sort of hyper-reality once the authorities took over. It was ugly and tragic and far too real.

"Honey?" came the voice. Meda looked up. It was Matt.

Meda jumped and took three quick steps before collapsing into him. She didn't cry, as she thought she might. Instead, she let out a long exhalation, one she felt like she'd been holding for hours. She didn't need him to ride in on a white horse to save her. She just needed the paralyzing absence to end.

"Hon, hon, I'm so sorry," said Matt, clutching her to him. "How're you doing?"

Meda took a moment to answer. Time was not of the essence. When she was ready she pulled just far enough away to look him in the eyes and whispered, "I'm okay. It's just been a lot. A lot to deal with."

"You can tell me about it when you're ready," said Matt. "Let's just get inside."

They made their way up to her apartment in contended silence. It was traumatizing to see such a wonderful woman die in such a terrible way and she wasn't sure if she would ever get some of those images out of her memories. But at least Matt's presence made her feel like she could begin to recover.

"Mrs. Javier and I," began Meda, without any prompting from Matt, "we were just outside talking. Like it was any other day. Then a tree branch fell. And, I don't know, Mrs. Javier wanted to get it off the sidewalk. I went to help her. But it all happened so fast. I didn't expect."

Meda's lip quivered and she began to shake her head, as if ruing her lack of urgency. Matt sensed her turmoil and said, "Come on honey, there's no way you could've seen it coming."

"That's just it," said Meda, her eyes growing wide as if to emote her sense of helplessness. "I never expected it. Who would? It happened so fast. One second Mrs. Javier was standing there talking to me and the next second this black car flashed by."

Meda trailed off, shaking her head again. Yet something in Matt's expression changed, a sense of inquisitiveness taking over it. "A black car? What kind of black car?"

"I don't know," said Meda with a shrug. "Like I said, it all happened so fast."

"No, I mean," insisted Matt, "was it a sedan? A sports car?"

"I don't remember, Matt," said Meda, growing agitated at the specificity of such details. "Why?"

"I ask," said Matt, "because I was almost run over this morning, too. And it was also a black car."

Meda bristled. (Does every story have to be about Matt? We were talking about Mrs. Javier here.) "What? What happened?"

"I was on my way to work. My mind was wandering and I was in my own world. Then this car revved up, out of nowhere, as if it was trying to hit me." Meda was reminded how the car that struck Mrs. Javier had revved its engine up as well and Matt saw the mild change in her demeanor. "What is it?"

Meda cocked her head to one side. She didn't want to get into this, she didn't want to entertain wild conspiracy theories anymore. Mrs. Javier was dead and it was a cold, terrible reality. Since Matt noticed her expression, though, she felt compelled to tell him. "It's not a big deal," she said, "but when Mrs. Javier was struck, I remember the car revving, like you just said. There was no brake squeal, no attempt to stop."

Matt listened intently, then asked, "You think she might've been run over on purpose?"

"No. No. I didn't say that," insisted Meda. "It just caught my attention when you mentioned the rev of the car's engine. That's all." But it was too late. She could intuit that Matt's mind was racing.

Matt saw she wanted to move off the topic and pleaded, "Wait. Hear me out. There's more to it."

"Okay."

"It's not simply the fact that Mrs. Javier was hit and that I was almost hit. It's important to remember both events were happening this morning at virtually the same time. The only reason I wasn't hit was because someone saved me." Matt appeared to waver, biting his lip momentarily as if to consider his words. "A man, he pushed me to the ground just before the car sped past."

Meda didn't want to appear unsympathetic. She was concerned for his safety and all. Yet his rambling was testing her patience against the backdrop of Mrs. Javier's passing.

When Meda said nothing, Matt continued. "What I'm saying is that, in both cases, it seems like the car was purposefully trying to run someone over. I was saved by that man. What if the car that hit Mrs. Javier wasn't intended for her? What if it meant to hit *you*?"

The question gave Meda pause. She hadn't even considered that. She didn't want to appropriate Mrs. Javier's passing to a narrative which shoved her to its center. But, recalling the details, she remembered that she had been jumping to Mrs. Javier's aid at the moment she was struck.

"And there's more," said Matt, gravely. Meda raised an eyebrow as if to tell him to go on. "I got a call from Magee on the way here. He'd tried to warn me that the Armenian mafia was out to get me."

"What?" said Meda, her burgeoning curiosity obliterated in an instant.

"I had the same reaction! I didn't take it seriously. Check it out, though, this is where it gets crazy: Magee knew that I hadn't taken his previous warning to heart so he did some more digging. He'd already been beaten up pretty bad once but he went to this ticket broker anyway. And the guy had a video recording from that night I hit the boy. Apparently the Armenians have it, too. And Meda: I'm on it."

Meda continued to listen, her stance combative with her fist notched into her hip.

"That night? I don't think I can trust my own memories. You know how I hit the boy, of course. But there's a second part to it." Matt paused for a beat, his eyes cast downward. "I—I can't believe this happened but, it's all there on the recording: I think I stabbed someone."

"What?" cried Meda, incredulous, angry.

"I didn't want to believe it myself. But Magee told me: I was definitely on the tape. This man that was stabbed? He was part of the Armenian mafia. That's why they're after us, you and me. They have the tape and they're finally catching up with us now. That night—though everything is such a blur—I do remember two bloody knives. I'd forgotten about them; probably on purpose, at some level. My mind couldn't handle the fact that I stabbed a man."

"No. No. No," Meda erupted, waving her hands in the air as if to physically wipe away everything Matt had just spewed. "I don't want to hear any more about this! I'm sorry, Matt, but I'm dealing with something *real* here. Mrs. Javier is dead. She died right in front of me. I'm still processing it. I'm still coming to terms with the fact that another human being is dead. So I don't have the time or the ability to deal with this. I'm sorry."

Matt was taken aback at her intensity but he continued. "I know it's hard to believe. But I'm right there on the tape. A guy was stabbed and he died that night. That's also real."

"You idiot," shot Meda in a tone which seethed with vitriol and disappointment. "If you stabbed this man, where was the blood? Did you have a single drop of blood on your clothes?"

"Well, no. But I was the only one there that night! There was no one else there to stab him."

At that Meda paused, her angry veneer giving way to one that was more pensive. She peered at Matt and, sensing the change, he waited for her to speak first. For Meda, it didn't seem like the time or place to entertain zany conspiracy theories yet she was stunned by the implications of her realization. And finally, she said, "Well, there was one other person there."

The comment entirely reframed the conversation. It was as if the Buddha himself had entered the room and both Matt and Meda became almost reverentially silent. The revelatory moment stretched on and it was clear that Matt was registering all of the implications as well.

Then, breaking the pin-drop silence, Matt said weakly, "You're suggesting that, if *I* wasn't the one who stabbed the man—"

"Yes," affirmed Meda, encouraging him to continue.

"That the only other person that could have done it—"

"Yes."

"Was the little boy?"

"Yes."

MATT

The thought that the boy had stabbed the man forced a sea change in Matt's worldview. Since the night of the accident, he had imagined the little boy as a passive, innocent victim—an inactive player in the whole drama. He'd never dreamt the boy may've been guilty of any wrongdoing himself.

"We have to talk to Magee," said Meda. "We have to get him on the phone with the ticket broker and explain that you didn't stab anyone. While you might be seen on the recording, the only reason you were there was because you'd pulled over after hitting the boy. You were in a car, driving. There was no way you could've stabbed him."

Matt could see she'd shifted into, "work mode," as if preparing to hammer out a plan of action with a problematic supplier. It wasn't a bad thing—her focus was on the facts, no nonsense. Yet it made Matt's hesitation that much harder to articulate. He recalled the image of that angry, toad-like man at the bar and he wasn't sure it was a good idea to contact Sergei. Clearly, Magee trusted him. Matt wasn't as convinced.

In the face of Matt's ponderous delay, though, Meda lost patience and reached across him in an attempt to snatch his phone from his pocket. "Oh, for the love of God, give me your phone. I'll call him."

"No, no," said Matt, drawing back and pulling out the phone himself. "I'll call, I'll call."

He dialed Magee's number and put it on speaker mode so both he and Meda could hear. "Magee, it's Matt. I'm here with Meda. We talked about the video, the one from the ticket broker."

"Sergei?"

"Yeah. We both know I didn't stab that guy, right?"

Matt waited for the confirmation from Magee and, after the briefest pause, he acceded, “Right.”

“Well Meda pointed out—I hadn’t even considered it—that the little boy might’ve done it. He might’ve stabbed the guy before I even got there.”

“The boy?” asked Magee, as if he couldn’t comprehend it.

“Yes,” said Matt. “When you think about it, we know nothing about him. What if he was trying to rob the guy? What if I hit the boy after he stabbed that man? It would explain why he wanted nothing to do with me afterward.”

Again, there was a pause and then Magee, sounding relieved, said, “Y’know...I think you guys are onto something.”

Meda flashed Matt an I-told-you-so glare and Magee continued. “Actually, I don’t think Sergei knows about the boy. The Armenians almost definitely don’t. They had the recording from the guy’s phone when he died and, once they saw you on it, they jumped to the conclusion that you were the culprit. They have no idea anyone else was there.”

“Exactly!” said Meda.

“Do you seriously think a kid would’ve stabbed the guy, though?” asked Magee.

“It doesn’t matter,” interrupted Meda. “The important part is that the Armenians find out about the boy, so they have some level of doubt, so they don’t try to kill Matt. They need to know Matt didn’t stab anyone.”

“I don’t know if that’s possible. I mean—”

“Magee!” snapped Meda. If they’d been seated across from each other Magee might’ve recoiled. “Do you have Sergei’s phone number?”

“Well, yes.”

“Then call him. Now.”

Matt glanced at Meda with a mix of appreciation and apprehension. He could see she was not going to be dissuaded.

"And make sure Matt and I stay on the line. Dial him in via conference call."

"I will. Jeez," said Magee, sounding flustered. "I don't use my conference feature that often."

There was a brief silence and a series of electronic beeps. Then Sergei answered. "You again?"

"I'm sorry. I don't mean to keep stalking you," said Magee sounding awkward and apologetic. "But this is important."

"I'm sure," replied Sergei.

"That friend of mine from the video? Matt? He's on the line, too. Along with his girlfriend."

"What?" Sergei half-shouted.

"Hold on, hold on. I can explain."

"Dammitt, Magee," said Sergei, his sense of betrayal apparent. "C'mon! This'd better be good."

"It is! We have proof Matt didn't stab the Armenian."

"How did I know you were going to say that?"

Sergei hadn't yet hung up so Magee launched in, trying his best to spew out as much as he could, as quickly as possible. "I understand why you won't believe us, but please listen. That night when Matt was recorded on the tape? He'd just hit a kid with his car. The only reason he was even out of the car was because he was checking on the boy. He never saw anyone else there. Which means the boy, as the only other person there, had to be the one that stabbed the Armenian. Matt, you said that the boy seemed to come out of nowhere, right? I bet he was running away from the encounter when you hit him."

Up until that point, both Matt and Meda had stayed silent and let Magee control the narrative. Growing more anxious with each passing second, however, Meda couldn't contain herself any longer. "Don't forget the blood. Matt had no blood on him at all. Which would've been impossible if he'd stabbed someone."

"That's right," said Magee enthusiastically.

Meda continued, "The Armenians don't know that the boy was there. It's important they know someone else was in the area in addition to Matt. *We* know Matt didn't do it. But at the very least those guys should know that Matt wasn't alone. They shouldn't try to kill him without being sure he was the one responsible."

Throughout, Sergei had been oddly quiet, conspicuously so. Then, finally, he asked, "Matt...where were you when you hit the boy? What street?"

"I'm sorry. I don't remember exactly where I was," said Matt sheepishly, eliciting a glare from Meda.

"You don't know where you were when you hit a little kid?" quizzed Sergei. Matt imagined his sneer through the phone.

"It was late. I was having a bad night. I was trying to take a quicker way home from the library."

"The library?" asked Sergei, the sneer's virtual presence only growing.

"Yeah. I was at the library working on my novel. I stayed too late and got kicked out. And I took the service road home because I thought it would be faster. I think I was out near East Elmhurst, maybe Flushing. I got turned around on the service road next to Astoria Boulevard."

"Hmmm. Okay. Okay," said Sergei, his tone shifting as he pondered, sounding less irascible.

An anticipatory silence arose and Meda, in nervous expectation, peered at Matt. In turn, he bit his lower lip to suggest he didn't understand the significance either. Then, unable to tolerate the quiet anymore, Magee asked, "Why does that matter?"

"It just connects a few dots. That's all," said Sergei, doing nothing to ease their curiosity.

"Connects what dots?" asked Meda.

"That area...there's a family that lives close by. Within walking distance. A couple weeks back this guy, a fellow, ah, *friend* of the Armenians, threatened Boris. He turns around and says something like, 'I'll get you when you least expect it.' Then this guy disappears for awhile after the stabbing. No one knows where he went. And when the guy reappears? He says he was on vacation with his wife. But that was only after the video of Matt surfaced."

As Sergei spoke, Meda's expression took the form of growing, restrained jubilation. Once he paused, though, she couldn't resist affirming, "So you think this guy might've stabbed Boris?"

"No, no," said Sergei, popping Meda's balloon. Then, the tone shifting yet again, he added, "I think it was his son."

Neither Meda nor Matt knew how to react. For a moment they had a solution at their fingertips, a culprit in the form of a different mobster. Instead, in his place, was the boy who'd been the initial impetus for the call. Except now the child had an identity; he was tangible and real. The implications piled up immediately.

"His son?" asked Matt.

"Yeah. The guy leaves town. Perfect alibi. Then his son does the job. He woulda got away with it, actually, if you hadn't been there."

Meda and Matt exchanged yet another glance, this one far more fearful than any traded previously. And, very slowly, Meda asked, "So what does that mean?"

"What does it mean? It means Matt's off the hook!" said Sergei, the first note of joy in his tone in the entire conversation. Then he added, "And it means the Armenians take care of the kid instead."

MATT

Four days later, Matt felt like he was clinically insane. Worse, actually. He felt like he was dead. If the guilt felt at the knowledge of the little boy's impending murder was a deluge—slow-moving and tidal—then Mrs. Javier's funeral represented the moment the brackish water arrived at the front step. Matt and Meda's relief at his apparent salvation had been morally conflicted from the start and that doubt had only intensified as they processed the implications: The boy had to die so that Matt might live and the old woman's funeral had forced them to confront the finality of such an outcome.

For her part, Meda had grown only angrier with time. From the start her ire had been focused on the men who'd killed Mrs. Javier. It was a natural reaction, a way for her to come to grips with the tragedy. Meda also recognized that she, not the old woman, was their target and her sense of responsibility drove this anger to new heights. Making matters even worse was the fact that she knew the culprits wouldn't be located. Unaccustomed to such a sense of impotence, her rage multiplied over and over again.

Matt wished he could feel such passion. He wanted to share Meda's sense of causation. Instead, he felt only an all-consuming despair at the horror enveloping him. Mrs. Javier was dead and the little boy would soon be next, and both were his fault. If he hadn't hit the boy none of the events would've been set in motion. How he wished he could go back to that night! Why had he been in such a rush to get home? What was so important that he couldn't have taken more time to assess the boy's condition, taken a moment longer to observe the area more fully? At the library he'd lost himself so absolutely—why had he allowed the real world to take hold of him so suddenly?

Mrs. Javier's funeral had been the previous Thursday and, in the interim, he'd focused on his day job. Though part of the reason had been functional, after taking so many days off, his real motivation had been distraction—he needed somewhere to focus his energies to avoid his torturous ruminations. He'd all but accepted there was nothing he could do to save the boy—or, more precisely, even if he could, it would most likely result in his own death. Yet the ghost of the boy, the knowledge that he could be dying at any moment, haunted his waking hours.

Further exacerbating Matt's condition was the fact that he couldn't concentrate well enough to write. How could he lose himself crafting fiction when he wasn't even sure who he was anymore? Thursday and Friday he'd plopped himself down after getting home from work, hoping for some, *any* kind of spark. Yet inspiration never came. The days slipped by and, by Saturday afternoon, the feeling of helplessness was overpowering.

Stifled, sitting dejectedly in front of the computer screen, he half-heartedly peered out the window. The world outside was cold and grey. It was October 22nd yet, because of the early cold snap, most of the leaves were already off the trees. It was hardly a day that inspired action—it would be so much easier to get cozy under a blanket or lose hours surfing the web. To be sure, a part of Matt wanted to do those exact things: Shut off his brain and forget the guilt that plagued him.

Instead, on a lark, he decided to do an internet search on the bar Magee had spoken about: Masis. He shouldn't have been surprised that very little information was available—based on the impression Magee had created, it didn't sound like a hip, trendy joint that'd engender online reviews. In fact, initially, the only search result for the bar was a generic white pages entry, a bare bones listing of its location and phone number. That was enough to tell Matt he'd found the right location, though. He scanned other results and then began to modify the terms to make them more precise. He didn't know what he hoped to find it bestowed a sense of purpose, at least. Then something caught his eye. Near the bar, perhaps four blocks away, was a grade school. By itself, that meant nothing. However, in one of the search results, he saw mention of Flushing, Queens. It was only a note in the preview of the search result but it was enough to get his attention—why was Flushing referenced in a story about a school at the bottom of Brooklyn? His curiosity piqued, he clicked and found a newsletter published by the school that showcased its current events. It was amateurish, only four pages long, and Matt was ready to click away. But at the last second he decided to follow through on his initial impulse. He searched the article for any mention of Flushing and was astonished at the results—it was referenced six times. A section devoted to academic achievement listed students' names and their borough of residence and, while most hailed from the Brooklyn, a surprising number lived in that specific area of Queens. How was that possible? Getting one's child into the right school was practically a contact sport in New York City and zoning requirements were uncompromisingly stringent. How could six students be brought in from a completely different borough to a singular school? It had to be the work of someone powerful, someone who could skirt the rules.

Matt peered out the window again. This time the gears in his mind were spinning—whirling like a dervish, more appropriately. The clouds outside hadn't passed yet suddenly the grey eased. Everything appeared different to Matt and two hours later he found himself emerging from a subway station in Brooklyn.

He knew he might be putting himself in grave danger and recognized that Magee had been beaten to a pulp doing the exact same thing. But he felt like he had to at least *try* to do something. Allowing the boy to be murdered was no longer an option.

As he walked towards Masis, he tried his best to appear natural. The area lacked foot traffic on an ordinary day, however, and on a Saturday morning it was all but deserted. So while there was effectively no one around to see him, his very presence made him conspicuous. Sauntering up to the front door of the bar wasn't an option yet, at the same time, it would be a challenge to blend in with the surroundings.

He'd readied himself for a visit that might prove to be anti-climactic—there was a good chance the bar wouldn't even be open. And a small, cowardly part of him might admit that he hoped to discover nothing. He was proud that he'd at least taken the leap, though.

He moved progressively closer and then, within a few blocks of the bar, he decided to linger on the street corner for a moment. He took out his phone to make it appear as if he was engaged in an important conversation and surveyed the area for an extended period. A slight breeze blew and a handful of cars passed but, otherwise, there was absolutely zero activity. Matt vacillated between a sense of fear that it had been a giant waste of time and a sense of relief that he'd found nothing to worry about. Then, far down the street, his eye caught the slightest movement. It was a quick flash, barely perceptible, and Matt wasn't even positive it was a person.

He craned his neck while trying to appear casual, still using his phone as a prop. Gradually coming into view from a dip in the road was a fierce looking man, bald and scowling. He was tall but not gangly, and he lumbered with heavy footfalls in his black boots. Then, more surprisingly, a young boy could be seen beside the man. He was perhaps ten or eleven years old, appeared just as ornery the man, and walked with an exaggerated swagger in his shoulders.

Matt's heart stopped. Was that the boy? The one he'd hit with his car? It was an incongruous pair to observe and, with growing unease, he realized they were likely headed to the bar. There was nothing else open for a three-block radius so, if they weren't headed there, they had to be lost. And judging by the man's appearance and the gait of his walk, he wasn't lost. Matt's mind searched for other explanations, tried to figure out why a boy so young might be headed to a bar like that on a Saturday morning, but no reason could be found.

Suddenly everything became more real—he'd begun the trip with low expectations, with no authentic sense of peril. Yet here was the opportunity to actually confront the boy and it terrified him. He experienced visions of the boy running away, only to be apprehended by the man, and he knew he'd have to do something. But the man had probably six inches and fifty pounds on him—his intervention might offer the boy a chance to escape but Matt wasn't positive he'd be so lucky.

Matt's sense of dread rose to new heights when the pair arrived at the bar, opened the door, and entered. There was no ceremony or drama involved—without exchanging a word the pair simply went in the building, as if it was the most customary thing to do on a Saturday morning. And Matt was left on his own.

He jogged down the sidewalk and, when he got within twenty feet, he slowed to approach the bar more cautiously. His thoughts were reeling with possibilities now. He needed a plan. Clearly, he couldn't simply walk in the front door—while it seemed the Armenians no longer intended to kill him, it would be insane to just waltz into their bar. On the other hand, it was equally crazy to think that any good could come from a grown man taking a boy into that bar on a Saturday morning. Even if the pair had nothing to do with the boy he'd hit, Matt could sense that something was very wrong.

Then it occurred to him: The police. Matt didn't have to engage in this dangerous adventure alone now that a literal crime had been committed. He considered the idea, notions of courage and recklessness battling within him. Involving the police might ruin the one, serendipitous chance he'd received to save the boy. Further, if they showed up and busted the bar, there was no guarantee they'd disrupt any plans to harm the child. Yet calling them remained the most logical, common sense course of action he could take.

He took a few steps back around the corner, just out of view of the bar, and stared at his phone for a long moment. He tried to consider every possibility, every potential repercussion of his decision. He thought of the boy inside and how he might've just walked into an ambush. And, if that was the case, Matt questioned what he could do to stop it. Yet he also considered the notion that the boy might be the man's son and that the pair might be merely watching a soccer match together—in which case, Matt would be putting himself in harm's way for no reason.

Seconds ticked by and, nervously, Matt peered about. Up ahead, directly beside the bar, was a derelict wooden fence with an alleyway behind it. He stared at it for a moment. Time was of the essence—if anything was going to happen to the boy, it was going to happen now, not an hour from now. And, all at once, he dialed 9-1-1, his eyes still trained on the fence. It rang once, then a second time. Matt's anticipation grew. He wasn't even positive he should be calling 911 and the delay gave him more time to reconsider. It rang a third time and Matt imagined the young boy inside the bar, blissfully unaware before the gun emerged. A fourth ring, and Matt's mood turned to disgust. If it took 911 this long to answer how long would it take for the police to arrive? It rang a fifth time and Matt shook his head. He finally heard a click but he was already in the process of punching the button to end the call. Knowing what he had to do, he turned the phone off and shoved it into his pocket. Then he strode down the concrete sidewalk, staring at the fence with determined resolve.

MAGEE

After a rough night bartending, an idea came to Magee in his sleep that solved a problem bedeviling his art. He'd been concerned about the way the paint was laying on the mirror but, in his dreamy haze, an epiphany had hit...he shouldn't be painting the front of it at all. The effect he hoped to achieve required a second pane of glass placed in front of the mirror's surface...it would create the depth and duality he couldn't manufacture on a single pane.

So when the phone rang the next morning, he very nearly ignored it. A distraction? He didn't need that now. It was nearby at the moment it rang, however, so with begrudging curiosity he craned his neck to at least see who was calling.

He didn't recognize the number, the area code wasn't any of the usual suspects, and it certainly wasn't his mother. Yet it seemed vaguely familiar. He took a step away, readied to return to his work, then it dawned on him: It was Sergei. What did he want? As far as Magee was concerned everything had worked itself out...Matt was no longer in danger...everyone could move on with their lives. But the phone was now on its third ring and a concern sprung forth: What if Matt wasn't safe after all? What is something had changed? The urgency compelled Magee to answer.

"Hey. It's Sergei."

"What's up?" asked Magee tentatively.

"Does your friend still want those tickets?"

"What?"

"The tickets to the opera. At the Met. Your friend was interested in buying 'em. That's how the whole thing got started."

Magee's mind caught up as Sergei spoke...it was a topic so far off Magee's radar that he didn't know what the guy was talking about at first. “Um...sure,” Magee blurted. “He’s still interested. Wow, I had completely forgotten about those.”

“I had, too. One of those things. Then this guy comes in, offering to sell. I thought of your friend.”

As Sergei continued, Magee realized he may have spoken too soon...in all actuality, he *wasn’t* positive Matt and Meda still wanted the tickets. It’d been a rough period for them and they might prefer to forget about the whole thing.

“It was weird actually,” continued Sergei. “It was like the guy was sent to me. He was tall, no emotion in his face. It was like he knew I’d want the tickets before he even offered.”

“And you bought them from him?” asked Magee.

“Course I bought them. Figured I’d help out your friend. Is there a problem?”

“No. Nothing’s wrong,” said Magee. “It just occurred to me that they might not be interested anymore.”

“Well...the show is tonight,” said Sergei, sounding irritated.

“That’s right,” muttered Magee. He’d been fully lost in his art and now found himself committing Matt and Meda to the opera that very night. He hoped he was making the right decision. “Okay. Fine. Where can I pick them up?”

“The usual. 7th and 20th. I’ll be there in an hour. You’re not going to leave me hanging, right?”

“No. I swear,” said Magee.

“Good,” said Sergei, before hanging up.

Magee put down the phone and began cleaning paint off his hands. Then he screwed the caps back on his paint bottles and dialed Meda.

MATT

Climbing the fence entailed a level of commitment Matt hadn't anticipated. Not only would he be trespassing and possibly injuring himself in the process, but he'd be spying on people who, only three days prior, had wanted him dead. He hesitated and then, with a gulp, placed his hands on the top of the wooden planks and began to pull himself up.

The fence was dilapidated, weathered to grey and white—Matt attempted to distract himself from that fact as he hoisted himself up and swung his leg over it. His position was precarious, straddling the rickety barrier as it tottered beneath him, and, in one rushed motion, he swung his other leg over and fell to the ground beyond. The momentum sent him sprawling when he landed, but at least he made it across.

He stood up, brushed off, and took stock of the alleyway. It was tight; the buildings on either side menaced overhead and allowed in very little light. Dank moss grew along the bottom of each and created a gross imitation of a forest floor—blackened chip bags and bottles served as vile replacements for sticks and leaves. The smell of decay was omnipresent and, Matt realized, it would be a terrible place to die.

He took his first step down the alley. As best he could tell, it shared the same wall as the bar next door. His plan hinged on there being access to the back of the bar, some window through which he could deduce what was happening inside.

As he crept closer, his hunch proved correct when he spied a door. It was grey and metal, institutional in its severity—meant for fire escape and security, nothing more. At eye level was a small window, crisscrossed with metal wire. The glass was filthy. From afar, it was hard to see through it at all. Grime from the city air had coagulated in spots where raindrops hit but at least it was some sort of portal to see inside.

Matt first attempted to get a better view by peering in at an angle from about three feet away. He could see movement beyond and could detect the muffled sounds of people talking, but he reasoned no one could see him unless they were expressly looking for him. Not satisfied, however, he took another tentative step closer. Immediately, he realized he could hear better, that he could make out distinct words. Then, growing more audacious, he took the end of his sleeve and carefully rubbed off some of the detritus. It helped. He could now see forms more clearly and soon spotted the young boy.

"How long?" came an older, gruff-sounding voice.

"Not long. He's coming from Queens," responded a younger voice, clearly that of the young boy.

"So what does that mean?" Another deep voice.

"It means that he should be there. At the right time. There'll be less things to go wrong." The young boy's voice again.

Matt's initial reaction was one of relief—the boy didn't sound as if he was in distress. If the boy sounded like he was in peril Matt would've needed to act decisively. Yet, deep down, he had no clue what he could actually do. His immediate concern satiated, he continued to listen and his attentiveness grew.

"But it'll be in a different spot. Remember that. Your guys will have to guide him," said the young boy, sounding instructive, nearly condescending to the men.

"Sure. Sure. We got that. What about his parents?"

Matt concentrated. It was clear the boy wasn't in danger. Not at all. Yet it also seemed like something else was at work.

"They'll be there, too. Of course. It's not as if he's driving himself to the opera. That's why we made sure his mom won three tickets. Lucky prize. All that."

"I still don't understand why we don't just do it at his house or whatever," came a third adult voice, dull and dispassionate.

Gone now was Matt's sense of relief. Instead, a different emotion took its place. He continued to listen to the conversation even as he didn't want to hear the words.

"Because we need to send a message. That's what Tibor wanted," said the boy. "It has to be in public, make the news. And it's too hard at our school. Darren saw what I meant."

"The kid is right. It is an impossible shot. Even from outside the building. The bullet passes through him...it could hit anybody else. Tibor does not want that."

Matt needed no further confirmation. Far from being an innocent victim, this child was actually setting up the boy Matt had hit. Suddenly it all became clear: All those whispers and cryptic warnings about an assassination attempt at *Götterdämmerung*? That was where they first intended to kill Matt! But now that he wasn't the target the attempt would be made on the little boy instead.

Matt's mind reeled and a corollary revelation occurred to him: He now had the actual means to save the little boy. He took a cautious step backward, still processing the results of his discovery. He wasn't listening as intently, though. And, vaguely, it dawned on him that the conversation on the other side of the door had ceased.

Dread spiked within him. He heard someone say, "What?"

Then, violently, the metal door flew open. It whizzed past him, a hair's width in front of his nose, and slammed into the brick wall with a jarring crash. Matt issued an involuntary grunt and fell backwards against the opposite wall of the alleyway. The back of his head struck it hard; he only barely avoided falling. And in front of him, glaring at him with violent resolve, were the Armenians.

MEDA

Meda's day was not going as planned. Her friend, Janet, had experienced abdominal pains and, rather than enjoying her baby shower, she'd been rushed to the emergency room. In addition, Meda hadn't heard from Matt since Mrs. Javier's funeral and, though only two dayspassed, the tribulations of the previous weeks cast a long shadow. With no baby shower to attend, she needed something to keep her worries for each at bay and had decided to run some errands instead. So when her phone began buzzing and she saw it was Magee she should've expected her day to encounter another swerve. And as she might've predicted, he did not disappoint, producing news of the opera tickets like a rabbit pulled out of a hat.

"Oh great! I'm in midtown. I can pick them up from him directly," said Meda.

"I'm not sure that's such a good idea," Magee responded, sounding guarded, tentative.

"Why?"

"The guy is a little weird. I mentioned that before."

"Yes, I remember," said Meda. "But now he knows me. We spoke on the phone. It shouldn't be a problem anymore, right?"

"I don't know," he said, pausing. "I just don't know."

Meda wasn't angry; she just thought Magee's concern was misplaced. She was only a couple subway stops away from the meeting point so there was no need for Magee, in Brooklyn, to go so far out of his way. And in a practical sense, she preferred to have the tickets in hand as soon as possible. The doors at the Met would open in a few hours. Any extra time to get ready was appreciated. "I'm across from a bank and I can get to 7th in ten minutes. It doesn't make sense for you to trek all the way in. You must have other stuff you'd rather be doing?"

There was a brief silence before Magee admitted, "I was on a bit of a roll here in the studio."

"Okay. That settles it then," said Meda. "I'm going to get the money now. I'm going to meet the guy. And I insist you get back to work immediately."

Again Magee hesitated before finally relenting. "Okay. Fine."

And in a sudden turn of events, Meda now found her day going down an entirely new path. Out of the blue, she and Matt were going to the opera after all (funny how life worked sometimes).

Meda withdrew the money and arrived at the designated corner with time to spare. She misidentified a few people as Sergei but then, when he finally did appear, Meda spotted him from a full block away. Despite no in-person introduction, she pegged him by his shifty eyes and guarded steps; clear departures from fellow pedestrians wrapped up in their own inner worlds. And by the time he reached the corner, Meda had already locked eyes with him and prepared to introduce herself.

"Where's Magee?" he grunted, before Meda had a chance to confirm he was the broker.

That his question skipped right over formality yet also demanded a response caused Meda to stutter. "Oh, hello. I'm Meda, Matt's girlfriend. Magee was getting the tickets for us. I was nearby so I decided to come on my own."

"Why is Magee always messin' things up?"

Meda giggled but the joviality was not commiserated. The gruffness in his question had caught Meda off guard yet again but, when it was clear he was serious, her mirth vanished. "I don't know. That's just the way he is, I guess."

Sergei peered at her with his toady eyes, as if to discern something more profound. Then, seemingly satisfied by some inscrutable assurance, he plunged his hand into the pocket of his overalls. "That'll be...$1,500. Different seats than you had last time, obviously."

"Oh, of course!" said Meda, digging into her purse after the abrupt change in tone. "Thank you so much for this. I didn't think we'd be able to go. You're a real life-saver."

Sergei said nothing. Instead, he simply held the tickets aloft towards her, practically tapping his toe in expectation. When his phone rang from inside his coveralls it seemed like a veritable relief for him, some place to put his attention.

"What?" Sergei growled almost immediately upon answering it. "He did what?" Prior to the call Sergei had appeared annoyed, albeit in a flippant, non-threatening way. As soon as the conversation began, however, his mood turned darker.

Meda located her wallet and began to count out the money but it was becoming clear Sergei was not paying attention. So intense was his concentration that he didn't even notice Meda take the tickets from his hand.

Then: "Are you kiddin' me?" he shouted. Meda jumped, despite the fact that they were standing on a busy sidewalk on a bright, sunny day.

"He's in the alley behind the bar?" Sergei seethed. Then, his eyes rolled up, staring at Meda from beneath his brow. His body stiffened as he listened, his eyes trained on her throughout. And his angry leer morphed into a smile, a terrible, monstrous smile that told Meda she should run. Now. Immediately. And, into the phone, he said, "Well you'll never guess who's here with me as we speak."

MATT

"You!" bellowed the largest, fiercest Armenian. It was, at once, both a howl of recognition and an incredulous question of Matt's audacity.

Matt ran. His first step was clumsy as he contorted to regain his center of gravity, but his ensuing steps became an unbridled charge down the alleyway. There was no thought involved—only immediate, instinctual response. He heard some shouting behind him, recognized that people were following, but beyond that there was no time for tactical considerations.

The fence. He was perhaps twenty feet away and closing. For a millisecond he considered charging through it, as if he were a linebacker. It wouldn't work, though. At ten feet and closing, he knew he'd have to hoist himself up and leap it in one single movement. He never got the chance.

As he neared the fence he was forced to slow down in the slightest. And in that moment, a hand landed on the back of his neck and yanked on his shirt collar. He was airborne for the briefest moment, his legs still in mid-stride, and he landed flat on his back, hard. The wind hoofed out of his lungs and refused to accept his next breath. And then a hard stomp to his gut followed.

Panic ensued. His mind felt as if it was in a different place than his body, as if he was watching from afar. His mind commanded his body to roll to the side and curl into a ball, even as another kick and another kick followed. In eye-bulging terror, he tried again to take in air but his lungs weren't cooperating. The kicks and the brutality were secondary to the fact that he couldn't breathe, couldn't speak. More boots followed, to his back and ribs. His face was buried in the repulsive moss of the alleyway, in the blackened cheese doodle bag, but none of that mattered: Air! He needed air!

A desperate gasp managed to re-inflate his lungs the slightest bit. It gave a sliver of hope even as the men continued to pummel him. There were three of them; a deluge of boots. They were cursing at him, demanding to know what he was doing there and that infuriated a back corner of Matt's mind: Why the hell were they asking him questions when it was clear he couldn't even breathe?

He took in another wheezing, pitiful gasp and, his need for oxygen barely satiated, the severity of the predicament hit him. As if hurtling through some sort of psychic tunnel, his mind came back to his body: He was in a desolate alleyway, hidden from view, and these men were not about to stop beating him until he was dead. He had to do something. But what?

"—fire—" he croaked, barely audible. Then, using oxygen he absolutely could not spare, he shouted, "Fire!"

It made the men pause. Matt couldn't see their reactions—his head was still buried in the crevice against the wall. It sounded as if they were snickering.

"Fire?" repeated one with a heavy accent. "Why is he saying that?"

Matt's mind went into overdrive. The gambit had worked. Long ago he'd heard that shouting, "fire," was far more likely to elicit help from strangers than shouting, "help." In this instance it had strewn temporary confusion in the men. Taking in another breath, Matt realized he had to press his momentary advantage, however slight it might be.

"Fire!" hollered Matt, even louder than the previous cry. It caused him to break into a coughing fit before, weakly, adding another, "—fire—"

The men guffawed and, for a beat, grew quiet. Matt dared not look but he sensed that his gambit had run its course. Then he heard one of them mutter in disgust, “To hell with this,” and a sharp boot connected with his back. Others immediately followed.

No, no, no! It hadn’t worked! It had only stalled them. Think, Matt, *think*! He couldn’t die like this!

Then came a voice, one without accent. “Hey! What’s going on back there?”

The beating ceased. For a moment there was silence—it was both brief yet seemed to stretch on forever.

Then there was a shout from the other end of the alleyway, from inside the bar. “Cops! Cops!”

“Oh shit,” muttered one of Matt’s attackers. They scampered away. And Matt heard the voice at the fence say, “Sherri! Sherri, we need back-up.”

Suddenly, miraculously, Matt was alone. The unexpectedness of it was jarring. For a long moment he stayed locked in place, as if the men might reappear at any moment. Then, gradually at first, he pulled his face out of the moss and garbage. It was a confusing, timorous state to be in—his body was still shot full of fight-or-flight chemicals yet he had no outlet to put that energy.

Squinting, he peered at the fence and then back to the door to the bar. Shouts were coming from inside, authoritative ones, ones without accent. There were also vague sounds of panicked movements—no words were spoken but, instead, there was the commotion of shuffling feet, drawers being opened and slammed shut.

Why had the police come? He was still trying to decide the best course of action when the fundamental question came to him. Why had they arrived at that precise moment? And then the answer came to him, causing his vision to swirl: The 911 call. He dialed it before investigating. If operators receive a call and the caller doesn't speak, they are obliged to investigate. The police had probably thought it to be a simple follow-up—it was only when they heard the attack in the alleyway that they realized something more nefarious was occurring.

Matt's knees wobbled as he stood and the full comprehension about how close he'd come to dying enveloped his thoughts with dread. If he had hung up on the call a millisecond earlier, before the operator answered? With his nerves and body still aflutter, Matt took his first step down the alleyway. Though terrified and shaking, he had to find out what was going on in the bar.

He arrived and peered in. The room was tight, with a freezer along one side and a paper-strewn desk nearly blocking passage on the other side. One of his attackers was against the wall with a uniformed police officer behind him locking him in handcuffs. In back of them was a different officer handcuffing another man. And behind them were five more men, each with them handcuffed, as well. Yet the child Matt had initially followed was nowhere in sight.

"They—they're going to kill a little boy," croaked Matt. It was weak, almost inaudible, yet everyone's gaze immediately landed on him.

The police officers appeared downright startled at his appearance. Then, glowering, the officer closest to Matt asked, "Who the hell are you?"

Matt didn't address the actual question. "I was listening in. I heard them planning it. At the opera tonight." As Matt continued to recover, his words grew more confident and forceful. "This boy, he killed one of their associates and they want to take revenge."

The officer closest to Matt, his stare still incredulous, asked, “What? Are you the guy that was getting beat up out there?”

“Yeah. I was the one that called 911,” answered Matt quickly before returning to his tale. “One of their friends died recently. I don’t know his name. Ask them. They were planning something.”

The officer then glanced to his partner, the pair virtually surrounded by the leering Armenians. His expression was something close to aggravation, a nod to the fact that the outnumbered officers had enough to handle at the moment. “Listen pal,” he said to Matt, “there’re more officers on the way. We’ll get your story in a second. For now: Just cool your jets, okay?”

Then something changed in the body language of the Armenian closest to Matt. He was the largest of the group, the one who had initially recognized Matt when the door flew open and, despite being handcuffed, his chest seemed to puff out defiantly. “It will not matter,” he said with an air of bravado.

The officer took notice. “Shut the hell up,” he said, attempting to regain control of the situation.

Matt’s sense of concern swelled, however. His curiosity hostile, he asked, “What?”

“It will not matter,” the man repeated, his arrogance growing.

“Both of you! Shut the hell up!” barked the officer, pushing the man against the wall for extra emphasis.

But Matt paid no heed. His eyes were locked with the Armenian’s and he hissed, “What are you talking about?”

“The plan is already in place. The little boy is practically dead already,” droned the man in his deep, heavy accent. “We will get off with a misdemeanor. And the child will be dead regardless."

"Listen to me: Shut *the hell* up!" hollered the officer again. No one was listening.

Matt glared at the man. His eyes became slits of rage.

Then, with a smirk below his cold, dead eyes, the man added, "My friends? They will have a nice surprise for him. They are probably getting ready as we speak."

Matt said nothing. Instead he continued to stare, unblinking. And, after a moment, bowing to the ferocity of Matt's glare, the edges of the man's smile fell in the slightest measure. Then Matt turned and ran.

"Get back here!" shouted the officer to Matt's back. He didn't stop, though. And when he hit the fence he pulled himself up and over with one mighty tug and didn't skip a beat as he leapt down to the concrete beyond.

MEDA

Meda launched into a sprint. She wasn't even sure why. There was just something about Sergei's smile that told her to go, *now*, while she had the chance. The logical portion of her mind reasoned she already had the tickets in hand anyway. It was the emotional, instinctual part that drove her to action.

"Hey!" called out Sergei. But she was already ten steps up the sidewalk.

She couldn't tell if he was giving chase and, at the intersection, she was met with a blaring car horn when she dashed across the street. She knew she might be embarrassing Magee tremendously. She didn't care. It was clear Sergei had made reference to her on his phone call and she wasn't ready to gamble on his intentions.

After the third block, dodging and weaving between pedestrians all the way, she turned to ascertain if he was following. She didn't see him immediately but it was hard to be certain with so many pedestrians impeding her vision. She decelerated to a light jog, stopped, and ducked into the doorway of a clothing store. As if searching for reassurance, she felt for the tickets and, satisfied, ducked her head out to get a sustained view of the sidewalk. Again, Sergei was nowhere to be seen. She began to rue dashing away from him (nice way to let fear control you, psycho-lady). Then she reassured herself with the notion that everything in her and Matt's life had been upended the previous weeks; she could be cut some slack when it came to overreaction.

She rested against the wall, her bag serving as a clunky pillow between herself and the concrete. After catching her breath, she pulled her phone out from inside her coat and considered calling Magee to explain her hasty departure. Before doing so, however, the phone came alive in her hand.

"Oh!" Startled by the buzzing, her other hand briefly shot to cover her chest before she peered at the phone. It was Matt. "Hello?"

"Honey. It's me. Where are you?" said Matt, rapid-fire.

"I'm in Manhattan. I can't believe you called. I—"

"Not now," he interrupted. "I'm in Brooklyn. I was just at that bar, Masis."

"What?" she cried.

"Yeah," he said, if only to acknowledge her anger. "I wanted to make sure the boy was okay. I couldn't just sit back and let them kill him. I put myself in danger—I'm sorry. We can talk about that later. For now, here is the important point: They're going to try to kill the boy tonight. At the opera."

Meda tried to process it all. She could hear Matt was out of breath and the urgency in his voice was obvious. But it was hard to absorb everything he was saying while she had so much to tell *him*. "Okay. Slow down."

"I can't. I think the cops might be after me."

"What?" cried Meda again, even more emphatically than the first.

"I'll explain later. Don't worry. I'm not in trouble. I'm wanted as a witness."

"Matt!"

"I know. I'm sorry. I had to run away from the bar. They openly admitted that they plan to kill the boy and the police won't be able to stop them in time. The Stoic Man told me as much."

"What? That again? Matt, you've got to slow down!"

"No. I'm about to get on the subway. We should meet at your place. We've got to figure out a way to get into the opera. There's—"

"Matt,"

"got to be"

"I have"

"a way."

"the tickets."

The conversation halted. Then, from Matt's end, "What?"

"I have the tickets to *Götterdämmerung*. I just picked them up. From Magee's friend, Sergei."

It was now Matt's turn to process the information and, after another brief pause, he asked, "Really?"

"Yes. Really," said Meda, her irritation evident. "And I haven't told you the half of it."

"What? What do you mean?"

"When I was picking them up from Sergei he got a phone call. And, it's hard to describe." Meda paused to gather her thoughts, her hand in the air as if she was talking to Matt in person and trying to convey a sense of insecurity. "He got the call and, at first, he was angry, surprised. Then he looked at me with this smile and it just didn't seem *right*. It's so hard to put into words but I felt this compulsion to get out of there. So I ran."

"What did he say before you ran? Why was he so angry?"

"It was like he couldn't believe what he was hearing. I'm forgetting the exact words now. But he was surprised someone was at a certain location. And then he said, 'You'll never guess who's here with me.' He was definitely talking about me. And I don't think it was in a good way."

"Meda," said Matt. She waited, expecting him to say more, but instead he stopped, as if he was in a state of awe.

"What? What is it?"

"From what you just said," Matt trailed off. Then, after a pause, he started again, "From what you just said, I think he was talking about me."

"You?"

"Yeah. He must've gotten a call from someone at the bar. They know who I am from the video. And Sergei was our contact to tell the Armenians I hadn't stabbed their friend. He's the only one who knows you're my girlfriend. Why else would he make such a specific reference to you?"

"Oh my God," muttered Meda.

"They caught me spying, knew I called the cops on them," Matt continued, "and then you were right there with Sergei when they called about me."

They both let the information sink in for a moment, Meda's jaw still agape.

"You did the right thing, honey," said Matt. "I'm so glad you followed your instincts. Who knows what he was he was going to do."

She was about to concur, to express her relief after such a close call. But before she said a word she looked up to find Sergei standing directly in front of her.

MATT

The phone went silent. Meda hadn't said goodbye, hadn't wrapped up the conversation. Instead, there was only dead air.

"Meda! Meda!" cried Matt, his knuckles white on the phone. "Can you hear me?"

He hung up, then frantically re-dialed. There was no answer. It went to voicemail and, in anguish, Matt let out a guttural cry.

He sprinted in the approximate direction of the subway. Then stopped. Then paced, scowling. The subway would take too long. And he'd have no phone reception—if she was desperately trying to reach him he'd be underground. Yet he had to get to her. He could try to find a cab but, in such an isolated location, that might become an exercise in futility. Time was of the essence—he couldn't wait on a random street corner and hope for the best.

All at once, he began punching in Magee's phone number.

"Magee. It's Matt. I need your help. I think Meda's in trouble. I need you to get to her."

"Okay," said Magee, instantly recognizing the urgency in Matt's tone, "I just spoke to her. She's in Manhattan."

"I know. She was picking up the tickets from Sergei. Something bad happened."

"Something bad?" said Magee, nearly speaking over Matt in the frenetic exchange.

"Yeah. I went to Masis."

"What?"

"I wanted to make sure the little boy would be okay. They spotted me. Beat the crap out of me."

"Are you crazy? Why would you go back there?"

"And the cops came," continued Matt, virtually ignoring Magee's concern. "The Armenian, he said they were going to kill the boy at the opera tonight. And someone from the bar must've called Sergei while Meda was getting the tickets from him."

"Oh no...."

"She ran. She got away. And she called me. But then the phone went dead. I'm afraid something happened to her."

"What do you need me to do?"

"First: Where was she meeting Sergei?"

"7th and 20th."

"Okay. Second: I need you to get there. I don't want to be unavailable if she calls so I'm going to try to find a cab. You can get there quicker by taking the subway, though."

"Yep. It should only take me fifteen minutes on the L line."

"Excellent. I don't know where she'll be now. I don't know why her phone cut out."

"Buddy. Buddy," interrupted Magee. "I understand. I got it. I'm leaving now. I'll call you and her once I'm off the train."

"Magee," said Matt in a purposefully calm tone, "thank you."

Matt hung up and then peered about the area. He had to find the nearest residential area or, at least, a main thoroughfare if he expected to find a cab. Complicating matters was the fact that he'd fled the bar without any destination in mind. He couldn't double-back the way he'd come without passing it. In fact, he essentially had to keep moving in the opposite direction lest he be detained by a converging police officer.

Flush with energy but with nowhere to direct it, he broke into a dash towards the nearest busy street. It wasn't the most well though-out plan but he needed to do something. He arrived at the corner and took stock: There were plenty of cars. Yet there wasn't a single yellow taxi in sight. His gaze shot up the street, then down, then back again. It was taking too long!

He felt like a downed power line, jumping about yet travelling nowhere.

This was his exact fear. Stagnation was the greatest enemy. He'd rather be travelling somewhere—anywhere—than remain stuck in place. The writing process had taught him it was better to make an active mistake, to summon ideas that may be deleted later, than to sit around waiting for inspiration that might not come. The only way to make something happen was to literally *make* it happen.

Matt gulped and jumped into the road. He was nearly run over. The first car swerved around him, its horn blaring. The second one—the driver's line of sight blocked by the first—veered a second late and came even closer to ending Matt.

He swung his arms in the air, attempting to flag down a car forcibly. Two more nearly ran him over and, behind them, an oncoming truck bore down. Matt knew that any car behind the truck would not have a proper view of the road, would not be able to maneuver into the other lane in time. But he refused to go back to the concrete.

The driver of the truck saw Matt and made an attempt to shift lanes. He was blocked by a car to his left, though. Matt did not budge. The car to the truck's side passed, the truck jumped lanes, and, at the last moment, the truck managed to careen around Matt. Behind the truck, another car.

That car's driver slammed on the brakes but it was still moving so fast. The sound of screeching tires ripped the air, the car did not stop. And when it came to a halt two feet in front of Matt, the entire chassis of the car continued to lean towards him with menace. Matt made eye contact with the driver. Then, the momentum lost, the car fell back. Distantly, Matt heard the hard thump of his heart. And then the driver's face contorted, changing from shock to unbridled anger.

Matt approached the driver's side door and he could hear the string of obscenities outside the car even though both windows were up. The driver was a middle-aged African-American man in a camouflage jacket with a beard and hard features. The car was at least ten years old with numerous home-fixes apparent. Matt, still flush with adrenaline, knocked on the window.

The man was irate as he rolled down the window. "Are you out of your damn mind? I coulda killed you! In fact, I outta—"

"My wife is in danger," said Matt. "$100 for a ride into Manhattan."

The man frowned even more deeply, peering at Matt in disbelief. But his tirade stopped and, for a moment, the only sound was that of other cars whooshing past.

Then: "Get in."

MEDA

This time Meda didn't question her instincts. She shoved a quick jab of her palm up into Sergei's face and slipped past him.

"Aggh!" he grunted, holding his nose.

But Meda was already darting down the sidewalk. Previously, she'd stopped to contact Matt. That was a mistake. This time she intended to run and keep running.

"Come back here!" hollered Sergei. But his words were plaintive and weak (he knew he'd blown his second chance).

She sprinted up the street and leapt between cars to make it as hard as possible for him to follow. (Think! Think! Think!) It wasn't easy to run and plot. While repeating the mantra to herself, it only served to distract her from actual thinking. Her first concern, she realized, was geography; she couldn't hem herself in. That meant she shouldn't run too far west towards the water and she had to avoid intersections where she might be forced to stop for protracted periods. The water was easily avoided by heading north; dodging traffic in Manhattan was another story. Chelsea's streets weren't necessarily packed with cars but the sidewalks were tight and crowds of people assembled at the corners quickly.

Meda took to the asphalt of 7th Avenue and avoided the sidewalk entirely. She was running against traffic, which helped her see oncoming cars, but it would be too dangerous to run in the street for long. She passed the 23rd Street subway station. It wasn't an option. Twenty minutes might pass before a train arrived and she'd be a sitting duck the entire time. No way. Better to keep moving.

The most sensible thing to do, of course, would be to flag down a police officer once she felt like she'd created enough distance. At least she'd be safe. But what could she possibly tell the officer? ("This guy is trying to kill me because my boyfriend uncovered a plot to kill a young child—don't ask why—at the opera.") And worse, based on what Matt said, the police were on the lookout for him as well. If she flagged down an officer she might not be allowed to leave the precinct until Matt was found.

(Think! Think! Think!) By 29th Street Meda's breath was getting short and she'd collided with five different pedestrians. She couldn't continue such a sprint forever; she had to come up with a long term strategy. For the first time she twirled to see if she could spot Sergei but didn't see him anywhere. That didn't necessarily mean she was safe, though; she'd learned that already.

She hit 30th Street, dodging increasingly more pedestrians as she closed in on midtown Manhattan proper. Then something came into view. Up ahead: Madison Square Garden. To that point, she'd been avoiding subway stations because they were veritable dead ends. But Madison Square Garden was different. Below it, Penn Station was sprawling and the security contingent throughout was unavoidable. She didn't have to get on a train; she could simply meld into the mass of people and bide her time.

She considered it. Re-considered it. Yet she could find no reason why it didn't make sense. For a moment her pace had begun to wane as she considered the choice. But with her path decided, she sped up once again and sprinted the final few blocks to her destination. And, as she ducked into the underground, she never noticed the GPS-enabled phone Sergei had dropped in her bag.

MAGEE

When Magee finally reached the subway station, he darted up the stairs to the sidewalk and immediately began checking his phone. He was flummoxed to find no messages, however. He'd expected to receive some sort of communication...some news, either good or bad. Silence hadn't even been a consideration. So for a moment he stood, indecisive and weighing his options. He could call Matt but, if he hadn't communicated yet, Magee doubted he had anything new to offer. Better to locate Meda first.

"Hello?" she answered, much to Magee's relief.

"Meda. Where are you? Are you okay?"

"Yes. Yes, I am. I'm in Penn Station," she replied, pausing briefly before adding, "How did you know I was in trouble?"

"Matt called me. He's coming too but he was farther out in Brooklyn. We figured I could get here quicker. I'm on 14th Street and 7th."

"I was in that area earlier. I ran away. Your buddy, Sergei, was about to—"

"I know. I heard. I'm so sorry. I'm just happy you got away." Momentarily, he considered reminding her that it was her idea to pick up the tickets herself. Instead, he asked, "You said you're at Penn Station? Where?"

"I'm in the Amtrak station. Near track number six. I'm behind a line of people waiting for the next train. I have cell phone service but it's been spotty."

"Okay," said Magee, taking in the information and then, all at once, bounding up the sidewalk. "Are you safe? Can you stay there for a second?"

"I think so," said Meda. "I've got a pretty good view of the whole room. Sergei won't be able to sneak up on me. And there are soldiers armed with machine guns standing watch."

"That's right," muttered Magee. Guards had been stationed there since 9/11...he was impressed with Meda's choice. "Okay. I'll be there in a couple minutes. I'll call Matt, too, and let him know where you are. You should lay low...don't worry about making any calls, just concentrate on the room. If you see Sergei just go stand directly beside one of those guards. He'd be crazy to try anything then. Once all three of us are together we can figure out what to do next. Does that make sense?"

Magee feared he'd spoken too long. Following their hyper-efficient exchange moments earlier, his plan felt like a drawn-out monologue in comparison. And as the utter silence from her end of the conversation stretched on, his apprehension grew.

"Meda?"

No response.

"Meda! Can you hear me? Are you there?"

No response.

MATT

R.A. didn't talk much. He'd insisted on seeing Matt's money before pulling away from sidewalk and, at first, he was moderately curious about Matt's plight. But when Matt explained that Meda was being chased by Armenian mobsters and added that he felt like he'd been going crazy lately, any semblance of interest retreated. So, instead, the pair drove in silence, Matt still possessed by a frenetic, nervous energy with nowhere to direct it.

Matt had tried to call Meda again but there was no answer. It did nothing to assuage his ever-increasing anxiety and, as he readied to call Magee, his friend called him first.

"Oh God, I'm glad you called."

"Matt, Meda is at Penn Station."

"Wow. Okay," said Matt, instantly relieved. "Are you with her?"

"No. Listen." His tone was grave and Matt's momentary sense of consolation vanished. "I'm heading there now on foot. I'm at 25th Street on 8th. I was on the phone with her. She seemed to be in a safe place. Then the line went dead."

"Again?" cried Matt, startling R.A. with his intensity.

"Yeah. But here's the thing: She was underground at the Amtrak station. Penn Station has cell service but she said it was spotty."

"I don't care. We have to assume the worst."

"I know. And I agree. I wanted you to know so you could head there."

Matt nodded then looked to R.A. with an expression that was equal parts pleading and demanding. "We need to go to Penn Station."

"What? You didn't say anything about Penn Station! I was going out of my way already with Chelsea!" It was clear his patience with this borderline crazy person was running thin.

"I know. I know. Fifty dollars more."

R.A. glared at Matt with an expression that all but verbalized the words, "Are you serious?" After a moment, though, his demeanor softened, transforming to grudging acceptance. He could see Matt was out of options. And it didn't seem like Matt was running a scam.

"Give me the money now," said R.A.

"Thank you so much," said Matt, digging into his wallet.

The change in destination wasn't drastic; Meda had already covered it on foot. But it meant entering a new level of traffic. They were already heading north on 6th Avenue and R.A. had intended to take a left on 20th to be done with Matt. If they were to go up to 34th Street, they'd run into much more congestion surrounding Herald Square. "In good conscience, I have to warn you," said R.A. thoughtfully, "once we hit the 30s, I don't know how fast we'll be moving. I'll take your money but...."

Matt grew pensive, understanding exactly what he was implying. "Okay. You're right. If you can get me to 8th Avenue and 30th Street I'll jump out and jog the rest of the way."

"I think that's a wise decision," said R.A. He paused then and, almost in spite of himself, asked, "Is your girl *really* in danger?"

"She is," said Matt. "And it's my fault because I was the one who introduced this craziness into our lives. The Armenian mafia is going to kill a little boy. I plan to stop them."

R.A. stared at Matt, his skepticism diminishing but not altogether gone. "That's not what you'd call a normal problem."

"It's not. You're right."

They arrived at their new destination and, when R.A. pulled his car over to temporarily double-park, he summoned forth a chorus of car horns. R.A. looked at Matt with a new expression, however, one that suggested he couldn't believe he was actually buying Matt's tale. "Keep the money," he said, pushing it back towards Matt. "If a man is willing to dive into oncoming traffic to get a ride, he's got to be pretty damn desperate. And a story like that? If even half of it is true I'm just happy to help you save that boy."

Matt stared at him in disbelief for a moment. Then, overwhelmed, he gushed, "Thank you! Thank you so much! You may have saved a life today."

"I sure hope I did," said R.A.

Then Matt leapt from the car and began sprinting up the avenue.

MEDA

It didn't happen quickly so much as it happened unexpectedly. Meda had been on the phone with Magee. He'd been prattling on with advice. Then the phone wasn't in her hand. There was split-second of panic as she saw it dropping, tumbling in mid-air. And then, out of nowhere, a hand caught it. All before she fully processed what'd happened.

It was only when she looked up that she had time to piece everything together. A man beside her had a duffel bag over his shoulder, a large one, and it had hit the top of her phone, knocking it out of her hand. However, the man had redeemed himself by making a miraculous catch, likely saving it from shattering on the floor. Though Meda had positioned herself strategically, he'd appeared out of nowhere and, due to her immediate sense of gratitude, she never questioned how he'd approached without notice. "Oh!" was all she had a chance to cry.

"Got it," said the man, as if to affirm to himself he'd caught it. Then, meeting her eyes, his demeanor changed and he became intensely apologetic. "I am sorry. I am so sorry."

"Wow," said Meda, still getting over the surprise.

The man was tall and barrel-chested, with eyes that appeared metallic, silver. Meda detected an accent in his voice but she couldn't place it. He possessed a rugged, weather-beaten face, yet, at the same time, his mannerisms appeared jumpy, like a teenager asking a girl out on a date. It was an incongruous air for such a formidable looking man. (Maybe he was nervous because he was foreign?)

"I am so, so sorry," the man continued, effusively. "I did not mean to. My bag."

"It's okay. It's okay," said Meda, annoyed but not angry. It was an honest mistake yet his incessant apologies and the fact that he was still clutching the phone were only making matters more awkward. He was bending at the waist, nearly bowing as he expressed his remorse, yet all Meda really wanted was to get Magee back on the phone.

"I am sorry," he said again, this time more slowly. "I should not ask. I need help. Help with just one thing."

Meda raised an eyebrow, not trying to hide her displeasure. "Look, can you give me the phone back first?"

"No, no. Wait," he insisted. Then he pointed over to the kiosks where train tickets were dispensed. "I need to get ticket. But I cannot read English. Can you...help me?"

She grimaced. At this point her phone was effectively held hostage. She could try to grab it from him but success was unlikely. Worse, it might draw attention, which was the absolute last thing she wanted. Better to be rid of the lummox sooner and prepare for Matt or Magee's arrival. "Okay," she acceded. "Let's go."

She strode ahead towards the kiosks. (If she was going to go out of her way to help him, she was going to do it on her terms.)

"Yes," proclaimed the man. "Thank you so, so much!"

Customarily, passengers picked up their tickets from one of the machines and then moved to the center of the room to check the board for a train's gate and arrival time. So there were far less people at the ticket terminals than her previous location. Meda arrived at the lonely kiosk, turned to the man, and said, "Okay, you need to swipe your credit card here."

She stopped speaking after that, however. She didn't trail off but, instead, completed her sentence on auto-pilot. Something had changed in the man's appearance. Gone was the goofy nervousness of a hapless tourist, replaced by a new level of confidence.

"You are coming with me," he said.

A chill went down Meda's back. "What?" she said, hoping in vain that she'd misheard him.

"You have. To come. With me," he said, the consonants in his words rigid and precise.

Clearly, this man was a member of the mafia. Meda had been suckered. And she had to think quickly. Shifting her stance to buy an extra second, she asked, "Why should I?"

"Because if you do not," said the man, anticipating the question so well that he sounded as if he was reading from a script, "Matt will die."

"What? What are you talking about?" asked Meda from behind a squint.

The man elaborated. "Your boyfriend. Matt. We know he is on his way to the opera. If he interferes, he will die.

"How do I know you're telling the truth?" It was a clumsy question. She was attempting to stall, to buy time to think, yet her confidence was wilting. She had options; she knew it and he knew it. She could start shrieking to draw attention. She could make a mad scramble to the soldiers standing at attention. She could attempt innumerable acts of resistance to create a scene. Yet none of those options would save Matt.

The Armenian appeared practically disappointed in the question and dismissed it entirely. "We will take care of our business with the boy tonight. That will happen despite anything you or Matt desire. We do not wish to kill Matt. My associates, however? They will kill him if sticks his nose where it does not belong. It would be a shame if it came to that, for you and for us. Therefore, I need you to come with me to talk him out of it."

Meda's poker face disintegrated. It was obvious the Armenians were already steps ahead of Matt. (She should've expected that, actually.) Meda knew all along that Matt was putting himself in danger yet she hadn't expected him to be walking into an outright trap. Saving the child was noble but there was no value in such a sacrifice if both he and the boy died anyway.

Sensing Meda's consternation, the man continued. "I am pleading with you to come with me. We honestly do not want to kill your boyfriend. He was in the wrong place at the wrong time. This is for his own good. I need you to come with me to make sure he does not do anything stupid."

Meda paused, thinking. "Wait. How does my presence deter Matt? What if he gets to the boy before we do?"

"He will see you before he sees the boy. We can guarantee it. If he sees you in person he will have no choice but to abort."

Again Meda paused, at a crossroads. She had every reason *not* to go with the man. For all she knew, they could be sneaking up on Matt at that very moment. Yet the plan made too much sense. At the end of the day, the Armenians had no reason to kill Matt. Why risk it? It was practically an act of desperation to ask for her help in the first place. The more nefarious part of the plan remained unaddressed, however. "Why, why do you have to kill the boy in the first place?" asked Meda haltingly. It was her last acquiescence to her conscience, even as her decision was almost made.

The man's eyes shot skyward, as if a nagging wife had reminded him of an errand. "If we stood back and allowed our brothers to die simply because the murderer was a child there would be none of us left. You know nothing. Children are pawns. This is how they get indoctrinated. Once they make their first kill they cannot go back. They are in the society forever. This boy? His life is gone already. Now it is about making the parents pay. So no one else repeats the same mistake."

His words were cold but rational. He might as well have been talking about the chemical composition of concrete and how it'd changed the modern world. Though it tore out a part of Meda's soul, she understood the perverse logic of the criminal: The boy had to die eventually. Matt was just too immature to accept it.

She bit her lip and peered up at the man. His expression was emotive, as if to give Meda enough space to make her own decision. Then, damning herself for doing so, she muttered, "Okay."

MAGEE

"Matt! Matt!"

Magee saw Matt coming first. It was lucky he did. If Magee hadn't stepped to the side and grabbed him he would've barreled over him and kept going.

Matt only barely halted and, as if broken out of a spell, shot an angry, bewildered glare at Magee. "Magee?" he uttered, blinking. Then, processing the implications of Magee's presence, he asked, "You didn't find her?"

"No, I only just got here myself. As far as I can tell, Meda's still down in Penn Station."

"Okay," said Matt, instantly bending at the knees and resuming his sprint. He ran into the street, dodging between cars as horns blared, and Magee was forced to follow. Magee had a perfect view as each vehicle came to a screeching halt and he cringed on Matt's behalf with each near-accident. Such a charge was unnecessary, dangerous even, and Magee needed to tell Matt to stop. He was going to get himself killed. "Matt! Wait!" he hollered, reaching for his shoulder.

Then, just as quickly as the dash had started, it was over. Matt came to halt, peering down as he did so. Magee looked over his shoulder to find that he'd pulled out his phone and it was vibrating. With relief in his eyes he quipped to Magee, "It's Meda."

Magee waited as Matt read the text, then quickly lost patience. "What is it? What'd she say?"

"She wrote," said Matt, faltering, his words arriving in batches, "that she's leaving Penn Station. And that she's heading to the Eastside."

"What?" said Magee, befuddled. "Why would she do that?"

"Here. Read it," said Matt, as confounded as Magee. The message read: "Leaving Penn. Too many people. Heading East. Meet me at Robert Moses Park. Near bridge."

In the moment Magee took to read the note, Matt grew more animated. "Okay. Okay," he said, beginning to bounce. "We have to get moving."

"Wait," said Magee, his palm towards Matt. His irritation at Meda was only barely counterbalanced by his desire to assess the situation. "This doesn't make any sense. Let's take a moment to think this through."

"Think what through?" said Matt, ready to dart.

"Why would Meda change the plan like that?" He wanted to give her the benefit of the doubt...it seemed so foolish.

"I don't know," said Matt, a bouncing jackrabbit of energy. "She said there were too many people. Whatever that means. Let's go!"

"No. Wait. Give me a second," pleaded Magee. "A crowd is a good thing. She'd be able to hide better. Can you write her back and tell her to stay at Penn?"

The green light was turning stale and Matt's frustrations boiled over. "We have to go. She said she was leaving. I don't know if she's still there. We have to go!"

Magee scowled before issuing a curt, "Fine."

The pair readied to take off again when, this time, Magee's phone lit up. "No!" Matt responded. "We don't have time."

He ignored his protests and yanked it out. It was Sergei.

"What? Screw him. Let's go."

Magee wanted to ignore the call...he had no interest in anything that guy had to say. Then, despite his regard for the man, he reconsidered. The guy was a valuable source of information. What if he knew something?

"Hello?" said Magee. And then, rather than Sergei's voice, he was surprised to hear Meda.

MEDA

Once Meda had the opportunity to think more logically, something began to gnaw at her: Penn Station was a big place. And she was virtually surrounded by people. So how did this guy find her? Even if he was aware she was in the Amtrak sub-section of Penn, it would still be remarkably hard to pick her out in such congestion. Anyone rooting around in an attempt to locate her would've stuck out like a sore thumb. Something didn't add up.

She continued to walk with the man while analyzing the sequence of events. As they passed the steps leading up to Madison Square Garden, it occurred to her that she'd also lost Sergei with comparatively little effort. The first time she ran he'd continued to trail her yet the second time she bolted he seemed to disappear the moment she escaped.

Once outside Penn Station, the Armenian stopped for a moment to get his bearings. They were on 8th Avenue with the cab stand in front of them and, in the distance, Meda thought she heard the echoing din of a series of car horns. The man began to guide them up the block to a less trafficked part of the sidewalk and, with surliness dripping from her words, Meda asked, "Are you at least going to give me my phone back?"

"No," he said without elaboration. Meda nearly stopped walking. She hadn't expected such a reply and her initial response was mute disgust.

"What? What do you mean? I'm going with you aren't I?"

Barely throwing a glance over his shoulder, the man replied, "We cannot risk you calling Matt. He might try to get clever. We need him to see you in person. I am sorry."

Again, Meda nearly came to a halt. (Who was this guy to start changing the arrangement now? She was going with him!

They had a deal!) Before she did so, however, before she even said a word, the situation spiraled. Two paces in front of her, the Armenian collided with a stranger chest-to-chest. It surprised her yet neither he nor the stranger seemed overly slighted. They crashed together, his arm shot into the pedestrian's stomach, and not a word was spoken. It was practically amicable. At the same moment a car screeched to a halt directly in front of them. And in one deft movement he ping-ponged off the stranger to the car, pulling Meda with him. It happened in an instant and, though she still had reservations regarding her cooperation, she was unprepared to fend off the man. She found herself grabbed at the arm and hip, ushered into the car without a chance to protest. She wanted to slow things down, to take a moment to think before falling into a stranger's car. But there was no opening to do so.

The Armenian dropped in beside her and she was forced to scoot sideways awkwardly with her purse against her back. "What the hell?" she shouted.

"What is the matter?" asked the man, all but yawning.

"You just shoved me into a car! That's the matter. I told you I'd come with you to help Matt. I didn't say you could kidnap me."

"You are not kidnapped," said the man. Yet there was something in his intonation that caused Meda to throw on a psychological emergency brake. When she'd used the word 'kidnap' she'd meant it sardonically, as an exaggeration. The literal articulation of it, however, forced her to confront the notion that she couldn't fully refute the term. She began to say something, stopped, then reined in her anger. Very quickly, she realized she'd better be wise with her words.

The facts were these: She was trapped in a speeding car with two violent men and she no longer had her phone. (Should've taken it back when she had the chance!) Irritated, borderline terrified, Meda glanced at the man's hands. She did a double-take, however, when she noticed something peculiar: He was no longer holding her phone. Had he put it in his pocket? Meda didn't think so; she'd been eying it up throughout their march. It was only after they'd leapt into the car that it disappeared. Or more precisely, Meda realized: Only after he'd run into that pedestrian. Suddenly, she began to connect the dots. No wonder neither he nor the pedestrian seemed surprised! It wasn't an accident; it was a handoff! The Armenian had given that man her phone.

Then, immediately following the revelation, a sinister feeling washed over her: *Why* had the Armenian given her phone away? And, just as importantly, how could the exchange have been so scripted? Meda turned her gaze out the window. She didn't want her expression seen. It was obvious the Armenian had lied about something but, even if she didn't know why, it was imperative that she continue to act natural. He had gone to pains to conceal the hand-off so her recognition of the exchange was her only advantage.

What possible use could they have of *her* phone? The Armenian already had possession of it at that time and there was no way she could overpower him to take it back. Also, she was cooperating and ready to travel with him. There would be no chance for her to make a call even if she had it. But what if, she realized, they weren't worried about *her* contacting anyone? What if they intended to send a message *from* it? Surely they would only have one recipient in mind: Matt.

Meda very nearly panicked. She kept her gaze fixed out the window but her body stiffened, as if anticipating a car accident. The Armenians were going to send Matt some sort of message, he would have no way of knowing it wasn't from her, and it was all her fault for losing the stupid phone in the first place. Her mental clatter hit a new high. She hadn't yet come to terms with the Armenian's plan for the little boy, much less how the Armenian had located her so easily at Penn Station. Yet now she found herself hurtling forward with no control of her destiny, in the backseat of a car as her bag jabbed her in her back.

The final thought hit her like a caveman's club. There was a hard object in her bag. What was it? With so many immediate distractions she hadn't focused on it and, on an unconscious level, had assumed it to be her phone. Obviously, it wasn't. So what was in her bag? She began to feel for it and let out a huffy sigh to give the impression she was settling into her seat. The Armenian glanced at her and sniffed, appearing to write-off the behavior as simple fussiness. Then, as discretely as possible, she pulled it out. It was a phone, but not her phone. Then illumination hit: The screen showed GPS coordinates. That was the reason the Armenian had found her so effortlessly. That was also why Sergei had given up the chase so easily. He must've shoved it in her bag when they ran into each other. It had been emitting some sort of signal the whole time (she could've run to Missouri and they still would've found her).

She wanted to throw the thing out the window. How dare they *track* her? Then a new thought sprung forth, though, a blinding flash amid all the other revelatory fireworks: She could use the phone to contact Matt. She wouldn't be able to talk to him outright but she might be able to warn him about messages originating from her phone. She surreptitiously began to dial, then stopped: What if he didn't answer? She would only have one chance at this and, if Matt was already receiving messages from her phone, he might not take the time to answer a call. (Particularly if forced to pick between messages from her and a call from Sergei, which would register as an unknown number.)

That was it, she realized: Call Magee. If it appeared the call was coming from Sergei, Magee would be far more likely to answer. He and Matt were on their way to find her and, logically, they would meet up at some point. Or so she hoped. The plan was dicey; it was risky not to call Matt directly. But she knew she had to make the most of her one chance (no extended texts, no hang-ups that risked a return call). Meda had no idea what message the Armenians intended to send Matt but, if the goal was to short-circuit their plan, Magee seemed to be the best option.

Still peering out the window, she dialed Magee's number with only a pair of artful glances. She waited a moment, then turned to the Armenian and asked, "So what do you plan to do?"

MATT

At the sound of Meda's voice Magee waved Matt over. First annoyed at the diversion, Matt turned grateful at Magee's levelheadedness. Also intuiting something odd about the conversation, a sense of eavesdropping, Magee held his finger to his lips before Matt could say anything.

"So what are you going to do?" Meda asked, sounding distant and somewhat muffled.

"You know," responded a deep, morose voice neither Magee nor Matt recognized.

They exchanged a glance, neither saying a word. It seemed evident that Meda had dialed Magee's number on the sly from Sergei's phone. Why she'd done so was still unclear.

"No, I mean," continued Meda, "I know you're going to kill the child. Why do it at *Götterdämmerung*?"

Both Matt and Magee registered the extra emphasis she'd put on the opera. Clearly, the text Matt had received from Meda's phone was a hoax and this was her way of letting them know the actual destination. Yet so many other questions remained unanswered.

There was a long period of silence and Matt could've sworn he heard the man sigh. Then, as if explaining something to a child, the man's voice droned, "I told you: We cannot let someone kill one of us, regardless of age. Those people used a child on purpose to indoctrinate him. The boy is all but dead already. We have to make it known that we—*we*—are the ones that killed him. To set an example."

For the second time, Matt and Magee exchanged a glance. While the first had been an expression of commiseration, this was one of trepidation.

For a long, tense moment all was silent. Then Meda asked, "So what do you plan to do with me?"

The man replied, as cold as ever, "That depends on what your boyfriend does."

"What does that mean?" Meda persisted, asking the question too quickly. Matt questioned her fearlessness.

"What I mean is: If your boyfriend shows up, you will have to tell him to leave."

"And what if I can't convince him?" Meda insisted.

"If you do not succeed, both of you, and the boy, will die."

His words dropped like a boulder in a deep, black pond and, momentarily, Meda's silence suggested she was done.

"And if I convince him it's not worth it we just leave? I don't believe you. Why would you just let us go?" She was unrelenting. Along with Matt, Magee became concerned as well. What did Meda think she was doing?

"Look: We have this covered," said the man, finally losing his laconic manner. "Matt is probably not going to show up anyway. You do not have to worry about such things. You are only along as a precaution. Okay? Now just be quiet."

Matt and Magee could feel the man's temper across the connection–it was as if he'd lost his composure over a buzzing fly.

After a long pause, a slight ruffling sound was heard. "What's going on?" asked Meda.

"We are here," said the man.

"Oh!" said Meda, sounding unprepared.

"Get out."

More rustling sounds were heard and then, abruptly, the call ended. Before Magee had a chance to make eye contact with Matt he'd already leapt into traffic and hailed a cab. "Okay. We need to get to the Metropolitan Opera immediately. Please hurry," said Matt.

"Actually, take us to 63rd Street at Amsterdam," Magee added. "There's a service entrance on that side."

MATT

The cab stopped in front of a nondescript metal rolling door and the pair jumped out, Magee trailing behind Matt. This was clearly Matt's journey but Magee wasn't about to let him go it alone. Matt hit the door in stride and immediately began yanking it open. It was heavy and required both of their efforts to hoist it. They took turns holding it aloft while the other snuck beneath and, once Magee was through, the door came down with hard rubber thud on the concrete.

They stood and, briefly, organized themselves. The décor was sparse, utilitarian—the floor was reinforced concrete with an institutional glaze atop and all fixtures and railings were unadorned steel. Three vans sat idle and, in the high-ceilinged depot, light diffused quickly.

The pair listened for a moment and heard echoing footfalls farther down a back hallway. They exchanged a glance, saying nothing. Then, though they only caught a few scant utterances, they registered the unmistakable accent. With no other humans in sight, they surmised that it had to be Meda and the Armenians. In the lowest whisper, Magee asked, "What do you plan to do?"

"I don't know," said Matt. And, with nothing more to add, he began to follow the echo to the hallway beyond.

It was a dangerous proposition. As compared to the depot, the hallway was illuminated well with harsh, unforgiving fluorescent light. The ceiling was low, the walls were made of cinder blocks painted a shiny ivory, and there were no large obstructions. If the Armenians doubled back or if Matt and Magee ran into security personnel there'd be no place to hide. Going down such a path committed the pair to their course.

Matt and Magee tried their best to keep their footfalls light but it was hard in the desolate hallway. In addition, the pair had to be mindful of distance, lest they approach too quickly and surprise the Armenians. Matt's mind was at work as they pursued, however, and, checking his watch, he saw it was 4:48. Showtime was at 6:00 so early arrivals would be milling about and finding their seats. If the Armenians hoped to kill the boy and his family—and if they also expected to escape—it was already too late for them to do so in the actual theater. They evidently had a different location in mind.

Matt and Magee arrived at a juncture in the hallway and stopped. The sounds of Meda and the Armenians' footfalls were clearly emanating from the path to the left. In fact, Magee had been instinctively following the sounds and had only halted when he saw that Matt had. He peered at his friend quizzically, as if to ask him what he was doing. But Matt's mind was racing. The other hallway to the right was as similarly utilitarian as the one they'd just traversed but, farther down it, Matt could see it truncated in a series of stairs.

Magee raised his eyebrows, as if to emphasize his confusion at Matt's indecision. Matt was busy formulating a plan, however, as he continued to mull the Armenian's options: They couldn't kill the boy at the entrance or on the floor of the opera—they needed some measure of solitude and they required a means to escape. That meant they'd have to head to some secluded area in the facility, some place away from the actual performance.

Matt put up the palm of his hand as if to calm Magee and, with hushed intensity, said, "They have to kill the boy in a private place. We can't keep following them."

Magee drew back. "What about Meda?"

Matt swallowed hard. He needed to save Meda but he wanted to save the boy, as well.

"We need to keep moving," insisted Magee, motioning down the hallway to the left. "If they get too far ahead we might lose them."

"I know," muttered Matt, weighing the possibilities. "I know."

He told himself that his notion of taking the alternate path wasn't expressly about the boy—it also allowed him to get the jump on the Armenians and keep Meda safe. Yet the rational part of his mind contested the idea, noting the obvious deduction that he had no way of knowing where the stairs led. Inasmuch as his plan allowed him to save both Meda and the boy, it nonetheless put all his eggs in one basket—if the path to the right took him in the wrong direction he'd be unable to save either. He was forced to ask himself: Was this about saving his future wife? Or was it about something more than that?

Matt glared down the hallway to the right. "We have to go up those stairs."

"What?" asked Magee in abject disbelief.

"We have to take the chance."

Magee tried again. "Matt, you're not thinking this through."

But Matt was already turned and sprinting towards the stairway.

MEDA

The march through the labyrinthine hallways below Lincoln Center was tortuous. With one of the Armenians in front of Meda and the other behind, there was no choice but to walk in lockstep. They hadn't encountered another person since entering the underground and she couldn't escape the feeling that she should be offering more resistance, more struggle. While she had no idea what she could do, she nonetheless felt a growing, slow-moving commitment the farther she moved away from civilization. Previously, on the sidewalk, she could've at least made a scene and hoped for someone to call the police. Now even that option was gone.

She'd done her best to convey her predicament to Magee. With no way to confirm he'd actually received the message, however, it required a great leap of faith to be confident she was doing the right thing. She didn't believe the Armenians would allow her and Matt to simply walk away yet she couldn't flee and leave Matt and Magee out to dry. It felt antithetical to her being to trust that things would simply work out but, in the interim, she needed to resist the urge to do anything rash.

For a long time the only sounds to be heard were those of their footfalls and the ambient, nearly imperceptible hum emitting from the concrete beneath such a structure. The solidity of the walls and the isolation from society made the atmosphere claustrophobic, heightening Meda's self-doubt. So when the second Armenian's phone buzzed, her neck snapped with amphetamine-like intensity. The lead Armenian said nothing, did not even turn around, and the second smirked at Meda's skittishness.

"It's Pietre," the second man announced. "Matt did not show up."

(What? What was that about Matt?)

"Of course," said the lead Armenian, utterly deadpan.

("Of course"? What did he mean by that?)

"What are you guys talking about?" blurted Meda, unable to contain herself.

"Quiet," said the second Armenian to Meda. "There's more."

He paused and Meda thought he would elaborate on Matt's status. Instead, it became readily apparent that he was addressing his compatriot directly. "He also says the plan remains."

"He has the kid?" asked the first.

"No. But his family is headed here now. We will have time to set up."

A shudder rippled down Meda's spine. She hadn't yet resolved the men's flip comments about Matt yet now discussion of the child was driving the situation into a new state of tangibility. She'd tacitly known they planned to kill the child; when she'd imagined a choice between Matt's life and his, it'd been easy to step aside and let the mafia handle its business. She hadn't literally envisioned the murder, however, or considered she'd be anywhere in the vicinity of the act when it occurred.

"Wait," she said, still walking. "What are you planning to do? Will I actually be there when it happens?"

"Shut up," said the lead Armenian.

"No, I won't shut up," said Meda, slowing her pace, then halting in defiance. "You just mentioned something about Matt and now you two are talking about killing the child. I cooperated with you when you said Matt would get hurt. Now you guys owe me some explanations."

The man in back nearly ran into her and it took the one in front a number of paces to realize she'd stopped. He turned and progressed towards her slowly, Meda's demands orphaned in the stark silence.

"We owe you nothing," was his initial reply, brutal in its simplicity. "We could have killed both the boy and Matt quite easily. We had no reason to involve you. It was only because you were there, with Sergei, that we decided to give you this opportunity."

The man's intensity couldn't stay hidden and, at times, it cracked through like lava beneath cooling rock. It gave his words urgency, despite the fact that Meda knew she couldn't trust the man, and on some level she also recognized she had no choice but to follow him anyway. Meda vacillated. And when she didn't respond immediately, he turned to walk again trusting that she would follow.

They passed through a set of double doors with, "AUTHORIZED PERSONNEL ONLY," lacquered across them. Then, traversing another nondescript hallway, they passed through a more formal set of doors and arrived at a staircase. It was covered in rich, luxurious carpet and it was clear they were approaching an area no longer restricted to employees.

Meda reassessed her options. (There was no good choice, only a few less-bad ones.) Now that they were entering a semi-public location again, she had the ability to make a scene, to scream and holler, if only to garner attention. But was that the best course of action? Matt and Magee were probably on their way. If she absconded in fear, she might be dooming either or both of them. Complicating matters, she was about to be party to the murder of a child, something she'd never considered when she agreed to accompany the man. Yet, with the men clearly in mode to commit such an act, she wondered what would happen to her if she created a distraction. Would they kill her? And what if she attempted to create some commotion but no one responded?

Without a word they proceeded up the stairs and the three of them arrived at a landing, long and wide, which was just as opulent as the stairway. Along either side of the corridor were gorgeous wooden doors, every one of them shut, with finely detailed mahogany chairs spaced between each. It appeared to Meda like a lounge meant to host cocktail parties or special events, now closed to the public. (Good thing she didn't try anything funny after all!) The first Armenian led the way down the expansive hall and, at the last door on the left, he opened it and ushered her inside.

The room was stark and barren while nonetheless possessing an ornate quality. The carpet was lavish, the trim richly decorated, and a radiant chandelier hung from the ceiling. Yet there were only two basic folding chairs present near the center of the back wall. The man signaled that Meda should take a seat and, as she did so, she glanced about the room further. It wasn't small yet the walls loomed with menace. There was nowhere to run now, no other options remaining.

"This is where it's going to happen?" she asked. She didn't need such confirmation but the gravity of the moment was weighing on her and she blurted the question out of sheer anxiety.

"Close your mouth. Or I will blow your brains out."

"Look, you don't need to be such an asshole," snapped Meda.

The man's body did not move but his gaze landed on her like a concrete block. It was too late for her to take back what she said. "My dear," he began, his words freezing the air brittle, "I do not believe you appreciate the seriousness of your situation. You see, I saw the phone."

"What?"

"The phone in your bag. Sergei's. I saw you take it out and dial."

Meda's mouth went dry. The air in her lungs felt ten pounds heavier.

"Yes. I knew you made the call and I knew our conversation was heard. That was why I was not surprised when Matt did not arrive at the rendezvous point."

(Rendezvous point? What?)

Meda's reaction spoke volumes, evidently. "Oh, you did not know?" continued the Armenian, himself surprised at Meda's ignorance. "Well no matter."

"What's that supposed to mean?" Meda croaked.

The first Armenian glanced to his partner with a smirk and he received a shrug in return. The second man then left the room and the attention of the first returned to Meda. He hesitated, as if deciding whether to tell her something, then cocked his head to the side and said, "The plan was to lure Matt to a different point. Then there would be no way for him to intervene. We needed your phone to do this. That was Plan A. You ruined it with your stupid phone call."

An edge appeared in his voice and Meda felt a pang of guilt: Had the Armenians been trying to keep Matt safe? Then she countered, "Once he arrived at that point, though. What were you going to do once he arrived there?"

The Armenian took a large swallow of air and said, "It was not our *intention* to harm him." His emphasis freed Meda of any residual feelings of guilt; he should've just admitted that they planned to kill him. Their primary goal might've been to keep him away from the opera but that didn't mean they had any compunction against killing him.

"If you planned to kill him," hissed Meda, ignoring the man's use of semantics, "then what did you need me for?"

He smirked again, as if it was all an amusing trifle. "You were Plan B. From the outset, you were a timely insurance policy. Most important was your phone. Any number of unforeseen things could occur to obstruct Plan A. Matt might change his mind, our associate might not succeed. So as long as you were available, we decided to take you as well."

He made it sound like he was at the store picking up groceries. Meda fumed. Yet, beneath such indignation, lay a stratum of fear. If this man could be so casually indifferent about kidnapping and murder, how little provocation would he require to actually pull the trigger?

"Once you made the call," the man went on, "everything changed. I played along because I knew, once you connected with Matt, he would not fall for the first plan. As soon as he heard your voice from the other phone he would suspect."

Meda wanted to correct him and tell him she'd called Magee, not Matt. She knew it wouldn't matter, though.

"At that point you stopped being an insurance policy."

The man said no more and the abrupt conclusion gave Meda pause. Against her better judgment, she asked, "What am I now, then?"

Before he could answer, the second Armenian darted back into the room and he was carrying a large mirror pane. "Right where Pietre said it would be," quipped the man, sounding altogether too jolly given the circumstance.

The man placed the mirror directly in front of her while the first propped it up with the other chair. She looked it up and down, sensing nefarious intent. "What? What's that for?"

"Simple," said the first man, with something resembling a smile. "Two-way mirror. We stay behind it. When the boy arrives, I shoot him. If your boyfriend shows up first, I shoot him. And then, when they're both dead, I shoot you."

MATT

"Matt, is this the right time to get *creative*?" asked Magee.

"I don't know the right time for anything anymore," replied Matt, galloping up another set of stairs.

Magee followed and the pair discovered another hallway at the top of the stairs, this one even more simple and unadorned. Whereas the previous hall had been luminous, almost blinding, this corridor was lit only by sparsely placed string lights like those found on a construction site. Clearly it was intended for employees only and it appeared barely utilized at that. Matt took that as a good sign.

"I'm serious, Matt," insisted Magee from behind. The corridor was narrow and it was impossible for Matt and Magee to walk side-by-side. "Your life could be at stake here. And Meda's."

"That's *why* I have to take this route," countered Matt. He was a man possessed. He recognized Magee's words and the truth in them but he remained undaunted.

Matt had no idea where he was going, of course. He just knew they couldn't follow Meda forever. Sooner or later the Armenians would arrive at their destination and then he and Magee would stumble upon them, losing the element of surprise. No. There had to be another way.

They continued down the corridor for a long stretch and, though Magee said nothing further, Matt could sense his misgivings. There were no outlets along the way, no chances to the leave the path, and the further they proceeded the more committed they became. If the corridor resulted in a dead-end all would be lost—they would've almost certainly lost Meda and the Armenians. And, even as he battled his own growing doubts, Matt feared he would soon lose Magee's confidence entirely.

Then Matt heard something that did not fit. It was faint, nearly indiscernible.

"Matt, I think—" began Magee before Matt shushed him with a single raised finger.

The sound danced at the periphery of Matt's attention like a gnat but he didn't stop moving. The sound was so slight and, despite the fact that individual voices were now becoming more distinct, they weren't the source of Matt's alarm. Something else, something apart from the drone was causing his mental churn.

"Matt. This is crazy. We—" began Magee, more insistent. Matt shushed him yet again.

Magee didn't see that Matt was straining to hear something. Recognizing this, Matt slowed and turned to assuage Magee. They were closing in on a doorway up ahead and Matt realized he should explain his dilemma before they got too close, lest anyone on the other side hear them. In that momentary pause, however, when no longer distracted by their footfalls or the rustling of their clothes, Matt divined the source of the sound. Before even saying a word to Magee, his eyes went wide at the epiphany. There was a reason the sound didn't fit in with the other murmurs: It was the voice of a young boy.

Magee realized as well, a moment late, and his eyes met Matt's. Clearly, there would be children at the opera apart from the one targeted by the Armenians. Probably not many, though. Matt nodded to Magee, wordlessly acknowledging that they were on to something. Then, practically on tip toes, they both approached the door.

Matt opened it a crack, unsure if he'd find a lively cocktail party, an angry security guard, or something much worse on the other side. But there was no one there. He craned his neck to get a better view of the room beyond and, once satisfied it was empty, he opened the door more fully.

He and Magee crept inside. The room was extravagantly cluttered and, while not as barren as the concrete corridor they'd been travelling, it was similarly ill-suited for public use. The carpet was stained, small stacks of opera programs were strewn in assorted piles, and racks of dinner glasses sat on an old oak table. Incongruously, surplus wiring sat beside a pair of expensive looking opera glasses and, fleetingly, Matt mused at what a treasure trove of ideas the materials represented. How many times does one see a stack of large, unadorned mirror panes leaning against an opera poster that might be worth thousands of dollars to the right collector? It was clear the room was an informal storage area for things the staff might need on the fly—the perfect spot for Matt and Magee to re-insert themselves without arousing suspicion.

A beat late, Matt realized the door on the opposite side of the room was ajar. He peered at it—it was an oxen slab of wood well-suited for 18th century castle—and noticed the keys dangling from the lock. It was only a matter of time before an employee noticed so he advanced towards the door, ready to close it, when he came to a halt.

He heard the boy's voice again. It was coming from the hallway beyond. And, putting two and two together, Matt realized the only reason he'd heard it in the first place was because the door had been left open. The voice defined his purpose now, supernaturally so. Doubt and fear had been growing in him when he thought he'd taken the wrong path but now the boy's voice was like a siren's call at sea, washing all doubt away. He was compelled to step out into the hallway beyond. Behind him, Magee hissed a harsh, "Matt." But it was too late.

Before Matt, farther down the hall, was a boy being led by the scruff of his neck by a large man in a leather coat. Though Matt's view was partially blocked by the hulking brute, the boy's shuffling steps and tight, nervous movements illustrated his fright. It had to be *the* boy.

Each second that passed seemed to lengthen exponentially. Matt stared without fear, the Armenian wholly unaware of his presence. He couldn't believe it. There was the boy. After everything that'd happened, *there* was the boy! Matt's bravado swelled as if he'd won a race, as if he'd defeated a monster. Somewhere, in a distant cave in his mind, a voice warned that he shouldn't stand there like a dummy—he should be *doing* something. But Matt was too invigorated to listen. Then, like the silent, slow-motion terror of a car gliding across a patch of ice before the inevitable crash, the Armenian looked in Matt's direction. At first it was casual, a mere glance after catching something out of the corner of his eye. Next, there was the double-take, the recognition of another person, the momentary face of confusion. And then there was anger.

After that, everything happened so fast. Too fast. The moment was at hand. Whether Matt was ready or not.

Matt whirled back into the room without conscious thought. He remembered the mirrors beside the doorway. As he spun back in, Matt's mind registered the concern on Magee's face, yet his body continued to act. He seized one of the panes—the glass heavy, solid—and twisted around to stick it out of the doorway.

There was a pop. Like a firecracker. And suddenly the mirror was much lighter. The front of it shattered and Matt flinched, dropping the remaining half. Shards of glass fell like tinkling, terrible rain, immediately followed by the crash of the other half of the mirror as it burst on the floor.

Purely on instinct, Matt jumped a half-step back into the room for protection. Then he heard screams—one was a boy's, the other a woman's. In a state of auto-pilot he then leapt and grabbed another mirror.

Magee hollered, "Matt!" and lunged to stop him. But it was too late. Matt was already charging down the hall, holding up the mirror as if it was a shield. The act was suicidal in its desperation—a pane of glass would offer no protection from a bullet. Yet at the fringes of his conscious mind, Matt had an inspiration he couldn't deny.

After five steps, he realized it was a two-way mirror—he could see through it. He saw the little boy running away from the man, down another corridor, yet the Armenian was running in the other direction, further down the landing. He appeared spooked and the observation offered Matt a fleeting moment of clarity—the man must've caught a glimpse of the gunfire in the mirror and hadn't realized he was looking at himself.

Then, to Matt's horror, the Armenian stopped, as if coming to his senses. He raised his gun to shoot. But he remained panicked, his hand was trembling. Matt saw the flashes erupt from the muzzle and heard two more bursts. Yet nothing happened to the mirror. Or to him.

The man's expression told a story of spiraling abandon; he appeared utterly unnerved that he'd missed Matt twice. Matt continued to rush forward and, for a terrible tick of the clock, the man merely stood with his mouth agape. Then, abruptly, he turned and sprinted towards the end of the landing again. Matt had no idea what the man saw in the mirror but he did not stop his charge—he was too committed to change course now. The man stopped at the last door and, in a moment that sent cold mercury through Matt's veins, stared at him again.

The Armenian was stationary—his aim would not be so shoddy this time and Matt was closing in.

Yet the man didn't shoot. His expressed conveyed abject terror, like that of a lone soldier completely surrounded, any semblance of strategic thought erased. He sent that horrified glare at Matt again and, in wild-eyed abandon, threw open the door instead.

Matt didn't fully fathom what he saw and heard next—his senses jumped into overdrive, the events too quick to comprehend in real time. Two, three, four quick firecrackers went off and the man took a step back. It was an awkward, ungainly movement and, zombie-like, the man raised his gun in response. He shot into the room, more fireworks cracking, not all of them in concert with the muzzle flashes from his gun. The man continued firing—Matt's conscious mind wondered why he was firing so many times. Yet he couldn't register all that was transpiring. He was recording the details without a translator. Amid the shots Matt heard a pane of glass shatter and, for the briefest instant, thought he'd been fired upon—from another direction maybe? But no, the mirror he held remained intact.

He also heard a woman screaming. It was coming from inside the room. And it sounded like Meda. "No," he gasped. It couldn't be her. How many shots had the man fired? She couldn't be in there, could she?

Matt saw that the man was still pulling the trigger, clicking and clicking—out of bullets. And the man was slouching, his right knee buckling. He began to connect the dots: The man had been shot when he threw open the door. And, in shock, he'd instinctually returned fire. Yet that revelation was mere background noise compared to his concern for Meda

Meda's scream created a myopic focus for Matt. She was all that mattered. He arrived at the door and tossed the mirror at the man, easily knocking him over. And by the time Matt heard the crash of glass, he was already beyond it, already focused on the scene inside the room.

There was blood. On the wall, on the carpet. One man was slumped on the floor, his expression locked in a state of ghastly surprise. Beside him was another man, face down in a pool of blood. Shards of mirrored glass were strewn around the pair, silvery reflections amid the blood and gore. Neither man was moving.

Then Matt located Meda. She was behind a chair. He couldn't see her well. She wasn't moving.

Three lunging steps into the room, he shouted, "Meda!"

Six steps in, nearly at her side, a dam inside Matt ready to break. And in one movement, he shoved the chair aside, slid on his hip, and crashed into her. It was clumsy, nearly rolling both onto broken glass. But in the process her arm moved. She was alive.

Relief burst forth inside Matt, gushing and unstoppable. He hugged her hard. He didn't care what happened next. She was *alive*!

After a moment he pulled away to get a better look at her. A quick survey found no apparent wounds. She appeared to be in shock, cowering with eyes that were wide and child-like. "I just. I just fell and rolled. I didn't know what else to do," she whispered, as if offering a guilty admission.

"You did the right thing," said Matt, nearly sobbing. "You're safe now, honey."

He clutched her tight again. She was shaking. He wanted to comfort her, to convey that the danger had passed. Unwittingly, he began rocking her back and forth in his arms. Then, after a period, he realized: No. She wasn't the one that was shaking. He was.

He looked up to see a large piece of the mirror still intact, balanced perfectly against the wall opposite him. Innumerable jagged fragments lay scattered about and a gradually increasing pool of blood threatened to engulf them. Yet this specific pane caught his attention. Even as he continued to clutch Meda, his body surging with both adrenaline and relief, his gaze stayed focused on it. He couldn't believe what he saw, a revelatory vision after all the turmoil and trauma. Rather than his own reflection in the mirror, Matt instead witnessed the image of the little boy.

MEDA

Of course the image Matt saw in the mirror of himself as a little boy was not the material representation of his youthful dream of becoming a writer. That would be impossible. But it didn't keep him from insisting as much in the days that followed. To Meda's chagrin he had seized on that narrative with a sense of talismanic awe and wouldn't be dissuaded by any reason or logic she presented. The fact that no child was located at the scene in the chaos that followed was all the proof he needed to confirm that the little boy was, in fact, him.

It didn't bother Meda, exactly. (Who was he hurting with such a belief?) She just thought it was weird. After everything they'd experienced in the preceding three weeks, she was disappointed *that* was his major takeaway. She knew Matt wasn't crazy, despite anything he might say to the contrary. Yet she couldn't wrap her head around such a metaphysical conclusion when actual bullets had been fired at them.

Thankfully, he hadn't asserted such an opinion to the staff or the police. The ushers at the Met had arrived first after hearing the gunshots, followed later by the cops. To his credit, Magee had been a virtuoso, explaining the situation and distracting gawkers while Matt and Meda recovered. This allowed them time to process the events more fully, each lost in thought even as they remained locked in embrace.

Meda remembered an overarching sense of fear which had no name, a type of rumination that only occurred after one was safe (two inches to the left and the body over there would've been her). She kept peering at one of the dead Armenians then looking away, over and over, as if it offered proof that she was alive and unharmed. In the background, she'd heard the screams of one of the ushers, and Magee explaining something, and the growing commotion. Yet her mind had remained locked on the inches that separated her from life and death.

The police hadn't been pleased with Matt. At all. In fact, it was only due to Magee's efforts that Matt hadn't blurted out his wild theory about the boy, potentially making the situation worse. Following the confrontation at Masis, the police were already en route to the opera when the events unfolded. And, once they caught up on everything, they were so disgusted by Matt's recklessness that they'd issued vague threats of arrest. But no one doubted that, had it not been for his efforts, the boy (wherever he ended up) would've been killed.

The fact that the Armenians had shot each other was the only thing that saved Matt and Meda from future retribution. After the police arrived, Meda had been shuttled to a quiet room and afforded the opportunity to compose herself. Almost immediately she'd feared for her and Matt's continued safety. Now that three of their own had died, she concluded there was no way the mafia would *not* come for her and Matt. The detective on the scene had calmed her, however, and pointed out an important fact: If anything at all happened to her or Matt, everyone would know who to blame. The violence at the opera had provided investigators with cause to look into their affairs and, since the shootings were bound to make the papers, the organization would become a target of suspicion. Therefore, the higher ranking members of their group would be forced to step in and quell any vendettas. The detective had summarized: Meda and Matt were safe because, if anything were to happen to either, it would be bad for business. His assurances didn't allay all of Meda's concerns but, in the days that followed, they allowed her to sleep at night at least. And after nearly dying that day, she would admit she was ready to move on and return to her regular life as soon as possible.

As far as Meda could tell, Matt appeared to return to his senses as well. Throughout the experience, he'd been focused on the welfare of the little boy. So, once he was positive the boy was safe, his previously-held angst vanished. Meda was glad that he'd stopped torturing himself (his bizarre theory about his reflection in the mirror notwithstanding) but she remained on alert for any signs of relapse. The recent troubles had appeared suddenly, seemingly out of the blue, and she intended to be on guard for any hint of another episode.

So when he'd insisted that she and Magee go with him to see something the following Friday, it wasn't as if Meda felt no hesitation. She presumed it wouldn't be dangerous and that Matt wouldn't go looking for trouble. But the fact that he'd been so secretive about the trip presented a red flag.

Matt pulled up in front of Meda's apartment and Magee hopped out to offer her the passenger seat. "So. What do you know about this?" asked Magee once Meda was settled.

"I have no clue," she said. "He won't give me any details either."

"I told you guys: It's a surprise. You," said Matt, addressing Magee, "will get a real kick out of it. And hon, I really want you to see this. It's important."

"As long as it doesn't involve the mafia," groused Meda.

They drove for a short time down a street that appeared vaguely familiar to both Meda and Magee. It was a service road, nondescript in every way. So when Matt flipped on his turn signal and began to guide the car to the side of the road, their curiosity perked up.

It was dark but Matt turned off the headlights even as the car was still rolling. He pulled over at an odd angle, though, resulting in an atrocious parking job that put the front-right tire up on the curb and left the back corner of the car butting into traffic.

"Matt," began Meda, incredulous.

"Hold on," said Matt, in return.

And, in one movement, he turned on the headlights again and popped out of the car. He was almost childlike in his glee and it took Meda and Magee a moment to identify what Matt was presenting.

Then: "No way," said Magee, with a whimsical, stupefied smile.

"What?" What?" said Meda.

Magee pushed his way out of the back seat to join Matt, Meda's question unaddressed. She couldn't get a good view, however, and, begrudgingly, she followed them out of the car.

"The Dirty Lord," said Magee, enthralled. "You'd mentioned it. But seeing it in person again...?"

"That's right," said Matt, beaming.

Meda caught up to them and saw the graffiti they were admiring. Magee was essentially speechless and Matt, unable to contain himself, jabbered, "Can you believe it? I re-discovered it two weeks ago. I was trying to find out what happened to the little boy and I just came upon it."

Then, addressing Meda, he said, "Hon, years ago Magee and I found this but we could never remember the location afterward. We decided it was the symbol for the Dirty Lord. See the 'D' and then the 'Y' there? And the 'L' there?"

Meda grimaced, her stare moving from Matt to Magee and back again.

Matt continued with no loss of momentum. "We decided he was the patron saint of wretches who live their lives out of their minds."

"Yes," added Magee. "The caretaker of nonsense and the source of insanity."

"Yes! Yes!" said Matt.

"I can't believe you found this, buddy," said Magee, his hand going to his chin. "How long ago was that? My God."

"I'm as surprised as you are," said Matt. Then he peered at Meda again, as if to invite her to partake in their enthusiasm, to ask why she wasn't more excited.

She glanced at Matt and then at Magee again, her brow furrowed in disbelief. Then she announced, "You two are idiots."

Matt and Magee's smiles drooped but, before Matt could protest, she asked, "Do either of you actually know what that is?"

"It's the Dirty Lord," said Matt, as if it was self-evident.

"No. It's the Flower of Life. It's a symbol present in the iconography of virtually all the world's major religions. It dates back thousands of years. Some say it represents the very formation of the universe. Da Vinci studied it. It symbolizes creation in the most basic sense, something coming from nothing." And stifling a giggle, she added, "I can assure you: It is not the Dirty Lord."

Silence. Matt looked at Magee and Magee looked back at Matt. Their smiles hadn't fully disappeared but, instead, the pair appeared perplexed. Beside them, cars continued to zoom past yet their presence did nothing to diminish the quiet that had dropped like a curtain between the threesome.

"Well," began Matt.

"No," said Meda, quashing his protest before it started. "Go home. Research it. I'm not making this up. While, yes, I can see where you guys might interpret some of the spray paint to be letters, the overall structure, the overlap of the circles, is most definitely the Flower of Life."

"All this time," said Magee, shaking his head at the revelation.

"It's fascinating how eternal the image is," continued Meda more congenially, as if to offer an escape from their embarrassment. "Religions the world over, ones whose followers were likely never in contact, have nonetheless used it at one time or another. There is no easy explanation for its prevalence. I'd say it's a little odd to see it scrawled under a bridge like this. In a more profound sense, though, it's compelling in its mystery."

Matt listened but Meda could see that he was still thinking, still reconciling the newfound revelation with his own outlook. "Let me throw this idea at you," he said.

"Yes?"

"What if the Flower of Life and the Dirty Lord *are* the same thing?" He paused for a moment dramatically, as if to let the notion to sink in. "What if the Flower of Life gave us the idea of the Dirty Lord and transformed *itself* into the Dirty Lord? It becomes self-referential, like the chicken and the egg. Did Magee and I create the Dirty Lord or did the Flower cause us to create the Dirty Lord out of itself?"

"I think," began Meda, forming her words, then stopping.

Matt continued, "If the Flower represents creation, then how does it create itself?"

"I," began Meda, stumbling again. Then, throwing her arms up, she said, "I don't know. I just think you shouldn't refer the Flower of Life as the Dirty Lord."

"But it can be both," persisted Matt, while Magee chucked and covered his face with his hand. "If the Flower of Life is the symbol of all creation, then creation flows not only out of it, but into it, as well. It can be called anything because it *is* everything."

Meda crossed her arms. "You're not going to let this go, are you?"

Matt smiled, goofy and proud. "No."

"Okay then!" announced Meda, bringing her hands together in a single, loud clap. "I can see we're not going to get anywhere on this topic."

Magee's chuckles turned into gales of laughter and, after a moment, Matt couldn't help but snort as well. The revelation was serious and important and enlightening, and neither Matt nor Magee wished to treat it disrespectfully. Yet there was simply nothing more to add.

Meda turned to go while Matt and Magee took an extra second to appreciate the design one final time. Each reminisced about how far they'd come since that fateful day they discovered it. Magee had remained committed to his art, yet he wasn't nearly as naïve as he was back then; Matt had also remained committed to his craft, though in a different way, and had survived a tempest to make sure the little boy lived. The pair remained transfixed and unmoving until, finally, Meda commanded, "Get in the car, idiots. Before somebody slams into your rear end."

DANI

For the sake of everything holy in this reality, Darqor must be defeated. Despite Dani's fatigue, despite the ever-tightening stitch in her side, she had to fight on. So far the villain had deflected nearly every blow from her Sword of Xe and she knew she couldn't keep up such a fierce battle forever. Yet she could not allow him to gain control of the Omniperion Gem. Though her muscles screamed in protest, she raised the sword once more and brought it down upon the monster. Darqor threw up his shield at the last moment, however, and when the weaponry clashed, the sword broke with feeble, Styrofoam 'clunkt.'

"Aw crap," moaned Donnie, immediately yanking off his Darqor helmet to inspect the damage to the sword. "I thought you said you'd fixed it, Dani?"

"I did. I thought I did," she said, clutching the shimmery, tinfoil-covered blade of the sword in one hand and the duct-taped handle in the other. At the joint between each was a farcical amount of dried glue, gobs and gobs that nonetheless failed to keep the Sword of Xe intact.

Dani Park and her best friend, Donnie, spent most Saturdays immersed in live action role playing, a fantastical escapade wherein one literally lives out fantasy with costumes and accessories. Most often, Dani played the role of Omega, the heroine of the Omega Zone novels, while Donnie played Darqor, the villain in the series. They spent countless hours honing their costumes to perfection, devouring the latest Omega Zone novels, and hatching storylines to perform. It required massive amounts of creativity, both from a creation standpoint—fashioning costumes and weapons from everyday items—and a functional standpoint—creating compelling storylines with only two participants. Dani and Donnie were the only ones at their high school interested in role playing apart from William Mor, and he was two grades younger and always insisted on "winning" the battles.

"I'm sorry," muttered Donnie as the pair continued to stare at the busted sword with disappointment. "I didn't mean to bring up the shield so hard."

"It's okay," said Dani, shrugging. "Won't be the first time we broke it."

Without a word they separated and began gathering the weapons and assorted regalia scattered about. A patch of woods behind Donnie's house offered the perfect spot to enact their adventures and, with the latest quest abruptly truncated, it was time to head home. Often they would get so engrossed in their adventures that they'd lose all track of time so, for once, Donnie could return before his mom called.

"Skype tonight?" asked Donnie as they walked back.

"Yep," said Dani. "Oh! Wait. My stupid cousin is going to be over with his family. I might not get on until later."

"That's okay," said Donnie cheerfully, obliviously. Dani had hoped for some commiseration at her plight but, clearly, Donnie was focused only on their next Skype session.

The pair separated and Dani began the six block walk home, already dreading the notion of spending the night with her cousin. Josh was their chief antagonist at school, often using the fact that he was Dani's relative as a shield. He'd tell the teachers—if they got involved at all—that he was only kidding. But he wasn't kidding; he was as mean and hurtful as a wasp. While virtually everyone in school treated Dani and Donnie shabbily, Josh's derision often went over the line, bordering on physical violence. And because of their familial relationship, neither Dani nor Donnie could get the respect from any authority figure to make the abuse end.

Dani hadn't even arrived at the front door when Josh's nasally whine assaulted her.

"Hey, it's the pixie back from pixieland." Her parents and her mom's sister's family all laughed. Dani did not.

"Hi everyone," said Dani, offering a brief, unenthusiastic wave.

"Did you have fun today" asked her mother, the smile from Josh's joke still present.

"Yeah," Dani shrugged, not daring to put down her bag of costumes and weapons.

"Who got turned into a dragon this time: You or Donnie?" chortled Josh. As irritating as his barbs were to begin with, they were made doubly infuriating by the fact that he didn't know what the heck he was talking about. Omega Zone didn't have anything to do with pixies or dragons. But Dani didn't have the patience to explain that to him, even if she thought he'd listen.

Dani didn't answer the question but, instead, stood shifting her feet at the front door. Her parents had chided her in the past for not being social enough—appearance was everything in a Korean family. Yet she'd barely entered her own home before being accosted and, frankly, she had nothing to say.

"Or let me guess," continued Josh. "A giant caterpillar came and stole all your gold so both of you had to turn into dragons to defeat him?"

"That's enough, Josh," said Dani's aunt half-heartedly between her giggles.

Dani turned to go up to her room. She'd had enough. At her back she heard Josh explaining how he was trying to help Dani. No one challenged such a ludicrous justification or attempted to defend Dani. Instead the adults simply changed the subject, just as they always did. Nothing changed.

Dani concealed her bag of costume gear in the back corner of her closet and sighed. She knew she'd have to go back downstairs eventually but, for the moment, she needed time away. To her pleasant surprise, Donnie was already on Skype. It was both a relief and a bewilderment: Did he sign on the second he got home or something?

"Hey, did you see the news?" blurted Donnie before Dani had a chance to say hello.

"No. What?"

"Turley is starting his own Badlands series. It was supposed to be a secret but it got leaked!"

Dani recognized the importance of the news immediately. Gene Turley was one of the most prominent writers in the Omega Zone series and the fact that he was joining the Badlands collective was tantamount to John F. Kennedy emigrating to the Soviet Union in the midst of the cold war. To an outsider, it might be a career move; to Dani and Donnie it was earthshaking.

"What?" she exclaimed, her fingers immediately going to work on the keyboard.

"Yeah, Mystik broke the news but a better article is on Keith Foster's site. Those two are buddies and he gives Turley's side of the story more coverage. Crazy right?"

Dani agreed, commiserating over such an incredible turn of events. Gone were any thoughts of her cousin or, even, her family, instead replaced by this insatiable curiosity. She lost herself again in the world she and Donnie inhabited. So engrossed was she that an hour passed, and then another, and then another, and she never did make her way downstairs. Only after the clock struck midnight did she realize the hour and, after grudgingly disconnecting from Skype, she wandered downstairs to find her cousin's family already gone.

That night Dani had a number of dreams, most instantly forgotten. One stuck, however, one which left clear and vivid details. In the dream, she was Omega and she was engaged in a ferocious battle with Darqor just like her live action role playing that afternoon. Except this time, she was actually fighting Darqor, in the flesh. She kept getting distracted, however, just when she had Darqor on the ropes. Out of nowhere, for example, she'd remember that she had to write a report for school. So she'd go do that, toiling away in her pajamas, while Darqor waited in a sort of stasis outside. And then she'd have to go on a trip to a local amusement park—which was weird since she'd visited the same place as a kid and loved it. And then she had to go to a beauty salon, of all places, while arguing that it was foolish to get her nails done when she was going to mess them up fighting Darqor anyway. She grew increasingly frustrated, fully aware that she had to go back and defeat him. The responsibility on her shoulders was massive because, according to the mythos of the Omega Zone novels, Darqor's defeat would bring about the end of the world of Ta and allow its citizens to ascend to the heavenly realm of Vikallydyl. She railed against her homework, and the vacation, and the beauty shop. But no one would listen to her.

Then Dani awoke to the harsh sounds of a fight between her parents. It was as familiar as it was exasperating: Her mother would manufacture some drama out of nowhere, her father wouldn't take it seriously, and the pair's anger would only escalate.

"All I'm saying," shouted her father, "is that I don't care what your co-worker thinks. I'm not taking her side. I'm not accusing you of anything. I'm merely saying I don't care about all these ridiculous fantasies you create when they don't actually exist."

"Oh that's crap and you know it," shouted Dani's mother in return. "You've seen the way Tina looks at you. Even you can't be that clueless."

"That's uncalled for."

"Well it's the reality. And you have to deal with it!"

Dani sighed and, approximately two seconds after that, she heard the front door slam. She still had the residual, nagging urge to defeat Darqor but, instead, found herself in the same old bed, in the same old house, where her parents had the same old fights. With a sigh, she forced herself to get up and go downstairs.

Her father was at the kitchen sink with his back to her, staring out the window. He was slumped, each palm flat on the countertop, and he hadn't heard her enter. Dani thought he was a complete dork, both in a good and bad way. He worked at some engineering firm—she barely saw him during the week—and he was hyper-logical, like a human-computer. But his sense of humor was weird and he got serious at all the wrong times. If he could just chill out she imagined he'd probably be a lot of fun.

"Hi," she said, as much to let her father know she was there as to literally say 'hello.'

It surprised him and he turned at the waist quickly, as if he'd been caught doing something improper. "Oh hi, Dani," he blinked. "You caught me daydreaming."

"I can see," giggled Dani. "Another freakout?"

Her father stepped away from the sink, his gaze downcast. "Yes," he said.

"She'll get over it. She always does."

"You...shouldn't talk about your mother like that," said her father, wholly unconvincingly.

Dani frowned. "You okay?"

"Oh yes. Everything's fine," he said, his moment of self-consciousness easing. He peered about the kitchen as if it might offer a clue what to say next and, eventually, asked, "How about you? How are you doing this fine morning?"

"Okay, I guess. Had a dream I almost killed Darqor so that was cool," she muttered.

"Oh, exciting indeed. And you were Omega?"

Dani blinked, then smiled. Her father had never let on that he knew anything about Omega Zone.

"Isn't that who you are?" he asked.

"Yeah. How did you know?"

He laughed. "You only spend every waking moment devoted to the stuff. Omega battles Darqor but first she must make sure the Skars don't get control of the Baga Pass, right?"

He was referring to a phase Dani had gone through a month earlier and he had totally mis-pronounced the Ba'Ka'Gen Pass. Still: Dani was impressed. And delighted. "You," she began but was too stunned to complete the sentence.

"Hey your old man isn't completely in the dark. I know Darqor isn't going down without a fight."

"But," started Dani again, flummoxed. "How long have you known about Omega Zone? And Darqor? And everything?"

"I don't know. I couldn't help overhearing."

Dani laughed. Her dad's slyness was a complete surprise. She wanted to play it cool but, secretly, she loved the fact that he had some interest in Omega Zone. "Yeah, well I almost killed Darqor in my dream. Course, that would've meant the end of the world. But...whatever."

Her father paused. "What was that again?"

"Oh, it's part of the storyline. When I—When Omega defeats Darqor, the world ends and everyone can go to Vikallydyl. It's this holy paradise."

"But," said her father, trying to process the notion, "how can the defeat of the bad guy...result in the end of the world? Shouldn't it be happily ever after?"

"It is."

"Not if the whole world blows up!" he laughed.

Dani rolled her eyes and grinned, cocking her head to one side. "It's not like that. It's a good thing. Everyone goes to this paradise, like I said."

"But that should be their choice, don't you think? What if they didn't want to go to paradise?"

"Who wouldn't want to go to paradise, Dad?"

"I don't know. Maybe some mother who hasn't delivered her first baby or some guitarist who hasn't played his first gig. Maybe some baby who hasn't lived yet. The point is that one person is making the choice on behalf of everyone else. It shouldn't be up to her to decide. If she knowingly defeats Darqor and creates this apocalypse, she's in essence playing God. Do you think that's okay?"

"Well...it's not that easy," said Dani, shifting her feet and trailing off. She wanted to convey how evil Darqor was or how great Vikallydyl would be. Every time she began to speak, however, she realized she wasn't countering his point effectively. The moment dragged on, Dani growing increasingly frustrated by both her father's stupid question and her own inability to address it.

Then, evidently, her father sensed her consternation and said, "I mean: I don't care, hon. I just thought it was odd. I was just making a joke."

"Yeah. Yeah," Dani nodded.

The silence persisted, adding to their mutual discomfort. Then, out of the blue, her father clapped his hands together and stated, "Well. The lawn isn't going to cut itself. I better get cracking before the rain."

He left and Dani, possessed by a vague, listless angst, meandered back to her room eventually. A part of her dismissed his comments—he was just an old guy who didn't get it. What could he possibly know about Omega Zone? He'd never even heard of the band, Happy Mudskippers, and he still tucked his shirt into his shorts—why should she care what he thought about Omega Zone? But another part of her knew it wasn't that easy. Deriding his opinion didn't make it any less valid.

Dani had been introduced to the series years ago and she'd immediately fallen in love with the chance to leave herself, her current reality for this fantastic new realm. It seemed so long ago, so hard to remember what life was like before Omega Zone. So immersed in the mythos for so long, it was an effort to separate where she ended and where Omega Zone began. So if she acknowledged her father's question had merit, what did that say about her and all the time she had spent lost in the fantasy world?

She arrived in her room and stood in the dead center of it, peering around at her computer, at the paraphernalia she'd amassed, at all the parts of her life that were intrinsically linked to the Omega Zone series. From the beginning, the mythos had stated how Ta would end. Yet that never took away from the suspense of the ever-expanding storylines. On a certain level it was essentially acknowledged that Darqor couldn't be defeated because, logically, that spelled the end of the series. As a figurehead, though, as the master manipulator who dispatched minions that actually could be beaten, his defeat remained the ultimate goal. Dani pondered the logic in a new way, revisiting the many assumptions made and the resultant commercially-informed implications on the series.

The ground began to shake. How could she have invested so much time in something with such a fundamental flaw? Try as she might to justify the overall genius of the series and the intricate web of stories that'd so enraptured her, she felt betrayed, embarrassed at her own stupidity. First and foremost, the Omega Series was a commercial enterprise that had to make money. Therefore, Darqor couldn't die. So if she truly believed he could, she was being played for a fool. Yet: How much energy had she spent defending the series to scoffing classmates? Were they aware of the problematic conclusion the whole time? And was that why they considered the series—and therefore her—so idiotic?

Tears welled up. And Dani's embarrassment spiraled. Bad enough she'd wasted so much time on such a childish story with a ridiculous ending. But now she was actually crying because of it? She felt suckered, taken advantage of by some faceless corporation that didn't care about anything. Santa Claus wasn't real. And neither was Omega.

She collapsed on her bed and buried her face in the pillow, unwilling to look at anything related to the Omega Zone stories. She heaved and lay there trembling, alone.

⋈ ⋈ ⋈

When Dani told Donnie she was done with Omega Zone he did not take the news well. At first, he was merely dismissive, unwilling to accept the notion that she would forsake everything so suddenly. They continued to Skpe that night but, without Omega Zone to discuss, the conversation was stilted and filled with awkward silences. A day passed, then another, and another, and, by that Thursday, his sense of betrayal was obvious. Following yet another pause in their conversation, he revolted. "Dani, come on! This sucks. Why are you doing this?"

"I don't know!" she cried. "It just...it just doesn't make sense anymore."

"Doesn't make sense? I'll tell you what doesn't make sense: You suddenly deciding one night, out of nowhere, that you don't like Omega Zone! That's what doesn't make sense to me."

"I'm sorry, Donnie. I really am. It's just that I realized how weird the ending is. It changes everything. And now? I don't know."

"How can you not know? You're not stupid. At least you didn't used to be," scolded Donnie.

Dani could see his frustration was boiling over but she had no way to articulate her feelings to him properly—she didn't even understand them herself. "It all," she said, her mannerisms like that of a wounded bunny. "It all just seems so...fake."

"Of course Omega Zone's fake! It's a story! It's fantasy!"

Dani felt a dagger plunge into her heart. Broken, she muttered, "Well...it wasn't for me."

Donnie began to say something else, something even more vitriolic, and Dani's hand crept to the power button on her laptop. Without a word, she pushed it, cutting Donnie off mid-sentence. It wasn't the right thing to do; she recognized that. Yet she also knew that he wouldn't give up, that he'd only continue to harangue her about her decision. So she decided to just cut ties, as rude as it might be.

It was only eight o'clock but she decided she was done with the day. In fact, it seemed like every day since her decision had been reduced to mere existence: Breakfast, aggravation at school, lunch, more aggravation, dinner and sleep. Each day had bled into the next and there was nothing left to look forward to. She was orphaned from Omega Zone and, as the result, her regular life had taken on a new, terrible clarity she wasn't sure she could accept. Now alienated from Donnie as well, she felt like a boat unmoored from the dock, drifting out to sea away from everything she loved.

Sleep would not come, though. Her thoughts were too tumultuous and, though she'd cocooned herself in her blankets, she could not escape her venomous lack of purpose. How could she continue to pretend such a fairy tale held value? Yet, if she couldn't, how could she cut it out of her life so impetuously? It was like lopping off a primary body part that had turned gangrenous. And, as she ruminated, her sense of alienation only grew.

She'd always put Omega Zone on a higher plane, something different than the dumb reality shows or hackneyed Hollywood movies others her age enjoyed. Yet, after the revelation unwittingly caused by her father's comments, Dani was forced to accept the notion that the Omega Zone series was just as commercial as any other entertainment. It wasn't a set of holy myths and, at the end of the day, it only kept going as long as it made money.

Yet, concurrent with that acceptance, Dani also resisted. Big deal if the producers were making money? That didn't mean the stories were worthless. It didn't disavow their meaning to her. The Omega Zone writers and the company that controlled the rights may have created a cross-marketing venture that made them lots of money. But they couldn't dictate the personal value of the stories. Once she took them and read them, they became hers.

A sense of rebellion arose. Too long she'd worried about what others thought and what Omega Zone represented. She was the master of her own identity, no matter what her classmates thought or what businessmen intended. The magic of Omega Zone may have begun in some studio in California but they were given form in her mind, in her creativity, in her literal self. It was her world.

And by the time morning rolled around, Dani had changed. The hours of meditation had been born of a crisis of identity but, through the night, a metamorphosis occurred. She emerged from her polymorphic tumult more unified, more free. Though the origination of the Omega Zone mythos may've been faulty, for Dani, no fault was recognized.

She arose from her bed weightlessly, as if floating on air. She didn't bother to call her school to feign sickness or to create contingency plans for the inevitable parental notification of her absence. Instead, with a playful grin, she snuck on tiptoes across her room to her bag of Omega Zone materials. In lithe silence she slid into her Omega costume and then appraised herself in the mirror for an extended period to make sure everything was perfect. Finally satisfied, she gave the slightest nod and spirited downstairs.

To be sure, she didn't know where this quixotic mission would take her. And she recognized that she'd need a healthy amount of imagination to locate an object to fill the role of Darqor. But the purity of her movements and the utter dearth of peripheral concerns assured her she was on the right path. She glided across the kitchen and an old remnant of herself was relieved to find evidence that her parents were gone. Dani's mother would've had a fit if she saw one of her butter knives stabbed and glued into either end of the broken Sword of Xe but a hasty repair was necessary.

With the sword functional once again, she held it aloft and scampered to the garage, ready for any danger that might present itself. At the doorway she peered about, her antennae up for any surprises. The dank, concrete floor alerted her to the fact that she was in the Cavern of Despair and the tools hanging from the wall bore an eerie resemblance to the Dartei, soulsuckers who would surely swoop down and attack if they sensed weakness. Through the open garage door, a modest amount of sunlight lit the front of the cave, eliciting ghostly shadows at the rear.

It took her a moment but, when she saw it, she could scarcely believe her eyes. There, beside the old Tarton Wheel: That old computer Dani's father refused to throw out. It faced away from her but the black hood shrouding it was unmistakable: Darqor's cape. And those USB ports in the back? Were they the holes in his cape, the holes that were his singular weakness, the only way to vanquish him for good? Face to face, Darqor was nigh impossible to defeat and, even if one succeeded temporarily, he inevitably returned. Yet here he was, distracted and unaware of her presence with his Achilles' heel fully exposed.

Wasting not a second she charged, emitting a fierce war cry that shook the cave. And with a warrior's might she plunged the Sword of Xe into the small of Darqor's back. He writhed in agony momentarily. The sword had hit its mark! Unwilling to lose such an opportunity should Darqor wriggle free, she gave the sword another thrust. Then another. He could not escape. He flailed, the horrific despot finally confronting his own mortality. Yet the Sword held firm.

Finally! After so many years, so many pitched battles and untold close calls, finally he was defeated. She was awestruck, unable to process the notion that it had actually happened. And for a long time she merely stared, a warrior who had fulfilled the warrior's mission. It was only after she stepped back to appraise the dying monster that the Sword of Xe dropped from her hand. She watched as Darqor's formerly fearsome body melted into a puddle of molten sludge and toxic chemical. She would've never believed it if she hadn't witnessed it herself.

Then, out of the corner of her eye, she saw something. It was far away on the horizon. The light. Without conscious thought, she stepped out of the garage towards it. The second sunrise grew, its intensity multiplying until it was nearly blinding. There was no sound, only the glorious, divine luminescence that shone first around, then through everything. And as it engulfed her and everything around her, Omega smiled.

MATT

Completing Dani's tale had been as cathartic as Matt's other stories, yet it also entailed something more. Matt couldn't put the sensation into words even if he wanted to, and it was never a good idea to try to explain a story. But upon completion he felt like he had become Dani—if only for a moment—just as Dani had become Omega. His words to Meda from a few nights earlier about the self-reflective nature of the Dirty Lord / Flower of Life still resonated and, just as Dani had created her own purpose so, too, did he. The little boy was fine, the danger had passed, and he was still writing as feverishly as he had during the crisis.

He never heard from the Stoic Man again, though. And that left him with an odd feeling of absence. Matt recognized that the man's appearance was intrinsically linked to the boy in some way—once the tumult had passed, the man had disappeared for good. And, obviously, Matt had no desire to return to that period in his life again. Yet, all the same, he felt like there was more he wanted to say to the man, like he had so many questions that'd never been addressed.

What's more, Matt felt a sense of reminiscence about their encounters. It was hard to fathom. Like that roommate he hated in college or that demeaning job he held when he was sixteen years old, the encounters with the man had been anything but enjoyable at the time they'd occurred. Yet, now that Matt was sure they'd never occur again, nostalgia had begun to fill in some of the blanks. He felt as if there'd been a level of kinship with the man—above and beyond the suspicion that the man had been guiding him in his own unfathomable way.

He mentioned his feelings to Meda one night in the easy silence following a large dinner. He hadn't ever fully described his encounters with the Stoic Man, so he wasn't sure how she'd react. Her response surprised him, however.

"I've been experiencing similar feelings," she said.

"You have?"

"Yes. About Mrs. Javier."

"You miss her?"

Meda gave a light nod and peered into the distance as she spoke. "I'm embarrassed to say it but I used to get very frustrated with her. It seemed like she was always hovering when I arrived home. After the worst days at work, without fail, she'd be underfoot and it made me resent her. It was wrong of me to feel that way. I know. It wasn't her fault."

"Oh, come on. Don't blame yourself, hon," said Matt, putting a hand on her arm.

"No, that's not what I'm trying to say. I don't blame myself. And I don't blame her. It's more than that." Meda paused, and, when she spoke again, she did so with eyes skyward, as if to convey her own sense of uncertainty. "I used to think that I was annoyed because she was an impediment, someone standing in the way of my goal. At the time, I was conflicted because she was an old lady and I thought I should be nicer to her. Lately though, I've begun to think that it was the opposite the whole time, that I was conflicted for an even deeper reason, one that I couldn't admit to myself. I feel like I may've resented her because of what she represented, what she symbolized to me. And I fear, rather than an impediment, she was actually an opportunity. And I wasted it."

"What? I'm not following, hon," said Matt. He had been concerned that she wouldn't understand his thoughts about the Stoic Man—he hadn't expected that she would have similarly complicated feelings about Mrs. Javier.

"Let me put it another way," she said, looking Matt in the eyes now and speaking with more direct diction. "All along, I'd been looking at her with a notion of pity. She was an old woman, she was looking for conversation, she was lonely. And all those presumptions, in a way, made me the center of that universe. When, in actuality, she was perfectly happy. She was at peace. I was the one resenting my job, my commute, everything."

She trailed off briefly and Matt was unsure if she had concluded or if she had merely paused. "Hon, you're being too hard on yourself," he said, feeling the urge to assuage her.

"No. Thank you, baby. But I don't need any of that," said Meda. She took a moment to pick her words and started again. "A moment ago you said how you've been missing that guy, the Stoic Man, right? How you were sad that you won't see him again?"

"Yeah," agreed Matt. It was a bit of an over-summarization but she had the basic idea.

"Well I feel the same way about Mrs. Javier. Not because I miss her in the classic sense. I do. But that's not what I mean." At that Meda smiled despite the apparent contradiction to her words. "And I'm not sad *for* her. I'm sure she's in a good place, wherever she is. I'm sad for *my* sake. Embarrassed. Because I didn't take this chance to grow while she was still alive. She was right there the whole time and I never appreciated her until it was too late. I'm going to miss seeing her. Worse, I'm going to miss her ability to see me."

Meda concluded and the pair remained silent for a long period. Matt no longer felt the impulse to comfort her; the grin on her face disarmed such notions. Then, in an apparent non sequitur, Meda announced, "I think I'm going to look for a choir to sing in this week." Her smile burst forth, broad and proud, and if Mrs. Javier was present she would've certainly remarked on the glow Meda emitted.

Matt peered up her, eyebrows raised. The change in the conversation topic was drastic but Matt trusted that she'd done so intentionally. "Oh yeah?"

"Yes. Screw work. I'll tell them I'll need to leave at a certain time on certain days and that appointment will be immutable. They'll just have to accept it." She nodded her head as she spoke, her chin bunched up under her lip in defiant determination.

"Wow, that's great, hon. I'm surprised."

"I know," admitted Meda. "It's been awhile. I'm not even sure where I plan to do it, exactly. I don't think a church choir is for me. And I probably don't have the chops for a theater league, no matter how amateur it might be. I just need to try something."

Matt reached across the table to hold her hand. She appeared ambitious but with a healthy sense of fear in her being. "So how far are you thinking of taking this? Are you suggesting a career change eventually?"

"No," said Meda flatly, almost chuckling at the notion. "No, no, no. Let's not get crazy here. As much as I welcome your enthusiasm, baby, that's not my goal. I'm not doing this to support myself or to make money. I'm doing it *for me*."

Matt stared at Meda, appreciating her. Her grin was unlike any she'd shown in a very long time—relaxed, almost sleepy in its satisfaction. She wasn't smiling for a picture or smiling when shaking someone's hand at a party; she was smiling because she couldn't *not* smile.

Later, they ate dessert. They watched television. They traded stories about their friends and items in the news. And, eventually, Matt left for the night.

On the walk home, he received a text from Magee: "Latest call from mama: She says if I'm not interested in blind date I should tell u. I tell her no, Matt runs over little kids with car.

She didn't get it." Matt was lost in contemplation and, unprepared for such wiseassery, he laughed out loud on the empty street. To a stranger's eyes he might've appeared crazy. Still smiling, he dialed Magee's number and launched in as soon as his friend answered, "I don't run over little kids, okay? No need to start spreading rumors."

Magee chuckled. "I needed to get my mother off my back. What can I say?"

"And that was the best you could come up with? You couldn't just say that I was practically married?"

"I figured you'd appreciate the villain I made you out to be. Though, the next time you meet her she may have a few questions for you."

"Great," said Matt, knowing full well Magee's mother wouldn't believe such tales anyway. Then, as an afterthought, he added, "You could offer that creep, Sergei. That'd definitely get your mom to leave you alone."

"Oh, I didn't get to tell you," said Magee, animated but in a less jovial way. "I spoke to my friend Taylor: Turns out Sergei moved away. He was afraid of the Armenians."

"Really?"

"Yeah, apparently, he figured that while you and Meda would be safe...there would still be elements within the group looking for their pound of flesh. And he feared he'd be the next logical target."

Matt pursed his lips—he'd only brought up Sergei's name as a joke. "I guess it serves him right," said Matt.

"Perhaps...perhaps," said Magee, sounding wistful.

"What? Why'd you say it like that?"

"I don't know," said Magee. His tone gave the impression of him fidgeting in his seat. "It's not like he introduced you guys to the mafia on purpose."

"He tried to kill Meda," said Matt, aghast.

"Well, slow down, buddy. He didn't literally try to kill anybody."

"Okay, okay. He tried to deliver Meda to someone who was going to kill her."

"And that guy found her anyway," added Magee.

"Still. C'mon, man. Why are you defending the guy? What's up?"

"I don't know," said Magee, retreating back into his hesitancy. "I sorta got the feeling that he had regrets, like he wanted to help...but he didn't know how to change things."

"Wanted to help? Really?"

"Okay, 'help' might not be the best word. He did show me that video of you, though. He didn't have to do that. And he went out of his way to warn me about the Armenians. I guess I felt like he wanted to do the right thing...but he was a hustler who got caught up in something bigger. He was probably out of his league. When we met him, he was trying to scalp some tickets. That's a trade that's got to be drying up, with the internet and all. So maybe his affiliation with the Armenians was out of necessity, just trying to make a buck."

"Maybe," repeated Matt, clearly skeptical.

"Oh, and get this: Sergei isn't even his real name," added Magee. "His name is actually Morgan. He went back to using it after he disappeared. Apparently, he'd adopted 'Sergei' when dealing with the Armenians. At least that's what Taylor said."

"Wow. That seems like a lot to juggle for a simple ticket scalping operation."

"Yep. Between the false persona and his paranoia, it was hard to get a bead on him. It makes me wonder what else he might be doing, why he went down that path."

"I guess," said Matt with a shrug, not sharing the same curiosity.

"I mean, I get it," continued Magee. "I recognize why you and Meda were never going to be best friends with the guy. It makes sense after everything that happened. But a part of me wonders if...and this is going to sound crazy...a part of me wonders if things might've been different in another life. If he and I might've had more in common."

"Yeah. You're right. That does sound crazy," said Matt. It was jocular, less a repudiation of Magee's musing and more a simple tension breaker. "About the only thing I can say in the guy's defense is that he actually came through with the tickets."

"Yep. Yet you still didn't get to see *Götterdämmerung*," laughed Magee.

"Nope. We never got to see the end of the world. We were a little, ah, busy that night," said Matt with faux lamentation. "Maybe next year."

"Well, I hope your disappointment wasn't too tremendous," said Magee.

"It was not. It's hard to be too disappointed when bullets are fired at you and none of them hit."

"Yep. Disappointment is a funny thing, isn't it?" added Magee.

The pair chuckled again and said their goodbyes. Matt continued on his walk home, lost in thought regarding how far he'd come and how far he had yet to go. October 22nd, the night of the opera, was weeks earlier yet the events of that night still reverberated among the trio.

It wasn't a tidy end to the journey they'd taken, and Matt, Meda, and Magee continued to discuss the outcomes. The little boy was never found, the Stoic Man dropped out of sight, and each of them continued to keep one eye over their shoulder for potential retribution by the Armenians. Yet life went on. Their stories continued to unfold.

Matt sometimes wondered what would've happened if he and Magee hadn't pursued Meda at the opera. Or if he hadn't jumped that fence and been caught snooping at the back of the bar. What would've happened to the boy then? What would Matt's own life look like? He tried not to spend too much time thinking of those paths, though. None of them seemed to end well.

He arrived at the crossroads at the end of Meda's block and stopped. A car was in the process of doing a U-turn in the middle of the intersection and, briefly, its high-beams landed on him, illuminating him with a blinding flash of light. He winced. Then he smiled. The car drove away and Matt recalled his hesitancy at the same spot weeks earlier, before he'd changed course and went searching for the little boy. This time, with his contended grin still present, he proceeded home without delay. After all, with twelve stories left to write, Matt had to go back to work.

The Author

Matthew Waterman created this work. It is his first published novel after two decades spent writing. Sometimes lucid, he is not an altogether terrible person. In fact, this one time he went right up to a stranger and gave that person a high-five. Matt's greatest singular talent may be over-thinking mundane matters. But at least his regrets have wings.

www.ingramcontent.com/pod-product-compliance
Lightning Source LLC
Chambersburg PA
CBHW061319170626
46817CB00001B/238

* 9 7 8 0 9 9 6 7 9 6 2 0 0 *